Isaac Asimov was born in Russia in 1920. At th
three he went with his fam
where he grew up. In 194
Columbia University and j
University School of Medic
Dr. Asimov is one of today
read authors. His books ran
pure science to history, reli
and humour. His recent nov selves',
was granted both the Nebula Award and the Hugo Award.
Dr. Asimov currently lives in New York City.

Edited by Isaac Asimov

Tomorrow's Children

18 Tales of Fantasy and Science Fiction

Illustrated by Emanuel Schongut

Futura Publications Limited
An Orbit Book

An Orbit Book

First published in Great Britain in 1974
by Futura Publications Limited

ISBN 0 8600 7821 3
Printed in Great Britain by
Hazell Watson & Viney Ltd
Aylesbury, Bucks

Futura Publications Limited
49 Poland Street,
London W1A 2LG

Acknowledgments

Grateful acknowledgment is made for the use of the following coyprighted material:

"The Ugly Little Boy," copyright © 1958 by Galaxy Publishing Corporation, from the book *Nine Tomorrows* by Isaac Asimov. Reprinted by permission of Doubleday & Company, Inc.

"It's a *Good* Life" by Jerome Bixby. Copyright 1953 by Ballantine Books, Inc. Reprinted by permission of the author.

"By the Waters of Babylon" ("The Place of the Gods") from *Selected Works of Stephen Vincent Benét,* published by Holt, Rinehart & Winston, Inc. Copyright 1937 by Stephen Vincent Benét. Copyright renewed 1964 by Thomas C. Benét, Stephanie B. Mahinand, Rachel Benét Lewis. Reprinted by permission of Brandt & Brandt.

"All Summer in a Day," copyright 1954 by Fantasy House, Inc., from the book *A Medicine for Melancholy* by Ray Bradbury. Reprinted by permission of Harold Matson Company, Inc.

"Star Bright" by Mark Clifton. Copyright 1952 by Mark Clifton. Reprinted by permission of Ann Elmo Agency.

"The Father-Thing" by Philip K. Dick. Copyright © 1954 by Mercury Press, Inc. Reprinted by permission of the author and the author's agents, Scott Meredith Literary Agency, Inc.

"The Wayward Cravat," copyright © 1958 by Gertrude Friedberg, from *The Wayward Cravat* by Gertrude Friedberg, *Short Story* 2. Reprinted by permission of the author and Charles Scribner's Sons.

"The Menace from Earth" by Robert A. Heinlein. Copyright © 1957 by Fantasy House, Inc. Reprinted by permission of the author.

"Gilead," copyright 1954 by Mercury Press, Inc., from the book *Pilgrimage: The Book of the People* by Zenna Henderson. Reprinted by permission of the author, Doubleday & Company, Inc., and Victor Gollancz, Ltd.

"The Little Terror" by Will F. Jenkins. Copyright 1953 by The Curtis Publishing Company. Reprinted by permission of the author and the author's agents, Littauer and Wilkinson.

"Cabin Boy" by Damon Knight. Copyright 1951 by Galaxy Publishing Corporation. Reprinted by permission of the author.

"A Pail of Air" by Fritz Leiber. Copyright 1951 by Galaxy Publishing Corporation. Reprinted by permission of the author and the author's agent, Robert P. Mills.

"Junior Achievement" by William Lee. Reprinted by permission of the author.

"When the Bough Breaks" by Lewis Padgett. Copyright 1944 by Street & Smith Publications, Inc., in the U.S.A. and Great Britain. Reprinted from *Astounding Science Fiction,* by permission of Harold Matson Company, Inc.

Contents

Introduction

Science fiction and fantasy serve many purposes, and surely one of them is to stave off age.

This branch of literature is particularly associated with youth; one has only to attend a national convention of s.f. fans to see that. There are not as many youngsters trailing the "big-name writers" as haunt the Beatles perhaps, but the science fiction fans make up in polysyllabic speech what they lack in decibelic screech.

There are some adults who disassociate themselves from science fiction and youth at the same time and say, rather proudly, "I haven't read science fiction since I was in high school." They sound as though they are praising themselves for a new-found maturity, when all they are really doing is celebrating a certain hardening of their mental arteries.

Wordsworth mourned the loss of the essence of youth, in religious terms, in a famous passage in his ode entitled "Intimations of Immortality from Recollections of Early Childhood":

Our birth is but a sleep and a forgetting;
The soul that rises with us, our life's star,
  Hath had elsewhere its setting,
    And cometh from afar:
  Not in entire forgetfulness,
  And not in utter nakedness,
But trailing clouds of glory do we come
  From God who is our home:
Heaven lies about us in our infancy!
Shades of the prison-house begin to close
  Upon the growing boy,
But he beholds the light, and whence it flows,
  He sees it in his joy;
The youth, who daily farther from the east

Must travel, still is Nature's priest,
And by the vision splendid
Is on his way attended;
At length the man perceives it die away,
And fade into the light of common day.

Alas, alas, in science fiction circles, we call the great property we sometimes lose with age "the sense of wonder."

How new and bright the world is when we are young; how fresh and inspired the simplest things; how welcome the extraordinary thoughts we can scarcely recognize as such, so extraordinary is even the ordinary. Science fiction and fantasy are not something to be enjoyed secretly as a semishameful substitute for reality; they are a glad extension of reality, the addition of still brighter colors to a bright universe.

As we age, the world sometimes ages with us; the colors grow drab as our hair grays; the paint cracks as our faces wrinkle; the sounds grow hoarse as our senses dull. We watch everything fade into the light of common day and then self-praise ourselves for the mechanical manner in which we face a monochromatic workaday world with a monochromatic workaday mind.

Is this inevitable? Does our sense of wonder necessarily die decades before we ourselves do? Is youth really the "toyland" Victor Herbert sings of, to which "once you pass its borders, you can ne'er return again."

I have better hopes than that. I think instead of a radio program put on in the late 1940s by Phil Harris, a show which featured a character who portrayed "Frank Remley," a drummer in Harris' band. Remley was pictured as the child in all of us; incapable of undertaking responsibility or of resisting temptation; a fool, liar, and cheat, but with all his weakness concentered into so small and personal a circle as to harm no one, not even himself; and so good-natured withal and innocent of all evil intention as to be completely lovable.

Every Christmas, Phil Harris reran a special program, one which revolved about the seemingly inevitable disillusionment of the Harris children, who were firmly convinced that Santa Claus would come even though some radio-show catastrophe prevented Harris from playing the role. Santa Claus *did* come of course, but only the children could see him—the children *and* Frank Remley. For that one show, a feeble halo flickered momentarily about Remley's foolish head and the listener, if properly moved (as I always was), wondered if the gain of responsibility and maturity was adequate payment for the loss of the sense of wonder.

We can turn to Wordsworth again and his sonnet "The World Is Too Much With Us":

> *—Great God! I'd rather be*
> *A pagan suckled in a creed outworn;*
> *So might I, standing on this pleasant lea,*
> *Have glimpses that would make me less forlorn;*
> *Have sight of Proteus rising from the sea;*
> *Or hear old Triton blow his wreathèd horn.*

Or, to translate: Would we rather be Remley, nurtured on folly, so that we might see Santa Claus coming down the chimney?

The choice is not so hard. Neither pagan creeds nor folly are the price we must pay for the sense of wonder.

I know many adults, neither pagans nor fools—indeed, intelligent, industrious, responsible men and women—who nevertheless enjoy the flexible delight of the youthful mind. Their ability to rejoice in good science fiction and fantasy is the outward sign of this inward blessedness.

Ah me, my friends grow older in body, along with me, for we are all mortal. But if our joints creak, our minds do not; and if our muscles soften, our brains do not; and if our tendons slacken, our imaginations do not.

The clouds of glory we trailed at birth need not and do not ever fade entirely after all.

But we are not the majority, of course. Writers of science fiction and fantasy, who find themselves surrounded by contemporaries who are increasingly immersed in the light of common day must occasionally turn away from the sad sight of butterflies flying into the cocoon and crawling out as caterpillars. They look back upon youth in their own special way and find it full of special powers.

—The power to adjust to a strange society of gadgets and nonhumans as their elders cannot.

—The power to endure and survive a society of ruin brought on by their elders.

—The power to make use of power, sometimes triumphantly and sometimes dreadfully, to the bemusement or even destruction of their elders.

Come, then, and meet some of tomorrow's children—

ISAAC ASIMOV

West Newton, Mass.
Christmas 1965

1

No Life of Their Own

CLIFFORD D. SIMAK

Before I was a writer, I was a proto-writer. That is, in junior high school, I read science fiction stories, absorbed them completely, and then passed them on, verbally, to a small but eager group of my classmates. I think I neglected telling them the stories were not exactly mine, since, if I had, that would have dimmed their admiration. Besides, if they found out they could read the stories for themselves, I would have lost my audience and even in junior high school I realized an audience was essential.

One of the stories with which I achieved a particular success was called "The World of the Red Sun" and it appeared in the December 1931 issue of Wonder Stories. *That, had I but realized it at the time, was my introduction to its author, Clifford D. Simak.*

Now here we are, over a generation later. I have long since graduated from telling other people's stories to telling my own. Cliff Simak has become a close friend of mine and, for heaven's sake, he is still at it too.

Even now he remains one of the mainstays of science fiction, refusing flatly to consider assuming the role of "elder statesman." He comes of a long-lived family and I thoroughly expect him to be writing for decades more.

What's more, Cliff manages to bring an atmosphere of his own to science fiction. Certainly one might expect that what suits science fiction best is a surrealist style, but Cliff is not bound by any such feeling.

No one is as skillful as he in combining the strangest of strange happenings on other worlds with a style that is downright bucolic. Let Cliff introduce you to the eternal aspects of childhood and present you with a bunch of odd children who would seem perfectly at home in Mark Twain's Hannibal, Missouri.

Ma and Pa were fighting again, not really mad at one another, but arguing pretty loud. They had been at it, off and on, for weeks.

"We just can't up and *leave!*" said Ma. "We have to think it out. We can't pull up and leave a place we've lived in all our lives without *some* thinking on it!"

"I *have* thought on it!" Pa said. "I've thought on it a *lot!* All these aliens moving in. There was a brood of new ones moved onto the Pierce place just a day or two ago."

"How do you know," asked Ma, "that you'll like one of the Homestead Planets once you settle on it? It might be worse than Earth."

"We can't be any more unlucky there than we been right

here! There ain't *anything* gone right. I don't mind telling you I am plumb discouraged."

And Pa sure-God was right about how unlucky we had been. The tomato crop had failed and two of the cows had died and a bear had robbed the bees and busted up the hives and the tractor had broken down and cost $78.90 to get fixed.

"Everyone has some bad luck," Ma argued. "You'd have it no matter where you go."

"Andy Carter doesn't have bad luck!" yelled Pa. "I don't know how he does it, but everything he does, it turns out to a hair. He could fall down in a puddle and come up dripping diamonds!"

"I don't know," said Ma philosophically. "We got enough to eat and clothes to cover us and a roof above our head. Maybe that's as much as anyone can expect these days."

"It ain't enough," Pa said. "A man shouldn't be content to just scrape along. I lay awake at night to figure out how I can manage better. I've laid out plans that should by rights have worked. But they never did. Like the time we tried that new adapted pea from Mars down on the bottom forty. It was sandy soil and they should have grown there. They ain't worth a damn on any land that will grow another thing. And that land was worthless; it should have been just right for those Martian peas. But I ask you, did they grow there?"

"No," said Ma, "now that I recollect, they didn't."

"And the next year, what happens? Andy Carter plants the same kind of peas just across the fence from where I tried to grow them. Same kind of land and all. And Andy gets bowlegged hauling those peas home."

What Pa said was true. He was a better farmer than Andy Carter could ever hope to be. And he was smarter, too. But let Pa try a thing and bad luck would beat him out. Let Andy try the same and it always went right.

And it wasn't Pa alone. It was the entire neighborhood. Everybody was just plain unlucky, except Andy Carter.

"I tell you," Pa swore, "just one more piece of bad luck and we'll throw in our hand and start over somewhere fresh. And the Homestead Planets seem the best to me. Why, you take . . ."

I didn't wait to hear any more. I knew it would go on the way it always had. So I snuck out without their seeing me and went down the road, and as I walked along, I worried that maybe one of these days they might make up their mind to move to one of the Homestead Planets. There had been an awful lot of our old neighbors who'd done exactly that.

It might be all right to emigrate, of course, but whenever I thought about it, I got a funny feeling at the thought of leaving Earth. Those other planets were so awful far away, one wouldn't have much chance of getting back again if he didn't like them. And all my friends were right in the neighborhood, and they were pretty good friends even if they were all aliens.

I got a little start when I thought of that. It was the first time it had occurred to me that they all were aliens. I had so much fun with them, I'd never thought of it.

It seemed a little queer to me that Ma and Pa should be talking about leaving Earth when all the farms that had been sold in our neighborhood had been bought up by aliens. The Homestead Planets weren't open to the aliens and that might be the reason they came to Earth. If they'd had a choice, maybe they would have gone to one of the Homesteads instead of settling down on Earth.

I walked past the Carter place and saw that the trees in the orchard were loaded down with fruit and I figured that some of us could sneak in and steal some of it when it got ripe. But we'd have to be careful, because Andy Carter was a stinker, and his hired man, Ozzie Burns, wasn't one bit better. I remembered the time we had been stealing watermelons and Andy had found us at it and I'd got caught in a barbed-wire fence when we ran away. Andy had walloped me, which was all right. But there'd been no call for him going to Pa and collecting seven dollars for the few melons we had stolen. Pa had paid up and then he'd walloped me again, worse than Andy did.

And after it was over, Pa had said bitterly that Andy was no great shakes of a neighbor. And Pa was right. He wasn't.

I got down to the old Adams place and Fancy Pants was out in the yard, just floating there and bouncing that old basketball of his.

We call him Fancy Pants because we can't pronounce his name. Some of these alien people have very funny names.

Fancy Pants was all dressed up as usual. He always is dressed up because he never gets the least bit dirty when he plays. Ma is always asking me why I can't keep neat and clean like Fancy Pants. I tell her it would be easy if I could float along like him and never had to walk, and if I could throw mud-balls like him without touching them.

This Sunday morning he was dressed up in a sky-blue shirt that looked like silk, and red britches that looked as if they might be velvet, and he had a green bow tied around his yellow curls that floated in the breeze. At first glance, Fancy Pants looked something like a girl—but you better never say so, because he'd mop up the road with you. He did with me the first time I saw him. He didn't even lay a hand on me while he was doing it, but sat up there, cross-legged, about three feet off the ground, smiling that sweet smile of his on his ugly face, and with his yellow curls floating in the breeze. And the worst of it was that I couldn't get back at him.

But that was long ago and we were good friends now.

We played catch for a while, but it wasn't too much fun.

Then Fancy Pants' pa came out of the house and he was glad to see me, too. He asked about the folks and wanted to know if the tractor was all right, now that we'd got it fixed. I answered him politely because I'm a little scared of Fancy Pants' pa.

He is sort of spooky—not the way he looks, the way he does things. From the looks of him, he wasn't meant to be a farmer, but he does all right at it. He doesn't use a plow to plow a field. He just sits cross-legged in the air and floats up and down the field, and when he passes over a strip of ground, that strip of ground is plowed—and not only plowed, but raked and harrowed until it is as fine as face powder. He does all his work that way. There aren't any weeds in any of his crops, for he just sails up and down the rows and the weeds come out slick and clean, with the roots intact, to lie on the ground and wither.

It doesn't take too much imagination to see what a guy like that could do if he ever caught a kid in any sort of mischief, so all of us are thoughtful and polite whenever he's around.

So I told him how we'd got the tractor all fixed up and about the bear busting up the beehives. Then I asked him about his time machine and he shook his head real sad.

"I don't know what's the matter, Steve," he said. "I put things into it and they disappear, and I should find them later, but I never have. If I'm moving them in time, I'm perhaps pushing them too far."

He would have told me more about his time machine, but there was an interruption.

While we had been talking, Fancy Pants' pa and me, the Fancy Pants dog had run a cat up a maple tree. That is the normal situation for any cat and dog—unless Fancy Pants is around.

For Fancy Pants wasn't one to leave a situation normal. He reached up into the tree—well, he didn't reach up with his hands, of course, but with whatever he reaches with—and he nailed this cat and sort of bundled it up so it couldn't move and brought it down to the ground.

Then he held the dog so the dog couldn't do more than twitch and he put that bundled-up cat down in front of the twitching dog, then let them loose with split-second timing.

The two of them exploded into a blur of motion, with the weirdest uproar you ever heard. The cat made it to the tree in the fastest time and nearly took off the bark swarming up the trunk. And the dog miscalculated and failed to put on his brakes in time and banged smack into the tree spread-eagled.

The cat by this time was up in the highest branches, hanging on and screaming, while the dog walked around in circles, acting kind of stunned.

Fancy Pants' pa broke off what he was saying to me and he looked at Fancy Pants. He didn't do or say a thing, but when he looked at Fancy Pants, Fancy Pants grew terribly pale and sort of wilted down.

"Let that teach you," said Fancy Pants' pa, "to leave those animals alone. You don't see Steve here or Nature Boy mistreating them that way, do you?"

"No, sir," mumbled Fancy Pants.

"And now get along, the two of you. You have things to do."

I got this to say for Fancy Pants' pa: he gives Fancy Pants his lickings, or whatever they may be, and then he forgets about it. He doesn't keep on harping at it for the rest of the day.

So Fancy Pants and me went down the road, me shuffling along, kicking up the dust, and Fancy Pants floating along beside me.

We got down to Nature Boy's place and he was waiting out

in front. I knew he had been hoping someone would come along. There were a couple of sparrows sitting on his shoulder and a rabbit hopping all around him and a chipmunk in the pocket of his pants, looking out at us with bright and beady eyes.

Nature Boy and I sat down underneath a tree and Fancy Pants came as close as he ever does to sitting down—floating about three inches off the ground—and we talked about what we ought to do. Trouble was, there wasn't really anything that needed any doing. So we sat there and talked and tossed pebbles and pulled stems of grass and put them in our mouths and chewed them, while Nature Boy's pet wild things gamboled all around us and didn't seem to be afraid at all. Except that they were a little leery of Fancy Pants. He is, when you come right down to it, a sort of sneaky rascal. Me they are fast friends with when I'm with Nature Boy, but let me meet them when I am alone and they keep their distance.

I can see how wild things might take to Nature Boy. He is fur all over, real sleek, glossy fur, and he wears nothing but that little pair of pants. Turn him loose without those pants and someone would be bound to take a shot at him.

So we sat there wondering what to do. Then I remembered that Pa had said a new family had moved onto the Pierce place and we decided to go down and see if they had any kids.

We went down the road to the old Pierce place and it turned out there was one just about our age. He was a sort of runty little kid, with a peaked face and big round eyes and a kind of eager look about him, like a stunted hoot owl.

He told us his name and it was even worse than Nature Boy's and Fancy Pants' names, so we had a vote on it and decided we would call him Butch. That suited him just fine.

Then he called out his family and they stood in a row, like a bunch of solemn, runty owls roosting on a limb, while he introduced them. There was his ma and pa and a little brother and a kid sister almost as big as he was. The rest of them went back into the house, but Butch's pa squatted down and began to talk with us.

You could see from the way he talked that he was a little scared of this farming business. He admitted he really was no farmer, but an optical worker, and explained to us that an optical worker designed lenses and ground them. But, he said, there was no future in a job like that back on his old home planet. He told us how glad he was to be on Earth and how he wanted to be a good citizen and a good neighbor, and a lot of other things like that.

When he started to run down, we got away from him. There ain't anything more embarrassing than a crazy adult who likes to talk with kids.

We decided that maybe we should show Butch around a bit and let him in on some of the things we had been doing.

So we struck off down Dark Hollow and we didn't make much time because all of these friends of Nature Boy were popping out to join him. Before very long, we were a sort of traveling menagerie—rabbits and chipmunks and a gopher or two and a couple of raccoons.

I like Nature Boy, of course, and I've had some good times with him, but he has spoiled a lot of fun as well. Before he showed up in the neighborhood, I did a lot of fishing and hunting, but that is all spoiled now. I can't shoot a squirrel or catch a fish without wondering if it is a friend of Nature Boy's.

After a while, we got down to the creek bed where we were digging out the lizard. We'd been at it all summer long and we hadn't uncovered very much of him, but we still figured that some day we might get him all dug out.

You understand that it wasn't a live lizard we were digging out, but a lizard that had turned to stone a zillion years ago.

There is a place where the stream runs down a limestone ledge and the limestone lies in layers. The lizard was between two of those layers. We'd got four or five feet of his tail uncovered. But the digging was getting harder, for we were working back into the limestone ledge and there was more of it to move.

Fancy Pants floated up above the limestone ledge and got himself set as solid as he could. Sitting there, he hit that limestone ledge a tremendous whack, being very careful not to crack the lizard. It was one of his better whacks, busting up a lot of stone, and while Fancy Pants rested up to take another one, the three of us piled in and threw out the busted rock.

But there was one big piece he had loosened up that we couldn't move.

"Hit it just a tap," I told him. "Break it up a little and we can get it out."

"I got it loose," he said. "It's up to you to get it out."

There was no sense arguing with him. So the three of us wrestled at the rock, but we couldn't budge it and Fancy Pants sat up there, fat and sassy, taking it easy and enjoying himself.

"You ought to have a crowbar," he told us. "If you had a crowbar, you could pry that rock out."

I was getting sick and tired of Fancy Pants, and so, just to get away from him for a while, I said I'd go and fetch a crowbar. And this new kid, this Butch, said he'd go along with me.

So we left Nature Boy and Fancy Pants and climbed up to the road and started out for my place. We didn't hurry any. It would serve Fancy Pants right if he had to wait, and Nature Boy as well, for all his showing off with his animals.

We walked along the road and talked. Butch told me about the planet he had come from and it sure was a poor-mouth place, and I told him about the neighborhood, and we were getting to be friends.

We reached the Carter place and were walking past the orchard when Butch stopped dead in the middle of the road and went sort of stiff, like a hunting dog will go when he scents a bird.

I was walking right behind him and I bumped into him, but he just stood there with those eager eyes agleam and his entire body tense—so tense it seemed to quiver when it really didn't.

"What's going on?" I asked.

He kept on looking at something in the orchard. I took a look where he was looking and I couldn't see a thing.

Then he turned around like a flash and jumped the fence on the downhill side of the road and went lickety-split down across the field opposite the orchard. I jumped the fence and ran after him and caught him just before he reached the woods. I grabbed him by the shoulder and spun him around to face me. It wasn't hard to do, he was such a spindly kid.

"What's the matter with you?" I hollered. "Where do you think you're going?"

"Home to get my gun!"

"Your *gun?* What for?"

"There's a whole bunch of them up there! We have to clean them out!"

He must have seen I didn't understand.

"Don't tell me," he said, "that you didn't see them?"

I shook my head. "There wasn't anything there."

"They're there, all right," he said. "Maybe you can't see them. Maybe you're like old folks."

There's no one who can accuse me of a thing like that. I doubled up my fist and poked it underneath his nose. He hurried up to explain.

"They're things that only kids can see. And they bring bad luck. You can't leave them around or you'll have bad luck all the time."

I didn't believe it right away. But after all the things I'd seen done by Nature Boy and Fancy Pants, you don't ever catch me saying straight out that a thing's impossible.

And after I'd thought it over for a minute, it made a silly sort of sense. For the folks certainly had been plagued by hard luck for a long time now and it didn't stand to reason that luck should be all bad and never any good unless there was something making it that way.

And it wasn't the folks alone, but all the other neighbors—all of them, of course, except Andy Carter, and Andy Carter was too mean to be bothered by bad luck.

We were, I thought, sure a hard-luck neighborhood.

"All right," I said to Butch. "Let's go and get that gun."

And I was thinking even as I said it that it must be a funny kind of gun that would shoot a thing one couldn't even see.

We made it back to the old Pierce place in almost no time at all. Butch's pa was sitting out underneath a tree, feeling sorry for himself. Butch came up to him and started jabbering and I couldn't understand a word.

His pa listened to him for a while and then broke in. "You should talk this planet's language, son. It is most impolite to do otherwise. And you want to become a good citizen of this great and glorious planet, I am sure, and there's no better way to do it than to talk its language and observe its customs and try to live the way its people do."

I'll say this much for him: Butch's pa sure knew how to fling around the words.

"Is it true, mister," I asked him, "that these things can bring bad luck?"

"Most assuredly," said Butch's pa. "Back on our old home planet, we know them well."

"Pa," asked Butch, "should I get my gun?"

"Now I don't know," said his pa. "It's something we have to give some study. Back on our home planet, there would be no question of it. But this is a different planet and it may have different ways. It may be that the man who has these creatures would object to your shooting them."

"But there isn't anyone really got them," I declared. "How can you have a thing when you can't even see it?"

"I was thinking about the gentleman in whose orchard they appeared."

"You mean Andy Carter. He doesn't know anything about them."

"That does not matter," said Butch's pa, with a great deal of righteousness. "It becomes, it would seem to me, a quite deep problem in ethics. On our home planet, no man would want these things; he'd be ashamed to have them. But here it might be different. They bring good luck, you see, to the ones that they adopt."

"You mean they bring good luck to Andy?" I asked him. "But I thought you said that they brought bad luck."

"So they do," said Butch's pa, "except to the ones that they adopt. To them they bring good luck, but bad luck to all the others. For it is an axiom that fortune for one man is misfortune for the rest. That is why we do not let them adopt any of us on our home planet."

"You think they have adopted Andy and that's why he has good luck?"

"You are most correct," said Butch's pa. "You have admirably grasped the concept."

"Well, gee, why don't we just go in and shoot them?"

"This Carter gentleman would not object to your doing so?"

"Of course he would, but that's what you would expect of him. He'd probably run us off the place before we got the job half done, but we could sneak back again . . ."

"No," Butch's Pa said flat out.

He was an awful stickler for doing the right thing, Butch's pa was—bound and determined he wasn't going to get caught off base doing something wrong.

"That is not the way to do," he said. "It is most unethical. You think that if this Carter knew he had these things, he would want to keep them?"

"I am sure he would. He doesn't care for anybody but himself."

Butch's pa heaved a big sigh and crawled to his feet. "Young man, would your father be at home?"

"He most likely would."

"We'll go and talk with him," he said. "He is a native of this planet and an honest man and he will tell us what is right."

"Mister," I asked him, "what do you call these things?"

"We have a name for them, but it does not translate into your tongue with anything like ease. We call them something that is neither here nor there, something that is halfway between. Halfling would be the word for it, if there is such a word."

"I don't know if there is or not," I said, "but it sounds right."

"Then," decided Butch's pa, "for sheer convenience we shall call them that."

At first, Pa was as flabbergasted as I was, but the more he listened to Butch's pa and the more he thought about it, the more he seemed to become convinced there might be something to it.

"There sure-God has been something causing all this hard luck of ours," he declared. "A man can't turn his hand to a thing but it goes wrong on him. And I must admit that it makes a man sore to have all these things happen to him and then look at Carter and see all the good luck he has."

"I am profoundly sorry," said Butch's pa, "to discover halflings exist on this planet. There were many on our old home planet and on some of the neighboring worlds, but I had no idea they had spread this far."

"What I don't rightly understand," said Pa, lighting up his pipe and settling down to hash the matter over, "is how they can be here and a man not see them."

"There is a most precise scientific explanation, but I have not the language to translate it. You might say that they are off-phase of this existence, but still not quite into it. The child eye is undulled, the mind unclosed, so that they can see somewhat, a fraction, just a little, beyond reality. And that is why they can be seen by children but are invisible to adults. I, in my time, when I was a child, saw and killed my share of them. You understand, sir, that on my planet, it is an accepted childish chore to be eternally on watch for them and vigilantly keep their numbers down."

Pa asked me: "You didn't see these things?"

"No, Pa," I said, "I didn't."

"And you didn't see them, either?" Pa asked Butch's pa.

"I lost my ability to see them many years ago," said Butch's pa. "So far as your boy is concerned, it may be that only the children of certain races—"

"But they must see us," Pa insisted. "Otherwise, how would they be able to bring good luck or bad?"

"They do see us. In that all are agreed. I assure you that the scientists of my planet have devoted many long and arduous years to the study of these beings."

"And another thing. What is their purpose in adopting people? What do they get out of it? Why should they show all this favoritism?"

"We are not sure," said Butch's pa. "There are several theories. One is that they have no life of their own, but must have a pattern in order to live. If they did not have a pattern, they would have no form nor senses and probably no perception. They are, it would seem, like parasites in many ways."

But Pa interrupted him. Pa was all wound up and had a lot of thinking that he had to do out loud.

"I don't suppose," he said, "that they are doing it just for the hell of it. There must be a solid reason—there is to everything. It seems reasonable to me that everything is planned, that there's nothing without purpose. There's nothing, when you get right down to it, that basically is bad. Maybe these things, with the bad luck that they bring, are part of a plan to make folks face up to adversity and develop character."

I swear it was the first time I had ever heard Pa sound like a preacher, but he sure did then.

"You may be right," said Butch's pa. "There is no agreement entirely on the reason for their being."

"They might," suggested Pa, "be a sort of gypsy tribe, just wandering around. They might up and move away."

Butch's pa sadly shook his head. "It almost never happens, sir, that they move away."

"When I was a kid, I once went to the city with my ma. I don't remember much about it, but I do remember standing in front of a great big window that was filled with toys and knowing that I never could have any one of them, and wishing hard that some day I might have just one of them. Maybe that's the way it is with these folks. Maybe they're just outside the window looking in on us."

"Your analogy is exceedingly picturesque," said Butch's pa with forthright admiration.

"But here I am running on," Pa said, "as if I took for gospel every word of it. I don't wish for the world to doubt you or what you've told us . . ."

"But you do and I cannot find it in my breast to blame you. Would you, perhaps, believe more readily if your son could tell you that he saw them?"

"Why, yes," Pa said thoughtfully. "I surely would."

"Before I came to Earth, I was a worker in the field of optics, and it may be possible that I can grind a set of lenses that would allow your son to see halflings. I am not sure he could, of course, but it is a chance worth taking. He is of the age to have still that ability to peer beyond reality. It may be that all his vision needs is a slight correction."

"If you could do that, if Steve here could really see these things, then I would believe you without the slightest question."

"I'll get on with it immediately," said Butch's pa. "Later on, we can discuss the ethics of the situation."

Pa sat watching Butch and his pa going down the road, and he sort of shuddered. "Some of these aliens sure-God come up with queer ideas. A man has got to watch himself or he might swallow some of them."

"These ones are all right," I told him.

Pa sat there thinking and I could almost see the wheels whirring in his brain. "I don't know too much about it, but the more one thinks about it, the more sense it makes. It seems reasonable to me that there might be just so much good luck and so much bad luck, and ordinarily both the good and the bad would be handed out in somewhat equal parts. But suppose something came along and corralled all the good luck for one particular man, then there ain't anything but bad luck left for the rest."

I wished that I could see it as clear as Pa. But the more I thought, the more like Greek it seemed.

"Maybe," said Pa, "when you get to the root of it, it's nothing more than simple competition. What is good luck for one man is bad luck for another. Say there is a job that everybody wants. One man gets it and that's good luck for him, but bad luck for the others. And say that this bear back in the woods just had to raid a hive. It would be bad luck for the man whose hive was raided, but good luck—or at least not bad luck—for the man whose hive the bear passed up. And say again that someone's tractor had to get busted . . ."

Pa went on like that for quite a while, but I don't think he even fooled himself. Both of us knew, I guess, that there would have to be more to it than that.

Fancy Pants and Nature Boy were sore at me for not coming back with the crowbar. They said I stood them up and I had to explain to them I hadn't and I had to tell them exactly what had happened before they would believe me. I suppose it might have been better if I had kept my mouth shut, but in the end I don't believe it made much difference.

Anyhow, we got to be friends again and we all liked Butch, so we had good times together. The other two kidded Butch a lot about the halflings at first, but Butch didn't seem to mind, so they gave it up.

We certainly had a good time that summer. There was the lizard and a lot of other things as well, including the family of skunks that fell in love with Nature Boy and followed him around. And there was the time Fancy Pants hauled all of Carter's machinery out into the back forty, with Andy hunting for it like lost cows and madder by the minute.

At home, and elsewhere in the neighborhood, there was still bad luck. The day the barn caved in, Pa was ready to admit flat out that there was something to what Butch's pa had said. It was all Ma could do to keep him from going up the road to see Andy Carter and talk to him by hand.

I had another birthday and the folks gave me a live-it set and that was something I had not expected. I had wanted one, of course, but I knew they cost a lot and with all the bad luck they had been having, the folks were short of money.

You know what a live-it is, of course. It's something like TV, only better. TV you only watch and with a live-it set you live it.

It's a viewer that you clamp onto your head and you look into it and you pick your channel and turn it on, then settle back and live the things you see.

It doesn't take any imagination to live it, because it all is there —the action and the sound and smell and even, to some extent, the actual feel of it.

My set was just a kid's set and I could only get the kid channels. But that was all right with me. I wouldn't have wanted to live through all that mushy stuff.

All morning I spent with my live-it. There was one thing called "Survey Incident" and it was all about what happened when a human survey team put down on an alien planet. Another one was about a hunting trip on a jungle world and a third was "Robin Hood." I think, of the three of them, I liked "Robin Hood" the best.

I was all puffed up with pleasure and pride and I wanted to show the kids what the folks had given me. So I took the live-it and went down to Fancy Pants' place. But I never got a chance to show the live-it to him.

Just before I got to the gate, I saw Fancy Pants floating along, silent and sneaky—and floating along beside him, not more than a yard away, was that poor, beat-up, bedraggled cat that Fancy Pants was always pestering. He had the cat all wrapped up in a tight bundle and it couldn't move a muscle, but I could see its eyes were wide with fright. If you ask me, that cat had a right to be afraid. There was scarcely anything in the book Fancy Pants hadn't done to it.

"Hi, Fancy Pants!" I yelled.

He put a finger to his lips and crooked another finger to let me know I could join him in whatever he was doing. So I jumped the fence and Fancy Pants floated lower until he was about my level.

"What's going on?" I asked him.

"He went away and forgot to close the padlock," whispered Fancy Pants.

"Who went away?"

"My pa. He forgot to lock the door to the old machine shed."

"But that's where—"

"Sure," said Fancy Pants. "That's where he's got the time machine."

"Fancy Pants, you don't intend to put that cat in there!"

"Why not? Pa ain't ever tried a living thing in it and I want to see what happens."

I didn't like it and yet I wanted awful bad to see that time machine. I wondered what one looked like. No one had seen the time machine except Fancy Pants' pa.

"What's the matter with you?" asked Fancy Pants. "Are you going chicken on me?"

"But the cat!"

"For the love of Mike, it's nothing but a cat."

And that was right, of course. It was nothing but a cat.

So I went along with him and we sneaked into the shed and pulled the door behind us. And there was the time machine in the middle of the floor.

It didn't look like much. It was a kind of hopper, and a bunch of things like coils ran around the throat where the hopper narrowed down, and that was all except for a crude control board that was nailed onto a post and hooked up to the hopper with a lot of wires.

The hopper came up to my chest and I put my live-it down on the edge of it and craned my neck to look into the throat to see what I could see.

At just that moment, Fancy Pants threw the switch that turned it on. I jerked away. For it was a scary business when you turned that hopper on.

When I sneaked back to have another look, it looked for all the world as if it were a whirlpool of cream, sort of thick and rich and shiny—and it was alive. You could see the liveness in it. And there was a feeling in it that maybe you should just jump in head first and I had to grip the edges of the hopper hard not to.

I *might* have dived in, if the cat at that very moment hadn't somehow wiggled free from Fancy Pants.

I don't know how that cat did it. Fancy Pants had it all rolled into a ball and really buttoned up. Maybe Fancy Pants got careless or maybe the cat had finally figured out an angle. But, anyhow, Fancy Pants had the cat poised above the hopper and was about to let it fall. The cat didn't get loose in part—it got loose entirely—and there it was, yowling and screaming, tail fluffed out, clawing at thin air to keep from falling down into the hopper. It managed to throw itself to one side as it fell and the claws of one paw hooked onto the hopper's edge while the other hooked into my live-it set.

I let out a yell and made a grab to try to save the live-it, but I was too late. The cat dragged it off balance and it slid down into that creamy whirlpool and was gone.

The cat shinnied up a post and up into the rafters and hung there, screaming and wailing.

Just then the door came open and there floated Fancy Pants' pa and we were caught red-handed.

I figured Fancy Pants' pa would give me the works right then and there.

But he didn't do a thing. He just floated there for a moment looking at the two of us.

Then he looked at me alone and said: "Steve, please leave."

I went out that door as fast as I could go, with just a fast glance back over my shoulder at Fancy Pants. He was pale and already beginning to appear a little shriveled. He knew what he had coming to him, and even while I realized that he deserved every bit of it, I still felt sorry for him.

But staying wouldn't help him and I was glad enough to get off scot-free.

Except that it wasn't scot-free.

I don't know what was the matter with me—just scared stiff, I guess. Anyhow, I went straight home and told Pa right out about it and he took down the strap from behind the door and let me have a few.

But it seemed to me that he didn't have his heart in it. He was getting a little uneasy about all these alien goings-on.

For several days I didn't go off the place. To have gone anywhere, I would have had to walk past Fancy Pants' house and I didn't want to see him—not for a while, at least.

Then one day Butch and his pa showed up and they had the glasses.

"I don't know if they'll fit," said Butch's pa. "I had to guess the fitting."

They looked just like any other glasses except that the lenses had funny lines running every which way, as if someone had taken the glass and twisted it until it was all crinkled out of shape.

I put them on and they were a bit loose and things looked different through them, but not a great deal different. I was looking at the barnyard when I put them on. The barnyard was still there, but it appeared strange and a little weird, although it was hard to put a finger on what was wrong with it. It was a bright, hot August day and the sun was shining hard, but when I put the glasses on, it seemed suddenly to get cloudy and a little cold. And that was some of the difference, but not all of it.

There was a feeling of strangeness that sent a shiver through me, and the light was wrong, and worst of all was the sense that I didn't belong. But there was nothing you could say flat out was absolutely wrong.

"Is it any different, son?" asked Pa.

"Some different," I answered.

"Let me see."

He took the glasses off me and put them on himself.

"I can't see a thing," he said. "Just a lot of color."

"I told you," said Butch's pa, "that only the young can see. You and I are too fixed in reality."

Pa took the glasses off and let them dangle in his hand.

"Did you see any halflings?" he asked me.

I shook my head.

"There are no halflings here," said Butch.

"To see the halflings," Butch's pa put in, "we must journey to the Carter place."

"Well, then," said Pa, "what are we waiting for?"

So the four of us went up the road to the Carter place.

There didn't seem to be anyone at home and that was rather queer, for either Carter himself or Mrs. Carter or Ozzie Burns, the hired man, always stayed at home if the others had to go to town or anywhere.

We stood in the road and Butch had himself a good look. There weren't any halflings around the buildings and there weren't any in the orchard or in any of the fields, so far as Butch could see. Pa was getting impatient. I knew what he was thinking—that he had been made a fool of by a bunch of aliens.

Then Butch said excitedly that he thought he saw a halfling

down in one corner of the pasture, just at the edge of the big Dark Hollow woods, where Andy had a hay barn, but it was so far away that he could not be sure.

"Give your boy the glasses," said Butch's pa, "and let him have a look."

Pa handed me the glasses and I put them on. I had a hard time getting familiar landmarks sorted out, but finally I did, and sure enough, down in the corner of the pasture, there were things moving around that looked like human beings, but mighty funny human beings. They had a sort of smoky look about them, as if you could blow them away.

"Well, what do you see?" asked Pa.

I told him what I saw and he stood there considering, rubbing his hand back and forth across his chin, with the whiskers grating.

"There doesn't seem to be a soul around," he said. "I don't suppose it would hurt if we went down there. If the things are there, I want Steve to have a good, hard look at them."

"You think it is all right?" asked Butch's pa, worried. "It's not unethical?"

"Well, sure," said Pa, "I suppose it is. But if we are quick about it and get out right away, Andy never needs to know."

So we crawled underneath the fence and went over the pasture and crossed into the woods so we could sneak up on the place where we had seen the halflings.

The going was a little rough, for in places the brush was rather heavy, and there were thick blackberry patches with the bushes loaded with black and shiny fruit.

But we sneaked along as quietly as we could and we finally reached a point opposite the place where we had seen the halflings.

Butch nudged me and whispered fiercely: "There they are!"

I put the glasses on and there they were, by golly.

Up at the edge of the hayfield, just beyond the woods, stood Andy's hay barn, really just a roof set on poles to cover the hay that Andy didn't have the room to get into his regular barn.

It was a rundown, dilapidated thing, and there was Andy standing up there on the roof, and some packs of shingles sat on the roof beside him, while climbing up a ladder with a bunch of shingles on his shoulder was Ozzie Burns, the hired man. Andy was reaching down to get the shingles that Ozzie was carrying up the ladder and at the foot of the ladder, hanging onto it so it wouldn't tip, was Mrs. Burns. And that was the reason none of them had been around—they were all down here, fixing to patch up the shingles on the barn.

And there were the halflings, a good two dozen of them. A bunch of them were up on the roof with Andy and a couple on the ladder with the hired man and a couple more of them helping to hold up the ladder. They looked busy and energetic and efficient, and every single one of them was the spitting image of Andy Carter.

Not that they really resembled Andy, for they didn't. They were actually wraithlike things that seemed to have but little substance to them. They were little more than a smoky outline, but those smoky outlines—every single one of them—was the squat, bulldog outline of Andy Carter. And they walked like him, with a belligerent swagger, and all their motions were like his, and you could sense the meanness in them.

In the time that I was gaping at them, Ozzie Burns had handed the shingles up to Andy and clambered up on the roof beside him and Mrs. Burns had stepped away from the ladder, not needing to hold it any longer, since Ozzie was safe up on the roof. I saw the ladder was standing on uneven ground and that was why she'd had to hold it.

Andy had been crouched down to lay the pack of shingles on the roof. Now he straightened up and looked toward the woods and he saw us standing there.

"What are you doing here?" he roared at us, and started down the ladder.

And now comes the funny part of it. I'll have to take it slow and try to tell it straight.

To me, it seemed the ladder separated and became two ladders. One was standing there against the hay barn and the other left it, and the top of this second ladder began to slide along the roof and was about to fall and carry Andy with it to the ground, just as sure as shooting.

I was about to shout for Andy to look out, although I don't know why I should have. If he fell and broke his neck, it'd have been all right with me.

But just as I was about to yell, two halflings moved fast and this second ladder disappeared. It had been sliding along the roof and was about to fall, with a second Andy clinging to it and beginning to look scared—and then suddenly there was just one ladder and one Andy instead of two.

I stood there, shaking, and I knew what I had seen, but at that moment I wouldn't admit it, not even to myself.

It was, I told myself, as if I had been looking at two separate times—at a time when the ladder should have fallen and at another time when it had not fallen because the halflings hadn't let it. I had seen good luck in actual operation. Or the averting of bad luck. Whichever it might be, it all came out the same.

And now Andy was almost at the ladder's foot and the halflings were coming down from off the roof in a helter-skelter fashion—some of them jumping off and others dropping off, and if they had been human instead of what they were, there would have been a flock of broken legs and necks.

Pa stepped out of the woods into the field and I stepped along with him. We knew we were walking into trouble, but we weren't ones to run. And trailing along behind us were Butch and his pa, but both of them looked scared and you could see they had no heart for it.

Then Andy was down off the ladder and walking straight toward us and he sure was on the warpath. And walking along beside him, in a line on either side of him, were all those halflings, and they kept in step with him and swung their arms like him and looked as mean as he did.

"Now, Andy," said Pa, trying to be conciliatory, "let us be reasonable." But it was quite an effort, I can tell you, for Pa to speak that way. He hated Andy Carter clear up from the ground and he sure-God had his reasons. Andy had been a rotten neighbor for an awful lot of years.

"Don't you tell me to be reasonable!" yelled Andy. "I been hearing all this talk about how you are blaming me for what you call hard luck. And I tell you to your face it ain't hard luck at all. It's plain downright shiftlessness and bad management. And if you think you're going to get anywhere with all this talk of yours, you are just plain crazy. You been taken in by a lot of alien nonsense. If I had my way, I'd run all those stinking aliens right off the planet."

Pa took a quick step forward and I thought he was about to

clobber Andy. But Butch's pa jumped forward and grabbed him by the arm.

"No! No!" he shouted. "There's no need to fight him! Let us go away!"

Pa stood there with Butch's pa hanging to his arm, and I wondered for a minute which one he would clobber, Butch's pa or Andy.

"I never liked you," Andy said to Pa, "from the first day I saw you. I had you figured for a bum and that is what you are. And this taking up with aliens is the lowest thing any human ever did. You ain't no better than they are. Now get off this place and don't you ever dare set foot on it again."

Pa jerked his arm and sent Butch's pa staggering to one side. Then he brought it up and back. I saw Andy's head start moving to one side, dropping over toward his shoulder, and for a second it looked like he had the beginning of two heads. And I knew that I was watching another accident beginning to unhappen, although it was no accident, for Pa sure meant to paste him.

But they weren't fast enough to get Andy's head tilted out of danger. They weren't dealing this time with a slowly sliding ladder.

There was a solid crack like someone had hit a tree with an axe on a frosty morning, and Andy's head jerked back and his feet came off the ground and he went tincup over teakettle, flat on his back.

And there were all those silly halflings standing in a row, with shocked looks upon their faces, as if they couldn't quite believe it. You could have bought the lot of them for no more than half a buck.

Pa turned around and held out his hand to me and said: "Come on, Steve. Let's go."

He said it in a quiet voice that was clear and level, and there was, I thought, a note of pride in it. And we turned around, the two of us, and we walked away from there, not hurrying any and not even looking back.

"I swear to God," said Pa, "I've meant to do that ever since I laid eyes on him fifteen years ago."

I hadn't noticed what had happened to Butch or to his pa and I wondered where they might have gone to, for there wasn't hide nor hair of them. But I didn't say anything to Pa about it, for I had a hunch he might not be harboring exactly friendly feelings toward Butch's pa.

But I needn't have worried about them, for when we got out to the road they were waiting for us, breathing kind of hard and considerably scratched up. The way they'd gone through that brush and all those blackberry patches must have been a caution.

"I am glad to see," said Butch's pa, "that you got back safely."

"Don't mention it," Pa told him coldly, and went on down the road, hanging tight onto my hand so that I had to trot along.

We got back home and went into the kitchen to get a drink of water.

Pa said to me, "Steve, have you got those glasses?"

I dug them out of my pocket and handed them to him. He put them on the shelf above the washstand.

"Leave them there," he said. "Don't touch them again--not ever. Do you understand me?"

"Yes, sir," I replied.

To tell the truth, I would have liked it better if he'd gone ranting up and down. I was afraid that what had happened out there in the woods had made him decide to go to one of the Homestead Planets. I told myself he maybe already had made up his mind and didn't need to rant.

But he never said a word about the fight with Andy nor about the Homestead Planets and he wasn't sore at me. He kept on being quiet and I knew that he still was mad clean through and I figured that he was mostly sore at Butch and Butch's pa for their having made a complete fool of him.

I did a lot of wondering about what I'd seen down there in Andy's hayfield. And the more I thought about it, the more I was convinced that I had grasped the secret of how the halflings operated.

For I must have been seeing in two different times when I'd been looking at the ladder. I must have looked into the future and seen the ladder slip. Except it never slipped, for the halflings, seeing that it would slip, had made one leg of it settle in the ground. And then, with the ladder sitting solid, it never slipped, of course. The halflings had done no more than look ahead a bit and then righted something that was about to happen before it had a chance to happen.

And that, I told myself, was the basis of good luck and bad. The halflings could spot disaster coming and try to head it off. Except they couldn't always make it. They had tried to protect Andy when Pa took a lick at him and they had failed. So I figured that they weren't infallible and that made me feel some better.

For if they could make good luck for Andy, it stood to reason they could make bad luck for the rest of us. All they had to do, if they had a mind to, was to see good luck heading for us and change it into bad.

It might even be possible, I told myself, that the halflings lived ahead of us, by a few seconds or so, and that the only thing which separated us from them was this matter of a different time.

But there was something else that troubled me a lot. Why had I been able to see two different times? It was clear to me that Butch and his people couldn't, for if they could, they'd have more answers to the halfling situation. They'd been studying it for years, and so far as I could figure, they didn't know for certain about this two-time business.

It seemed to me, when I thought about it, that Butch's pa might have ground better than he knew when he made my glasses. He might have put in something or taken out something or done something he didn't know about at all.

Or it might be that the human race had a different kind of vision, or maybe just a little different, and when you added the correction for Butch's kind of vision to our kind of vision, you brought out a thing you couldn't even guess at.

I tried and tried to get it clear within my mind, but I couldn't do it. I just went around in circles.

I stayed close to home for several days because I had a feeling that I should be ignoring Butch to uphold the family honor and that is how I missed the big hassle between Fancy Pants and Nature Boy.

It seems that Nature Boy got sick and tired of how Fancy Pants was mistreating that poor, bedraggled cat. So he took one member of the skunk family that had fallen in love with him and he clipped and dyed that skunk to look exactly like the cat. And one day he sneaked over to Fancy Pants' place and switched the skunk for the cat without anyone seeing him.

The skunk didn't want to be Fancy Pants' skunk; he belonged to Nature Boy. So he started beating it back home as fast as he could go, which wasn't very fast.

Just then Fancy Pants floated out of the door and he saw the skunk going through the gate. He thought the cat was trying to sneak away from him, so he reached out and grabbed it up and rolled it into a ball and tossed it pretty high into the air, sort of careless like, to teach that cat a lesson.

It went up in the air and came down smack-dab on top of Fancy Pants, who was floating out there in the yard a few feet off the ground.

The skunk was scared witless. As soon as it got its claws fastened into Fancy Pants and had some leverage, it retaliated with enthusiasm. And for the first time in his life, Fancy Pants thumped down to the ground and, among other things, he got his clothes as dirty as any other kid.

I would give a zillion dollars to have seen it.

For a while, they figured that they might have to take Fancy Pants out somewhere and bury him for a week or two to make him presentable again. But they finally got him to a point where one could come near him.

Fancy Pants' pa went storming down to talk with Nature Boy's pa and the two of them put on a ruckus that had the neighborhood chuckling for a week.

And now I was really strapped for playmates. I was still cold-shouldering Butch and I knew better than to take up again with either Nature Boy or Fancy Pants. They both were mean cusses when they set their mind to it. I was sure we hadn't heard the last of this feud of theirs and I didn't want to get tangled up in it by being friends with either one of them.

It was plenty tough, let me tell you. Here I was with vacation almost ended and no one to pal around with and my live-it gone. I watched the days slip past and regretted every minute of it.

Then one day the sheriff drove up to the house.

Pa and I were out in the barnyard trying to tinker up a corn binder that was all tied together with haywire and other makeshift odds and ends. Pa had been threatening to buy one for a long time now, but with all the tough luck we'd been having, there wasn't any money.

"Good morning, Henry," the sheriff said to Pa.

Pa said good morning back.

"I hear you been having a little trouble with your neighbors," said the sheriff.

"Not what you would call real trouble," Pa told him. "I busted one in the snoot the other day is all."

"Right on his own farm, too."

Pa quit working on the binder and squatted back on his heels to look up at the sheriff. "Andy been around complaining?"

"He was in the other day. Said you had swallowed some fool story that this new alien family started. About some kind of bad-luck critters he'd been harboring on his farm."

"And you talked him out of it?"

"Well, now," said the sheriff, "I am a peaceable man and I hate to see two neighbors fighting. Andy wanted to put you under peace bond, but I said I'd come over and have a talk with you."

"All right," invited Pa. "Go ahead and talk."

"Now look here, Henry. You know the story about them hard-luck critters is so much poppycock. I'm surprised you took any stock in it."

Pa got up slowly. He had a hard look on his face and I thought for a minute he was about to bust the sheriff. I was scared, I tell you, for that is something no one should ever do—up and bust a sheriff.

I don't know what he might have done or what he might have said, for at that moment Nature Boy's pa came tearing down the road in his old jalopy and pulled in behind the sheriff's car, intending to park there. But he miscalculated some and he smacked into the sheriff's car hard enough to skid it ahead six feet or so with the brakes all set.

The sheriff broke into a run. "By God!" he said. "It isn't even safe to drive out into this corner of the county!"

The two of us ran along behind him. I was running just because there was some excitement, but I figure maybe Pa was running so he could help Nature Boy's pa if the sheriff should take it into his head to get feisty with him.

And the funny thing about it was that Nature Boy's pa, instead of sitting there and waiting for the sheriff, had jumped out of his car and was running up the slope to meet us.

"They told me I'd find you here," he panted to the sheriff.

"You found me, all right," said the sheriff, practically breathing fire. "Now I'm going to—"

"My boy is gone!" yelled Nature Boy's pa. "He wasn't home last night . . ."

The sheriff grabbed him and said to him: "Now let's take this easy. Tell me exactly what happened."

"He went off yesterday, early in the morning, and he didn't show up for meals, but we didn't think too much of it—he often goes off for an entire day. He has a lot of friends out there in the woods."

"And he didn't come home last night?"

Nature Boy's pa shook his head. "Along about dusk, we got worried. I went out and hunted for him and I didn't find him. I hunted all night long, but there wasn't any sign of him. I thought maybe he'd just holed up for the night with one of his friends in the woods. I thought maybe he'd show up when it got light, but he never did."

"Well, all right," said the sheriff, "you leave it to me. We'll rouse out all the neighbors and organize a hunt. We'll find him." He said to me: "You know the lad? You did some playing with him?"

"All the time," I answered.

"Lead us to all the places where you played. We'll look there first."

Pa said: "I'll start phoning the neighbors. I'll get them here right away."

He ran up the hill toward the house.

In an hour or less, there were a hundred people gathered and the sheriff took them all in hand. He divided them into posses and appointed captains for each posse and told them where to hunt.

It was the most excitement we've ever had in the neighborhood.

The sheriff took me with the posse he headed up and we went down Dark Hollow. I took them to the place where we were digging out the lizard and the place where we had started to dig ourselves a cave and the hole in the creek where Nature

Boy had made friends with some whopping trout, and some other places, too. We found some old tracks of Nature Boy's, but there was no fresh sign, although we hunted up and down the hollow clear to where it flowed into the river, and we trailed back come night, and I was tuckered out.

And a little scared as well.

For an awful suspicion had come to me.

And no matter how hard I tried to keep from thinking of it, I couldn't help myself, for all the time I was trying to remember if the hopper in that time machine had been big enough to take a kid the size of Nature Boy.

Ma fed me and sent me up to bed and later she came up and tucked me in and kissed me. She hadn't done that in years. She knew I was too big to be tucked in and kissed, but she did it anyhow.

And then she went downstairs and I lay there listening to some men who still were out there in the yard, talking among themselves. Some of the others still were hunting and I knew that I should be out there hunting with them, but I knew Ma wouldn't let me go and I was glad of it. For I was tired all through and the woods at night can be a scary place.

I should by rights have gone straight to sleep. Any other night I would have. But I lay there thinking about that hopper in the time machine and I wondered how long it would take before someone told the sheriff about the ruckus between Fancy Pants and Nature Boy, and I thought perhaps they had already. And if so, the sheriff probably was looking into it right now, for the sheriff was nobody's fool.

I wondered if I should tell him myself if no one else had. But that was one fight I didn't have any hankering to get tangled up in.

Finally I went to sleep and it seemed to me I hadn't been asleep any time at all when something woke me up. It still was dark, but there was a red glow shining through the window. I sat up quick, with my hair standing half on end.

I thought at first it might be our barn or the machine shed, but then I saw it wasn't that close. I skinned out of bed and over to the window. That fire was a big one and it wasn't too far up the road.

It looked as if it was on the Carter place, but I knew that

must be wrong, for if bad luck like that struck anyone, it wouldn't be Andy Carter. Unless, of course, he was loaded with insurance.

I went downstairs in my bare feet and Ma was standing at the door, looking up the road toward the blaze.

"What is it, Ma?" I asked.

"It's the barn on the Carter place," she said. "They phoned the neighborhood for help, but all the men are out hunting Nature Boy."

We stood there, Ma and me, and watched until the blaze almost died out, and then Ma hiked me off to bed.

I crawled underneath the covers, weak with this new excitement. I wondered why we should tag along for months with nothing happening, and then all at once have it busting out all over.

I lay there and thought about Andy Carter's barn and there was something wrong about it. Andy had been the luckiest man in seven counties and now, without any warning, he was having bad luck just like the rest of us.

I wondered if the halflings might have gone off and left him, and if that was the case, I wondered why they had. Maybe, I told myself, they had gotten plain disgusted with Andy's meanness.

It was broad daylight when I woke again and I jumped straight out of bed and climbed into my clothes. I rushed downstairs to see if there was any word of Nature Boy.

Ma said there wasn't, that the men were still out hunting. She had breakfast ready for me and insisted I eat it and warned me about wandering off or trying to join one of the searching parties. She said it wasn't safe for me to be out in the woods with so many bears about. And that was funny, for she had never worried about the bears before.

But she made me promise I wouldn't.

As soon as I got out, I zipped down the road as fast as I could go. I had to see the place where the Carter barn had burned down and I just had to talk with someone. And Butch was the only one left that I could talk to.

There wasn't much to see at the Carter place, just burned and blackened timbers that still were smoking some. I stood out in the road a while and then I saw Andy come out of the house and he stood there for a minute looking straight at me. So I got out of there.

I went past Fancy Pants' place real fast, hoping I wouldn't see him. At the moment, I didn't want a thing to do with Fancy Pants.

When I got to Butch's place, his ma told me he was sick in bed. She didn't think it was catching, she said, so I went up to see him.

Butch sure looked terrible lying there—more like a runty hoot owl than he ever had before—but he was glad to see me. I asked him how he was and he said he felt better. He made me promise I wouldn't tell his ma, then told me that he'd got sick from eating green apples he'd pinched off the Carter orchard. He'd heard about Nature Boy and I told him in a whisper the suspicions I had.

He lay there looking at me solemnly and finally he said: "Steve, I should have told you this before. That is no time machine."

"No time machine? How do you know?"

"Because I saw the stuff that Fancy Pants' pa put through it. It didn't go anywhere. It still is lying there."

"You saw . . ." And then I had it. "You mean it went to where the halflings are?"

"That's what I mean," said Butch.

Sitting there on the edge of the bed, I tried to think it through, but there were so many questions bubbling up in me that I couldn't do it.

"Butch," I asked, "where is this place that the halflings are?"

"I don't know," said Butch. "It's close to us, almost in this world, but not really."

And I remembered something Pa had said several weeks before. "You mean it's like a place behind a plate-glass window that's between our world and theirs?"

"Something like that."

"And if Nature Boy is there, what would happen to him?"

Butch shuddered. "I don't know."

"Would he be all right? Could he breathe in there?"

"I suppose he could," said Butch. "I think the halflings do."

I got up from the bed and started for the door. Then I turned back again.

"Butch, what are the halflings doing? What are they hanging around for?"

"No one's sure," said Butch. "There are a lot of ideas about what they are after. One is that they have to be near something that is living before they can live themselves. They can't live a life themselves; they've got to have a life to—well, like imitate, only that's not the word."

"They need a pattern," I said, remembering what Butch's pa had said that day, before Pa choked him off with his own rambling about what the halflings might be after.

"I guess you could call it that," said Butch.

And I stood there thinking what a lousy life the halflings must have led, using Andy Carter as their pattern.

But that wasn't so, for the halflings, that time I had seen them, had sure-God been happy. They'd been running around up there on the roof and keeping themselves busy and enjoying themselves.

And they had, every one of them, looked like Andy Carter. And of course they would, with Andy as their pattern.

Thinking about it, I could see how someone like Andy, with his kind of disposition, might enjoy being mean as dirt and ornery with his neighbors. He'd have a sense of independence and the feel of every hand being raised against him and him standing there like a mighty warrior, defying all of them. And from that he'd get a sense of strength and domination. All in all, I supposed, Andy, for a man like him, might be living a pretty darned satisfactory life.

I started for the door, and Butch called after me, "Where are you going, Steve?"

"I'm going to find Nature Boy," I said.

"I'll go with you."

"No, you stay in bed. Your ma will skin both of us if you don't."

I got out of the house and headed fast for home, and as I ran, I kept on thinking about how the halflings had no life of their own, but had to find another life and pattern themselves on it.

Sometimes they'd be mighty lucky and fasten onto someone who'd give them a good and exciting life, or maybe a good and contented life, but other times they'd get a mighty poor one.

But you had to say this for them—they gave all the help they could to the one they'd picked out as a pattern, and they kept working at it.

And I wondered how many persons who had been great successes might have been watched over by the halflings. What an awful letdown it would be if they were to learn that they had not become great or rich or famous through any particular effort or brilliance of their own, but by the grace of a bunch of things that helped them from outside.

I got home and went into the kitchen and over to the sink.

"Is that you, Steve?" Ma called from the living room.

"I'm getting a drink," I told her.

"Where you been?"

"Just around."

"Now don't you go running off," she warned.

"No, ma'am, I won't."

And all the time I was talking to her, I was climbing on a chair so I could reach those glasses where Pa had put them on the shelf and told me not to touch them again—not ever.

Then I had them in my pocket and was climbing off the chair.

I heard Ma heading for the kitchen and I hurried out as quietly as I could.

I didn't put the glasses on until I got to where the Carter farm cornered on the road. I went along the road, watching carefully, and finally I found a bunch of halflings down in a fence corner just beyond the orchard. They were standing there and squabbling over something and they didn't seem to notice me until I got real close.

Then they all swung around and stood facing me. They seemed to be talking among themselves and pointed at me.

And there on the head of one of them, pushed up on his forehead, was the live-it set I had lost down the time machine.

When I saw that, I realized Butch actually had seen the stuff that Fancy Pants' pa had put through the time machine.

At first I don't think they realized that I could see them, but after I stood there for a while, staring at them, they began to move up closer to me.

I could feel the hair rearing right up on my head. There was nothing I wanted to do more than turn around and run. But I told myself they couldn't reach me and there was nothing to be scared of, so I stood my ground.

They reminded me of a bunch of crows. They must have seen I didn't have a gun, or maybe this particular bunch didn't know about the guns Butch's people had. And they crowded up real close to me, like a flock of crows is not afraid of an empty-handed man, but will keep their distance when he has a gun.

I could see their mouths moving at me, but naturally I couldn't hear a thing, and they kept pointing at the one that had my live-it on his head.

To tell the honest truth, I didn't pay too close attention to what they might have been doing at the start of it. I was too busy looking at them and trying to figure out what might have happened to them. There was one thing certain—this either was a different bunch than I had seen down in Andy Carter's hay-field or they had changed a lot. There was still some of Andy in them, although not as much of him as someone else, as if Andy and someone else had gotten sort of scrambled together.

Finally I made out that they were pointing at the one with the live-it on his head and then tapping their own heads, and I figured out that each of them was asking for a live-it too.

I don't know what I would have said to them or how I would have said it, if I had had the chance, only I never had the chance. They suddenly parted, as if someone from behind had pushed them to one side, and there was Nature Boy, standing face to face with me.

We stood there and looked at one another for a good long time, not saying anything, not making any motion. Then he stepped forward and I stepped forward until we were almost nose to nose. I was afraid there, for a moment, we'd walk right through each other. What would have happened then? Probably nothing much.

"You O.K.?" I asked him, thinking maybe he could read my lips even if he couldn't hear me, but he shook his head. So I asked him once again, talking slowly and forming my words as distinctly as I could. But he shook his head again.

Then I thought of something else.

I lifted up my hand and stuck out my finger and pretended I was writing on the imaginary window that separated us.

"YOU O.K.?" I wrote, taking it slow, because he'd have to read it backwards.

He didn't get it right away and I did it once again and this time he understood.

"O.K.," he wrote. And then he wrote real slow: "GET ME OUT!"

I stood there looking at him and it was horrible, for there he was and here I was, and so far as I could see, there was no way to get him out.

He must have sensed what I was thinking, because all at once his mouth trembled and that was the first time I'd ever seen Nature Boy even close to crying. Not even that time when we were digging out the lizard and a big rock fell on his toe.

I thought how bad it must have been for him, trapped in that place and able to see out, but knowing that no one could see in. He might even have followed some of the searching parties, hoping that someone might accidentally glimpse him, but knowing they couldn't. Maybe he had trailed along behind his pa, as close as he could get to him, and his pa not knowing it. And maybe he'd gone back home and watched his family and been all the lonelier for their not knowing he was there. And undoubtedly he'd hunted around for Butch, who he knew could see him, only Butch had been sick in bed.

And while I was thinking all of this, I got a faint idea. I told myself that it probably wouldn't work, but the more I thought about it, the more it seemed it might.

So I reached up with my finger and I wrote: "MEET ME AT FANCY PANTS'."

I pocketed my glasses and hurried along home. I circled around the house because I didn't want to take the chance of Ma seeing me and not letting me go. I went into the machine shed and found a length of rope and hunted up a hacksaw.

Lugging these, I made my way back to Fancy Pants' place. The machine shed was back of the barn, so no one from the house could see me, and anyhow no one seemed to be around. I knew that Fancy Pants' pa, and maybe Fancy Pants himself, would be out with the searchers, floating around over places where it would be impossible for the men on foot to go.

I laid down the rope and hacksaw and put on my glasses and Nature Boy was there, right beside the machine shed door.

He had some of the halflings with him, including the one who still had the live-it perched up on his forehead. And scattered all around the place, just like Butch had said, were tea cups and pie plates and children's blocks and a lot of other junk—the stuff that Fancy Pants' pa had fed into the time machine.

I looked at the halflings again and all at once I knew what was different about them. They were still some of Andy, but they were Nature Boy as well. And then I knew why Andy's barn had burned. These halflings of his had been so busy tagging around after Nature Boy that they had not been able to give Andy their attention.

It seemed only natural, of course. A halfling would get a lot more good out of a real live human inside that world of theirs than they would someone they could only see from behind a plate-glass window.

I took the glasses off and put them in my pocket and got to work. It was no easy job to saw through that padlock. The steel was awfully hard and the blade was dull and I was afraid it might break before I got through the steel. I cussed myself for not thinking to bring along an extra blade or two.

The sawing made an awful racket because I had forgotten to bring along some oil to squirt into the cut. But nobody heard the sawing.

Finally I got through.

I opened the door and stepped into the shed and the time machine was there, just the way I remembered it. I laid down the rope and went over to the control board and studied it, but it wasn't very complicated.

I got it turned on and the creamy whirlpool was sliding in the hopper's throat.

I picked up the rope and put my glasses on and got an awful fright. The machine shed was built on a gentle slope and the floor I was standing on was four or five feet above the ground and there I was, standing in the air, or so it seemed to me.

I had a sense, not of falling, but that by rights I should be falling, that any minute now I would begin to fall. I knew I wouldn't, naturally—I was standing on a transparent but solid floor. But knowing that didn't help much. That horrible, dreamlike feeling that I was about to tumble to the ground still kept hold of me.

And to make it even worse, there was Nature Boy, standing underneath me, with his head about level with my feet, looking up at me. His face was hopeful and he was motioning me to get busy with the rope.

Moving cautiously, even if there was no need of caution, I took one end of the rope and tossed it down the hopper and felt the suck and tug of the creamy whirlpool pulling down the rope. Down underneath the hopper, I could see the rope coming out, dangling into that place where Nature Boy was trapped. He moved over quickly and grabbed hold of the rope and I could feel the weight of the pull he put on it.

Nature Boy was about my size, perhaps a little smaller, and I knew I'd have to pull as hard as ever I could to get him out of there. I even wound a hitch around my hand to make sure it wouldn't slip. I pulled with all my might. And that rope didn't budge. It felt as if I were pulling against a house. I couldn't gain an inch.

So I quit pulling and knelt down, still hanging to the rope, peering at the base of the time machine.

It was a funny thing. The rope went to the bottom of the hopper's throat and then it skipped a foot or two. There was a foot or so of sidewise space where there wasn't any rope, and then the rope took up again, dangling down into that other place where Nature Boy had hold of it.

It didn't make sense. That rope should have gone into that other world in a straight and simple line. But the fact was that it didn't. It went off somewhere else before it fell into the other world.

And that, I figured, was the reason I couldn't pull it out. You could put a thing through the time machine, but you couldn't pull it back.

I looked down at Nature Boy and he looked back at me. I knew he'd seen it and knew as well as I did exactly what it meant. He looked pretty pitiful and I don't suppose I looked any better.

Just then the machine shed door screeched open.

I jumped up, still hanging to the rope, and there was Fancy Pants' pa.

He was all burned up and I couldn't blame him. Not after seeing how I had sawed the padlock to break into the place.

"Steve," he said, and you could hear him fighting to keep his voice level, "I thought I told you to keep out of here."

"Yes, sir," I said, "but Nature Boy's in there."

"Nature Boy!" he shouted. Then his voice dropped. "You don't know what you're talking about. How could he get in?"

"I don't know," I said, though I could have told him.

"Those glasses you are wearing," asked Fancy Pants' pa. "Are those the ones that were made for you by Butch's father?"

I nodded.

"Then you can see?"

"I can see Nature Boy," I said. "Just as plain as day."

I let go of the rope to take my glasses off and the rope slid down that hopper slicker than a whistle.

"It's all right, I guess," I said. "I couldn't pull him out."

"Steve," said Fancy Pants' pa, "I want you to tell me the truth. You're not just thinking up a story? You are not pretending?"

He was awful pale and I saw what he was thinking—if Nature Boy had gone down that hopper, the entire neighborhood would be down on him like a ton of bricks.

I crossed my heart. "And hope to die," I added.

That seemed good enough for him.

He shut off the time machine, then went outdoors. I followed him.

"Now," he said, "you stay right here. I'll be back immediately."

He floated off in somewhat of a hurry, zooming away above the pasture woods. He was out of sight in no time.

I sat down with my back against the machine shed and I was feeling pretty low. I knew I should put on my glasses, but I kept them in my pocket. I couldn't have stood the sight of Nature Boy looking out at me.

It was done and over with, I knew. There was no way in the world for me or anyone to rescue Nature Boy. He was gone for good and all. He was worse than gone.

And sitting there, I thought up some pretty dreadful things to do to Fancy Pants. For there was no doubt in my mind that Fancy Pants had got into the shed and had grabbed Nature

Boy, just like he did the cat, and dumped him down the hopper.

He was pretty sore, I knew, about the trick that Nature Boy had played on him with that skunk disguised as a cat. There was nothing he would have stopped at to get even.

I was sitting there and thinking when Fancy Pants' pa came floating up the road, and panting along behind him were Pa and the sheriff and Butch's pa and Nature Boy's pa and some other neighbors.

The sheriff came straight for me and he grabbed me by the shoulders and gave me a good, sharp shake.

"Now," he bellowed, "what is all this foolishness? I warn you, boy, it will go hard with you if you've been pulling our leg."

I tried to break away from him, but he wouldn't let me go. Then Pa stepped up and flung out his arm so that it caught the sheriff straight across the chest and sent him staggering back.

"You keep your hands off him," Pa said to the sheriff.

"But that story," blustered the sheriff. "You surely don't believe—"

"I do," said Pa. "I believe every word of it. My boy doesn't lie."

I'll say this for Pa: He may storm around and yell and he may take the strap to you for a lot of trifling things, but when it comes down to the pinch, he's standing there beside you.

"I'll remind you, Henry," said the sheriff, bristling, "that you're not entirely in the clear yourself. There's that business of the breach of peace I talked Andy Carter out of."

"Andy Carter," said Pa, speaking more slowly than one would expect him to. "He's the man who lives just down the road, if I recall correctly. Has there been any of you who have seen him lately?"

He looked around the crowd and it seemed that no one had.

"Last time I talked to Andy," said Pa, "was when I called him on the phone and told him we needed help. He said he was too busy to go hunting any alien whelp. He said it would be good riddance if all of them got lost."

He looked around the crowd and no one spoke a word. I don't suppose it was quite polite of Pa to say what he had, with Nature Boy's pa and Butch's pa and all the rest of those alien people standing there before us. But it sure-God was the truth, and they needed it right then, and Pa was the one who was not afraid to give it to them right between the eyes.

Then someone spoke up from the crowd and there were so many of them I couldn't be sure exactly who it was. But whoever it was said: "I tell you, folks, it was nothing but plain justice when Andy's barn burned down."

The sheriff bristled up. "If I thought one of you had a hand in that, I would–"

"You wouldn't do a thing," said Pa. He turned to me. "All right, Steve, tell us what you have to tell. I promise you that everyone will listen and there won't be any interruptions."

He looked straight at the sheriff when he was saying it.

"Just a second, sir," said Butch's pa. "I want to voice one important point. I know this boy can see the halflings, for I myself am the one who made the glasses for him. I know it is immodest of me to say a thing like this, but if I am nothing else, I am one fine optician."

"Thank you, sir," Pa said. "And now, Steve, go ahead."

But I never got a chance to say a single word, for Butch came stumbling around the barn and he had the gun with him. Or at least I took it for the gun, although it didn't look like one. It was a sticklike thing and it glittered in the sunlight from all sorts of prisms and mirrors set into it at all kinds of crazy angles.

"Pa," yelled Butch, "I heard about it and I brought the gun. I hope I'm not too late."

He ran up to his pa and his pa took the gun away from him and held it with everyone looking at him.

"Thank you, son," said Butch's pa. "It was good of you, but we won't need a gun. We aren't shooting anything today."

Then Butch cried out: "There he is, Pa! There's Nature Boy!"

I am not too sure that all of them believed I had found Nature Boy. Some might have had their reservations, and kept quiet about it because they didn't want to tangle with my pa. But Butch was a different matter. He could see these things without any silly glasses. And he was an alien, and everyone expected aliens to do these sort of crazy things.

"All right," admitted the sheriff, "so I guess he must be there. Now what do we do?"

"There doesn't seem to be much to go on," said Pa, "but we can't leave the boy in there." He looked at Nature Boy's pa. "Don't you worry. We'll figure a way to get him out."

But he spoke with so much confidence that I knew he was only talking so that Nature Boy's pa would know we weren't giving up.

Personally, I could see no hope. If you couldn't get him out the way he had gotten in, there didn't seem to be any other way. There were no doors into that other place.

"Gentlemen," said Butch's pa, "I have a small idea."

We all turned and waited.

"This gun," he said, "is used to keep down the number of halflings. It ruptures the wall between the two worlds sufficiently to let a bullet through. There might be an adaptation made of it, and we can do that later, or have someone do it for us, if that be necessary. But it seems possible to me we could use the gun itself."

"But we don't want to shoot the boy," the sheriff protested. "What we want to do is get him out."

"I have no intention, sir, of shooting him. There will be no bullet in the gun. All we'll use is the device to rupture the curtain or whatever it may be that lies between the worlds. And I can—what is the word?—tinker, I believe. I can tinker up the gun so that rupture will be greater."

He sat down on the ground and began working on the gun, shifting prisms here and there and adjusting tiny mirrors.

"There is just one thing," he said. "The rupture will last for but a moment. The boy must be immediate to take advantage of it. He must leap outward instantly the rupture should appear."

He turned to me. "Steve, can you communicate with him?"

"Communicate?"

"Talk to him. With signs, perhaps? Or the reading of the lips? Or some other way?"

"Sure, I can do that."

"Please, would you do it then?"

So I put on my glasses and looked around until I found Nature Boy. I had quite a time making him understand what we planned to do. It wasn't any easier to talk with him with all those crazy halflings standing all around him and making motions at me and pointing at the live-it, then tapping their own heads.

I was sweating plenty, for I was afraid that I had not got it all across to him, but I knew that any more of it would do no more than confuse him.

So I told Butch's pa that we were all set, and Butch's pa handed Butch the gun, and the rest stepped back a ways, and there was Butch with the gun and me standing right behind him. And there was Nature Boy standing in that other place, and a bunch of those silly halflings clustered all about him, and they sure didn't know about the alien gun or they'd not have been standing there. And Nature Boy looked like someone who'd been stood against a wall and was being executed without even any blindfold.

Out of the tail of my eye, I saw Fancy Pants floating off to one side of us, and he was the saddest-looking sack you ever saw.

Suddenly there was a strange white flash of brilliance as all the prisms and the mirrors moved on the gun that Butch was holding. He had pulled a trigger, or whatever it was.

For a second, straight in front of us, a funny sort of hole seemed to open up in the place that should not have been there at all—a jagged, ragged hole that appeared in nothingness. And I caught sight of Nature Boy jumping through the hole the second it stayed open.

And there he was, staggering a bit from the jump that he had made—only he was not alone. He had one of the halflings with him!

He had him by the wrist in a good tight grip and it was plain to see that he had jerked him through with him, for the halfling did not seem at all happy about what had happened to him. I saw at once that it was the halfling who had the live-it on his head.

Butch pushed the halfling toward me and he said: "Here, Steve. It was the only way I could get your live-it back."

I saw that Butch was letting go of the halfling and I grabbed him quick by the other wrist and was somewhat surprised to find that he was solid. I would not have been astonished if my hand had gone right through him, for he still had that swirly-smoky look about him, although it seemed to me he might be hardening up a bit and becoming more substantial.

Pa moved over close beside me, saying, "You be careful, Steve!"

"Aw, he's all right," I said. "He's not even trying to get away from me."

Someone raised a shout and I whirled around and stared.

A half dozen of the halflings had grabbed hold of the edges of that door into the other world, and they were tugging for dear life so it would stay open, and pouring out of it was that entire herd of halflings! They were shoving and pushing and scrambling to get through, and there were a lot more of them, it seemed to me, than I had thought there were.

We just stood there and watched them until they all were through. We didn't do a thing because there was not a thing we could do. And they stood there in a bunch, packed tight together, staring back at us.

The sheriff came alongside Pa. He pushed back his hat until it roosted on his neck. You could see that the sheriff was flabbergasted and I enjoyed it, for it had been apparent from the very first that the sheriff hadn't believed a word he'd heard about the halflings.

I don't know, maybe he still was thinking that it might be nothing but some sort of alien joke. You could see, without half trying, that the sheriff didn't cotton to any aliens.

"How come," he asked suspiciously, "that this one here has got a live-it on?"

So I told him and he blinked at me, dazed and dumbfounded, but he said nothing back. I sure had shut him up.

Fancy Pants' pa had floated up while I was telling it and he said I told the truth, for he'd been there and seen it.

Everyone began to talk at once, but Fancy Pants' pa floated up a little higher and held up his hand to command attention.

"Just a moment, if you please," he said. "Before we get down to more serious business, I have something you must hear. As you may suspect, knowing the episode of the skunk, my family undoubtedly has a great deal to answer for in this incident."

A human saying things like that would sound silly and pompous, but Fancy Pants' pa could get away with it.

"So," said Fancy Pants' pa, "I now announce to you that my malefactor son, for the forthcoming thirty days, must walk upon his feet. He must not float an inch. If the punishment does not seem sufficient—"

"It's enough," Pa cut in. "The boy has to learn his lesson, but there is no use being harsh with him."

"Now, sir," said Nature Boy's pa, being very formal, "it is not necessary—"

"I insist," Fancy Pants' pa said. "I really must insist. It can be no other way."

"Say," bawled the sheriff, "will someone explain to me what this is all about?"

"Sheriff," Pa said to him, "your understanding of this matter is of no great importance and it would take too long to explain. We have more important business we should be attending to." He turned around a bit so he faced the crowd. "Well, gentlemen, what do we do next? It appears to me that we have some guests. And remembering that these critters are bearers of good luck, it would seem to me we should treat them as kindly as we can."

"Pa," I said, tugging at his coat sleeve, "I know how we can get them over on our side. Every one of them wants a live-it set."

"That's right," spoke up Nature Boy. "All the time I was in there, they pestered me and pestered me about how to get the sets. All the time they squabbled over who would get to use Steve's set next."

"You mean," the sheriff asked, in a weak voice, "that these things can talk?"

"Why, sure they can," said Nature Boy. "They learn a lot more back in that world of theirs than you could ever guess."

"Well, now," Pa said with a lot of satisfaction, "if that is all they want, it's not too great a price for us to pay to get us some good luck. We'll just buy a lot of live-it sets. We can probably get them wholesale—"

"But if we get the live-its," objected Butch's pa, "they'll just lie around and use them and be of no help to us at all. They won't need us any more. They'll have all these patterns they need from the live-it sets."

"Well, anyhow," said Pa, "even if that should be true, we'll get them off our necks. They won't pester us with this bad luck they commit."

"It won't do us any good however you look at it," declared

Butch's pa, who had a mighty low opinion of the halflings. "They all live together. That's the way it's always been. They never helped an entire neighborhood, but just one man or family in the neighborhood. A whole tribe of them comes in and they give one family all the benefit. You couldn't get them to split up and work for all of us."

"If you jerks would listen," said the halfling with the live-it on his head, "I can get you straightened out."

It was a shock, I tell you, to hear him speak at all. He was the kind of thing you'd figure shouldn't speak at all—just a sort of dummy. And the way he spoke and the tone he used made it even worse. It was the way Andy Carter always talked—either wild and blustering, or out of the corner of his mouth, sarcastic. After listening to Andy all these years, that poor halfling didn't know any different.

Everyone just stood there, staring at the halfling who had spoken, while all the other halflings were nodding their heads in such mad agreement with him that I thought they'd snap their necks.

Pa was the first one to get his feet back under him.

"Go ahead," he said to the halfling. "We all are listening."

"We'll make a deal with you," said the halfling, using ornery words but speaking most respectful, "but you'll have to level with us, see? We'll work hard for you and guard against mishap, but we got to have the live-its and no mistake about it. One for each of us—and if I was you, mister, I wouldn't try to chisel."

"Well, now," said Pa, "that sounds fair enough. But you mean all of us?"

"All of you," the live-it halfling said.

"You mean you will split up?" asked Pa. "Each of us will have at least one of you? You won't all live together anymore?"

"I think, sir," said Fancy Pants' pa, "that we can depend on that. I believe I understand what this gentleman is thinking. It is something that happened with the human race on Earth."

"What happened here on Earth?" asked Pa, sort of flabbergasted.

"Why," said Fancy Pants' pa, "the elimination of the need for social clustering. There was a time when the human race found it necessary to congregate in families and tribes for companionship and entertainment. Then the race got the record player and the radio and TV and there was less need for get-togethers. A man had entertainment of his own in his home. He need not move beyond his living room to be entertained. So the spectator and group sports simply petered out."

"And you think," asked Pa, "that the same thing will happen with the halflings if we gave them live-its?"

"Certainly," said Fancy Pants' pa. "We supply them, as it were, entertainment for the home, personal entertainment. There will be no further need for tribal living."

"You said it, pal!" the halfling said enthusiastically.

All the rest of them were nodding in agreement.

"But it's still no good," yelped Butch's pa, getting real riled up. "They're in this world now, and how do you get them back? And while they're here, can they do anything for us?"

"You can stop shooting off your mouth right now," the halfling said to Butch's pa with utmost respect. "We can't do anything here for you, that's sure. In this world of yours, we can't see ahead. And to do you any good, we have to see ahead."

"You mean that if we give you live-its, you'll go back home again?" asked Pa.

"Sure," said the halfling. "Back there is our home. Just try to keep us from it."

"We won't even try," Pa said. "We might even push you back. We'll give you the live-its and you get back there and start to work for us."

"We'll work for you hard," said the halfling, "but not all the time. We take out some time for looking at the live-it. That all right with you?"

"Sure," Pa agreed. "Sure, that's O.K. with us."

"All right," said the halfling, "get us back where we belong."

I turned around and walked out of the crowd, out to the edge of it. For it was all settled now and I had a belly full of it. It would be all right with me if we never had any more excitement in the neighborhood.

Up by the barn, I saw Fancy Pants limping along on the ground. He was having a tough time walking. But I didn't feel the least bit sorry for him. He had it coming.

I figured in just a little while I'd go up around the barn and clobber him for that time he mopped up the road with me.

It should be an easy job, I told myself, with him grounded by his pa for thirty days.

2

The Accountant

ROBERT SHECKLEY

The real science fiction writer is born. From the moment he can read he is fascinated by science fiction. And from the moment he reads science fiction he is overwhelmed by the desire to write science fiction. And from the moment he begins to write science fiction, he never stops until he has published science fiction.

I can name you any number of people for whom this is virtually a life story, whether the third act—that of publication—comes early or late. For Robert Sheckley it came quite early.

But there is not always a happy ending; at least, not for the science fiction addict of the second class—the one who does not write himself but longs to read the work of those who do.

Sometimes the science fiction writer, in his zoom upward, moves right through the ceiling and ends up writing all sorts of dubious material (such as straight novels, television scripts, screenplays) for no better reason than that they bring one untold gold. And as far as "straight science fiction" is concerned, he is lost.

Alas, the greater the talent, the greater the chance of such a tragedy, and Bob Sheckley is in enormous danger of such a fate. He was a mere novice when I was already an established "name" and I can well remember patting him paternally on the head, and predicting future greatness. Now look at him! It is from a story of his that the top-ranking movie The Tenth Victim *(starring Marcello Mastroianni and Ursula Andress) was taken.*

Can Bob resist the lure of the outside world? Or will he remain faithful to us who need him so?

If you doubt the extent of the need, let Robert Sheckley introduce you to Mr. Dee and his black-sheep son, Morton, in a delightful satire.

Mr. Dee was seated in the big armchair, his belt loosened, the evening papers strewn around his knees. Peacefully he smoked his pipe, and considered how wonderful the world was. Today he had sold two amulets and a philter; his wife was bustling around the kitchen, preparing a delicious meal; and his pipe was drawing well. With a sigh of contentment Mr. Dee yawned and stretched.

Morton, his nine-year-old son, hurried across the living room, laden with books.

"How'd school go today?" Mr. Dee called.

"Okay," the boy said, slowing down, but still moving toward his room.

"What have you got there?" Mr. Dee asked, gesturing at his son's tall pile of books.

"Just some more accounting stuff," Morton said, not looking at his father. He hurried into his room.

Mr. Dee shook his head. Somewhere, the lad had picked up the notion that he wanted to be an accountant. An accountant! True, Morton was quick with figures, but he would have to forget this nonsense. Bigger things were in store for him.

The doorbell rang.

Mr. Dee tightened his belt, hastily stuffed in his shirt and opened the front door. There stood Miss Greeb, his son's fourth-grade teacher.

"Come in, Miss Greeb," said Dee. "Can I offer you something?"

"I have no time," said Miss Greeb. She stood in the doorway, her arms akimbo. With her gray, tangled hair, her thin, long-nosed face and red runny eyes, she looked exactly like a witch. And this was as it should be, for Miss Greeb *was* a witch.

"I've come to speak to you about your son," she said.

At this moment Mrs. Dee hurried out of the kitchen, wiping her hands on her apron.

"I hope he hasn't been naughty," Mrs. Dee said anxiously.

Miss Greeb sniffed ominously. "Today I gave the yearly tests. Your son failed miserably."

"Oh dear," Mrs. Dee said. "It's spring. Perhaps—"

"Spring has nothing to do with it," said Miss Greeb. "Last week I assigned the Greater Spells of Cordus, section one. You know how easy *they* are. He didn't learn a single one."

"Hm," said Mr. Dee succinctly.

"In Biology he doesn't have the slightest notion which are the basic conjuring herbs. Not the slightest."

"This is unthinkable," said Mr. Dee.

Miss Greeb laughed sourly. "Moreover, he has forgotten all the Secret Alphabet which he learned in third grade. He has forgotten the Protective Formula, forgotten the names of the ninety-nine lesser imps of the Third Circle, forgotten what little he knew of the Geography of Greater Hell. And what's more, he doesn't want to learn."

Mr. and Mrs. Dee looked at each other silently. This was very serious indeed. A certain amount of boyish inattentiveness was allowable; encouraged, even, for it showed spirit. But a child *had* to learn the basics, if he ever hoped to become a full-fledged wizard.

"I can tell you right here and now," said Miss Greeb, "if this were the old days, I'd flunk him without another thought. But there are so few of us left."

Mr. Dee nodded sadly. Witchcraft had been steadily declining over the centuries. The old families died out, or were snatched by demoniac forces, or became scientists. And the fickle public showed no interest whatsoever in the charms and enchantments of ancient days.

Now, only a scattered handful possessed the Old Lore, guarding it, teaching it in places like Miss Greeb's private school for the children of wizards. It was a heritage, a sacred trust.

"It's this accounting nonsense," said Miss Greeb. "I don't know where he got the notion." She stared accusingly at Dee. "And I don't know why it wasn't nipped in the bud."

Mr. Dee felt his cheeks grow hot.

"But I do know this. As long as Morton has *that* on his mind, he can't give his attention to Thaumaturgy."

Mr. Dee looked away from the witch's red eyes. It was his fault. He should never have brought home that toy adding machine. And when he first saw Morton playing at double-entry bookkeeping, he should have burned the ledger.

But how could he know it would grow into an obsession?

Mrs. Dee smoothed out her apron, and said, "Miss Greeb, you know you have our complete confidence. What would you suggest?"

"All I can do I have done," said Miss Greeb. "The only remaining thing is to call up Boarbas, the Demon of Children. And that, naturally, is up to you."

"Oh, I don't think it's that serious yet," Mr. Dee said quickly. "Calling up Boarbas is a serious measure."

"As I said, that's up to you," Miss Greeb said. "Call Boarbas or not, as you see fit. As things stand now, your son will never be a wizard." She turned and started to leave.

"Won't you stay for a cup of tea?" Mrs. Dee asked hastily.

"No, I must attend a Witches' Coven in Cincinnati," said Miss Greeb, and vanished in a puff of orange smoke.

Mr. Dee fanned the smoke with his hands and closed the door. "Phew," he said. "You'd think she'd use a perfumed brand."

"She's old-fashioned," Mrs. Dee murmured.

They stood by the door in silence. Mr. Dee was just beginning to feel the shock. It was hard to believe that his son, his own flesh and blood, didn't want to carry on the family tradition. It couldn't be true!

"After dinner," Dee said, finally, "I'll have a man-to-man talk with him. I'm sure we won't need any demoniac intervention."

"Good," Mrs. Dee said. "I'm sure you can make the boy understand." She smiled, and Dee caught a glimpse of the old witch-light flickering behind her eyes.

"My roast!" Mrs. Dee gasped suddenly, the witch-light dying. She hurried back to her kitchen.

Dinner was a quiet meal. Morton knew that Miss Greeb had been there, and he ate in guilty silence, glancing occasionally at his father. Mr. Dee sliced and served the roast, frowning deeply. Mrs. Dee didn't even attempt any small talk.

After bolting his dessert, the boy hurried to his room.

"Now we'll see," Mr. Dee said to his wife. He finished the last of his coffee, wiped his mouth and stood up. "I am going to reason with him now. Where is my Amulet of Persuasion?"

Mrs. Dee thought deeply for a moment. Then she walked across the room to the bookcase. "Here it is," she said, lifting it from the pages of a brightly jacketed novel. "I was using it as a marker."

Mr. Dee slipped the amulet into his pocket, took a deep breath, and entered his son's room.

Morton was seated at his desk. In front of him was a notebook, scribbled with figures and tiny, precise notations. On his desk were six carefully sharpened pencils, a soap eraser, an abacus, and a toy adding machine. His books hung precariously over the edge of the desk; there was *Money*, by Rimraamer, *Bank Accounting Practice*, by Johnson and Calhoun, *Ellman's Studies for the CPA*, and a dozen others.

Mr. Dee pushed aside a mound of clothes and made room for himself on the bed. "How's it going, son?" he asked in his kindest voice.

"Fine, Dad," Morton answered eagerly. "I'm up to chapter four in *Basic Accounting,* and I answered all the questions—"

"Son," Dee broke in, speaking very softly, "how about your regular homework?"

Morton looked uncomfortable and scuffed his feet on the floor.

"You know, not many boys have a chance to become wizards in this day and age."

"Yes, sir, I know." Morton looked away abruptly. In a high, nervous voice he said, "But, Dad, I want to be an accountant. I really do. Dad?"

Mr. Dee shook his head. "Morton, there's always been a wizard in our family. For eighteen hundred years the Dees have been famous in supernatural circles."

Morton continued to look out the window and scuff his feet.

"You wouldn't want to disappoint me, would you, son?" Dee smiled sadly. "You know, anyone can be an *accountant.* But only a chosen few can master the Black Arts."

Morton turned away from the window. He picked up a pencil, inspected the point, and began to turn it slowly in his fingers.

"How about it, boy? Won't you work harder for Miss Greeb?"

Morton shook his head. "I want to be an accountant."

Mr. Dee contained his sudden rush of anger with difficulty. What was wrong with the Amulet of Persuasion? Could the spell have run down? He should have recharged it. Nevertheless, he went on.

"Morton," he said in a husky voice, "I'm only a Third Degree Adept, you know. My parents were very poor. They couldn't send me to The University."

"I know," the boy said in a whisper.

"I want you to have all the things I never had. Morton, you can be a First Degree Adept." He shook his head wistfully. "It'll be difficult. But your mother and I have a little put away, and we'll scrape the rest together somehow."

Morton was biting his lip and turning the pencil rapidly in his fingers.

"How about it, son? You know, as a First Degree Adept, you won't have to work in a store. You can be a Direct Agent of The Black One. A Direct Agent! What do you say, boy?"

For a moment Dee thought his son was moved. Morton's lips were parted, and there was a suspicious brightness in his eyes. But then the boy glanced at his accounting books, his little abacus, his toy adding machine.

"I'm going to be an accountant," he said.

"We'll see!" Mr. Dee shouted, all patience gone. "You will *not* be an accountant, young man. You will be a wizard. It was good enough for the rest of your family, and by all that's damnable, it'll be good enough for you. You haven't heard the last of this, young man." And he stormed out of the room.

Immediately Morton returned to his accounting books.

Mr. and Mrs. Dee sat together on the couch, not talking. Mrs. Dee was busily knotting a wind-cord, but her mind wasn't on it. Mr. Dee stared moodily at a worn spot on the living room rug.

Finally, Dee said, "I've spoiled him. Boarbas is the only solution."

"Oh, no," Mrs. Dee said hastily. "He's so young."

"Do you want your son to be an accountant?" Mr. Dee asked bitterly. "Do you want him to grow up scribbling with figures instead of doing The Black One's important work?"

"Of course not," said Mrs. Dee. "But Boarbas—"

"I know. I feel like a murderer already."

They thought for a few moments. Then Mrs. Dee said, "Perhaps his grandfather can do something. He was always fond of the boy."

"Perhaps he can," Mr. Dee said thoughtfully. "But I don't know if we should disturb him. After all, the old gentleman has been dead for three years."

"I know," Mrs. Dee said, undoing an incorrect knot in the wind-cord. "But it's either that or Boarbas."

Mr. Dee agreed. Unsettling as it would be to Morton's grandfather, Boarbas was infinitely worse. Immediately Dee made preparations for calling up his dead father.

He gathered together the henbane, the ground unicorn's

horn, the hemlock, together with a morsel of dragon's tooth. These he placed on the rug.

"Where's my wand?" he asked his wife.

"I put it in the bag with your golfsticks," she told him.

Mr. Dee got his wand and waved it over the ingredients. He muttered the three words of The Unbinding, and called out his father's name.

Immediately a wisp of smoke arose from the rug.

"Hello, Grandpa Dee," Mrs. Dee said.

"Dad, I'm sorry to disturb you," Mr. Dee said. "But my son—your grandson—refuses to become a wizard. He wants to be an—accountant."

The wisp of smoke trembled, then straightened out and described a character of the Old Language.

"Yes," Mr. Dee said. "We tried persuasion. The boy is adamant."

Again the smoke trembled, and formed another character.

"I suppose that's best," Mr. Dee said. "If you frighten him out of his wits once and for all, he'll forget this accounting nonsense. It's cruel—but it's better than Boarbas."

The wisp of smoke nodded, and streamed toward the boy's room. Mr. and Mrs. Dee sat down on the couch.

The door of Morton's room was slammed open, as though by a gigantic wind. Morton looked up, frowned, and returned to his books.

The wisp of smoke turned into a winged lion with the tail of a shark. It roared hideously, crouched, snarled, and gathered itself for a spring.

Morton glanced at it, raised both eyebrows, and proceeded to jot down a column of figures.

The lion changed into a three-headed lizard, its flanks reeking horribly of blood. Breathing gusts of fire, the lizard advanced on the boy.

Morton finished adding the column of figures, checked the result on his abacus, and looked at the lizard.

With a screech the lizard changed into a giant gibbering bat. It fluttered around the boy's head, moaning and gibbering.

Morton grinned, and turned back to his books.

Mr. Dee was unable to stand it any longer. "Damn it," he shouted, "aren't you scared?"

"Why should I be?" Morton asked. "It's only Grandpa."

Upon the word, the bat dissolved into a plume of smoke. It nodded sadly to Mr. Dee, bowed to Mrs. Dee, and vanished.

"Good-bye, Grandpa," Morton called. He got up and closed his door.

"That does it," Mr. Dee said. "The boy is too cocksure of himself. We must call up Boarbas."

"No!" his wife said.

"What, then?"

"I just don't know anymore," Mrs. Dee said, on the verge of tears. "You *know* what Boarbas does to children. They're never the same afterwards."

Mr. Dee's face was hard as granite. "I know. It can't be helped."

"He's so young!" Mrs. Dee wailed. "It—it will be traumatic!"

"If so, we will use all the resources of modern psychology to heal him," Mr. Dee said soothingly. "He will have the best psychoanalysts money can buy. But the boy must be a wizard!"

"Go ahead then," Mrs. Dee said, crying openly. "But please don't ask me to assist you."

How like a woman, Dee thought. Always turning into jelly at the moment when firmness was indicated. With a heavy heart, he made the preparations for calling up Boarbas, Demon of Children.

First came the intricate sketching of the pentagon, and the twelve-pointed star within it, and the endless spiral within that. Then came the herbs and essences; expensive items, but absolutely necessary for the conjuring. Then came the inscribing of the Protective Spell, so that Boarbas might not break loose and destroy them all. Then came the three drops of hippogriff blood—

"Where is my hippogriff blood?" Mr. Dee asked, rummaging through the living-room cabinet.

"In the kitchen, in the aspirin bottle," Mrs. Dee said, wiping her eyes.

Dee found it, and then all was in readiness. He lighted the black candles and chanted the Unlocking Spell.

The room was suddenly very warm, and there remained only the Naming of the Name.

"Morton," Mr. Dee called. "Come here."

Morton opened the door and stepped out, holding one of his accounting books tightly, looking very young and defenseless.

"Morton, I am about to call up the Demon of Children. Don't make me do it, Morton."

The boy turned pale and shrank back against the door. But stubbornly he shook his head.

"Very well," Mr. Dee said. "BOARBAS!"

There was an ear-splitting clap of thunder and a wave of heat, and Boarbas appeared, as tall as the ceiling, chuckling evilly.

"Ah!" cried Boarbas, in a voice that shook the room. "A little boy."

Morton gaped, his jaw open and eyes bulging.

"A naughty little boy," Boarbas said, and laughed. The demon marched forward, shaking the house with every stride.

"Send him away!" Mrs. Dee cried.

"I can't," Dee said, his voice breaking. "I can't do anything until he's finished."

The demon's great horned hands reached for Morton; but quickly the boy opened the accounting book. "Save me!" he screamed.

In that instant, a tall, terribly thin old man appeared, covered with worn pen points and ledger sheets, his eyes two empty zeroes.

"*Zico Pico Reel!*" chanted Boarbas, turning to grapple with the newcomer. But the thin old man laughed, and said, "A contract of a corporation which is *ultra vires* is not voidable only, but utterly void."

At these words Boarbas was flung back, breaking a chair as he fell. He scrambled to his feet, his skin glowing red-hot with rage, and intoned the Demoniac Master-Spell: "VRAT, HAT, HO!"

But the thin old man shielded Morton with his body, and cried the words of Dissolution. "Expiration, Repeal, Occurrence, Surrender, Abandonment, and Death!"

Boarbas squeaked in agony. Hastily he backed away, fumbling in the air until he found The Opening. He jumped through this, and was gone.

The tall, thin old man turned to Mr. and Mrs. Dee, cowering

in a corner of the living room, and said, "Know that I am The Accountant. And Know, Moreover, that this Child has signed a Compact with Me, to enter My Apprenticeship and be My Servant. And in return for Services Rendered, I, THE ACCOUNTANT, am teaching him the Damnation of Souls, by means of ensnaring them in a cursed web of Figures, Forms, Torts, and Reprisals. And behold, this is My Mark upon him!"

The Accountant held up Morton's right hand, and showed the ink smudge on the third finger.

He turned to Morton, and in a softer voice said, "Tomorrow, lad, we will consider some aspects of Income Tax Evasion as a Path to Damnation."

"Yes *sir,*" Morton said eagerly.

And with another sharp look at the Dees, The Accountant vanished.

For long seconds there was silence. Then Dee turned to his wife.

"Well," Dee said, "if the boy wants to be an accountant *that* badly, I'm sure I'm not going to stand in his way."

3

Novice

JAMES H. SCHMITZ

One day recently I was engaged in one of my favorite early morning occupations—that of staring in the mirror at my hair and wondering if I was getting gray enough to notice. As usual, I decided that I wasn't. I was still holding up, yes, sir!

With a certain satisfaction I thought of an old, faraway friend whom I hadn't seen in years and who, when I last had seen him (at a time when he was considerably younger than I am now), was all gray, *How delightful!*

That night the old friend called. He was passing through Boston and had arrived, in fact, that morning at just about the time that I was thinking of him. I told him so and he said, inevitably, "Telepathy!"

And like the dull old conservative I am, I said, "No! Coincidence! Do you know how many times I think of old, faraway friends who then don't *call me?"*

But such rational arguments are useless. Everyone wants to believe in telepathy and seizes on every pretext to do so.

Why this should be, I don't know. Consider the trouble we get into by talking. Even though every one of us is remarkably adept at weasel-words and outright lies, still, if we talk long enough, we convict ourselves every time. (Think of the deadly nature of the newspaper interview in which someone is quoted correctly.)

Why then should anyone want to communicate by thought, when the chances of control are less and the chances of disaster infinitely greater? But mind-reading is fun to play with in science fiction, at least, so let James H. Schmitz introduce you to a young lady who is involved with both mind-reading and extraterrestrials to produce the combination he calls "xenotelepathy"

There was, Telzey Amberdon thought, someone besides TT and herself in the garden. Not, of course, Aunt Halet, who was in the house waiting for an early visitor to arrive, and not one of the servants. Someone or something else must be concealed among the thickets of magnificently flowering native Jontarou shrubs about Telzey.

She could think of no other way to account for Tick-Tock's spooked behavior—or, to be honest about it, for the manner her own nerves were acting up without visible cause this morning.

Telzey plucked a blade of grass, slipped the end between her lips and chewed it gently, her face puzzled and concerned. She wasn't ordinarily afflicted with nervousness. Fifteen years old, genius level, brown as a berry and not at all bad-looking in her sunbriefs, she was the youngest member of one of Orado's most prominent families and a second-year law student at one of the most exclusive schools in the Federation of the Hub. Her physical, mental, and emotional health, she'd always been informed, were excellent. Aunt Halet's frequent cracks about the inherent instability of the genius level could be ignored; Halet's own stability seemed questionable at best.

But none of that made the present odd situation any less disagreeable . . .

The trouble might have begun, Telzey decided, during the night, within an hour after they arrived from the spaceport at the guest house Halet had rented in Port Nichay for their vacation on Jontarou. Telzey had retired at once to her second-story bedroom with Tick-Tock; but she barely got to sleep before something awakened her again. Turning over, she discovered TT reared up before the window, her forepaws on the sill, big cat-head outlined against the star-hazed night sky, staring fixedly down into the garden.

Telzey, only curious at that point, climbed out of bed and joined TT at the window. There was nothing in particular to be seen, and if the scents and minor night-sounds which came from the garden weren't exactly what they were used to, Jontarou was after all an unfamiliar planet. What else would one expect here?

But Tick-Tock's muscular back felt tense and rigid when Telzey laid her arm across it, and except for an absent-minded dig with her forehead against Telzey's shoulder, TT refused to let her attention be distracted from whatever had absorbed it. Now and then, a low, ominous rumble came from her furry throat, a half-angry, half-questioning sound. Telzey began to feel a little uncomfortable. She managed finally to coax Tick-Tock away from the window, but neither of them slept well the rest of the night. At breakfast Aunt Halet made one of her typical nasty-sweet remarks.

"You look so fatigued, dear—as if you were under some severe mental strain . . . which, of course, you might be," Halet added musingly. With her gold-blond hair piled high on her head and her peaches and cream complexion, Halet looked fresh as a daisy herself . . . a malicious daisy. "Now wasn't I right in insisting to Jessamine that you needed a vacation away from that terribly intellectual school?" She smiled gently.

"Absolutely," Telzey agreed, restraining the impulse to fling a spoonful of egg yolk at her father's younger sister. Aunt Halet often inspired such impulses, but Telzey had promised her mother to avoid actual battles on the Jontarou trip, if possible. After breakfast she went out into the back garden with Tick-Tock, who immediately walked into a thicket, camouflaged herself, and vanished from sight. It seemed to add up to something. But what?

Telzey strolled about the garden awhile, maintaining a pretense of nonchalant interest in Jontarou's flowers and colorful bug life. She experienced the most curious little chills of alarm from time to time, but discovered no signs of a lurking intruder, or of TT either. Then, for half an hour or more, she'd just sat cross-legged in the grass, waiting quietly for Tick-Tock to show up of her own accord. And the big lunkhead hadn't obliged.

Telzey scratched a tanned kneecap, scowling at Port Nichay's park trees beyond the garden wall. It seemed idiotic to feel scared when she couldn't even tell whether there was anything to be scared about! And, aside from that, another unreasonable feeling kept growing stronger by the minute now. This was to the effect that she should be doing some unstated but specific thing . . .

In fact, that Tick-Tock *wanted* her to do some specific thing!

Completely idiotic!

Abruptly Telzey closed her eyes, thought sharply, "Tick-Tock?" and waited—suddenly very angry at herself for having given in to her fancies to this extent—for whatever might happen.

She had never really established that she was able to tell, by a kind of symbolic mind-picture method, like a short waking dream, approximately what TT was thinking and feeling. Five years before, when she'd discovered Tick-Tock—an odd-looking and odder-behaved stray kitten then—in the woods near the Amberdons' summer home on Orado, Telzey had thought so. But it might never have been more than a colorful play of her imagination; and after she got into law school and grew increasingly absorbed in her studies, she almost forgot the matter again.

Today, perhaps because she was disturbed about Tick-Tock's behavior, the customary response was extraordinarily prompt.

The warm glow of sunlight shining through her closed eyelids faded out quickly and was replaced by some inner darkness. In the darkness there appeared then an image of Tick-Tock sitting a little way off beside an open door in an old stone wall, green eyes fixed on Telzey. Telzey got the impression that TT was inviting her to go through the door, and, for some reason, the thought frightened her.

Again there was an immediate reaction. The scene with Tick-Tock and the door vanished; and Telzey felt she was standing in a pitch-black room, knowing that if she moved even one step forward, something that was waiting there silently would reach out and grab her.

Naturally she recoiled . . . and at once found herself sitting, eyes still closed and the sunlight bathing her lids, in the grass of the guest house garden.

She opened her eyes, looked around. Her heart was thumping rapidly. The experience couldn't have lasted more than four or five seconds, but it had been extremely vivid, a whole, compact little nightmare. None of her earlier experiments at getting into mental communication with TT had been like that.

It served her right, Telzey thought, for trying such a childish stunt at the moment! What she should have done at once was to make a methodical search for the foolish beast—TT was bound to be *somewhere* nearby—locate her behind her camouflage, and hang on to her then until this nonsense in the garden was explained! Talented as Tick-Tock was at blotting herself out, it usually was possible to spot her if one directed one's attention to shadow patterns. Telzey began a surreptitious study of the flowering bushes about her.

Three minutes later, off to her right, where the ground was banked beneath a six-foot step in the garden's terraces, Tick-Tock's outline suddenly caught her eye. Flat on her belly, head lifted above her paws, quite motionless, TT seemed like a transparent wraith stretched out along the terrace, barely discernible even when stared at directly. It was a convincing illusion; but what seemed to be rocks, plant leaves, and sun-splotched earth seen through the wraith-outline was simply the camouflage pattern TT had printed for the moment on her hide. She could have changed it completely in an instant to conform to a different background.

Telzey pointed an accusing finger.

"See you!" she announced, feeling a surge of relief which seemed as unaccountable as the rest of it.

The wraith twitched one ear in acknowledgment, the head outlines shifting as the camouflaged face turned towards Telzey. Then the inwardly uncamouflaged, very substantial-looking mouth opened slowly, showing Tick-Tock's red tongue and curved white tusks. The mouth stretched in a wide yawn, snapped shut with a click of meshing teeth, became indistinguishable again. Next, a pair of camouflaged lids drew back from TT's round, brilliant-green eyes. The eyes stared across the lawn at Telzey.

Telzey said irritably, "Quit clowning around, TT!"

The eyes blinked, and Tick-Tock's natural bronze-brown color suddenly flowed over her head, down her neck, and across her body into legs and tail. Against the side of the terrace, as if materializing into solidity at that moment, appeared two hundred pounds of supple, rangy, long-tailed cat . . . or catlike creature. TT's actual origin had never been established. The best guesses were that what Telzey had found playing around in the woods five years ago was either a biostructural experiment which had got away from a private laboratory on Orado, or some spaceman's lost pet, brought to the capital planet from one of the remote colonies beyond the Hub. On top of TT's head was a large, fluffy pompon of white fur, which might have looked ridiculous on another animal, but didn't on her. Even as a fat kitten, hanging head down from the side of a wall by the broad sucker pads in her paws, TT had possessed enormous dignity.

Telzey studied her, the feeling of relief fading again. Tick-Tock, ordinarily the most restful and composed of companions, definitely was still tensed up about something. That big, lazy yawn a moment ago, the attitude of stretched-out relaxation . . . all pure sham!

"What is eating you?" she asked in exasperation.

The green eyes stared at her, solemn, watchful, seeming for that fleeting instant quite alien. And why, Telzey thought, should the old question of what Tick-Tock really was pass through her mind just now? After her rather alarming rate of growth began to taper off last year, nobody had cared any more.

For a moment Telzey had the uncanny certainty of having had the answer to this situation almost in her grasp. An answer which appeared to involve the world of Jontarou, Tick-Tock, and—of all unlikely factors—Aunt Halet.

She shook her head. TT's impassive green eyes blinked.

Jontarou? The planet lay outside Telzey's sphere of personal interests, but she'd read up on it on the way here from Orado. Among all the worlds of the Hub, Jontarou was *the* paradise for zoologists and sportsmen, a gigantic animal preserve, its continents and seas swarming with magnificent game. Under Federation law, it was being retained deliberately in the primitive state in which it had been discovered. Port Nichay, the only city, actually the only inhabited point on Jontarou, was beautiful and quiet, a pattern of vast but elegantly slender towers, each separated from the others by four or five miles of rolling parkland and interconnected only by the threads of transparent skyways. Near the horizon, just visible from the garden, rose the tallest towers of all, the green and gold spires of the Shikaris' Club, a center of Federation affairs and of social activity. From the aircar which brought them across Port Nichay the evening before, Telzey had seen occasional strings of guest houses, similar to the one Halet had rented, nestling along the park slopes.

Nothing very sinister about Port Nichay or green Jontarou, surely!

Halet? That blond, slinky, would-be Machiavelli? What could—?

Telzey's eyes narrowed reflectively. There'd been a minor occurrence—at least, it had seemed minor—just before the spaceliner docked last night. A young woman from one of the newscasting services had asked for an interview with the daughter of Federation Councilwoman Jessamine Amberdon. This happened occasionally; and Telzey had no objections until the newshen's gossipy persistence in inquiring about the "unusual pet" she was bringing to Port Nichay with her began to be annoying. TT might be somewhat unusual, but that was not a matter of general interest; and Telzey said so. Then Halet moved smoothly into the act and held forth on Tick-Tock's appearance, habits, and mysterious antecedents, in considerable detail.

Telzey had assumed that Halet was simply going out of her way to be irritating, as usual. Looking back on the incident, however, it occurred to her that the chatter between her aunt and the newscast woman had sounded oddly stilted—almost like something the two might have rehearsed.

Rehearsed for what purpose? Tick-Tock . . . Jontarou.

Telzey chewed gently on her lower lip. A vacation on Jontarou for the two of them and TT had been Halet's idea, and Halet had enthused about it so much that Telzey's mother at last talked her into accepting. Halet, Jessamine explained privately to Telzey, had felt they were intruders in the Amberdon family, had bitterly resented Jessamine's political honors and, more recently, Telzey's own emerging promise of brilliance. This invitation was Halet's way of indicating a change of heart. Wouldn't Telzey oblige?

So Telzey had obliged, though she took very little stock in Halet's change of heart. She wasn't, in fact, putting it past her aunt to have some involved dirty trick up her sleeve with this trip to Jontarou. Halet's mind worked like that.

So far there had been no actual indications of purposeful mischief. But logic did seem to require a connection between the various puzzling events here . . . A newscaster's rather forced-looking interest in Tick-Tock—Halet could easily have paid for that interview. Then TT's disturbed behavior during their first night in Port Nichay, and Telzey's own formless anxieties and fancies in connection with the guest house garden.

The last remained hard to explain. But Tick-Tock . . . and Halet . . . might know something about Jontarou that she didn't know.

Her mind returned to the results of the half-serious attempt she'd made to find out whether there was something Tick-Tock "wanted her to do." An open door? A darkness where somebody waited to grab her if she took even one step forward? It couldn't have had any significance. Or could it?

So you'd like to try magic, Telzey scoffed at herself. Baby games . . . How far would you have got at law school if you'd asked TT to help with your problems?

Then why had she been thinking about it again?

She shivered, because an eerie stillness seemed to settle on the garden. From the side of the terrace, TT's green eyes watched her.

Telzey had a feeling of sinking down slowly into a sunlit dream, into something very remote from law school problems.

"Should I go through the door?" she whispered.

The bronze cat-shape raised its head slowly. TT began to purr.

Tick-Tock's name had been derived in kittenhood from the manner in which she purred—a measured, oscillating sound, shifting from high to low, as comfortable and often as continuous as the unobtrusive pulse of an old clock. It was the first time, Telzey realized now, that she'd heard the sound since their arrival on Jontarou. It went on for a dozen seconds or so, then stopped. Tick-Tock continued to look at her.

It appeared to have been an expression of definite assent . . .

The dreamlike sensation increased, hazing over Telzey's thoughts. If there was nothing to this mind-communication thing, what harm could symbols do? This time, she wouldn't let them alarm her. And if they did mean something . . .

She closed her eyes.

The sunglow outside faded instantly. Telzey caught a fleeting picture of the door in the wall, and knew in the same moment that she'd already passed through it.

She was not in the dark room then, but poised at the edge of a brightness which seemed featureless and without limit, spread out around her with a feeling-tone like "sea" or "sky." But it was an unquiet place. There was a sense of unseen things on all sides watching her and waiting.

Was this another form of the dark room—a trap set up in her mind? Telzey's attention did a quick shift. She was seated in the grass again; the sunlight beyond her closed eyelids seemed to shine in quietly through rose-tinted curtains. Cautiously she let her awareness return to the bright area; and *it* was still there. She had a moment of excited elation. She was controlling this! And why not, she asked herself. These things were happening in *her* mind, after all!

She would find out what they seemed to mean; but she would be in no rush to . . .

An impression as if, behind her, Tick-Tock had thought, "Now I can help again!"

Then a feeling of being swept swiftly, irresistibly forward, thrust out and down. The brightness exploded in thundering colors around her. In fright she made the effort to snap her eyes open, to be back in the garden; but now she couldn't make it work. The colors continued to roar about her, like a confusion of excited, laughing, triumphant voices. Telzey felt caught in the middle of it all, suspended in invisible spiderwebs. Tick-Tock seemed to be somewhere nearby, looking on. Faithless, treacherous TT!

Telzey's mind made another wrenching effort, and there was a change. She hadn't got back into the garden, but the noisy, swirling colors were gone and she had the feeling of reading a rapidly moving microtape now, though she didn't actually see the tape.

The tape, she realized, was another symbol for what was happening, a symbol easier for her to understand. There were voices, or what might be voices, around her; on the invisible tape she seemed to be reading what they said.

A number of speakers, apparently involved in a fast, hot argument about what to do with her. Impressions flashed past . . .

Why waste time with her? It was clear that kitten-talk was all she was capable of! . . . Not necessarily; that was a normal first step. Give her a little time! . . . But what—exasperatedly—could *such* a small-bite *possibly* know that would be of significant value?

There was a slow, blurred, awkward-seeming interruption. Its content was not comprehensible to Telzey at all, but in some unmistakable manner it was defined as Tick-Tock's thought.

A pause as the circle of speakers stopped to consider whatever TT had thrown into the debate.

Then another impression . . . one that sent a shock of fear through Telzey as it rose heavily into her awareness. Its sheer intensity momentarily displaced the tape-reading symbolism. A savage voice seemed to rumble:

"Toss the tender small-bite to *me*"—malevolent crimson eyes fixed on Telzey from somewhere not far away—"and let's be done here!"

Startled, stammering protest from Tick-Tock, accompanied by gusts of laughter from the circle. Great sense of humor these characters had, Telzey thought bitterly. That crimson-eyed thing wasn't joking at all!

More laughter as the circle caught her thought. Then a kind of majority opinion found sudden expression:

"Small-bite *is* learning! No harm to wait. We'll find out quickly. Let's . . ."

The tape ended; the voices faded; the colors went blank. In whatever jumbled-up form she'd been getting the impressions at that point—Telzey couldn't have begun to describe it—the whole thing suddenly stopped.

She found herself sitting in the grass, shaky, scared, eyes open. Tick-Tock stood beside the terrace, looking at her. An air of hazy unreality still hung about the garden.

She might have flipped! She didn't think so; but it certainly seemed possible! Otherwise . . . Telzey made an attempt to sort over what had happened.

Something *had* been in the garden! Something had been inside her mind. Something that was at home on Jontarou.

There'd been a feeling of perhaps fifty or sixty of these . . . well, beings. Alarming beings! Reckless, wild, hard . . . and that red-eyed nightmare! Telzey shuddered.

They'd contacted Tick-Tock first, during the night. TT understood them better than she could. Why? Telzey found no immediate answer.

Then Tick-Tock had tricked her into letting her mind be invaded by these beings. There must have been a very definite reason for that.

She looked over at Tick-Tock. TT looked back. Nothing stirred in Telzey's thoughts. Between *them* there was still no direct communication.

Then how had the beings been able to get through to her?

Telzey wrinkled her nose. Assuming this was real, it seemed clear that the game of symbols she'd made up between herself and TT had provided the opening. Her whole experience just now had been in the form of symbols, translating whatever occurred into something she could consciously grasp.

"Kitten-talk" was how the beings referred to the use of symbols; they seemed contemptuous of it. Never mind, Telzey told herself; they'd agreed she was learning.

The air over the grass appeared to flicker. Again she had the impression of reading words off a quickly moving, not quite visible tape.

"You're being taught and you're learning," was what she

seemed to read. "The question was whether you were capable of partial understanding as your friend insisted. Since you were, everything else that can be done will be accomplished very quickly."

A pause, then with a touch of approval, "You're a well-informed mind, small-bite! Odd and with incomprehensibilities, but well-informed—"

One of the beings, and a fairly friendly one—at least not unfriendly. Telzey framed a tentative mental question. "Who are you?"

"You'll know very soon." The flickering ended; she realized she and the question had been dismissed for the moment. She looked over at Tick-Tock again.

"Can't *you* talk to me now, TT?" she asked silently.

A feeling of hesitation.

"Kitten-talk!" was the impression that formed itself with difficulty then. It was awkward, searching; but it came unquestionably from TT. "Still learning too, Telzey!" TT seemed half anxious, half angry. "We—"

A sharp buzz-note reached Telzey's ears, wiping out the groping thought-impression. She jumped a little, glanced down. Her wrist-talker was signaling. For a moment she seemed poised uncertainly between a world where unseen, dangerous-sounding beings referred to one as small-bite and where TT was learning to talk, and the familiar other world where wrist-communications buzzed periodically in a matter-of-fact manner. Settling back into the more familiar world, she switched on the talker.

"Yes?" she said. Her voice sounded husky.

"Telzey, dear," Halet murmured honey-sweet from the talker, "would you come back into the house, please? The living room. We have a visitor who very much wants to meet you."

Telzey hesitated, eyes narrowing. Halet's visitor wanted to meet *her?*

"Why?" she asked.

"He has something *very* interesting to tell you, dear." The edge of triumphant malice showed for an instant, vanished in murmuring sweetness again. "So please hurry!"

"All right." Telzey stood up. "I'm coming."

"Fine, dear!" The talker went dead.

Telzey switched off the instrument, noticed that Tick-Tock had chosen to disappear meanwhile.

Flipped? she wondered, starting up towards the house. It was clear Aunt Halet had prepared some unpleasant surprise to spring on her, which was hardly more than normal behavior for Halet. The other business? She couldn't be certain of anything there. Leaving out TT's strange actions—which might have a number of causes, after all—that entire string of events could have been created inside her head. There was no contradictory evidence so far.

But it could do no harm to take what *seemed* to have happened at face value. Some pretty grim event might be shaping up, in a very real way, around here . . .

"You reason logically!" The impression now was of a voice speaking to her, a voice that made no audible sound. It was the same being who'd addressed her a minute or two ago.

The two worlds between which Telzey had felt suspended seemed to glide slowly together and become one.

"I go to law school," she explained to the being, almost absently.

Amused agreement. "So we heard."

"What do you want of me?" Telzey inquired.

"You'll know soon enough."

"Why not tell me now?" Telzey urged. It seemed about to dismiss her again.

Quick impatience flared at her. "Kitten-pictures! Kitten-thoughts! Kitten-talk! Too slow, too slow! YOUR pictures—too much YOU! Wait till the . . ."

Circuits close . . . channels open . . . Obstructions clear? What *had* it said? There'd been only the blurred image of a finicky, delicate, but perfectly normal technical operation of some kind.

". . . . Minutes now!" the voice concluded. A pause, then another thought tossed carelessly at her. "This is more important to you, small-bite, than to *us!*" The voice impression ended as sharply as if a communicator had snapped off.

Not *too* friendly! Telzey walked on towards the house, a new fear growing inside her . . . a fear like the awareness of a storm gathered nearby, still quiet—deadly quiet, but ready to break.

"Kitten-pictures!" a voice seemed to jeer distantly, a whispering in the park trees beyond the garden wall.

Halet's cheeks were lightly pinked; her blue eyes sparkled. She looked downright stunning, which meant to anyone who knew her that the worst side of Halet's nature was champing at the bit again. On uninformed males it had a dazzling effect, however; and Telzey wasn't surprised to find their visitor wearing a tranced expression when she came into the living room. He was a tall, outdoorsy man with a tanned, bony face, a neatly trained black mustache, and a scar down one cheek which would have seemed dashing if it hadn't been for the stupefied look. Beside his chair stood a large, clumsy instrument which might have been some kind of telecamera.

Halet performed introductions. Their visitor was Dr. Droon, a zoologist. He had been tuned in on Telzey's newscast interview on the liner the night before, and wondered whether Telzey would care to discuss Tick-Tock with him.

"Frankly, no," Telzey said.

Dr. Droon came awake and gave Telzey a surprised look. Halet smiled easily.

"My niece doesn't intend to be discourteous, Doctor," she explained.

"Of course not," the zoologist agreed doubtfully.

"It's just," Halet went on, "that Telzey is a little, oh, sensitive where Tick-Tock is concerned. In her own way, she's attached to the animal. Aren't you, dear?"

"Yes," Telzey said blandly.

"Well, we hope this isn't going to disturb you too much, dear." Halet glanced significantly at Dr. Droon. "Dr. Droon, you must understand, is simply doing . . . well, there is something very important he must tell you now."

Telzey transferred her gaze back to the zoologist. Dr. Droon cleared his throat. "I, ah, understand, Miss Amberdon, that you're unaware of what kind of creature your, ah, Tick-Tock is?"

Telzey started to speak, then checked herself, frowning. She had been about to state that she knew exactly what kind of creature TT was . . . but she didn't, of course!

Or did she? She . . .

She scowled absent-mindedly at Dr. Droon, biting her lip.

"Telzey!" Halet prompted gently.

"Huh?" Telzey said. "Oh . . . please go on, Doctor!"

Dr. Droon steepled his fingers. "Well," he said, "she . . . your pet . . . is, ah, a young crest cat. Nearly full-grown now, apparently, and—"

"Why, yes!" Telzey cried.

The zoologist looked at her. "You knew that—"

"Well, not really," Telzey admitted. "Or sort of." She laughed, her cheeks flushed. "This is the most . . . go ahead please! Sorry I interrupted." She stared at the wall beyond Dr. Droon with a rapt expression.

The zoologist and Halet exchanged glances. Then Dr. Droon resumed cautiously. The crest cats, he said, were a species native to Jontarou. Their existence had been known for only eight years. The species appeared to have had a somewhat limited range—the Baluit mountains on the opposite side of the huge continent on which Port Nichay had been built . . .

Telzey barely heard him. A very curious thing was happening. For every sentence Dr. Droon uttered, a dozen other sentences appeared in her awareness. More accurately, it was as if an instantaneous smooth flow of information relevant to whatever he said arose continuously from what might have been almost her own memory, but wasn't. Within a minute or two she knew more about the crest cats of Jontarou than Dr. Droon could have told her in hours . . . much more than he'd ever known.

She realized suddenly that he'd stopped talking, that he had asked her a question. "Miss Amberdon?" he repeated now, with a note of uncertainty.

"Yar-rrr-REE!" Telzey told him softly. "I'll drink your blood!"

"Eh?"

Telzey blinked, focused on Dr. Droon, wrenching her mind away from a splendid view of the misty-blue peaks of the Baluit range.

"Sorry," she said briskly. "Just a joke!" She smiled. "Now what were you saying?"

The zoologist looked at her in a rather odd manner for a moment. "I was inquiring," he said then, "whether you were familiar with the sporting rules established by the various hunting associations of the Hub in connection with the taking of game trophies?"

Telzey shook her head. "No, I never heard of them."

The rules, Dr. Droon explained, laid down the type of equipment . . . weapons, spotting and tracking instruments, number of assistants, and so forth . . . a sportsman could legitimately use in the pursuit of any specific type of game. "Before the end of the first year after their discovery," he went on, "the Baluit crest cats had been placed in the ultra-equipment class."

"What's ultra-equipment?" Telzey asked.

"Well," Dr. Droon said thoughtfully, "it doesn't quite involve the use of full battle armor . . . not quite! And, of course, even with that classification the sporting principle of mutual accessibility must be observed."

"Mutual . . . oh, I see!" Telzey paused as another wave of silent information rose into her awareness; went on, "So the game has to be able to get at the sportsman too, eh?"

"That's correct. Except in the pursuit of various classes of flying animals, a shikari would not, for example, be permitted the use of an aircar other than as a means of simple transportation. Under these conditions, it was soon established that crest cats were being obtained by sportsmen who went after them at a rather consistent one-to-one ratio."

Telzey's eyes widened. She'd gathered something similar from her other information source but hadn't quite believed it. "One hunter killed for each cat bagged?" she said. "That's pretty rough sport, isn't it?"

"Extremely rough sport!" Dr. Droon agreed dryly. "In fact, when the statistics were published, the sporting interest in winning a Baluit cat trophy appears to have suffered a sudden and sharp decline. On the other hand, a more scientific interest in these remarkable animals was coincidingly created, and many permits for their acquisition by the agents of museums, universities, public and private collections were issued. Sporting rules, of course, do not apply to that activity."

Telzey nodded absently. "I see! *They* used aircars, didn't they? A sort of heavy knockout gun—"

"Aircars, long-range detectors, and stunguns are standard

equipment in such work," Dr. Droon acknowledged. "Gas and poison are employed, of course, as circumstances dictate. The collectors were relatively successful for a while.

"And then a curious thing happened. Less than two years after their existence became known, the crest cats of the Baluit range were extinct! The inroads made on their numbers by man cannot begin to account for this, so it must be assumed that a sudden plague wiped them out. At any rate, not another living member of the species has been seen on Jontarou until you landed here with your pet last night."

Telzey sat silent for some seconds. Not because of what he had said, but because the other knowledge was still flowing into her mind. On one very important point *that* was at variance with what the zoologist had stated; and from there a coldly logical pattern was building up. Telzey didn't grasp the pattern in complete detail yet, but what she saw of it stirred her with a half incredulous dread.

She asked, shaping the words carefully but with only a small part of her attention on what she was really saying, "Just what does all that have to do with Tick-Tock, Dr. Droon?"

Dr. Droon glanced at Halet, and returned his gaze to Telzey. Looking very uncomfortable but quite determined, he told her, "Miss Amberdon, there is a Federation law which states that when a species is threatened with extinction, any available survivors must be transferred to the Life Banks of the University League, to insure their indefinite preservation. Under the circumstances, this law applies to, ah, Tick-Tock!"

So that had been Halet's trick. She'd found out about the crest cats, might have put in as much as a few months arranging to make the discovery of TT's origin on Jontarou seem a regrettable mischance—something no one could have foreseen or prevented. In the Life Banks, from what Telzey had heard of them, TT would cease to exist as an individual awareness while scientists tinkered around with the possibilities of reconstructing her species.

Telzey studied her aunt's carefully sympathizing face for an instant, asked Dr. Droon, "What about the other crest cats you said were collected before they became extinct here? Wouldn't they be enough for what the Life Banks need?"

He shook his head. "Two immature male specimens are known to exist, and they are at present in the Life Banks. The others that were taken alive at the time have been destroyed . . . often under nearly disastrous circumstances. They are enormously cunning, enormously savage creatures, Miss Amberdon! The additional fact that they can conceal themselves to the point of being virtually indetectable except by the use of instruments makes them one of the most dangerous animals known. Since the young female which you raised as a pet has remained docile . . . so far . . . you may not really be able to appreciate that."

"Perhaps I can," Telzey said. She nodded at the heavy-looking instrument standing beside his chair. "And that's—?"

"It's a life detector combined with a stungun, Miss Amberdon. I have no intention of harming your pet, but we can't take chances with an animal of that type. The gun's charge will knock it unconscious for several minutes—just long enough to let me secure it with paralysis belts."

"You're a collector for the Life Banks, Dr. Droon?"

"That's correct."

"Dr. Droon," Halet remarked, "has obtained a permit from the Planetary Moderator, authorizing him to claim Tick-Tock for the University League and remove her from the planet, dear. So you see there is simply nothing we can do about the matter! Your mother wouldn't like us to attempt to obstruct the law, would she?" Halet paused. "The permit should have your signature, Telzey, but I can sign in your stead if necessary."

That was Halet's way of saying it would do no good to appeal to Jontarou's Planetary Moderator. She'd taken the precaution of getting his assent to the matter first.

"So now if you'll just call Tick-Tock, dear . . ." Halet went on.

Telzey barely heard the last words. She felt herself stiffening slowly, while the living room almost faded from her sight. Perhaps, in that instant, some additional new circuit had closed in her mind, or some additional new channel had opened, for TT's purpose in tricking her into contact with the reckless, mocking beings outside was suddenly and numbingly clear.

And what it meant immediately was that she'd have to get out of the house without being spotted at it, and go someplace where she could be undisturbed for half an hour.

She realized that Halet and the zoologist were both staring at her.

"Are you ill, dear?"

"No." Telzey stood up. It would be worse than useless to try to tell these two anything! Her face must be pretty white at the moment—she could feel it—but they assumed, of course, that the shock of losing TT had just now sunk in on her.

"I'll have to check on that law you mentioned before I sign anything," she told Dr. Droon.

"Why, yes . . ." He started to get out of his chair. "I'm sure that can be arranged, Miss Amberdon!"

"Don't bother to call the Moderator's office," Telzey said. "I brought my law library along. I'll look it up myself." She turned to leave the room.

"My niece," Halet explained to Dr. Droon who was beginning to look puzzled, "attends law school. She's always so absorbed in her studies . . . Telzey?"

"Yes, Halet?" Telzey paused at the door.

"I'm very glad you've decided to be sensible about this, dear. But don't take too long, will you? We don't want to waste Dr. Droon's time."

"It shouldn't take more than five or ten minutes," Telzey told her agreeably. She closed the door behind her, and went directly to her bedroom on the second floor. One of her two valises was still unpacked. She locked the door behind her, opened the unpacked valise, took out a pocket edition law library and sat down at the table with it.

She clicked on the library's view-screen, tapped the clearing and index buttons. Behind the screen, one of the multiple rows of pinhead tapes shifted slightly as the index was flicked into reading position. Half a minute later she was glancing over the legal section on which Dr. Droon had based his claim. The library confirmed what he had said.

Very neat of Halet, Telzey thought, very nasty . . . and pretty idiotic! Even a second-year law student could think immediately of two or three ways in which a case like that could have been dragged out in the Federation's courts for a couple of decades before the question of handing Tick-Tock over to the Life Banks became too acute.

Well, Halet simply wasn't really intelligent. And the plot to shanghai TT was hardly even a side issue now.

Telzey snapped the tiny library shut, fastened it to the belt of her sunsuit, and went over to the open window. A two-foot ledge passed beneath the window, leading to the roof of a patio on the right. Fifty yards beyond the patio, the garden ended in a natural-stone wall. Behind it lay one of the big wooded park areas which formed most of the ground level of Port Nichay.

Tick-Tock wasn't in sight. A sound of voices came from ground-floor windows on the left. Halet had brought her maid and chauffeur along; and a chef had showed up in time to make breakfast this morning, as part of the city's guest house service. Telzey took the empty valise to the window, set it on end against the left side of the frame, and let the window slide down until its lower edge rested on the valise. She went back to the house guard-screen panel beside the door, put her finger against the lock button, and pushed.

The sound of voices from the lower floor was cut off as outer doors and windows slid silently shut all about the house. Telzey glanced back at the window. The valise had creaked a little as the guard field drove the frame down on it, but it was supporting the thrust. She returned to the window, wriggled feet foremost through the opening, twisted around and got a footing on the ledge.

A minute later she was scrambling quietly down a vine-covered patio trellis to the ground. Even after they discovered she was gone, the guard screen would keep everybody in the house for some little while. They'd either have to disengage the screen's main mechanisms and start poking around in them, or force open the door to her bedroom and get the lock unset. Either approach would involve confusion, upset tempers, and generally delay any organized pursuit.

Telzey edged around the patio and started towards the wall, keeping close to the side of the house so she couldn't be seen from the windows. The shrubbery made minor rustling noises as she threaded her way through it . . . and then there was a different stirring which might have been no more than a slow, steady current of air moving among the bushes behind her. She shivered involuntarily but didn't look back.

She came to the wall, stood still, measuring its height, jumped and got an arm across it, swung up a knee and squirmed up and over. She came down on her feet with a small thump in the grass on the other side, glanced back once at the guest house, crossed a path and went on among the park trees.

Within a few hundred yards it became apparent that she had an escort. She didn't look around for them, but spread out to right and left like a skirmish line, keeping abreast with her, occasional shadows slid silently through patches of open, sunlit ground, disappeared again under the trees. Otherwise, there was hardly anyone in sight. Port Nichay's human residents appeared to make almost no personal use of the vast parkland spread out beneath their tower apartments; and its traffic moved over the airways, visible from the ground only as rainbow-hued ribbons which bisected the sky between the upper tower levels. An occasional private aircar went by overhead.

Wisps of thought which were not her own thoughts flicked through Telzey's mind from moment to moment as the silent line of shadows moved deeper into the park with her. She realized she was being sized up, judged, evaluated again. No more information was coming through; they had given her as much information as she needed. In the main perhaps, they were simply curious now. This was the first human mind they'd been able to make heads or tails of, and that hadn't seemed deaf and silent to their form of communication. They were taking time out to study it. They'd been assured she would have something of genuine importance to tell them; and there was some derision about that. But they were willing to wait a little, and find out. They were curious and they liked games. At the moment, Telzey and what she might try to do to change their plans was the game on which their attention was fixed.

Twelve minutes passed before the talker on Telzey's wrist began to buzz. It continued to signal off and on for another few minutes, then stopped. Back in the guest house they couldn't be sure yet whether she wasn't simply locked inside her room and refusing to answer them. But Telzey quickened her pace.

The park's trees gradually became more massive, reached higher above her, stood spaced more widely apart. She passed through the morning shadow of the residential tower nearest the guest house, and emerged from it presently on the shore of a small lake. On the other side of the lake, a number of dappled grazing animals like long-necked, tall horses lifted their heads to watch her. For some seconds they seemed only mildly interested, but then a breeze moved across the lake, crinkling the surface of the water; and as it touched the opposite shore, abrupt panic exploded among the grazers. They wheeled, went flashing away in effortless twenty-foot strides, and were gone among the trees.

Telzey felt a crawling along her spine. It was the first objective indication she'd had of the nature of the company she had brought to the lake, and while it hardly came as a surprise, for a moment her urge was to follow the example of the grazers.

"Tick-Tock?" she whispered, suddenly a little short of breath.

A single up-and-down purring note replied from the bushes on her right. TT was still around, for whatever good that might do. Not too much, Telzey thought, if it came to serious trouble. But the knowledge was somewhat reassuring . . . and this, meanwhile, appeared to be as far as she needed to get from the guest house. They'd be looking for her by aircar presently, but there was nothing to tell them in which direction to turn first.

She climbed the bank of the lake to a point where she was screened both by thick, green shrubbery and the top of a single immense tree from the sky, sat down on some dry, mossy growth, took the law library from her belt, opened it and placed it in her lap. Vague stirrings indicated that her escort was also settling down in an irregular circle about her; and apprehension shivered on Telzey's skin again. It wasn't that their attitude was hostile; they were simply overawing. And no one could predict what they might do next. Without looking up, she asked a question in her mind.

"Ready?"

Sense of multiple acknowledgment, variously tinged—sardonic, interestedly amused, attentive, doubtful. Impatience quivered through it too, only tentatively held in restraint, and Telzey's forehead was suddenly wet. Some of them seemed on the verge of expressing disapproval with what was being done here—

Her fingers quickly flicked in the index tape, and the stir of feeling about her subsided, their attention captured again for the moment. Her thoughts became to some degree detached, ready to dissect another problem in the familiar ways and present the answers to it. Not a very involved problem essentially, but this time it wasn't a school exercise. Her company waited, withdrawn, silent, aloof once more, while the index blurred, checked, blurred and checked. Within a minute and a half she had noted a dozen reference symbols. She tapped in another of the pinhead tapes, glanced over a few paragraphs, licked salty sweat from her lip, and said in her thoughts, emphasizing the meaning of each detail of the sentence so that there would be no misunderstanding, "This is the Federation law that applies to the situation which existed originally on this planet . . ."

There were no interruptions, no commenting thoughts, no intrusions of any kind, as she went step by step through the section, turned to another one, and another. In perhaps twelve minutes she came to the end of the last one, and stopped. Instantly argument exploded about her.

Telzey was not involved in the argument; in fact, she could grasp only scraps of it. Either they were excluding her deliberately, or the exchange was too swift, practiced and varied to allow her to keep up. But their vehemence was not encouraging. And was it reasonable to assume that the Federation's laws would have any meaning for minds like these? Telzey snapped the library shut with fingers that had begun to tremble, and placed it on the ground. Then she stiffened. In the sensations washing about her, a special excitement rose suddenly, a surge of almost gleeful wildness that choked away her breath. Awareness followed of a pair of malignant crimson eyes fastened on her, moving steadily closer. A kind of nightmare paralysis seized Telzey—they'd turned her over to that red-eyed horror! She sat still, feeling mouse-sized.

Something came out with a crash from a thicket behind her. Her muscles went tight. But it was TT who rubbed a hard head against her shoulder, took another three stiff-legged steps forward and stopped between Telzey and the bushes on their right, back rigid, neck fur erect, tail twisting.

Expectant silence closed in about them. The circle was waiting. In the greenery on the right something made a slow, heavy stir.

TT's lips peeled back from her teeth. Her head swung towards the motion, ears flattening, transformed to a split, snarling demon-mask. A long shriek ripped from her lungs, raw with fury, blood lust, and challenge.

The sound died away. For some seconds the tension about them held; then came a sense of gradual relaxation mingled with a partly amused approval. Telzey was shaking violently. It had been, she was telling herself, a deliberate test . . . not of herself, of course, but of TT. And Tick-Tock had passed with honors. That *her* nerves had been half ruined in the process would seem a matter of no consequence to this rugged crew . . .

She realized next that someone here was addressing her personally.

It took a few moments to steady her jittering thoughts enough to gain a more definite impression than that. This speaker, she discovered then, was a member of the circle of whom she hadn't been aware before. The thought-impressions came hard and cold as iron—a personage who was very evidently in the habit of making major decisions and seeing them carried out. The circle, its moment of sport over, was listening with more than a suggestion of deference. Tick-Tock, far from conciliated, green eyes still blazing, nevertheless was settling down to listen too.

Telzey began to understand.

Her suggestions, Iron Thoughts informed her, might appear without value to a number of foolish minds here, but *he* intended to see they were given a fair trial. Did he perhaps hear, he inquired next of the circle, throwing in a casual but horridly vivid impression of snapping spines and slashed shaggy throats spouting blood, any objection to that?

Dead stillness all around. There was definitely no objection! Tick-Tock began to grin like a pleased kitten.

That point having been settled in an orderly manner now, Iron Thoughts went on coldly to Telzey, what specifically did she propose they should do?

Halet's long, pearl-gray sportscar showed up above the park trees twenty minutes later. Telzey, face turned down towards the open law library in her lap, watched the car from the corner of her eyes. She was in plain view, sitting beside the lake, apparently absorbed in legal research. Tick-Tock, camouflaged among the bushes thirty feet higher up the bank, had spotted the car an instant before she did and announced the fact with a three-second break in her purring. Neither of them made any other move.

The car was approaching the lake but still a good distance off. Its canopy was down, and Telzey could just make out the heads of three people inside. Delquos, Halet's chauffeur, would be flying the vehicle, while Halet and Dr. Droon looked around for her from the sides. Three hundred yards away, the aircar began a turn to the right. Delquos didn't like his employer much; at a guess, he had just spotted Telzey and was trying to warn her off.

Telzey closed the library and put it down, picked up a handful of pebbles and began flicking them idly, one at a time, into the water. The aircar vanished to her left.

Three minutes later she watched its shadow glide across the surface of the lake towards her. Her heart began to thump almost audibly, but she didn't look up. Tick-Tock's purring continued, on its regular, unhurried note. The car came to a stop almost directly overhead. After a couple of seconds, there was a clicking noise. The purring ended abruptly.

Telzey climbed to her feet as Delquos brought the car down to the bank of the lake. The chauffeur grinned ruefully at her. A side door had been opened, and Halet and Dr. Droon stood behind it. Halet watched Telzey with a small smile while the naturalist put the heavy life-detector-and-stungun device carefully down on the floorboards.

"If you're looking for Tick-Tock," Telzey said, "she isn't here."

Halet just shook her head sorrowfully.

"There's no use lying to us, dear! Dr. Droon just stunned her."

They found TT collapsed on her side among the shrubs, wearing her natural color. Her eyes were shut; her chest rose and fell in a slow breathing motion. Dr. Droon, looking rather apologetic, pointed out to Telzey that her pet was in no pain, that the stungun had simply put her comfortably to sleep. He also explained the use of the two sets of webbed paralysis belts which he fastened about TT's legs. The effect of the stun charge would wear off in a few minutes, and contact with the inner surfaces of the energized belts would then keep TT anesthetized and unable to move until the belts were removed. She would, he repeated, be suffering no pain throughout the process.

Telzey didn't comment. She watched Delquos raise TT's limp body above the level of the bushes with a gravity hoist belonging to Dr. Droon, and maneuver her back to the car, the others following. Delquos climbed into the car first, opened the big trunk compartment in the rear. TT was slid inside and the trunk compartment locked.

"Where are you taking her?" Telzey asked sullenly as Delquos lifted the car into the air.

"To the spaceport, dear," Halet said. "Dr. Droon and I both felt it would be better to spare your feelings by not prolonging the matter unnecessarily."

Telzey wrinkled her nose disdainfully, and walked up the aircar to stand behind Delquos' seat. She leaned against the back of the seat for an instant. Her legs felt shaky.

The chauffeur gave her a sober wink from the side.

"That's a dirty trick she's played on you, Miss Telzey!" he murmured. "I tried to warn you."

"I know." Telzey took a deep breath. "Look, Delquos, in just a minute something's going to happen! It'll look dangerous, but it won't be. Don't let it get you nervous . . . right?"

"Huh?" Delquos appeared startled, but kept his voice low. "Just *what's* going to happen?"

"No time to tell you. Remember what I said."

Telzey moved back a few steps from the driver's seat, turned around, said unsteadily, "Halet . . . Dr. Droon—"

Halet had been speaking quietly to Dr. Droon; they both looked up.

"If you don't move, and don't do anything stupid," Telzey said rapidly, "you won't get hurt. If you do . . . well, I don't know! You see, there's another crest cat in the car . . ." In her mind she added, "Now!"

It was impossible to tell in just what section of the car Iron Thoughts had been lurking. The carpeting near the rear passenger seats seemed to blur for an instant. Then he was there, camouflage dropped, sitting on the floorboards five feet from the naturalist and Halet.

Halet's mouth opened wide; she tried to scream but fainted

instead. Dr. Droon's right hand started out quickly towards the big stungun device beside his seat. Then he checked himself and sat still, ashen-faced.

Telzey didn't blame him for changing his mind. She felt he must be a remarkably brave man to have moved at all. Iron Thoughts, twice as broad across the back as Tick-Tock, twice as massively muscled, looked like a devil-beast even to her. His dark-green marbled hide was crisscrossed with old scar patterns; half his tossing crimson crest appeared to have been ripped away. He reached out now in a fluid, silent motion, hooked a paw under the stungun and flicked upwards. The big instrument rose in an incredibly swift, steep arc eighty feet into the air, various parts flying away from it, before it started curving down towards the treetops below the car. Iron Thoughts lazily swung his head around and looked at Telzey with yellow fire-eyes.

"Miss Telzey! Miss Telzey!" Delquos was muttering behind her. "You're *sure* it won't . . ."

Telzey swallowed. At the moment she felt barely mouse-sized again. "Just relax!" she told Delquos in a shaky voice. "He's really quite t-t-t-tame."

Iron Thoughts produced a harsh but not unamiable chuckle in her mind.

The pearl-gray sportscar, covered now by its streamlining canopy, drifted down presently to a parking platform outside the suite of offices of Jontarou's Planetary Moderator, on the fourteenth floor of the Shikaris' Club Tower. An attendant waved it on into a vacant slot.

Inside the car Delquos set the brakes, switched off the engine, asked, "Now what?"

"I think," Telzey said reflectively, "we'd better lock you in the trunk compartment with my aunt and Dr. Droon while I talk to the Moderator."

The chauffeur shrugged. He'd regained most of his aplomb during the unhurried trip across the parklands. Iron Thoughts had done nothing but sit in the center of the car, eyes half shut, looking like instant death enjoying a dignified nap and occasionally emitting a ripsawing noise which might have been either his style of purring or a snore. And Tick-Tock, when Delquos peeled the paralysis belts off her legs at Telzey's direction, had greeted him with her usual reserved affability. What the chauffeur was suffering from at the moment was intense curiosity, which Telzey had done nothing to relieve.

"Just as you say, Miss Telzey," he agreed. "I hate to miss whatever you're going to be doing here, but if you *don't* lock me up now, Miss Halet will figure I was helping you and fire me as soon as you let her out."

Telzey nodded, then cocked her head in the direction of the rear compartment. Faint sounds coming through the door indicated that Halet had regained consciousness and was having hysterics.

"You might tell her," Telzey suggested, "that there'll be a grown-up crest cat sitting outside the compartment door." This wasn't true, but neither Delquos nor Halet could know it. "If there's too much racket before I get back, it's likely to irritate him . . ."

A minute later, she set both car doors on lock and went outside, wishing she were less informally clothed. Sunbriefs and sandals tended to make her look juvenile.

The parking attendant appeared startled when she approached him with Tick-Tock striding alongside.

"They'll never let you into the offices with that thing, miss," he informed her. "Why, it doesn't even have a collar!"

"Don't worry about it," Telzey told him aloofly.

She dropped a two-credit piece she'd taken from Halet's purse into his hand, and continued on towards the building entrance. The attendant squinted after her, trying unsuccessfully to dispel an odd impression that the big catlike animal with the girl was throwing a double shadow.

The Moderator's chief receptionist also had some doubts about TT, and possibly about the sunbriefs, though she seemed impressed when Telzey's identification tag informed her she was speaking to the daughter of Federation Councilwoman Jessamine Amberdon.

"You feel you can discuss this . . . emergency . . . only with the Moderator himself, Miss Amberdon?" she repeated.

"Exactly," Telzey said firmly. A buzzer sounded as she spoke. The receptionist excused herself and picked up an earphone. She listened a moment, said blandly, "Yes . . . Of course . . . Yes, I understand," replaced the earphone and stood up, smiling at Telzey.

"Would you come with me, Miss Amberdon?" she said. "I think the Moderator will see you immediately . . ."

Telzey followed her, chewing thoughtfully at her lip. This was easier than she'd expected—in fact, too easy! Halet's work? Probably. A few comments to the effect of "A highly imaginative child . . . overexcitable," while Halet was arranging to have the Moderator's office authorize Tick-Tock's transfer to the Life Banks, along with the implication that Jessamine Amberdon would appreciate a discreet handling of any disturbance Telzey might create as a result.

It was the sort of notion that would appeal to Halet . . .

They passed through a series of elegantly equipped offices and hallways, Telzey grasping TT's neck-fur in lieu of a leash, their appearance creating a tactfully restrained wave of surprise among secretaries and clerks. And if somebody here and there was troubled by a fleeting, uncanny impression that not one large beast but two seemed to be trailing the Moderator's visitor down the aisles, no mention was made of what could have been only a momentary visual distortion. Finally, a pair of sliding doors opened ahead, and the receptionist ushered Telzey into a large, cool balcony garden on the shaded side of the great building. A tall, gray-haired man stood up from the desk at which he was working, and bowed to Telzey. The receptionist withdrew again.

"My pleasure, Miss Amberdon," Jontarou's Planetary Moderator said. "Be seated, please." He studied Tick-Tock with more than casual interest while Telzey was settling herself into a chair, added, "and what may I and my office do for you?"

Telzey hesitated. She'd observed his type on Orado in her mother's circle of acquaintances—a senior diplomat, a man not easy to impress. It was a safe bet that he'd had her brought out to his balcony office only to keep her occupied while Halet was quietly informed where the Amberdon problem child was and requested to come over and take charge.

What she had to tell him now would have sounded rather wild even if presented by a presumably responsible adult. She could provide proof, but until the Moderator was already nearly sold on her story, that would be a very unsafe thing to do. Old Iron Thoughts was backing her up, but if it didn't look as if her plans were likely to succeed, he would be willing to ride herd on his devil's pack just so long . . .

Better start the ball rolling without any preliminaries, Telzey decided. The Moderator's picture of her must be that of a spoiled, neurotic brat in a stew about the threatened loss of a pet animal. He expected her to start arguing with him immediately about Tick-Tock.

She said, "Do you have a personal interest in keeping the Baluit crest cats from becoming extinct?"

Surprise flickered in his eyes for an instant. Then he smiled.

"I admit I do, Miss Amberdon," he said pleasantly. "I should like to see the species re-established. I count myself almost uniquely fortunate in having had the opportunity to bag two of the magnificent brutes before disease wiped them out on the planet."

The last seemed a less than fortunate statement just now. Telzey felt a sharp tingle of alarm, then sensed that in the minds which were drawing the meaning of the Moderator's speech from her mind there had been only a brief stir of interest.

She cleared her throat, said, "The point is that they weren't wiped out by disease."

He considered her quizzically, seemed to wonder what she was trying to lead up to. Telzey gathered her courage, plunged on. "Would you like to hear what did happen?"

"I should be much interested, Miss Amberdon," the Moderator said without change of expression. "But first, if you'll excuse me a moment . . ."

There had been some signal from his desk which Telzey hadn't noticed, because he picked up a small communicator now, said, "Yes?" After a few seconds, he resumed, "That's rather curious, isn't it? . . . Yes, I'd try that . . . No, that shouldn't be necessary . . . Yes, please do. Thank you." He replaced the communicator, his face very sober; then, his eyes flicking for an instant to TT, he drew one of the upper desk drawers open a few inches, and turned back to Telzey.

"Now, Miss Amberdon," he said affably, "you were about to say? About these crest cats . . ."

Telzey swallowed. She hadn't heard the other side of the conversation, but she could guess what it had been about. His office had called the guest house, had been told by Halet's maid that Halet, the chauffeur, and Dr. Droon were out looking for Miss Telzey and her pet. The Moderator's office had then checked on the sportscar's communication number and attempted to call it. And, of course, there had been no response.

To the Moderator, considering what Halet would have told him, it must add up to the grim possibility that the young lunatic he was talking to had let her three-quarters-grown crest cat slaughter her aunt and the two men when they caught up with her! The office would be notifying the police now to conduct an immediate search for the missing aircar.

When it would occur to them to look for it on the Moderator's parking terrace was something Telzey couldn't know. But if Halet and Dr. Droon were released before the Moderator accepted her own version of what had occurred, and the two reported the presence of wild crest cats in Port Nichay, there would be almost no possibility of keeping the situation under control. Somebody was bound to make some idiotic move, and the fat would be in the fire . . .

Two things might be in her favor. The Moderator seemed to have the sort of steady nerve one would expect in a man who had bagged two Baluit crest cats. The partly opened desk drawer beside him must have a gun in it; apparently he considered that a sufficient precaution against an attack by TT. He wasn't likely to react in a panicky manner. And the mere fact that he suspected Telzey of homicidal tendencies would make him give the closest attention to what she said. Whether he believed her then was another matter, of course.

Slightly encouraged, Telzey began to talk. It did sound like a thoroughly wild story, but the Moderator listened with an appearance of intent interest. When she had told him as much as she felt he could be expected to swallow for a start, he said musingly, "So they weren't wiped out—they went into hiding! Do I understand you to say they did it to avoid being hunted?"

Telzey chewed her lip frowningly before replying. "There's something about that part I don't quite get," she admitted. "Of course I don't quite get either why you'd want to go hunting . . .

twice . . . for something that's just as likely to bag you instead!"

"Well, those are, ah, merely the statistical odds," the Moderator explained. "If one has enough confidence, you see—"

"I don't really. But the crest cats seem to have felt the same way—at first. They were getting around one hunter for every cat that got shot. Humans were the most exciting game they'd ever run into.

"But then that ended, and the humans started knocking them out with stunguns from aircars where they couldn't be got at, and hauling them off while they were helpless. After it had gone on for a while, they decided to keep out of sight.

"But they're still around . . . thousands and thousands of them! Another thing nobody's known about them is that they weren't only in the Baluit mountains. There were crest cats scattered all through the big forests along the other side of the continent."

"Very interesting," the Moderator commented. "Very interesting, indeed!" He glanced towards the communicator, then returned his gaze to Telzey, drumming his fingers lightly on the desktop.

She could tell nothing at all from his expression now, but she guessed he was thinking hard. There was supposed to be no native intelligent life in the legal sense on Jontarou, and she had been careful to say nothing so far to make the Baluit cats look like more than rather exceptionally intelligent animals. The next—rather large—question should be how she'd come by such information.

If the Moderator asked her that, Telzey thought, she could feel she'd made a beginning at getting him to buy the whole story.

"Well," he said abruptly, "if the crest cats are not extinct or threatened with extinction, the Life Banks obviously have no claim on your pet." He smiled confidingly at her. "And that's the reason you're here, isn't it?"

"Well, no," Telzey began, dismayed. "I—"

"Oh, it's quite all right, Miss Amberdon! I'll simply rescind the permit which was issued for the purpose. You need feel no further concern about that." He paused. "Now, just one question . . . do you happen to know where your aunt is at present?"

Telzey had a dead, sinking feeling. So he hadn't believed a word she said. He'd been stalling her along until the aircar could be found.

She took a deep breath. "You'd better listen to the rest of it."

"Why, is there more?" the Moderator asked politely.

"Yes. The important part! The kind of creatures they are, they wouldn't go into hiding indefinitely just because someone was after them."

Was there a flicker of something beyond watchfulness in his expression. "What would they do, Miss Amberdon?" he asked quietly.

"If they couldn't get at the men in the aircars and couldn't communicate with them"—the flicker again!—"they'd start looking for the place the men came from, wouldn't they? It might take them some years to work their way across the continent and locate us here in Port Nichay. But supposing they did it finally and a few thousand of them are sitting around in the parks down there right now? They could come up the side of these towers as easily as they go up the side of a mountain. And supposing they'd decided that the only way to handle the problem was to clean out the human beings in Port Nichay?"

The Moderator stared at her in silence a few seconds. "You're saying," he observed then, "that they're rational beings—above the Critical I.Q. level."

"Well," Telzey said, "legally they're rational. I checked on that. About as rational as we are, I suppose."

"Would you mind telling me now how you happen to know this?"

"They told me," Telzey said.

He was silent again, studying her face. "You mentioned, Miss Amberdon, that they have been unable to communicate with other human beings. This suggests then that you are a xenotelepath . . ."

"I am?" Telzey hadn't heard the term before. "If it means that I can tell what the cats are thinking, and they can tell what I'm thinking, I guess that's the word for it." She considered him, decided she had him almost on the ropes, went on quickly.

"I looked up the laws, and told them they could conclude a treaty with the Federation which would establish them as an

Affiliated Species . . . and that would settle everything the way they would want it settled, without trouble. Some of them believed me. They decided to wait until I could talk to you. If it works out, fine! If it doesn't"—she felt her voice falter for an instant—"they're going to cut loose fast!"

The Moderator seemed undisturbed. "What am I supposed to do?"

"I told them you'd contact the Council of the Federation on Orado."

"Contact the Council?" he repeated coolly. "With no more proof for this story than your word, Miss Amberdon?"

Telzey felt a quick, angry stirring begin about her, felt her face whiten.

"All right," she said. "I'll give you proof! I'll have to now. But that'll be it. Once they've tipped their hand all the way, you'll have about thirty seconds left to make the right move. I hope you remember that!"

He cleared his throat. "I—"

"NOW!" Telzey said.

Along the walls of the balcony garden, beside the ornamental flower stands, against the edges of the rock pool, the crest cats appeared. Perhaps thirty of them. None quite as physically impressive as Iron Thoughts who stood closest to the Moderator; but none very far from it. Motionless as rocks, frightening as gargoyles, they waited, eyes glowing with hellish excitement.

"This is *their* council, you see," Telzey heard herself saying.

The Moderator's face had also paled. But he was, after all, an old shikari and a senior diplomat. He took an unhurried look around the circle, said quietly, "Accept my profound apologies for doubting you, Miss Amberdon!" and reached for the desk communicator.

Iron Thoughts swung his demon head in Telzey's direction. For an instant she picked up the mental impression of a fierce yellow eye closing in an approving wink.

". . . An open transmitter line to Orado," the Moderator was saying into the communicator. "The Council. And snap it up! Some very important visitors are waiting . . ."

The offices of Jontarou's Planetary Moderator became an extremely busy and interesting area then. Quite two hours passed before it occurred to anyone to ask Telzey again whether she knew where her aunt was at present.

Telzey smote her forehead.

"Forgot all about that!" she admitted, fishing the sportscar's keys out of the pocket of her sunbriefs. "They're out on the parking platform . . ."

The preliminary treaty arrangements between the Federation of the Hub and the new Affiliated Species of the Planet of Jontarou were formally ratified two weeks later, the ceremony taking place on Jontarou, in the Champagne Hall of the Shikaris' Club.

Telzey was able to follow the event only by news viewer in her ship-cabin, she and Halet being on the return trip to Orado by then. She wasn't too interested in the treaty's details—they conformed almost exactly to what she had read out to Iron Thoughts and his co-chiefs and companions in the park. It was the smooth bridging of the wide language gap between the contracting parties by a row of interpreting machines and a handful of human xenotelepaths which held her attention.

As she switched off the viewer, Halet came wandering in from the adjoining cabin.

"I was watching it too!" Halet observed. She smiled. "I was hoping to see dear Tick-Tock."

Telzey looked over at her. "Well, TT would hardly be likely to show up in Port Nichay," she said. "She's having too good a time now finding out what life in the Baluit range is like."

"I suppose so," Halet agreed doubtfully, sitting down on a hassock. "But I'm glad she promised to get in touch with us again in a few years. I'll miss her."

Telzey regarded her aunt with a reflective frown. Halet meant it quite sincerely, of course; she had undergone a profound change of heart during the past two weeks. But Telzey wasn't without some doubts about the actual value of a change of heart brought on by telepathic means. The learning process the crest cats had started in her mind appeared to have continued automatically several days longer than her rugged teachers had really intended; and Telzey had reason to believe that by the end of that time she'd developed associated latent abilities of which the crest cats had never heard. She'd barely begun to get it all sorted out yet, but . . . as an example . . . she'd found it remarkably easy to turn Halet's more obnoxious attitudes virtually upside down. It had taken her a couple of days to get the hang of her aunt's personal symbolism, but after that there had been no problem.

She was reasonably certain she'd broken no laws so far, though the sections in the law library covering the use and abuse of psionic abilities were veiled in such intricate and downright obscuring phrasing—deliberately, Telzey suspected—that it was really difficult to say what they did mean. But even aside from that, there were a number of arguments in favor of exercising great caution.

Jessamine, for one thing, was bound to start worrying about her sister-in-law's health if Halet turned up on Orado in her present state of mind, even though it would make for a far more agreeable atmosphere in the Amberdon household.

"Halet," Telzey inquired mentally, "do you remember what an all-out stinker you used to be?"

"Of course, dear," Halet said aloud. "I can hardly wait to tell dear Jessamine how much I regret the many times I . . ."

"Well," Telzey went on, still verbalizing it silently, "I think you'd really enjoy life more if you were, let's say, about halfway between your old nasty self and the sort of sickening-good kind you are now."

"Why, Telzey!" Halet cried out with dopey amiability. "What a delightful idea!"

"Let's try it," Telzey said.

There was silence in the cabin for some twenty minutes then while she went painstakingly about remolding a number of Halet's character traits for the second time. She still felt some misgiving about it; but if it became necessary, she probably could always restore the old Halet *in toto*.

These, she told herself, definitely were powers one should treat with respect! Better rattle through law school first; then, with that out of the way, she could start hunting around to see who in the Federation was qualified to instruct a genius-level novice in the proper handling of psionics . . .

4

Child of Void

MARGARET ST. CLAIR

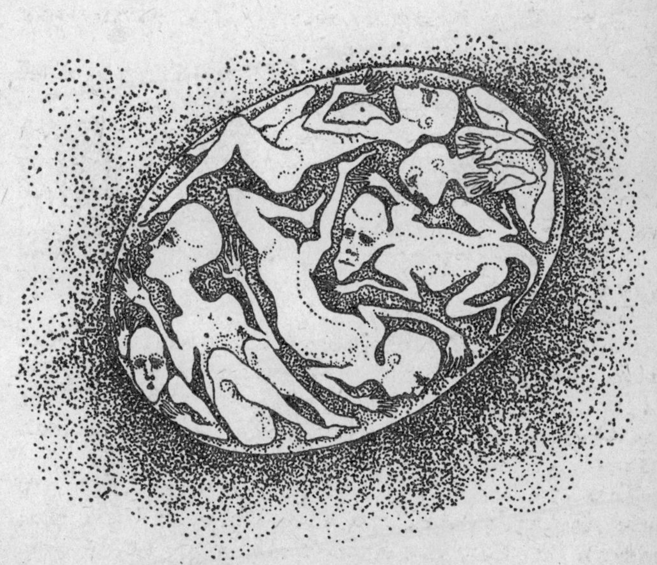

A perennial source of discomfort to me is the confusion in the minds of part of the public about science fiction fans and flying saucer enthusiasts.

To be sure, flying saucer enthusiasts like to present their "unidentified flying objects" as spaceships from other worlds manned by individuals of advanced technologies and surely this sounds like science fiction. (Incidentally, these people are not the least interested in unidentified flying objects and are furious with scientists who wish to leave them unidentified until more information is in. No, no, these enthusiasts instantly identify every such object in full and foolish detail.)

But consider the differences. The flying saucer enthusiast often postulates creatures that are humanoid in form, are dressed in robes, are benign of purpose, and are constantly speaking like storybook preachers. Doesn't this sound familiar? Are we not in a kind of pseudoscientific spirit world, one that has dropped the ectoplasm and "higher planes" of the earlier spiritualists to take up the mysterious space-drives and other planets of a new breed of mystic?

What has that sort of nonsense to do with real science fiction?

Science fiction is man-centered rather than spirit-centered. Man's problems must be solved, or not solved, by man, and there are no creatures (whether spirits or robed benignities from Venus) to take care of us. If creatures from outer space do reach us, they are very apt to add to our problems and pose new crises.

Let Margaret St. Clair introduce a youngster who finds himself in the midst of just such a problem, and see how he and his family handle it (or do they?).

Ischeenar is his name, and he lives in the big toe of my left foot. He's fairly quiet during the day, except that now and then he makes my foot twitch. But at night he comes out and sits on my knee and says all sorts of hateful things. Once he suggested—

But I didn't mean to tell about Ischeenar yet. I suppose I got off on him thinking about the fire and all that. It was after the fire that he got into my foot. But I want to tell this in order, the way it happened, and I ought to begin at the beginning. I suppose that means telling about how we happened to go to Hidden Valley to live.

Uncle Albert killed himself and left Hidden Valley to Mom in his will. I didn't want to go there. We had visited Hidden Valley once or twice when I was little, and I hated it. It gave me the creeps. It was the kind of place you see articles about in the Sunday supplement—a place where water flows uphill and half the time the laws of gravity don't work, a place where sometimes a rubber ball will weigh three or four pounds and you can look out the upstairs window and see a big blue lake where the vegetable garden ought to be. You never could depend on things being normal and right.

But Mom wanted to go. She said there was a nice little house we could live in, an artesian well with the best water in the world, and good rich soil for growing our own vegetables. There were even a cow and some chickens. Mom said we could be a lot more comfortable there than in the city, and live better. She said we'd get used to the funny things and they wouldn't bother us. And though she didn't say so, I knew she thought I'd be happier away from people, on a farm.

Mom's been awfully good to me. She kept on with the massage and exercises for my back for years after the doctors said it was no use. I wish I could do more for her. Her ideas are usually pretty good, and when I've gone against them I've been sorry. When you think about it, Mom is generally right.

So we went to Hidden Valley, Mom and Donnie (that's my younger brother) and I. It was worse than I had thought it was going to be. The place was still queer enough to scare you purple, but besides that there was something new, a kind of heavy depression in the air.

It was terrible. At first it made you feel like you'd like to put your head up and howl the way a dog does; then you felt too worn out and miserable and unhappy to have energy left for howling.

It got worse with every hour we stayed there. By the time we'd been in Hidden Valley for two days, Mom and I were looking at each other and wondering which of us would be the first to suggest going back to the city. I kept thinking about how sensible Uncle Albert had been to blow himself up with the dynamite. Even Donnie and his kitten felt the depression; they sat huddled up together in a corner and looked miserable.

Finally Mom said, in a kind of desperate way, "Eddie, why don't you see what you can get on your radio set? It might cheer you up." Mom doesn't give up easily.

I thought it was a silly idea. I've been a ham operator ever since I was fifteen, and it's a lot of fun. I enjoy it more than anything. But when you're feeling as bad as I was then, you don't want to talk to anyone. You just want to sit and wonder about dying and things like that.

My stuff had been dumped down all in a corner of the little beaverboarded living room. I hadn't felt chipper enough to do anything about getting it set up, though Uncle Albert had put in a private power system and there was electricity in the house. After Mom asked me for the second time, though, I got up and hobbled over to my equipment. And here a funny thing happened. I'd hardly started hunting around for a table to put my stuff on when my depression began to lift.

It was wonderful. It was like being lost in the middle of a dark, choking fog and then having the fog blow away and the bright sun shine out.

The others were affected the same way. Donnie got a piece of string and began playing with the kitten, and the kitten sat back and batted at the string with its paws the way cats do when they're playful. Mom stood watching me for a while, smiling, and then she went out in the kitchen and began to get supper. I could smell the bacon frying and hear her whistling "Onward, Christian Soldiers." Mom whistles that way when she's feeling good.

We didn't go back to feeling depressed again, either. The funny things about Hidden Valley stopped bothering us, and we all enjoyed ourselves. We had fresh eggs, and milk so rich you could hardly drink it, and lettuce and peas and tomatoes and everything. It was a dry year, but we had plenty of water for irrigation. We lived off the fat of the land; you'd have to have a hundred dollars a week to live like that in the city.

Donnie liked school (he walked about a mile to the school bus) better than he had in the city because the kids were more friendly, and Mom got a big bang out of taking care of the cow and the chickens. I was outside all day long, working in the garden, and I got a fine tan and put on some weight. Mom said I never looked so well. She went into town in the jalopy twice a month to get me books from the county library, and I had all kinds of interesting things to read.

The only thing that bothered me—and it didn't really *bother* me, at that—was that I couldn't contact any other hams with my station. I never got a single signal from anyone. I don't know what the trouble was, really—what it looked like was that radio waves couldn't get into or out of the valley. I did everything I could to soup up my equipment. I had Mom get me a dozen books from the county library, and I stayed up half the night studying them. I tore my equipment down and built it up again eight or ten times and put in all sorts of fancy stuff. Nothing helped. I might as well have held a rock to my ear and listened to it.

But outside of that, as I say, I thought Hidden Valley was wonderful. I was glad Mom had made me and Donnie go there. Everything was doing fine, until Donnie fell in the cave.

It happened when he went out after lunch to hunt his kitten—it was Saturday—and he didn't come back and he didn't come back. At last Mom, getting worried, sent me out to look for him.

I went to all the usual places first, and then, not finding him, went farther away. At last, high up on a hillside, I found a big, fresh-looking hole. It was about five feet across, and from the look of the grass on the edges, the earth had just recently caved in. It seemed to be six or seven feet deep. Could Donnie be down in there? If there's a hole to fall in, a kid will fall in it.

I put my ear over the edge and listened. I couldn't see anything when I looked. After a moment I heard a sound like sobbing, pretty much muffled.

"Donnie!" I yelled. "Oh, Donnie!" There wasn't any answer, but the sobbing seemed to get louder. I figured if he was down there, he was either hurt or too scared to answer my call.

I hobbled back to the house as quick as I could and got a stepladder. I didn't tell Mom—no use in worrying her any more. I managed to get the ladder to the hole and down inside. Then I went down myself. I've got lots of strength in my arms.

Donnie wasn't at the bottom. Some light was coming in at the top, and I could see that the cave went on sloping down. I listened carefully and heard the crying again.

The slope was pretty steep, about twenty degrees. I went forward carefully, feeling my way along the side and listening. Everything was as dark as the inside of a cow. Now and then I'd yell Donnie's name.

The crying got louder. It did sound like Donnie's voice. Pretty soon I heard a faint "Eddie!" from ahead. And almost at the same moment I saw a faint gleam.

When I got up to it, Donnie was there. I could just make him out silhouetted against the dim yellowish glow. When I said his name this time, he gulped and swallowed. He crawled up to me as quick as he could and threw his arms around my legs.

"Ooooh, Eddie," he said, "I'm so glad you came! I fell in and hurt myself. I didn't know how to get out. I crawled away down here. I've been awful scared."

I put my arms around him and patted him. I certainly was glad to see him. But my attention wasn't all on him. Part of it was fixed on the egg.

It wasn't really an egg, of course. Even at the time I knew that. But it looked like a reptile's egg, somehow, a huge, big egg. It was about the size of a cardboard packing box, oval-shaped, and it seemed to be covered over with a tough and yet gelatinous skin. It glowed faintly with a pale orange light, as if it were translucent and the light were coming through it from behind. Shadows moved slowly inside.

Donnie was holding onto my legs so tightly I was afraid he'd stop the circulation. I could feel his heart pounding against me, and when I patted him his face was wet with tears. "I'm awful glad you came, Eddie," he said again. "You know that ol' egg there? It's been making me see all sorts of things. I was awful scared."

Donnie never lies. "It's all right now, kid," I said, looking at the egg. "We won't let it show you any more bad things."

"Oh, they weren't bad!" Donnie drew away from me. "The egg's bad, but the things weren't! They were awful nice."

I knew I ought to get him out, but I was curious. I was so curious I couldn't stand it. I said, "What kind of things, Quack-quack?" (That's his pet name, because his name is Donald.)

"Oh . . ." Donnie's voice was dreamy. His heartbeat was calming down. "Books and toys and candy. A great big Erector set. A toy farm and fire truck and a cowboy suit. And ice cream—I wish you could have some of the ice cream, Eddie. I had sodas and malteds and Eskimo bars and Cokes. Oh, and I won first prize in the spelling contest. Mom was awful glad."

"You mean—the egg let you have all these things?" I asked, feeling dazed.

"Naw." Donnie's tone held disgust. "But I could have 'em, all that and a lot more, if I'd do what the egg wanted."

"Oh."

"But I wouldn't do it." Donnie's voice was virtuous. "I said no to 'em. That egg's bad."

"What did the egg want you to do?"

"Aw, they wouldn't tell me." Donnie's tone was full of antagonism. "They never did say. C'm on, let's get out of here. You help me, I don't like it here."

I didn't answer. I didn't move. I couldn't. The egg . . . was showing me things.

What sort of things? The things I wanted most, just as it had with Donnie. Things I wanted so much I wouldn't even admit to wanting them. I saw myself healthy and normal and strong, with a straight back and powerful limbs. I was going to college, I was captain of the football team. I made the touchdown that won the big game. I was graduated with honors while Mom and my girl friend—such a pretty, jolly girl—looked on, their faces bright with pride. I got an important research job in radio. And so on—foolish ambitions, impossible hopes. Crazy dreams.

But they weren't dreams when the egg was showing them to me. They were real, they weren't something I had to hide or laugh at any longer. And all the time a voice inside my brain was saying, "You can have this. You can have all this.

"Won't you help us, won't you please help us? We're harmless, we're trapped and hurt. We came here from our own place to colonize, and we can't get out and we can't get back.

"It would be easy for you to help us. And we'll be grateful. We'll give you all you saw. And more. All you have to do . . ."

I took a step forward. Of course I wanted what they had shown me. I wanted them very much. And besides, I felt sorry for the things, the harmless things imprisoned in the egg. I've known what it is to feel helpless and trapped.

Donnie was beating on my thigh with his fists and screaming. I tried to shake him off so I could go on listening to the other voice. He hung on, pummeling me, and finally, in desperation, grabbed at my hand and bit it hard with his sharp little teeth.

"Eddie, Eddie, Eddie! Come out of it, please come out of it!"

That roused me. I looked at him, dazed and resentful. Why wouldn't he let me listen so I could help the poor things in the egg? "Be quiet, Quack-quack," I mumbled to him.

"You gotta listen, Eddie! Don't let them get you! 'Member what happened to Uncle Albert? 'Member how we felt when we first came to the farm?"

The words penetrated. My normal caution was waking up. "But they say they don't mean us any harm," I argued weakly. I was talking to Donnie just like he was grown up.

"Aw, they're big liars. They can't help hurting us. It's something they put into the air, like, by just being alive. They can stop it for a while, if they try hard. But that's the way they really are. Like poison oak or a rattlesnake. 'Sides, I think they like it. They like being the way they are."

Poison oak and rattlers, I translated to myself, aren't consciously evil. They don't will their nature. But it's their nature to be poisonous. If Donnie was right in thinking that the things in the egg gave out, as a part of their metabolism, a vibration which was hostile to human life . . . Uncle Albert had committed suicide by blowing himself up with dynamite.

"We'd better get rid of the egg, Quack-quack," I said.

"Yes, Eddie."

I helped him up the shaft to the mouth of the cave. He'd sprained his ankle. On the way I asked, "What are the things in the egg like, Donnie?" I had an idea, but I wanted to check it with him. I felt his young mind and senses were keener and more reliable in this than mine.

"Like radio. Or 'lectricity."

"Where did they come from?"

"Another—not like where we live. Everything's different. It's not like here. It's right here beside us. An' it's a long way off."

I nodded. I helped him up the ladder and left him sitting on the hillside. Then I went back to the house for my .22 and a can of kerosene.

Donnie watched me anxiously as I went down with them. I don't mind admitting I was pretty nervous myself.

A .22 isn't an elephant gun. Still, at a two-foot range it ought to have some penetrating power. It didn't. The bullets just bounced off from the side of the egg. I could hear them spatting against the walls of the cave. I used three clips before I gave up.

That left the kerosene. There hadn't been any more attempts to show me pictures or bring me around. In a silence that seemed bitterly hostile I poured kerosene all over the egg. I used plenty. Then I stood back and tossed a match at it.

Heat boiled up. It got so hot I retreated nearly to where Donnie had fallen in. But when it cooled off enough so that I could go back, I found the egg sitting there as good as new. There wasn't even any soot on it.

I was beaten. I couldn't think of anything more to do. I went up the ladder with the empty kerosene can and my gun. Donnie seemed to know I'd failed. He was crying when I came up to him. "Don't tell Mom," I said, and he nodded dutifully.

Would the egg let it go at that? I didn't think so. After supper I said to Mom, "You know, sometimes I think it would be nice to go back to the city for a while."

She looked at me as if she couldn't believe her ears. "Are you crazy, Eddie? We never had it so good before." Her eyes narrowed and she began to get worried. "What's the matter, honey? Aren't you feeling well?"

I couldn't tell her. I knew she'd believe me; that was just the trouble. If she knew there was a chance I could be cured, be made healthy and strong the way she wanted me to be, she'd make a dicker with the things in the egg, come hell or high water. It wouldn't make any difference to her whether they were good or bad, if she thought they could help *me*. Mom's like that.

"Oh, I feel fine," I said as heartily as I could. "It was just an idea. How's for seconds on the strawberry shortcake? It's even better than usual, Mom."

Her face relaxed. But I didn't sleep much that night.

The breakfast Mom cooked next morning was punk. I wasn't hungry, but I couldn't help noticing. The toast was burned, the eggs were leathery and cold, the coffee was the color of tea. There was even a fly in the pitcher of orange juice. I thought she must be worried about Donnie. I had bandaged his foot according to the picture in the first-aid book, but the ankle had swelled up like a balloon, and it looked sore and bad.

After breakfast Mom said, "Eddie, you seem worn out. I

think carrying Donnie so far was bad for you. I don't want you to do any work today. You just sit around and rest."

"I don't feel like resting," I objected.

"Well–" Her face brightened. "I know," she said, sounding pleased. "Why don't you see what you can get on your radio set? The cord's long enough you could take it out on the side porch and be out in the fresh air. It's been a long time since you worked with it. Maybe you could get some of the stations you used to get."

She sounded so pleased with herself for having thought of the radio that I didn't have the heart to argue with her. She helped me move the table and the equipment outside, and I sat down and began to fiddle with it. It was nice and cool out on the porch.

I didn't get any signals, of course. Pretty soon Donnie came limping out. He was supposed to stay on the couch in the living room, but it's hard for a kid to keep still.

"What's the matter, Donnie?" I asked, looking at him. He was frowning, and his face was puckered up and serious. "Foot hurt?"

"Oh, some . . . But Eddie . . . you know that old egg?"

I picked up my headphones and turned them a bit. "Um," I said.

"Well, I don't think you should'a built that fire around it. It was a bad thing to do."

I put the headphones down. I wanted to tell Donnie to shut up and not bother me; I know that was because I didn't like what he was saying. "Why was it bad?" I asked.

"Because it stirred the things in the egg up. I kin feel it. It's like you have a station with more juice, you can get farther. The fire gave them more juice."

I didn't know what to say. I figured he was right, and I felt scared. After a minute I made myself laugh. "Nothing to worry about, Quack-quack," I said. "We can lick any old egg."

His face relaxed a little. "I guess so," he said. He sat down in the porch swing.

Mom stuck her head around the edge of the door. "Did you get anything on your radio, Eddie?" she asked.

"No," I said a little shortly.

"That's too bad." She went back in the kitchen and hung

her apron up, and then she came out on the porch. She was rubbing her forehead with the back of her hand as if her head ached.

To please her, I put on my headphones and twiddled the dials. No dice, of course. Mom frowned. She went around to the other side of the table and stood looking at the wiring, something I'd never seen her do before. "How would it be if you moved this from here to here?" she said. Her voice was a little high.

I leaned over to see what she was pointing at. "That would just burn out the tubes."

"Oh." She stood there for a moment. Then her hand darted out, and before I could stop her, before I even had any idea what she was up to, she moved the wire she'd been talking about.

"Hey!" I squawked, "stop that!" I said it too late. There was a crackle and a flash and all the tubes burned out. My station was completely dead.

Mom rubbed her forehead and looked at me. "I don't know what made me do that, Eddie," she said apologetically. "It was just like something moved my hand! I'm awfully sorry, son."

"Oh, that's okay," I said. "Don't worry about it. The station wasn't good for anything."

"I know, but . . . My head's been feeling queer all morning. I think it must be the weather. Doesn't the air feel heavy and oppressive to you?"

The air did have a thick, discouraging feel, but I hadn't noticed it before she burned out the radio tubes. I opened my mouth to say something, but before I could say it, Donnie yelled, "Look at Fluffie! She's walking on the air!"

We both jerked around. There Fluffie was, about ten feet up, making motions with her paws as if she were trying to walk. She was mewing a blue streak. Now and then she'd slip down three or four feet and then go up to the former level, just as if a hand had caught at her. Her fur was standing up all over, and her tail was three times its usual size. Finally she went up about twenty feet and then came sailing down in a long curve. She landed on the ground with a thump. And that was the beginning of all the phenomena.

It wasn't so much that we felt depressed at first, though we certainly did. But we could stand it; the depression wasn't as bad as it had been when we first came to Hidden Valley. I guess that was because the things in the egg were more spread out now. Whether that was the reason or not, most of the phenomena were physical.

You could hardly get into the living room. It was like pushing your way through big wet bladders to go into it. If you sat on the sofa you had a sense of being crowded and pushed, and pretty soon you'd find yourself down at the far end of it, squeezed into a corner. When Mom struck matches to make a fire for lunch, the matches were twitched out of her hand and went sailing around the room. We had to eat cold things; she was afraid of burning down the place.

At first Mom tried to pretend there was nothing wrong; after all, you couldn't *see* anything. But I went out in the kitchen at suppertime and found her crying quietly. She said it was because she'd been trying to cut bread for sandwiches and the knife in her hand kept rising up toward her throat. I knew that if Mom was crying it had been pretty bad. So I told her about the egg in the cave and all that.

"They're out of the egg now," she said unhappily when I had finished. "My burning out the tubes this morning let them out. We've got to go back to the city, Eddie. It's the only thing to do."

"And leave them loose?" I said sharply. "We can't do that. If it was just a case of deserting the valley and having them stay here, it would be all right. But they won't stay here. They came to Earth to colonize. That means they'll increase and spread out.

"Remember how it was when we came here? Remember how we felt? Suppose it was like that over most of the Earth!"

Mom shook her head till her gray curls bobbed. "This can't be real, Eddie," she said in a sort of wail. "We must be having hallucinations or something. I keep telling myself, this can't be real."

Donnie, outside, gave a sudden horrible shriek. Mom turned as white as a ghost. Then she darted out, with me after her.

Donnie was standing over Fluffie's body, crying with rage. He was so mad and so miserable he could hardly talk. "They killed her! They killed her!" he said at last. "She was way up in the air, and they pushed her down hard and she squashed when she hit the ground. She's all mashed flat!"

There wasn't anything to say. I left Mom to try to comfort Donnie, and went off by myself to try to think.

I didn't get anywhere with my thinking. How do you fight anything you can't see or understand? The things from the egg were immaterial but could produce material phenomena; Donnie had said they were like electricity or radio. Even if that were true, how did it help? I thought up a dozen fragmentary schemes, each with some major flaw, for getting rid of them, and in the end I had to give up.

None of us went to bed that night. We stayed up in the kitchen huddled together for comfort and protection, while the house went crazy around us. The things that happened were ridiculous and horrible. They made you feel mentally outraged. It was like being lowered down into a well filled with craziness.

About three o'clock the light in the kitchen went slowly out. The house calmed down and everything got quiet. I guess the things from the egg had revenged themselves on us enough for having tried to get rid of them, and now they were going about their own business, perhaps beginning to increase. Because from then on the feeling of depression got worse. It was worse than it had ever been before.

It seemed like years and years until four o'clock. I sat there in the dark, holding Mom's and Donnie's hands and wondering how much longer I could stand it. I had a vision of life, then, that people in asylums must have, an expanse filled with unbearable horror and pain and misery.

By the time it was getting light I couldn't stand it any longer. There was a way out; I didn't have to go on seeing Hell opening in front of me. I pulled my hands from Mom's and Donnie's and stood up. I knew where Uncle Albert had kept the dynamite. I was going to kill myself.

Donnie's eyes opened and he looked at me. I'd known he wasn't asleep. "Don't do it, Eddie," he said in a thread of a voice. "It'll only give them more juice."

Part of my mind knew dimly what he meant. The things from the egg weren't driving me to suicide deliberately; they didn't care enough about me for that. But my death—or any human's death—would be a nice little event, a tidbit, for them. Life is electrical. My death would release a little juice.

It didn't matter, it wasn't important. I knew what I was going to do.

Mom hadn't moved or looked at me. Her face was drawn and gray and blotched. I knew, somehow, that what she was enduring was worse than what I had endured. Her vision was darker than mine had been. She was too deep in it to be able to think or speak or move.

The dynamite was in a box in the shed. I hunted around until I found the detonator and the fuse. I stuffed the waxy, candle-like sticks inside the waistband of my trousers and picked up the other things. I was going to kill myself, but part of me felt a certain compunction at the thought of blowing up Mom and Donnie. I went outside and began to walk uphill.

The sun was coming up in a blaze of red and gold and there was a soft little breeze. I could smell wood smoke a long way off. It was going to be a fine day. I looked around me critically for a good place to blow myself up.

They say suicides are often very particular; I know I was. This spot was too open and that one too enclosed; there was too much grass here and not quite enough at the other place. It wasn't that I had cold feet. I hadn't. But I wanted everything to go off smoothly and well, without any hitches or fuss. I kept wandering around and looking, and pretty soon, without realizing it, I was near the hillside with the cave.

For a moment I thought of going down in the cave to do what I had to do. I decided against it. The explosion, in that confined space, might blow up the whole valley. I moved on. And suddenly I felt a tug at my mind.

It wasn't all around, like the feeling of depression was, something that seemed to be broadcast generally into the air. And it wasn't like the voice inside my head I'd heard in the cave. The best way I can express the feeling is by saying that it was like walking past a furnace with your eyes shut.

I hesitated. I was still feeling suicidal; I never wavered in that. But I felt a faint curiosity and something a lot fainter that you might call, if you exaggerated, the first beginnings of hope.

I went to the mouth of the cave and let myself down through the opening.

The egg, when I reached it, was different from the way I remembered it. It was bigger and the edges were misty. But the chief difference was that it was rotating around its long axis at a really fancy rate of speed. It reminded me of the rotation of a generator. The sensation I felt was coming out from it.

Watching the thing's luminous, mazy whirling, I got the idea that it and the things which had come out of it represented opposite poles. It was as alive as they were, though in an opposite way, and its motion provided the energy for them to operate.

I pulled the sticks of dynamite out of my belt and began setting them up. There really wasn't much danger of blowing up the valley, and as long as I was going to do away with myself, I might as well take the egg with me, or try to. That was the way I looked at it.

No attempt was made to stop me. This may have been because the things from the egg weren't interested in human beings, except spasmodically, but I think it more likely was because they, being polar opposites from the egg, had to keep their distance from it. Anyhow, I got my connections made without interference. I stood back a foot or two.

I closed the switch.

The next thing I knew, my head was on Mom's lap. She was shaking me desperately by the shoulders and crying something about fire.

Now, I don't see how I could have been responsible for the fire. The earthquake, possibly. Apparently when the dynamite exploded, the egg tried to absorb the energy. (That's why I wasn't hurt more.) It got an overload. And the overload, somehow, blew it clean out of our space. I got a glimpse of the space it was blown into, I think, just before my head hit the rock. But anyhow, a thing like that might possibly have caused an earthquake. All the country around Hidden Valley is over a fault.

Anyhow, there'd been earthquakes, several of them. Mom and Donnie had gone out hunting me as soon as the worst shocks were over, and found me lying at the mouth of the cave. They got me up somehow; I don't weigh much. Mom was nearly crazy with worry because I was still unconscious. For the last two hours or so she'd been smelling the smoke and hearing the crackling of the fire.

Some camper up in the mountains, I guess, started it. It was an awfully dry year. Anyhow, by the time I was conscious and on my feet again, it was too late to think about running. We didn't even have time to grab a suitcase. Mom and Donnie and I went down the flume.

That was some trip. When we got to Portsmouth, we found the whole town ready to pick up and leave, the fire was that close. They got it out in time, though. And then we found out that we were refugees.

There were pieces about the three of us in the city papers, with scare heads and everything. The photographers took pictures of all of us, even me, and they tried to make out we were heroes because we'd gone down the flume and hadn't got burned up in the fire. That was a lot of foolishness; there isn't anything heroic in saving your own life. And Mom hated those pictures. She said they made her look like she was in her seventies and heading for the grave.

One of the papers took up a collection for us, and we got a couple of hundred dollars out of it. It was a big help to us, because all we had in the world was the clothes we were standing in. After all, though, we hadn't really expected to be alive. And we'd got rid of the things from the egg.

As Mom says, we have a lot to be thankful for.

I could be more thankful, though, if I didn't have Ischeenar. I've tried and tried to figure out why he didn't die when the rest of the things did, when the egg was blown into another space. The only thing I can think of is that maybe, having been born here on Earth, he's different from the rest of them. Anyhow, he's here with us. I've managed to keep Mom from finding out, but, as I say, he lives in my big toe.

Sometimes I feel almost sorry for him. He's little and helpless, and alone in a big and hostile world. He's different from everything around him. Like us, he's a refugee.

But I wish I could get rid of him. He's not so bad now while he's young. He's really not dangerous. But I wish to *God* I could get rid of him.

He's going to be a stinker when he grows up.

5

When the Bough Breaks

LEWIS PADGETT

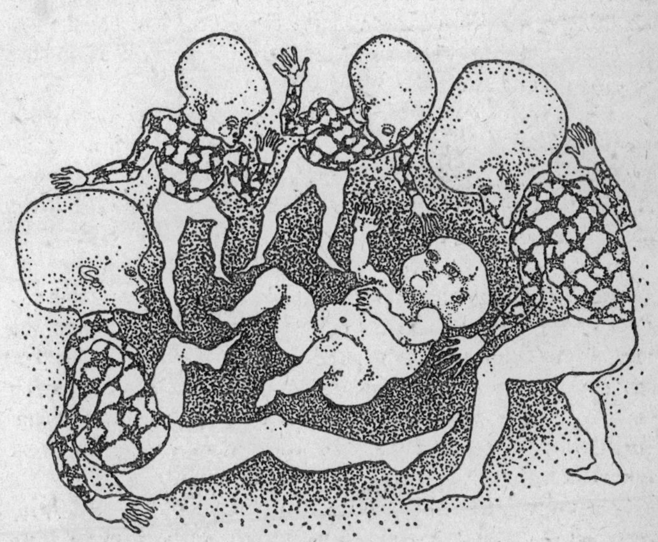

Lewis Padgett, whose real name was Henry Kuttner, died in February 1958. I was in Baltimore at the time getting ready to give a 9 A.M. *talk to some students at the University of Maryland Medical School. I was up quite early, therefore, and read the* New York Times *over scrambled eggs and coffee. I saw the notation—a little two-column box on the obituary page—and passed it by without a tremor.*

I discarded the paper, gave my talk, and then, after returning to the hotel, thought back on what I had read and went racing down to the lobby for a second New York Times. *I turned to the obituary page and it was horrifyingly true; it was* my *Henry Kuttner. I had never encountered such a situation before, so it had just never occurred to me a science fiction writer could make the* New York Times *obituary page. I had initially taken it for granted that it was another Henry Kuttner.*

Other science fiction writers have, alas, made the obituary page since, but it has never had quite the same impact upon me as that first time.

Henry was only forty-three, and who knows how many wonderful science fiction stories died with him. I had met him only once, about fifteen years before, during the war. There was a group of us, all of us loudmouths, all of us brassy, all of us demanding—writer-like—our share of the limelight. All of us but Henry. He sat in the background, quietly holding hands with his wife, Catherine L. Moore (herself a fantasy writer of note), needing only her to be happy.

Henry and Catherine often collaborated and it is hard to tell where one left off and the other began but, however that might be, let Lewis Padgett introduce yoü to the kind of terrifying infant that no one can dream up in quite so thoroughly and uncomfortably real a manner as a science fiction writer.

They were surprised at getting the apartment, what with high rents and written-in clauses in the lease, and Joe Calderon felt himself lucky to be only ten minutes' subway ride from the University. His wife, Myra, fluffed up her red hair in a distracted fashion and said that landlords presumably expected parthenogenesis in their tenants, if that was what she meant. Anyhow, it was where an organism split in two and the result was two mature specimens. Calderon grinned, said, "Binary fission, chump," and watched young Alexander, aged eighteen months, backing up on all fours across the carpet, preparatory to assuming a standing position on his fat bowlegs.

It was a pleasant apartment, at that. The sun came into it at times, and there were more rooms than they had any right to expect, for the price. The next-door neighbor, a billowy blonde who talked of little except her migraine, said that it was hard to keep tenants in 4-D. It wasn't exactly haunted, but it had the queerest visitors. The last lessee, an insurance man who drank heavily, moved out one day talking about little men who came ringing the bell at all hours asking for a Mr. Pott, or somebody like that. Not until some time later did Joe identify Pott with Caldron—or Calderon.

They were sitting on the couch in a pleased manner, looking at Alexander. He was quite a baby. Like all infants, he had a collar of fat at the back of his neck, and his legs, Calderon said, were like two vast and trunkless limbs of stone—at least they gave that effect. The eyes stopped at their incredible bulging pinkness, fascinated. Alexander laughed like a fool, rose to his feet, and staggered drunkenly toward his parents, muttering unintelligible gibberish. "Madman," Myra said fondly, and tossed the child a floppy velvet pig of whom he was enamored.

"So we're all set for the winter," Calderon said. He was a tall, thin, harassed-looking man, a fine research physicist, and very much interested in his work at the University. Myra was a rather fragile redhead, with a tilted nose and sardonic red-brown eyes. She made deprecatory noises.

"If we can get a maid. Otherwise I'll char."

"You sound like a lost soul," Calderon said. "What do you mean, you'll char?"

"Like a charwoman. Sweep, cook, clean. Babies are a great trial. Still, they're worth it."

"Not in front of Alexander. He'll get above himself."

The doorbell rang. Calderon uncoiled himself, wandered vaguely across the room, and opened the door. He blinked at nothing. Then he lowered his gaze somewhat, and what he saw was sufficient to make him stare a little.

Four tiny men were standing in the hall. That is, they were tiny below the brows. Their craniums were immense, watermelon large and watermelon shaped, or else they were wearing abnormally huge helmets of glistening metal. Their faces were wizened, peaked tiny masks that were nests of lines and wrinkles. Their clothes were garish, unpleasantly colored, and seemed to be made of paper.

"Oh?" Calderon said blankly.

Swift looks were exchanged among the four. One of them said, "Are you Joseph Calderon?"

"Yeah."

"We," said the most wrinkled of the quartet, "are your son's descendants. He's a superchild. We're here to educate him."

"Yes," Calderon said. "Yes, of course. I . . . *listen!*"

"To what?"

"Super—"

"There he is," another dwarf cried. "It's Alexander! We've hit the right time at last!" He scuttled past Calderon's legs and into the room. Calderon made a few futile snatches, but the small men easily evaded him. When he turned, they were gathered around Alexander. Myra had drawn up her legs under her and was watching with an amazed expression.

"Look at that," a dwarf said. "See his potential tefeetzie?" It sounded like tefeetzie.

"But his skull, Bordent," another put in. "That's the important part. The vyrings are almost perfectly coblastably."

"Beautiful," Bordent acknowledged. He leaned forward. Alexander reached forward into the nest of wrinkles, seized Bordent's nose, and twisted painfully. Bordent bore it stoically until the grip relaxed.

"Undeveloped," he said tolerantly. "We'll develop him."

Myra sprang from the couch, picked up her child, and stood at bay, facing the little men. "Joe," she said, "are you going to stand for this? Who are these bad-mannered goblins?"

"Lord knows," Calderon said. He moistened his lips. "What kind of a gag is that? Who sent you?"

"Alexander," Bordent said. "From the year . . . ah . . . about 2450, reckoning roughly. He's practically immortal. Only violence can kill one of the supers, and there's none of that in 2450."

Calderon sighed. "No, I mean it. A gag's a gag. But—"

"Time and again we've tried. In 1940, 1944, 1947—all around this era. We were either too early or too late. But now we've hit on the right time-sector. It's our job to educate Alexander. You should feel proud of being his parents. We worship you, you know. Father and mother of the new race."

"Tuh!" Calderon said. "Come off it!"

"They need proof, Dobish," someone said. "Remember, this is their first inkling that Alexander is homo superior."

"Homo nuts," Myra said. "Alexander's a perfectly normal baby."

"He's perfectly supernormal," Dobish said. "We're his descendants."

"That makes you a superman," Calderon said skeptically, eyeing the small man.

"Not in toto. There aren't many of the X Free type. The biological norm is specialization. Only a few are straight-line super. Some specialize in logic, others in vervainity, others—like us—are guides. If we were X Free supers, you couldn't stand there and talk to us. Or look at us. We're only parts. Those like Alexander are the glorious whole."

"Oh, send them away," Myra said, getting tired of it. "I feel like a Thurber woman."

Calderon nodded. "Okay. Blow, gentlemen. Take a powder. I mean it."

"Yes," Dobish said, "they need proof. What'll we do? Skyskinate?"

"Too twisty," Bordent objected. "Object lesson, eh? The stiller."

"Stiller?" Myra asked.

Bordent took an object from his paper clothes and spun it in his hands. His fingers were all double-jointed. Calderon felt a tiny electric shock go through him.

"Joe," Myra said, white-faced. "I can't move."

"Neither can I. Take it easy. This is . . . it's—" He slowed and stopped.

"Sit down," Bordent said, still twirling the object. Calderon and Myra backed up to the couch and sat down. Their tongues froze with the rest of them.

Dobish came over, clambered up, and pried Alexander out of his mother's grip. Horror moved in his eyes.

"We won't hurt him," Dobish said. "We just want to give him his first lesson. Have you got the basics, Finn?"

"In the bag." Finn extracted a foot-long bag from his garments. Things came out of that bag. They came out incredibly. Soon the carpet was littered with stuff—problematical in design, nature, and use. Calderon recognized a tesseract.

The fourth dwarf, whose name, it turned out, was Quat, smiled consolingly at the distressed parents. "You watch. You can't learn; you've not got the potential. You're homo saps. But Alexander, now—"

Alexander was in one of his moods. He was diabolically gay. With the devil-possession of all babies, he refused to collaborate. He crept rapidly backwards. He burst into loud, squalling sobs. He regarded his feet with amazed joy. He stuffed his fist into his mouth and cried bitterly at the result. He talked about invisible things in a soft, cryptic monotone. He punched Dobish in the eye.

The little men had inexhaustible patience. Two hours later they were through. Calderon couldn't see that Alexander had learned much.

Bordent twirled the object again. He nodded affably, and led the retreat. The four little men went out of the apartment, and a moment later Calderon and Myra could move.

She jumped up, staggering on numbed legs, seized Alexander, and collapsed on the couch. Calderon rushed to the door and flung it open. The hall was empty.

"Joe—" Myra said, her voice small and afraid. Calderon came back and smoothed her hair. He looked down at the bright fuzzy head of Alexander.

"Joe. We've got to do—do something."

"I don't know," he said. "If it happened—"

"It happened. They took those things with them. Alexander. Oh!"

"They didn't try to hurt him," Calderon said hesitatingly.

"Our *baby!* He's no superchild."

"Well," Calderon said, "I'll get out my revolver. What else can I do?"

"I'll do something," Myra promised. "Nasty little goblins! I'll do something, just wait."

And yet there wasn't a great deal they could do.

Tacitly they ignored the subject the next day. But at 4 P.M., the same time as the original visitation, they were with Alexander in a theater, watching the latest Technicolor film. The four little men could scarcely find them here—

Calderon felt Myra stiffen, and even as he turned, he suspected the worst. Myra sprang up, her breath catching. Her fingers tightened on his arm.

"He's gone!"

"G-gone?"

"He just vanished. I was holding him . . . Let's get out of here."

"Maybe you dropped him," Calderon said inanely, and lit a match. There were cries from behind. Myra was already pushing her way toward the aisle. There were no babies under the seat, and Calderon caught up with his wife in the lobby.

"He disappeared," Myra was babbling. "Like that. Maybe he's in the future. Joe, what'll we do?"

Calderon, through some miracle, got a taxi. "We'll go home. That's the most likely place. I hope."

"Yes. Of course it is. Give me a cigarette."

"He'll be in the apartment—"

He was, squatting on his haunches, taking a decided interest in the gadget Quat was demonstrating. The gadget was a gayly colored eggbeater with four-dimensional attachments, and it talked in a thin, high voice. Not in English.

Bordent flipped out the stiller and began to twirl it as the couple came in. Calderon got hold of Myra's arms and held her back. "Hold on," he said urgently. "That isn't necessary. We won't try anything."

"Joe!" Myra tried to wriggle free. "Are you going to let them—"

"Quiet!" he said. "Bordent, put that thing down. We want to talk to you."

"Well, if you promise not to interrupt . . ."

"We promise." Calderon forcibly led Myra to the couch and held her there. "Look, darling. Alexander's all right. They're not hurting him."

"Hurt him, indeed!" Finn said. "He'd skin us alive in the future if we hurt him in the past."

"Be quiet," Bordent commanded. He seemed to be the leader of the four. "I'm glad you're cooperating, Joseph Calderon. It goes against my grain to use force on a demigod. After all, you're *Alexander*'s father."

Alexander put out a fat paw and tried to touch the whirling

rainbow eggbeater. He seemed to be fascinated. Quat said, "The kivelish is sparking. Shall I vastinate?"

"Not too fast," Bordent said. "He'll be rational in a week, and then we can speed up the process. Now, Calderon, please relax. Anything you want?"

"A drink."

"They mean alcohol," Finn said. "The Rubáiyát mentions it, remember?"

"Rubáiyát?"

"The singing red gem in Twelve Library."

"Oh, yes," Bordent said. "That one. I was thinking of the Yahweh slab, the one with the thunder effects. Do you want to make some alcohol, Finn?"

Calderon swallowed. "Don't bother. I have some in that sideboard. May I—"

"You're not *prisoners*." Bordent's voice was shocked. "It's just that we've got to make you listen to a few explanations, and after that—well, it'll be different."

Myra shook her head when Calderon handed her a drink, but he scowled at her meaningly. "You won't feel it. Go ahead."

She hadn't once taken her gaze from Alexander. The baby was imitating the thin noise of the eggbeater now. It was subtly unpleasant.

"The ray is working," Quat said. "The viewer shows some slight cortical resistance, though."

"Angle the power," Bordent told him.

Alexander said, "Modjewabba?"

"What's that?" Myra asked in a strained voice. "Super language?"

Bordent smiled at her. "No, just baby talk."

Alexander burst into sobs. Myra said, "Superbaby or not, when he cries like that, there's a good reason. Does your tutoring extend to that point?"

"Certainly," Quat said calmly. He and Finn carried Alexander out. Bordent smiled again.

"You're beginning to believe," he said. "That helps."

Calderon drank, feeling the hot fumes of whiskey along the backs of his cheeks. His stomach was crawling with cold uneasiness.

"If you were human . . ." he said doubtfully.

"If we were, we wouldn't be here. The old order changeth. It had to start sometime. Alexander is the first homo superior."

"But why us?" Myra asked.

"Genetics. You've both worked with radioactivity and certain shortwave radiations that effected the germ plasm. The mutation just happened. It'll happen again from now on. But you happen to be the first. You'll die, but Alexander will live on. Perhaps a thousand years."

Calderon said, "This business of coming from the future . . . you say Alexander sent you?"

"The adult Alexander. The mature superman. It's a different culture, of course—beyond your comprehension. Alexander is one of the X Frees. He said to me, through the interpreting-machine, of course, 'Bordent, I wasn't recognized as a super till I was thirty years old. I had only ordinary homo sap development till then. I didn't know my potential myself. And that's bad.' It *is* bad, you know," Bordent digressed. "The full capabilities of an organism can't emerge unless it's given the fullest chance of expansion from birth on. Or at least from infancy. Alexander said to me, 'It's about five hundred years ago that I was born. Take a few guides and go into the past. Locate me as an infant. Give me specialized training, from the beginning. I think it'll expand me.'"

"The past," Calderon said. "You mean it's plastic?"

"Well, it affects the future. You can't alter the past without altering the future too. But things tend to drift back. There's a temporal norm, a general level. In the original time sector, Alexander wasn't visited by us. Now that's changed. So the future will be changed. But not tremendously. No crucial temporal apexes are involved, no keystones. The only result will be that the mature Alexander will have his potential more fully realized."

Alexander was carried back into the room, beaming. Quat resumed his lesson with the eggbeater.

"There isn't a great deal you can do about it," Bordent said. "I think you realize that now."

Myra said, "Is Alexander going to look like you?" Her face was strained.

"Oh, no. He's a perfect physical specimen. I've never seen him, of course, but—"

Calderon said, "Heir to all the ages. Myra, are you beginning to get the idea?"

"Yes. A superman. But he's our baby."

"He'll remain so," Bordent put in anxiously. "We don't want to remove him from the beneficial home and parental influence. An infant needs that. In fact, tolerance for the young is an evolutionary trait aimed at providing for the superman's appearance, just as the vanishing appendix is such a preparation. At certain eras of history mankind is receptive to the preparation of the new race. It's never been quite successful before—there were anthropological miscarriages, so to speak. My squeevers, it's *important!* Infants are awfully irritating. They're helpless for a very long time, a great trial to the patience of the parents—the lower the order of the animal, the faster the infant develops. With mankind it takes years for the young to reach an independent state. So the parental tolerance increases in proportion. The superchild won't mature, actually, till he's about twenty."

Myra said, "Alexander will still be a baby then?"

"He'll have the physical standards of an eight-year-old specimen of homo sap. Mentally . . . well, call it irrationality. He won't be leveled out to an intellectual or emotional norm. He won't be sane, any more than any baby is. Selectivity takes quite a while to develop. But his peaks will be far, far above the peaks of, say, *you* as a child."

"Thanks," Calderon said.

"His horizons will be broader. His mind is capable of grasping and assimilating far more than yours. The world is really his oyster. He won't be limited. But it'll take a while for his mind, his personality, to shake down."

"I want another drink," Myra said.

Calderon got it. Alexander inserted his thumb in Quat's eye and tried to gouge it out. Quat submitted passively.

"Alexander!" Myra said.

"Sit still," Bordent said. "Quat's tolerance in this regard is naturally higher developed than yours."

"If he puts Quat's eye out," Calderon said, "it'll be just too bad."

"Quat isn't important, compared to Alexander. He knows it, too."

Luckily for Quat's binocular vision, Alexander suddenly tired of his new toy and fell to staring at the eggbeater again. Dobish and Finn leaned over the baby and looked at him. But there was more to it than that, Calderon felt.

"Induced telepathy," Bordent said. "It takes a long time to develop, but we're starting now. I tell you, it was a relief to hit the right time at last. I've rung this doorbell at least a hundred times. But never till now—"

"Move," Alexander said clearly. "Real. Move."

Bordent nodded. "Enough for today. We'll be here again tomorrow. You'll be ready?"

"As ready," Myra said, "as we'll ever be, I suppose." She finished her drink.

They got fairly high that night and talked it over. Their arguments were biased by their realization of the four little men's obvious resources. Neither doubted any more. They knew that Bordent and his companions had come from five hundred years in the future, at the command of a future Alexander who had matured into a fine specimen of superman.

"Amazing, isn't it?" Myra said. "That fat little blob in the bedroom turning into a twelfth-power Quiz Kid."

"Well, it's got to start somewhere. As Bordent pointed out."

"And as long as he isn't going to look like those goblins—ugh!"

"He'll be super. Deucalion and what's-her-name—that's us. Parents of a new race."

"I feel funny," Myra said. "As though I'd given birth to a moose."

"That could never happen," Calderon said consolingly. "Have another slug."

"It might as well have happened. Alexander is a swoose."

"Swoose?"

"I can use that goblin's doubletalk too. Vopishly woggle in the grand foyer. So there."

"It's a language to them," Calderon said.

"Alexander's going to talk English. I've got my rights."

"Well, Bordent doesn't seem anxious to infringe on them. He said Alexander needed a home environment."

"That's the only reason I haven't gone crazy," Myra said. "As long as he . . . they . . . don't take our baby away from us . . ."

A week later it was thoroughly clear that Bordent had no intention of encroaching on parental rights—at least, any more than was necessary, for two hours a day. During that period the four little men fulfilled their orders by cramming Alexander with all the knowledge his infantile but super brain could hold. They did not depend on blocks or nursery rhymes or the abacus. Their weapons in the battle were cryptic, futuristic, but effective. And they taught Alexander, there was no doubt of that. As B-1 poured on a plant's roots forces growth, so the vitamin teaching of the dwarfs soaked into Alexander, and his potentially superhuman brain responded, expanding with brilliant, erratic speed.

He had talked intelligibly on the fourth day. On the seventh day he was easily able to hold conversations, though his baby muscles, lingually undeveloped, tired easily. His cheeks were still sucking-disks; he was not yet fully human, except in sporadic flashes. Yet those flashes came oftener now, and closer together.

The carpet was a mess. The little men no longer took their equipment back with them; they left it for Alexander to use. The infant crept—he no longer bothered to walk much, for he could crawl with more efficiency—among the Objects, selected some of them, and put them together. Myra had gone out to shop. The little men wouldn't show up for half an hour. Calderon, tired from his day's work at the University, fingered a highball and looked at his offspring.

"Alexander," he said.

Alexander didn't answer. He fitted a gadget to a Thing, inserted it peculiarly in a Something Else, and sat back with an air of satisfaction. Then—"Yes?" he said. It wasn't perfect pronunciation, but it was unmistakable. Alexander talked somewhat like a toothless old man.

"What are you doing?" Calderon said.

"No."

"What's that?"

"No."

"No?"

"I understand it," Alexander said. "That's enough."

"I see." Calderon regarded the prodigy with faint apprehension. "You don't want to tell me."

"No."

"Well, all right."

"Get me a drink," Alexander said. For a moment Calderon had the mad idea that the infant was demanding a highball. Then he sighed, rose, and returned with a bottle.

"Milk," Alexander said, refusing the potation.

"You said a drink. Water's a drink, isn't it?" My God, Calderon thought, I'm arguing with the kid. I'm treating him like . . . like an adult. But he isn't. He's a fat little baby squatting on his behind on the carpet, playing with a tinkertoy.

The tinkertoy said something in a thin voice. Alexander murmured, "Repeat." The tinkertoy did.

Calderon said, "What was that?"

"No."

"Nuts." Calderon went out to the kitchen and got milk. He poured himself another shot. This was like having relatives drop in suddenly, relatives you hadn't seen for ten years. How the devil did you *act* with a superchild?

He stayed in the kitchen, after supplying Alexander with his milk. Presently Myra's key turned in the outer door. Her cry brought Calderon hurrying.

Alexander was vomiting, with the air of a research man absorbed in a fascinating phenomenon.

"Alexander!" Myra cried. "Darling, are you sick?"

"No," Alexander said. "I'm testing my regurgitative processes. I must learn to control my digestive organs."

Calderon leaned against the door, grinning crookedly. "Yeah. You'd better start now, too."

"I'm finished," Alexander said. "Clean it up."

Three days later the infant decided that his lungs needed developing. He cried. He cried at all hours, with interesting variations—whoops, squalls, wails, and high-pitched bellows. Nor would he stop till he was satisfied. The neighbors complained. Myra said, "Darling, is there a pin sticking you? Let me look—"

"Go away," Alexander said. "You're too warm. Open the window. I want fresh air."

"Yes, d-darling. Of course." She came back to bed and Calderon put his arm around her. He knew there would be shadows under her eyes in the morning. In his crib Alexander cried on.

So it went. The four little men came daily and gave Alexander his lessons. They were pleased with the infant's progress. They did not complain when Alexander indulged in his idiosyncrasies, such as batting them heavily on the nose or ripping their paper garments to shreds. Bordent tapped his metal helmet and smiled triumphantly at Calderon.

"He's coming along. He's developing."

"I'm wondering. What about discipline?"

Alexander looked up from his rapport with Quat. "Homo sap discipline doesn't apply to me, Joseph Calderon."

"Don't call me Joseph Calderon. I'm your father, after all."

"A primitive biological necessity. You are not sufficiently well developed to provide the discipline I require. Your purpose is to give me parental care."

"Which makes me an incubator," Calderon said.

"But a deified one," Bordent soothed him. "Practically a logos. The father of the new race."

"I feel more like Prometheus," the father of the new race said dourly. "He was helpful, too. And he ended up with a vulture eating his liver."

"You will learn a great deal from Alexander."

"He says I'm incapable of understanding it."

"Well, aren't you?"

"Sure. I'm just the papa bird," Calderon said, and subsided into a sad silence, watching Alexander, under Quat's tutelary eye, put together a gadget of shimmering glass and twisted metal. Bordent said suddenly, "Quat! Be careful of the egg!" And Finn seized a bluish ovoid just before Alexander's chubby hand could grasp it.

"It isn't dangerous," Quat said. "It isn't connected."

"He might have connected it."

"I want that," Alexander said. "Give it to me."

"Not yet, Alexander," Bordent refused. "You must learn the correct way of connecting it first. Otherwise it might harm you."

"I could do it."

"You are not logical enough to balance your capabilities and lacks as yet. Later it will be safe. I think now, perhaps, a little philosophy, Dobish—eh?"

Dobish squatted and went en rapport with Alexander. Myra

came out of the kitchen, took a quick look at the tableau, and retreated. Calderon followed her out.

"I will never get used to it if I live a thousand years," she said with slow emphasis, hacking at the doughy rim of a pie. "He's my baby only when he's asleep."

"We won't live a thousand years," Calderon told her. "Alexander will, though. I wish we could get a maid."

"I tried again today," Myra said wearily. "No use. They're all in war plants. I mention a baby—"

"You can't do all this alone."

"You help," she said, "when you can. But you're working hard too, fella. It won't be forever."

"I wonder if we had another baby . . . if—"

Her sober gaze met his. "I've wondered that too. But I should think mutations aren't as cheap as that. Once in a lifetime. Still, we don't know."

"Well, it doesn't matter now, anyway. One infant's enough for the moment."

Myra glanced toward the door. "Everything all right in there? Take a look. I worry."

"It's all right."

"I know, but that blue egg—Bordent said it was dangerous, you know. I heard him."

Calderon peeped through the door crack. The four dwarfs were sitting facing Alexander, whose eyes were closed. Now they opened. The infant scowled at Calderon.

"Stay out," he requested. "You're breaking the rapport."

"I'm so sorry," Calderon said, retreating. "He's okay, Myra. His own dictatorial little self."

"Well, he *is* a superman," she said doubtfully.

"No. He's a superbaby. There's all the difference."

"His latest trick," Myra said, busy with the oven, "is riddles. Or something like riddles. I feel so small when he catches me up. But he says it's good for his ego. It compensates for his physical frailness."

"Riddles, eh? I know a few too."

"They won't work on Alexander," Myra said, with grim assurance.

Nor did they. "What goes up a chimney up?" was treated with the contempt it deserved; Alexander examined his father's riddles, turned them over in his logical mind, analyzed them for flaws in semantics and logic, and rejected them. Or else he answered them, with such fine accuracy that Calderon was too embarrassed to give the correct answers. He was reduced to asking why a raven was like a writing desk, and since not even the Mad Hatter had been able to answer his own riddle, was slightly terrified to find himself listening to a dissertation on comparative ornithology. After that, he let Alexander needle him with infantile gags about the relations of gamma rays to photons, and tried to be philosophical. There are few things as irritating as a child's riddles. His mocking triumph pulverizes itself into the dust in which you grovel.

"Oh, leave your father alone," Myra said, coming in with her hair disarranged. "He's trying to read the paper."

"That news is unimportant."

"I'm reading the comics," Calderon said. "I want to see if the Katzenjammers get even with the Captain for hanging them under a waterfall."

"The formula for the humor of an incongruity predicament," Alexander began learnedly, but Calderon disgustedly went into the bedroom, where Myra joined him. "He's asking me riddles again," she said. "Let's see what the Katzenjammers did."

"You look rather miserable. Got a cold?"

"I'm not wearing makeup. Alexander says the smell makes him ill."

"So what? He's no petunia."

"Well," Myra said, "he does get ill. But of course he does it on purpose."

"Listen. There he goes again. What now?"

But Alexander merely wanted an audience. He had found a new way of making imbecilic noises with his fingers and lips. At times the child's normal phases were more trying than his super periods. After a month had passed, however, Calderon felt that the worst was yet to come. Alexander had progressed into fields of knowledge hitherto untouched by homo sap, and he had developed a leechlike habit of sucking his father's brains dry of every scrap of knowledge the wretched man possessed.

It was the same with Myra. The world was indeed Alexander's oyster. He had an insatiable curiosity about everything, and there was no longer any privacy in the apartment. Calderon took to locking the bedroom door against his son at night—Alexander's crib was now in another room—but furious squalls might waken him at any hour.

In the midst of preparing dinner, Myra would be forced to stop and explain the caloric mysteries of the oven to Alexander. He learned all she knew, took a jump into more abstruse aspects of the matter, and sneered at her ignorance. He found out Calderon was a physicist, a fact which the man had hitherto kept carefully concealed, and thereafter pumped his father dry. He asked questions about geodetics and geopolitics. He inquired about monotremes and monorails. He was curious about biremes and biology. And he was skeptical, doubting the depth of his father's knowledge. "But," he said, "you and Myra Calderon are my closest contacts with homo sap as yet, and it's a beginning. Put out that cigarette. It isn't good for my lungs."

"All right," Calderon said. He rose wearily, with his usual feeling these days of being driven from room to room of the apartment, and went in search of Myra. "Bordent's about due. We can go out somewhere. Okay?"

"Swell." She was at the mirror, fixing her hair, in a trice. "I need a permanent. If I only had the time!"

"I'll take off tomorrow and stay here. You need a rest."

"Darling, no. The exams are coming up. You simply can't do it."

Alexander yelled. It developed that he wanted his mother to sing for him. He was curious about the tonal range of homo sap and the probable emotional and soporific effect of lullabies. Calderon mixed himself a drink, sat in the kitchen and smoked, and thought about the glorious destiny of his son. When Myra stopped singing, he listened for Alexander's wails, but there was no sound till a slightly hysterical Myra burst in on him, dithering and wide-eyed.

"Joe!" She fell into Calderon's arms. "Quick, give me a drink or . . . or hold me tight or something."

"What is it?" He thrust the bottle into her hands, went to the door, and looked out. "Alexander? He's quiet. Eating candy."

Myra didn't bother with a glass. The bottle's neck clicked against her teeth. "Look at me. Just look at me. I'm a mess."

"What happened?"

"Oh, nothing. Nothing at all. Alexander's turned into a black magician, that's all." She dropped into a chair and passed a palm across her forehead. "Do you know what that genius son of ours just did?"

"Bit you," Calderon hazarded, not doubting it for a minute.

"Worse, far worse. He started asking me for candy. I said there wasn't any in the house. He told me to go down to the grocery for some. I said I'd have to get dressed first, and I was too tired."

"Why didn't you ask me to go?"

"I didn't have the chance. Before I could say boo that infantile Merlin waved a magic wand or something. I . . . I was down at the grocery. Behind the candy counter."

Calderon blinked. "Induced amnesia?"

"There wasn't any time-lapse. It was just *phweet*—and there I was. In this rag of a dress, without a speck of makeup on, and my hair coming down in tassels. Mrs. Busherman was there too, buying a chicken—that cat across the hall. She was kind enough to tell me I ought to take more care of myself. Meow," Myra ended furiously.

"Good Lord."

"Teleportation. That's what Alexander says it is. Something new he's picked up. I'm not going to stand for it, Joe. I'm not a rag doll, after all." She was half hysterical.

Calderon went into the next room and stood regarding his child. There was chocolate smeared around Alexander's mouth.

"Listen, wise guy," he said. "You leave your mother alone, hear me?"

"I didn't hurt her," the prodigy pointed out, in a blobby voice. "I was simply being efficient."

"Well, don't be so efficient. Where did you learn that trick, anyhow?"

"Teleportation? Quat showed me last night. He can't do it himself, but I'm X Free super, so I can. The power isn't disciplined yet. If I'd tried to teleport Myra Calderon over to Jersey, say, I might have dropped her in the Hudson by mistake."

Calderon muttered something uncomplimentary. Alexander said, "Is that an Anglo-Saxon derivative?"

"Never mind about that. You shouldn't have all that chocolate, anyway. You'll make yourself sick. You've already made your mother sick. And you nauseate me."

"Go away," Alexander said. "I want to concentrate on the taste."

"No. I said you'd make yourself sick. Chocolate's too rich for you. Give it here. You've had enough." Calderon reached for the paper sack. Alexander disappeared. In the kitchen Myra shrieked.

Calderon moaned despondently, and turned. As he had expected, Alexander was in the kitchen, on top of the stove, hoggishly stuffing candy into his mouth. Myra was concentrating on the bottle.

"What a household," Calderon said. "The baby teleporting himself all over the apartment, you getting stewed in the kitchen, and me heading for a nervous breakdown." He started to laugh. "Okay, Alexander. You can keep the candy. I know when to shorten my defensive lines strategically."

"Myra Calderon," Alexander said, "I want to go back into the other room."

"Fly in," Calderon suggested. "Here, I'll carry you."

"Not you. Her. She has a better rhythm when she walks."

"Staggers, you mean," Myra said, but she obediently put aside the bottle, got up, and laid hold of Alexander. She went out. Calderon was not much surprised to hear her scream a moment later. When he joined the happy family, Myra was sitting on the floor, rubbing her arms and biting her lips. Alexander was laughing.

"What now?"

"H-he sh-shocked me," Myra said in a child's voice. "He's like an electric eel. He d-did it on purpose, too. Oh, Alexander, will you *stop* laughing!"

"You fell down," the infant crowed in triumph. "You yelled and fell down."

Calderon looked at Myra, and his mouth tightened. "Did you do that on purpose?" he asked.

"Yes. She fell down. She looked funny."

"You're going to look a lot funnier in a minute. X Free super or not, what you need is a good paddling."

"Joe—" Myra said.

"Never mind. He's got to learn to be considerate of the rights of others."

"I'm homo superior," Alexander said, with the air of one clinching an argument.

"It's homo posterior I'm going to deal with," Calderon announced, and attempted to capture his son. There was a stinging blaze of jolting nervous energy that blasted up through his synapses; he went backwards ignominiously, and slammed into the wall, cracking his head hard against it. Alexander laughed like an idiot.

"You fell down too," he crowed. "You look funny."

"Joe," Myra said. "Joe. Are you hurt?"

Calderon said sourly that he supposed he'd survive. Though, he added, it would probably be wise to lay in a few splints and a supply of blood plasma. "In case he gets interested in vivisection."

Myra regarded Alexander with troubled speculation. "You're kidding, I hope."

"I hope so too."

"Well—here's Bordent. Let's talk to him."

Calderon answered the door. The four little men came in solemnly. They wasted no time. They gathered about Alexander, unfolded fresh apparatus from the recesses of their paper clothes, and set to work. The infant said, "I teleported *her* about eight thousand feet."

"That far, eh?" Quat said. "Were you fatigued at all?"

"Not a bit."

Calderon dragged Bordent aside. "I want to talk to you. I think Alexander needs a spanking."

"By voraster!" the dwarf said, shocked. "But he's *Alexander!* He's X Free type super!"

"Not yet. He's still a baby."

"But a superbaby. No, no, Joseph Calderon. I must tell you again that disciplinary measures can be applied only by sufficiently intelligent authorities."

"You?"

"Oh, not yet," Bordent said. "We don't want to overwork him. There's a limit even to super brainpower, especially in the very formative period. He's got enough to do, and his attitudes for social contacts won't need forming for a while yet."

Myra joined them. "I don't agree with you there. Like all babies, he's antisocial. He may have superhuman powers but he's subhuman as far as mental and emotional balance go."

"Yeah," Calderon agreed. "This business of giving us electric shocks—"

"He's only playing," Bordent said.

"And teleportation. Suppose he teleports me to Times Square when I'm taking a shower?"

"It's only his play. He's a baby still."

"But what about us?"

"You have the hereditary characteristic of parental tolerance," Bordent explained. "As I told you before, Alexander and his race are the reason why tolerance was created in the first place. There's no great need for it with homo sap. I mean there's a wide space between normal tolerance and normal provocation. An ordinary baby may try his parents severely for a few moments at a time, but that's about all. The provocation is far too small to require the tremendous store of tolerance the parents have. But with the X Free type, it's a different matter."

"There's a limit even to tolerance," Calderon said. "I'm wondering about a crèche."

Bordent shook his shiny metallic-sheathed head. "He needs you."

"But," Myra said, "but can't you give him just a little discipline?"

"Oh, it isn't necessary. His mind's still immature, and he must concentrate on more important things. You'll tolerate him."

"It's not as though he's our baby any more," she murmured. "He's not Alexander."

"But he is. That's just it. *He's Alexander!*"

"Look, it's normal for a mother to want to hug her baby. But how can she do that if she expects him to throw her halfway across the room?"

Calderon was brooding. "Will he pick up more . . . more super powers as he goes along?"

"Why, yes. Naturally."

"He's a menace to life and limb. I still say he needs discipline. Next time I'll wear rubber gloves."

"That won't help," Bordent said, frowning. "Besides, I must insist . . . no, Joseph Calderon, it won't do. You mustn't interfere. You're not capable of giving him the right sort of discipline—which he doesn't need yet anyway."

"Just one spanking," Calderon said wistfully. "Not for revenge. Only to show him he's got to consider the rights of others."

"He'll learn to consider the rights of other X Free supers. You must not attempt anything of the sort. A spanking—even if you succeeded, which is far from probable—might warp him psychologically. We are his tutors, his mentors. We must *protect* him. You understand?"

"I think so," Calderon said slowly. "That's a threat."

"You are Alexander's parents, but it's Alexander who is important. If I must apply disciplinary measures to you, I must."

"Oh, forget it," Myra sighed. "Joe, let's go out and walk in the park while Bordent's here."

"Be back in two hours," the little man said. "Good-bye."

As time went past, Calderon could not decide whether Alexander's moronic phases or his periods of keen intelligence were more irritating. The prodigy had learned new powers; the worst of that was that Calderon never knew what to expect, or when some astounding gag would be sprung on him. Such as the time when a mess of sticky taffy had materialized in his bed, filched from the grocery by deft teleportation. Alexander thought it was very funny. He laughed.

And, when Calderon refused to go to the store to buy candy because he said he had no money—"Now don't try to teleport me. I'm broke."—Alexander had utilized mental energy, warping gravity lines shockingly. Calderon found himself hanging upside-down in mid-air, being shaken, while loose coins cascaded out of his pocket. He went after the candy.

Humor is a developed sense, stemming basically from cruelty. The more primitive a mind, the less selectivity exists. A cannibal would probably be profoundly amused by the squirmings of his victim in the seething kettle. A man slips on a banana peel and breaks his back. The adult stops laughing at that point, the child does not. And a civilized ego finds embarrassment as acutely distressing as physical pain. A baby, a child, a moron, is incapable of practicing empathy. He cannot identify himself with another individual. He is regrettably autistic; his own rules are arbitrary, and garbage strewn around the bedroom was funny to neither Myra nor Calderon.

There was a little stranger in the house. Nobody rejoiced. Except Alexander. He had a lot of fun.

"No privacy," Calderon said. "He materializes everywhere, at all hours. Darling, I wish you'd see a doctor."

"What would he advise?" Myra asked. "Rest, that's all. Do you realize it's been two months since Bordent took over?"

"And we've made marvelous progress," Bordent said, coming over to them. Quat was en rapport with Alexander on the carpet, while the other two dwarfs prepared the makings of a new gadget. "Or, rather, Alexander has made remarkable progress."

"We need a rest," Calderon growled. "If I lose my job, who'll support that genius of yours?" Myra looked at her husband quickly, noting the possessive pronoun he had used.

Bordent was concerned. "You are in difficulty?"

"The Dean's spoken to me once or twice. I can't control my classes any more. I'm too irritable."

"You don't need to expend tolerance on your students. As for money, we can keep you supplied. I'll arrange to get some negotiable currency for you."

"But I want to work. I like my job."

"Alexander is your job."

"I need a maid," Myra said, looking hopeless. "Can't you make me a robot or something? Alexander scares every maid I've managed to hire. They won't stay a day in this madhouse."

"A mechanical intelligence would have a bad effect on Alexander," Bordent said. "No."

"I wish we could have guests in once in a while. Or go out visiting. Or just be alone," Myra sighed.

"Some day Alexander will be mature, and you'll reap your reward. The parents of Alexander. Did I ever tell you that we have images of you two in the Great Fogy Hall?"

"They must look terrible," Calderon said. "I know we do now."

"Be patient. Consider the destiny of your son."

"I do. Often. But he gets a little wearing sometimes. That's quite an understatement."

"Which is where tolerance comes in," Bordent said. "Nature planned well for the new race."

"Mm-m-m."

"He is working on sixth-dimensional abstractions now. Everything is progressing beautifully."

"Yeah," Calderon said. And he went away, muttering, to join Myra in the kitchen.

Alexander worked with facility at his gadgets, his pudgy fingers already stronger and surer. He still had an illicit passion for the blue ovoid, but under Bordent's watchful eye he could use it only along the restricted lines laid out by his mentors. When the lesson was finished, Quat selected a few of the objects and locked them in a cupboard, as was his custom. The rest he left on the carpet to provide exercise for Alexander's ingenuity.

"He develops," Bordent said. "Today we've made a great step."

Myra and Calderon came in in time to hear this. "What goes?" he asked.

"A psychic bloc removal. Alexander will no longer need to sleep."

"What?" Myra said.

"He won't require sleep. It's an artificial habit anyway. The super race has no need of it."

"He won't sleep any more, eh?" Calderon said. He had grown a little pale.

"Correct. He'll develop faster now, twice as fast."

At 3:30 A.M. Calderon and Myra lay in bed, wide awake, looking through the open door into the full blaze of light where Alexander played. Seen there clearly, as if upon a lighted stage, he did not look quite like himself any more. The difference was subtle, but it was there. Under the golden down his head had changed shape slightly, and there was a look of intelligence and purpose upon the blobby features. It was not an attractive look. It didn't belong there. It made Alexander look less like a superbaby than a debased oldster. All a child's normal cruelty and selfishness—perfectly healthy, natural traits in the developing infant—flickered across Alexander's face as he played absorbedly with solid crystal blocks which he was fitting into one another like a Chinese puzzle. It was quite a shocking face to watch.

Calderon heard Myra sigh beside him.

"He isn't our Alexander any more," she said. "Not a bit."

Alexander glanced up and his face suddenly suffused. The look of paradoxical age and degeneracy upon it vanished as he opened his mouth and bawled with rage, tossing the blocks in all directions. Calderon watched one roll through the bedroom door and come to rest upon the carpet, spilling out of its solidity a cascade of smaller and smaller solid blocks that tumbled winking toward him. Alexander's cries filled the apartment. After a moment windows began to slam across the court, and presently the phone rang. Calderon reached for it, sighing.

When he hung up he looked across at Myra and grimaced. Above the steady roars he said, "Well, we have notice to move."

Myra said, "Oh. Oh, well."

"That about covers it."

They were silent for a moment. Then Calderon said, "Nineteen years more of it. I think we can expect about that. They did say he'd mature at twenty, didn't they?"

"He'll be an orphan long before then," Myra groaned. "Oh, my head! I think I caught cold when he teleported us up to the roof just before dinner. Joe, do you suppose we're the first parents who ever got . . . got caught like this?"

"What do you mean?"

"I mean, was there ever another superbaby before Alexander? It does seem like a waste of a lot of tolerance if we're the first to need it."

"We could use a lot more. We'll need a lot." He said nothing more for a while, but he lay there thinking and trying not to hear his superchild's rhythmic howling. Tolerance. Every parent needed a great deal of it. Every child was intolerable from time to time. The race had certainly needed parental love in vast quantities to permit its infants to survive. But no parents before had ever been tried consistently up to the very last degree of tolerance. No parents before had ever had to face twenty years of it, day and night, strained to the final notch. Parental love is a great and all-encompassing emotion, but . . .

"I wonder," he said thoughtfully. "I wonder if we *are* the first."

Myra's speculations had been veering. "I suppose it's like tonsils and appendix," she murmured. "They've outlived their use, but they still hang on. This tolerance is vestigial in reverse. It's been hanging on all these millenniums, waiting for Alexander."

"Maybe. I wonder . . . Still, if there ever had been an Alexander before now, we'd have heard of him. So . . ."

Myra rose on one elbow and looked at her husband. "You think so?" she said softly. "I'm not so sure. I think it might have happened before."

Alexander suddenly quieted. The apartment rang with silence for a moment. Then a familiar voice, without words, spoke in both their brains simultaneously.

"Get me some more milk. And I want it just warm, not hot."

Joe and Myra looked at one another again, speechless. Myra sighed and pushed the covers back. "I'll go this time," she said. "Something new, eh? I—"

"Don't dawdle," said the wordless voice, and Myra jumped and gave a little shriek. Electricity crackled audibly through the room, and Alexander's bawling laughter was heard through the doorway.

"He's about as civilized now as a well-trained monkey, I suppose," Joe remarked, getting out of bed. "I'll go. You crawl back in. And in another year he may reach the elevation of a bushman. After that, if we're still alive, we'll have the pleasure of living with a superpowered cannibal. Eventually he may work up to the level of practical joker. That ought to be interesting." He went out, muttering to himself.

Ten minutes later, returning to bed, Joe found Myra clasping her knees and looking into space.

"We aren't the first, Joe," she said, not glancing at him. "I've been thinking. I'm pretty sure we aren't."

"But we've never heard of any supermen developing . . ."

She turned her head and gave him a long, thoughtful look. "No," she said.

They were silent. Then he nodded "Yes, I see what you mean."

Something crashed in the living room. Alexander chuckled and the sound of splintering wood was loud in the silence of the night. Another window banged somewhere outside.

"There's a breaking point," Myra said quietly. "There's got to be."

"Saturation," Joe murmured. "Tolerance saturation—or something. It could have happened."

Alexander trundled into sight, clutching something blue. He sat down and began to fiddle with bright wires. Myra rose suddenly.

"Joe, he's got that blue egg! He must have broken into the cupboard."

Calderon said, "But Quat told him—"

"It's dangerous!"

Alexander looked at them, grinned, and bent the wires into a cradle shape the size of the egg.

Calderon found himself out of bed and halfway to the door. He stopped before he reached it. "You know," he said slowly, "he might hurt himself with that thing."

"We'll have to get it away from him," Myra agreed, heaving herself up with tired reluctance.

"Look at him," Calderon urged. "Just look."

Alexander was dealing competently with the wires, his hands flickering into sight and out again as he balanced a tesseract beneath the cradle. That curious veil of knowledge gave his chubby face the debased look of senility which they had come to know so well.

"This will go on and on, you know," Calderon murmured. "Tomorrow he'll look a little less like himself than today. Next week—next month—what will he be like in a year?"

"I know," Myra's voice was an echo. "Still, I suppose we'll have to . . ." Her voice trailed to a halt. She stood barefoot beside her husband, watching.

"I suppose the gadget will be finished," she said, "once he connects up that last wire. We ought to take it away from him."

"Think we could?"

"We ought to try."

They looked at each other. Calderon said, "It looks like an Easter egg. I never heard of an Easter egg hurting anybody."

"I suppose we're doing him a favor, really," Myra said in a low voice. "A burnt child dreads the fire. Once a kid burns himself on a match, he stays away from matches."

They stood in silence, watching.

It took Alexander about three more minutes to succeed in his design, whatever it was. The results were phenomenally effective. There was a flash of white light, a crackle of split air, and Alexander vanished in the dazzle, leaving only a faint burnt smell behind him.

When the two could see again, they blinked distrustfully at the empty place. "Teleportation?" Myra whispered dazedly.

"I'll make sure." Calderon crossed the floor and stood looking down at a damp spot on the carpet, with Alexander's shoes in it. He said, "No. Not teleportation." Then he took a long breath. "He's gone, all right. So he never grew up and sent Bordent back in time to move in on us. It never happened."

"We weren't the first," Myra said in an unsteady, bemused voice. "There's a breaking point, that's all. How sorry I feel for the first parents who don't reach it!"

She turned away suddenly, but not so suddenly that he could not see she was crying. He hesitated, watching the door. He thought he had better not follow her just yet.

6

A Pail of Air

FRITZ LEIBER

Those of us in the Northeast aren't going to forget the gigantic power failure of November 9, 1965.

The lights in my house went out just as dinner was about to be served. We calmly lit a number of candles and ate. The children didn't mind since anything novel was rather exciting and they relied in full security on their parents' protection. My wife having managed to finish the cooking before the blackout and feeling rich in candles, wasn't worried either.

Only I grew uneasy. After all, I have an electric typewriter and the thought that I was in no position to write—in case the mood came upon me, as it does almost constantly—set my fingers to twitching helplessly. (My son, in a gesture of touching loyalty, offered me his non-electric typewriter and a candle, but that would scarcely do.)

So I called Boston Edison and the line was busy. My next step was to go down to the garage and turn on one of the car radios. (We had no transistor radios that night; we now have three.) The first thing I heard was the astonishing phrase, "blackout all over New England and New York."

I raced upstairs, put out all the candles but one, placed the flashlights out of reach, and sternly announced that I was instituting strict rationing. I have been immersed in science fiction catastrophes for too many years to take such matters lightly.

Of course, the current went on a few hours later and my family has never forgiven me for making a military emergency out of what might have been a lark.

But here is one of the stories that influenced me on that occasion. Let the tall and handsome Fritz Leiber (son of the Shakespearean actor, and looking it every inch) describe a youngster facing the results of an almost ultimate catastrophe and doing so with a resilience that fills one with hope for the human race.

Pa had sent me out to get an extra pail of air. I'd just about scooped it full and most of the warmth had leaked from my fingers when I saw the thing.

You know, at first I thought it was a young lady. Yes, a beautiful young lady's face all glowing in the dark and looking at me from the fifth floor of the opposite apartment, which hereabouts is the floor just above the white blanket of frozen air. I'd never seen a live young lady before, except in the old magazines—Sis is just a kid and Ma is pretty sick and miserable—and it gave me such a start that I dropped the pail. Who wouldn't, knowing everyone on Earth was dead except Pa and Ma and Sis and you?

Even at that, I don't suppose I should have been surprised. We all see things now and then. Ma has some pretty bad ones, to judge from the way she bugs her eyes at nothing and just screams and screams and huddles back against the blankets hanging around the Nest. Pa says it is natural we should react like that sometimes.

When I'd recovered the pail and could look again at the opposite apartment, I got an idea of what Ma might be feeling at those times, for I saw it wasn't a young lady at all but simply a light—a tiny light that moved stealthily from window to window, just as if one of the cruel little stars had come down out of the airless sky to investigate why the Earth had gone away from the Sun, and maybe to hunt down something to torment or terrify, now that the Earth didn't have the Sun's protection.

I tell you, the thought of it gave me the creeps. I just stood there shaking, and almost froze my feet and did frost my helmet so solid on the inside that I couldn't have seen the light even if it had come out of one of the windows to get me. Then I had the wit to go back inside.

Pretty soon I was feeling my familiar way through the thirty or so blankets and rugs Pa has got hung around to slow down the escape of air from the Nest, and I wasn't quite so scared. I began to hear the tick-ticking of the clocks in the Nest and knew I was getting back into air, because there's no sound outside in the vacuum, of course. But my mind was still crawly and uneasy as I pushed through the last blankets—Pa's got them faced with aluminum foil to hold in the heat—and came into the Nest.

Let me tell you about the Nest. It's low and snug, just room for the four of us and our things. The floor is covered with thick woolly rugs. Three of the sides are blankets, and the blankets roofing it touch Pa's head. He tells me it's inside a much bigger room, but I've never seen the real walls or ceiling.

Against one of the blanket-walls is a big set of shelves, with tools and books and other stuff, and on top of it a whole row of clocks. Pa's very fussy about keeping them wound. He says we must never forget time, and without a sun or moon, that would be easy to do.

The fourth wall has blankets all over except around the fireplace, in which there is a fire that must never go out. It keeps us from freezing and does a lot more besides. One of us must always watch it. Some of the clocks are alarm and we can use them to remind us. In the early days there was only Ma to take turns with Pa—I think of that when she gets difficult—but now there's me to help, and Sis too.

It's Pa who is the chief guardian of the fire, though. I always think of him that way: a tall man sitting cross-legged, frowning anxiously at the fire, his lined face golden in its light, and every so often carefully placing on it a piece of coal from the big heap beside it. Pa tells me there used to be guardians of the fire sometimes in the very old days—vestal virgins, he calls them—although there was unfrozen air all around then and you didn't really need them.

He was sitting just that way now, though he got up quick to take the pail from me and bawl me out for loitering—he'd spotted my frozen helmet right off. That roused Ma and she joined in picking on me. She's always trying to get the load off her feelings, Pa explains. He shut her up pretty fast. Sis let off a couple of silly squeals too.

Pa handled the pail of air in a twist of cloth. Now that it was inside the Nest, you could really feel its coldness. It just seemed to suck the heat out of everything. Even the flames cringed away from it as Pa put it down close by the fire.

Yet it's that glimmery white stuff in the pail that keeps us alive. It slowly melts and vanishes and refreshes the Nest and feeds the fire. The blankets keep it from escaping too fast. Pa'd like to seal the whole place, but he can't—building's too earthquake-twisted, and besides he has to leave the chimney open for smoke.

Pa says air is tiny molecules that fly away like a flash if there isn't something to stop them. We have to watch sharp not to let the air run low. Pa always keeps a big reserve supply of it in buckets behind the first blankets, along with extra coal and cans of food and other things, such as pails of snow to melt for water. We have to go way down to the bottom floor for that stuff, which is a mean trip, and get it through a door to outside.

You see, when the Earth got cold, all the water in the air froze first and made a blanket ten feet thick or so everywhere, and then down on top of that dropped the crystals of frozen air, making another white blanket sixty or seventy feet thick maybe.

Of course, all the parts of the air didn't freeze and snow down at the same time.

First to drop out was the carbon dioxide—when you're shoveling for water, you have to make sure you don't go too high and get any of that stuff mixed in, for it would put you to sleep, maybe for good, and make the fire go out. Next there's the nitrogen, which doesn't count one way or the other, though it's the biggest part of the blanket. On top of that and easy to get at, which is lucky for us, there's the oxygen that keeps us alive. Pa says we live better than kings ever did, breathing pure oxygen, but we're used to it and don't notice. Finally, at the very top, there's a slick of liquid helium, which is funny stuff. All of these gases in neat separate layers. Like a pussy caffay, Pa laughingly says, whatever that is.

I was busting to tell them all about what I'd seen, and so as soon as I'd ducked out of my helmet and while I was still climbing out of my suit, I cut loose. Right away Ma got nervous and began making eyes at the entry-slit in the blankets and wringing her hands together—the hand where she'd lost three fingers from frostbite inside the good one, as usual. I could tell that Pa was annoyed at me scaring her and wanted to explain it all away quickly, yet could see I wasn't fooling.

"And you watched this light for some time, son?" he asked when I finished.

I hadn't said anything about first thinking it was a young lady's face. Somehow that part embarrassed me.

"Long enough for it to pass five windows and go to the next floor."

"And it didn't look like stray electricity or crawling liquid or starlight focussed by a growing crystal, or anything like that?"

He wasn't just making up those ideas. Odd things happen in a world that's about as cold as can be, and just when you think matter would be frozen dead, it takes on a strange new life. A slimy stuff comes crawling toward the Nest, just like an animal snuffing for heat—that's the liquid helium. And once, when I was little, a bolt of lightning—not even Pa could figure where it came from—hit the nearby steeple and crawled up and down it for weeks, until the glow finally died.

"Not like anything I ever saw," I told him.

He stood for a moment frowning. Then, "I'll go out with you, and you show it to me," he said.

Ma raised a howl at the idea of being left alone, and Sis joined in too, but Pa quieted them. We started climbing into our outside clothes—mine had been warming by the fire. Pa made them. They have plastic headpieces that were once big double-duty transparent food cans, but they keep heat and air in and can replace the air for a little while, long enough for our trips for water and coal and food and so on.

Ma started moaning again, "I've always known there was something outside there, waiting to get us. I've felt it for years —something that's part of the cold and hates all warmth and wants to destroy the Nest. It's been watching us all this time, and now it's coming after us. It'll get you and then come for me. Don't go, Harry!"

Pa had everything on but his helmet. He knelt by the fireplace and reached in and shook the long metal rod that goes up the chimney and knocks off the ice that keeps trying to clog it. Once a week he goes up on the roof to check if it's working all right. That's our worst trip and Pa won't let me make it alone.

"Sis," Pa said quietly, "come watch the fire. Keep an eye on the air, too. If it gets low or doesn't seem to be boiling fast enough, fetch another bucket from behind the blanket. But mind your hands. Use the cloth to pick up the bucket."

Sis quit helping Ma be frightened and came over and did as she was told. Ma quieted down pretty suddenly, though her eyes were still kind of wild as she watched Pa fix on his helmet tight and pick up a pail and the two of us go out.

Pa led the way and I took hold of his belt. It's a funny thing, I'm not afraid to go by myself, but when Pa's along I always want to hold on to him. Habit, I guess, and then there's no denying that this time I was a bit scared.

You see, it's this way. We know that everything is dead out there. Pa heard the last radio voices fade away years ago, and had seen some of the last folks die who weren't as lucky or well protected as us. So we knew that if there was something groping around out there, it couldn't be anything human or friendly.

Besides that, there's a feeling that comes with it always being night, *cold* night. Pa says there used to be some of that feeling even in the old days, but then every morning the Sun would come and chase it away. I have to take his word for that, not ever remembering the Sun as being anything more than a big star. You see, I hadn't been born when the dark star snatched us away from the Sun, and by now it's dragged us out beyond the orbit of the planet Pluto, Pa says, and taking us farther out all the time.

I found myself wondering whether there mightn't be something on the dark star that wanted us, and if that was why it had captured the Earth. Just then we came to the end of the corridor and I followed Pa out on the balcony.

I don't know what the city looked like in the old days, but now it's beautiful. The starlight lets you see it pretty well—there's quite a bit of light in those steady points speckling the blackness above. (Pa says the stars used to twinkle once, but that was because there was air.) We are on a hill and the shimmery plain drops away from us and then flattens out, cut up into neat squares by the troughs that used to be streets. I sometimes make my mashed potatoes look like it, before I pour on the gravy.

Some taller buildings push up out of the feathery plain, topped by rounded caps of air crystals, like the fur hood Ma wears, only whiter. On those buildings you can see the darker squares of windows, underlined by white dashes of air crystals. Some of them are on a slant, for many of the buildings are pretty badly twisted by the quakes and all the rest that happened when the dark star captured the Earth.

Here and there a few icicles hang, water icicles from the first days of the cold, other icicles of frozen air that melted on the roofs and dripped and froze again. Sometimes one of those icicles will catch the light of a star and send it to you so brightly you think the star has swooped into the city. That was one of the things Pa had been thinking of when I told him about the light, but I had thought of it myself first and known it wasn't so.

He touched his helmet to mine so we could talk easier and he asked me to point out the windows to him. But there wasn't any light moving around inside them now, or anywhere else. To my surprise, Pa didn't bawl me out and tell me I'd been seeing things. He looked all around quite a while after filling his pail, and just as we were going inside he whipped around without warning, as if to take some peeping thing off guard.

I could feel it too. The old peace was gone. There was something lurking out there, watching, waiting, getting ready.

Inside, he said to me, touching helmets, "If you see something like that again, son, don't tell the others. Your Ma's sort of nervous these days and we owe her all the feeling of safety we can give her. Once—it was when your sister was born—I was ready to give up and die, but your Mother kept me trying. Another time she kept the fire going a whole week all by herself when I was sick. Nursed me and took care of the two of you too.

"You know that game we sometimes play, sitting in a square in the Nest, tossing a ball around? Courage is like a ball, son. A person can hold it only so long, and then he's got to toss it to someone else. When it's tossed your way, you've got to catch it and hold it tight—and hope there'll be someone else to toss it to when you get tired of being brave."

His talking to me that way made me feel grown-up and good. But it didn't wipe away the thing outside from the back of my mind—or the fact that Pa took it seriously.

It's hard to hide your feelings about such a thing. When we got back in the Nest and took off our outside clothes, Pa laughed about it all and told them it was nothing and kidded me for having such an imagination, but his words fell flat. He didn't convince Ma and Sis any more than he did me. It looked for a minute like we were all fumbling the courage-ball. Something had to be done, and almost before I knew what I was going to say, I heard myself asking Pa to tell us about the old days, and how it all happened.

He sometimes doesn't mind telling that story, and Sis and I sure like to listen to it, and he got my idea. So we were all settled around the fire in a wink, and Ma pushed up some cans to thaw for supper, and Pa began. Before he did, though, I noticed him casually get a hammer from the shelf and lay it down beside him.

It was the same old story as always—I think I could recite the main thread of it in my sleep—though Pa always puts in a new detail or two and keeps improving it in spots.

He told us how the Earth had been swinging around the Sun ever so steady and warm, and the people on it fixing to make money and wars and have a good time and get power and treat each other right or wrong, when without warning there comes charging out of space this dead star, this burned-out sun, and upsets everything.

You know, I find it hard to believe in the way those people felt, any more than I can believe in the swarming number of them. Imagine people getting ready for the horrible sort of war they were cooking up. Wanting it even, or at least wishing it were over so as to end their nervousness. As if all folks didn't have to hang together and pool every bit of warmth just to keep alive. And how can they have hoped to end danger, any more than we can hope to end the cold?

Sometimes I think Pa exaggerates and makes things out too black. He's cross with us once in a while and was probably cross with all those folks. Still, some of the things I read in the old magazines sound pretty wild. He may be right.

The dark star, as Pa went on telling it, rushed in pretty fast and there wasn't much time to get ready. At the beginning they tried to keep it a secret from most people, but then the truth came out, what with the earthquakes and floods—imagine, oceans of *unfrozen* water!—and people seeing stars blotted out by something on a clear night. First off they thought it would hit the Sun, and then they thought it would hit the Earth. There was even the start of a rush to get to a place called China, because people thought the star would hit on the other side. But then they found it wasn't going to hit either side, but was going to come very close to the Earth.

Most of the other planets were on the other side of the Sun and didn't get involved. The Sun and the newcomer fought over the Earth for a little while—pulling it this way and that, like two dogs growling over a bone, Pa described it this time—and then the newcomer won and carried us off. The Sun got a consolation prize, though. At the last minute it managed to hold on to the Moon.

That was the time of the monster earthquakes and floods, twenty times worse than anything before. It was also the time of the Big Jerk, as Pa calls it, when all Earth got yanked suddenly, just as Pa has done to me once or twice, grabbing me by the collar to do it, when I've been sitting too far from the fire.

You see, the dark star was going through space faster than the Sun, and in the opposite direction, and it had to wrench the world considerably in order to take it away.

The Big Jerk didn't last long. It was over as soon as the Earth was settled down in its new orbit around the dark star. But it was pretty terrible while it lasted. Pa says that all sorts of cliffs and buildings toppled, oceans slopped over, swamps and sandy deserts gave great sliding surges that buried nearby lands. Earth was almost jerked out of its atmosphere blanket and the air got so thin in spots that people keeled over and fainted—though of course, at the same time, they were getting knocked down by the Big Jerk and maybe their bones broke or skulls cracked.

We've often asked Pa how people acted during that time, whether they were scared or brave or crazy or stunned, or all four, but he's sort of leery of the subject, and he was again tonight. He says he was mostly too busy to notice.

You see, Pa and some scientist friends of his had figured out part of what was going to happen—they'd known we'd get captured and our air would freeze—and they'd been working like mad to fix up a place with airtight walls and doors, and insulation against the cold, and big supplies of food and fuel and water and bottled air. But the place got smashed in the last earthquakes and all Pa's friends were killed then and in the Big Jerk. So he had to start over and throw the Nest together quick without any advantages, just using any stuff he could lay his hands on.

I guess he's telling pretty much the truth when he says he didn't have any time to keep an eye on how other folks behaved, either then or in the Big Freeze that followed—followed very quick, you know, both because the dark star was pulling us away very fast and because Earth's rotation had been slowed in the tug-of-war, so that the nights were ten old nights long.

Still, I've got an idea of some of the things that happened from the frozen folk I've seen, a few of them in other rooms in our building, others clustered around the furnaces in the basements where we go for coal.

In one of the rooms, an old man sits stiff in a chair, with an arm and a leg in splints. In another, a man and woman are huddled together in a bed with heaps of covers over them. You can just see their heads peeking out, close together. And in another a beautiful young lady is sitting with a pile of wraps huddled around her, looking hopefully toward the door, as if waiting for someone who never came back with warmth and food. They're all still and stiff as statues, of course, but just like life.

Pa showed them to me once in quick winks of his flashlight, when he still had a fair supply of batteries and could afford to waste a little light. They scared me pretty bad and made my heart pound, especially the young lady.

Now, with Pa telling his story for the umpteenth time to take our minds off another scare, I got to thinking of the frozen folk again. All of a sudden I got an idea that scared me worse than anything yet. You see, I'd just remembered the face I'd thought I'd seen in the window. I'd forgotten about that on account of trying to hide it from the others.

What, I asked myself, if the frozen folk were coming to life? What if they were like the liquid helium that got a new lease on life and started crawling toward the heat just when you thought its molecules ought to freeze solid forever? Or like the electricity that moves endlessly when it's just about as cold as that? What if the ever-growing cold, with the temperature creeping down the last few degrees to the last zero, had mysteriously wakened the frozen folk to life—not warm-blooded life, but something icy and horrible?

That was a worse idea than the one about something coming down from the dark star to get us.

Or maybe, I thought, both ideas might be true. Something coming down from the dark star and making the frozen folk move, using them to do its work. That would fit with both things I'd seen—the beautiful young lady and the moving, star-like light.

The frozen folk with minds from the dark star behind their unwinking eyes, creeping, crawling, snuffing the way, following the heat to the Nest.

I tell you, that thought gave me a very bad turn and I wanted very badly to tell the others my fears, but I remembered what Pa had said and clenched my teeth and didn't speak.

We were all sitting very still. Even the fire was burning silently. There was just the sound of Pa's voice and the clocks.

And then, from beyond the blankets, I thought I heard a tiny noise. My skin tightened all over me.

Pa was telling about the early years in the Nest and had come to the place where he philosophizes.

"So I asked myself then," he said, "what's the use of going on? What's the use of dragging it out for a few years? Why prolong a doomed existence of hard work and cold and loneliness? The human race is done. The Earth is done. Why not give up? I asked myself—and all of a sudden I got the answer."

Again I heard the noise, louder this time, a kind of uncertain, shuffling tread, coming closer. I couldn't breathe.

"Life's always been a business of working hard and fighting the cold," Pa was saying. "The earth's always been a lonely place, millions of miles from the next planet. And no matter how long the human race might have lived, the end would have come some night. Those things don't matter. What matters is that life is good. It has a lovely texture, like some rich cloth or fur, or the petals of flowers—you've seen pictures of those, but I can't describe how they feel—or the fire's glow. It makes everything else worth while. And that's as true for the last man as the first."

And still the steps kept shuffling closer. It seemed to me that the inmost blanket trembled and bulged a little. Just as if they were burned into my imagination, I kept seeing those peering, frozen eyes.

"So right then and there," Pa went on, and now I could tell that he heard the steps too, and was talking loud so we maybe wouldn't hear them, "right then and there I told myself that I was going on as if we had all eternity ahead of us. I'd have children and teach them all I could. I'd get them to read books. I'd plan for the future, try to enlarge and seal the Nest. I'd do what I could to keep everything beautiful and growing. I'd keep alive my feeling of wonder even at the cold and the dark and the distant stars."

But then the blanket actually did move and lift. And there was a bright light somewhere behind it. Pa's voice stopped and his eyes turned to the widening slit and his hand went out until it touched and gripped the handle of the hammer beside him.

In through the blanket stepped the beautiful young lady. She stood there looking at us the strangest way, and she carried something bright and unwinking in her hand. And two other faces peered over her shoulders—men's faces, white and staring.

Well, my heart couldn't have been stopped for more than four or five beats before I realized she was wearing a suit and helmet like Pa's homemade ones, only fancier, and that the men were too—and that the frozen folk certainly wouldn't be wearing those. Also, I noticed that the bright thing in her hand was just a kind of flashlight.

The silence kept on while I swallowed hard a couple of times, and after that there was all sorts of jabbering and commotion.

They were simply people, you see. We hadn't been the only ones to survive; we'd just thought so, for natural enough reasons. These three people had survived, and quite a few others with them. And when we found out *how* they'd survived, Pa let out the biggest whoop of joy.

They were from Los Alamos and they were getting their heat and power from atomic energy. Just using the uranium and plutonium intended for bombs, they had enough to go on for thousands of years. They had a regular little airtight city, with airlocks and all. They even generated electric light and grew plants and animals by it. (At this Pa let out a second whoop, waking Ma from her faint.)

But if we were flabbergasted at them, they were double-flabbergasted at us.

One of the men kept saying, "But it's impossible, I tell you. You can't maintain an air supply without hermetic sealing. It's simply impossible."

That was after he had got his helmet off and was using our air. Meanwhile the young lady kept looking around at us as if we were saints, and telling us we'd done something amazing, and suddenly she broke down and cried.

They'd been scouting around for survivors, but they never expected to find any in a place like this. They had rocket ships at

Los Alamos and plenty of chemical fuel. As for liquid oxygen, all you had to do was go out and shovel the air blanket at the top level. So after they'd got things going smoothly at Los Alamos, which had taken years, they'd decided to make some trips to likely places where there might be other survivors. No good trying long-distance radio signals, of course, since there was no atmosphere to carry them around the curve of the Earth.

Well, they'd found other colonies at Argonne and Brookhaven and way around the world at Harwell and Tanna Tuva. And now they'd been giving our city a look, not really expecting to find anything. But they had an instrument that noticed the faintest heat waves and it had told them there was something warm down here, so they'd landed to investigate. Of course we hadn't heard them land, since there was no air to carry the sound, and they'd had to investigate around quite a while before finding us. Their instruments had given them a wrong steer and they'd wasted some time in the building across the street.

By now, all five adults were talking like sixty. Pa was demonstrating to the men how he worked the fire and got rid of the ice in the chimney and all that. Ma had perked up wonderfully and was showing the young lady her cooking and sewing stuff, and even asking about how the women dressed at Los Alamos. The strangers marveled at everything and praised it to the skies. I could tell from the way they wrinkled their noses that they found the Nest a bit smelly, but they never mentioned that at all and just asked bushels of questions.

In fact, there was so much talking and excitement that Pa forgot about things, and it wasn't until they were all getting groggy that he looked and found the air had all boiled away in the pail. He got another bucket of air quick from behind the blankets. Of course that started them all laughing and jabbering again. The newcomers even got a little drunk. They weren't used to so much oxygen.

Funny thing, though—I didn't do much talking at all and Sis hung on to Ma all the time and hid her face when anybody looked at her. I felt pretty uncomfortable and disturbed myself, even about the young lady. Glimpsing her outside there, I'd had all sorts of mushy thoughts, but now I was just embarrassed and scared of her, even though she tried to be nice as anything to me.

I sort of wished they'd all quit crowding the Nest and let us be alone and get our feelings straightened out.

And when the newcomers began to talk about our all going to Los Alamos, as if that were taken for granted, I could see that something of the same feeling struck Pa and Ma too. Pa got very silent all of a sudden and Ma kept telling the young lady, "But I wouldn't know how to act there and I haven't any clothes."

The strangers were puzzled like anything at first, but then they got the idea. As Pa kept saying, "It just doesn't seem right to let this fire go out."

Well, the strangers are gone, but they're coming back. It hasn't been decided yet just what will happen. Maybe the Nest will be kept up as what one of the strangers called a "survival school." Or maybe we will join the pioneers who are going to try to establish a new colony at the uranium mines at Great Slave Lake or in the Congo.

Of course, now that the strangers are gone, I've been thinking a lot about Los Alamos and those other tremendous colonies. I have a hankering to see them for myself.

You ask me, Pa wants to see them too. He's been getting pretty thoughtful, watching Ma and Sis perk up.

"It's different, now that we know others are alive," he explains to me. "Your mother doesn't feel so hopeless any more. Neither do I, for that matter, not having to carry the whole responsibility for keeping the human race going, so to speak. It scares a person."

I looked around at the blanket walls and the fire and the pails of air boiling away and Ma and Sis sleeping in the warmth and the flickering light.

"It's not going to be easy to leave the Nest," I said, wanting to cry, kind of. "It's so small and there's just the four of us. I get scared at the idea of big places and a lot of strangers."

He nodded and put another piece of coal on the fire. Then he looked at the little pile and grinned suddenly and put a couple of handfuls on, just as if it was one of our birthdays or Christmas.

"You'll quickly get over that feeling, son," he said. "The

trouble with the world was that it kept getting smaller and smaller, till it ended with just the Nest. Now it'll be good to have a real huge world again, the way it was in the beginning."

I guess he's right. You think the beautiful young lady will wait for me till I grow up? I'll be twenty in only ten years.

7

Junior Achievement

WILLIAM LEE

The teenager is king these days, I am told. As controller of a sizable fraction of the nation's spending money, he must be catered to by those who put out movies, television shows, and musical recordings. The rest of us must endure it all.

And yet teenage enthusiasms are not actually murderous. Listening to the Beatles may make you wish you were dead (if you are over nineteen), but you don't really die, however much your hair turns gray. And if you listen to them long enough you may even find a perverted liking for them growing within you. I have—to my own horror—been seduced into listening to them and then found myself singing some of their songs with every sensation of pleasure.

And teenage accomplishments can be admirable, too. At the age of eighteen the English chemist William Henry Perkin prepared the first synthetic dye, recognized what he had, quit school, opened a factory, singlehandedly designed the necessary equipment, refined the necessary chemicals, and founded a giant industry. He retired at thirty-five, a millionaire many times over.

The American chemist Charles Martin Hall, having heard that the man who first worked out a practical method for producing aluminum cheaply would make himself a millionaire, went home, worked out such a method, and became filthy rich. Of course, he wasn't quite a teenager—just an old man of twenty-two.

So let William Lee introduce you to a number of kids in an upbeat, non-Beatle view of what kids might be like.

"What would you think," I asked Marjorie over supper, "if I should undertake to lead a junior achievement group this summer?"

She pondered it while she went to the kitchen to bring in the dessert. It was dried apricot pie, and very tasty, I might add.

"Why Donald," she said, "it could be quite interesting, if I understand what a junior achievement group is. What gave you the idea?"

"It wasn't my idea, really," I admitted. "Mr. McCormack called me to the office today, and told me that some of the children in the lower grades wanted to start one. They need adult guidance of course, and one of the group suggested my name."

I should explain, perhaps, that I teach a course in general

science in our Ridgeville Junior High School, and another in general physics in the Senior High School. It's a privilege which I'm sure many educators must envy, teaching in Ridgeville, for our new school is a fine one, and our academic standards are high. On the other hand, the fathers of most of my students work for the Commission and a constant awareness of the Commission and its work pervades the town. It is an uneasy privilege then, at least sometimes, to teach my old-fashioned brand of science to these children of a new age.

"That's very nice," said Marjorie. "What does a junior achievement group do?"

"It has the purpose," I told her, "of teaching the members something about commerce and industry. They manufacture simple compositions like polishing waxes and sell them from door to door. Some groups have built up tidy little bank accounts which are available for later educational expenses."

"Gracious, you wouldn't have to sell from door to door, would you?"

"Of course not. I'd just tell the kids how to do it."

Marjorie put back her head and laughed, and I was forced to join her, for we both recognize that my understanding and "feel" for commercial matters—if I may use that expression—is almost nonexistent.

"Oh, all right," I said, "laugh at my commercial aspirations. But don't worry about it, really. Mr. McCormack said we could get Mr. Wells from Commercial Department to help out if he was needed. There is one problem, though. Mr. McCormack is going to put up fifty dollars to buy any raw materials wanted and he rather suggested that I might advance another fifty. The question is, could we do it?"

Marjorie did mental arithmetic. "Yes," she said, "yes, if it's something you'd like to do."

We've had to watch such things rather closely for the last ten—no, eleven years. Back in the old Ridgeville, fifty odd miles to the south, we had our home almost paid for, when the accident occurred. It was in the path of the heaviest fallout, and we couldn't have kept on living there even if the town had stayed. When Ridgeville moved to its present site, so, of course, did we, which meant starting mortgage payments all over again.

Thus it was that on a Wednesday morning about three weeks later, I was sitting at one end of a plank picnic table with five boys and girls lined up along the sides. This was to be our headquarters and factory for the summer—a roomy unused barn belonging to the parents of one of the group members, Tommy Miller.

"Okay," I said, "let's relax. You don't need to treat me as a teacher, you know. I stopped being a schoolteacher when the final grades went in last Friday. I'm on vacation now. My job here is only to advise, and I'm going to do that as little as possible. You're going to decide what to do, and if it's safe and legal and possible to do with the starting capital we have, I'll go along with it and help in any way I can. This is your meeting."

Mr. McCormack had told me, and in some detail, about the youngsters I'd be dealing with. The three who were sitting to my left were the ones who had proposed the group in the first place.

Doris Enright was a grave young lady of ten years, who might, I thought, be quite a beauty in a few more years but was at the moment rather angular—all shoulders and elbows. Peter Cope, Jr., and Hilary Matlack were skinny kids too. The three were of an age and were all tall for ten-year-olds.

I had the impression during that first meeting that they looked rather alike, but this wasn't so. Their features were quite different. Perhaps from association—for they were close friends—they had just come to have a certain similarity of restrained gesture and of modulated voice. And they were all tanned by sun and wind to a degree that made their eyes seem light and their teeth startlingly white.

The two on my right were cast in a different mold. Mary McCready was a big husky redhead of twelve, with a face full of freckles and an infectious laugh, and Tommy Miller, a few months younger, was just an average extroverted well-adjusted youngster, noisy and restless, T-shirted and butch barbered.

The group exchanged looks to see who would lead off, and Peter Cope seemed to be elected.

"Well, Mr. Henderson, a junior achievement group is a bunch of kids who get together to manufacture and sell things, and maybe make some money."

"Is that what you want to do," I asked, "make money?"

"Why not?" Tommy asked. "There's something wrong with making money?"

"Well, sure, I suppose we want to," said Hilary. "We'll need some money to do the things we want to do later."

"And what sort of things would you like to make and sell?" I asked.

The usual products, of course, with these junior achievement efforts, are chemical specialties that can be made safely and that people will buy and use without misgivings—solvent to free up rusty bolts, cleaner to remove road tar, mechanics hand soap—that sort of thing. Mr. McCormack had told me, though, that I might find these youngsters a bit more ambitious. "The Miller boy and Mary McCready," he had said, "have exceptionally high I.Q.'s—around one forty or one fifty. The other three are hard to classify. They have some of the attributes of exceptional pupils, but much of the time they seem to have little interest in their studies. The junior achievement idea has sparked their imaginations. Maybe it'll be just what they need."

Mary said, "Why don't we make a freckle remover? I'd be our first customer."

"The thing to do," Tommy offered, "is to figure out what people in Ridgeville want to buy, then sell it to them."

"I'd like to make something by powder metallurgy techniques," said Pete. He fixed me with a challenging eye. "You should be able to make ball bearings by molding, then densify them by electroplating."

"And all we'd need is a hydraulic press," I told him, "which, on a guess, might cost ten thousand dollars. Let's think of something easier."

Pete mulled it over and nodded reluctantly. "Then maybe something in the electronics field. A hi-fi sub assembly of some kind."

"How about a new detergent?" Hilary put in.

"Like the liquid dishwashing detergents?" I asked.

He was scornful. "No, they're formulations—you know, mixtures. That's cookbook chemistry. I mean a brand-new synthetic detergent. I've got an idea for one that ought to be good even in the hard water we've got around here."

"Well now," I said, "organic synthesis sounds like another

operation calling for capital investment. If we should keep the achievement group going for several summers, it might be possible later on to carry out a safe synthesis of some sort. You're Dr. Matlack's son, aren't you? Been dipping into your father's library?"

"Some," said Hilary, "and I've got a home laboratory."

"How about you, Doris," I prompted, "do you have a special field of interest?"

"No." She shook her head in mock despondency. "I'm not very technical. Just sort of miscellaneous. But if the group wanted to raise some mice, I'd be willing to turn over a project I've had going at home."

"You could sell mice?" Tommy demanded incredulously.

"Mice," I echoed, then sat back and thought about it. "Are they a pure strain? One of the recognized laboratory strains? Healthy mice of the right strain," I explained to Tommy, "might be sold to laboratories. I have an idea the Commission buys a supply every month."

"No," said Doris, "these aren't laboratory mice. They're fancy ones. I got the first four pairs from a pet shop in Denver, but they're red—sort of chipmunk color, you know. I've carried them through seventeen generations of careful selection."

"Well, now," I admitted, "the market for red mice might be rather limited. Why don't you consider making an aftershave lotion? Denatured alcohol, glycerine, water, a little color and perfume. You could buy some bottles and have some labels printed. You'd be in business before you knew it."

There was a pause, then Tommy inquired, "How do you sell it?"

"Door to door."

He made a face. "Never build up any volume. Unless it did something extra. You say we'd put color in it. How about enough color to leave your face looking tanned? Men won't use cosmetics and junk, but if they didn't have to admit it, they might like the shave lotion."

Hilary had been deep in thought. He said suddenly, "Gosh, I think I know how to make a—what do you want to call it?—a before-shave lotion."

"What would that be?" I asked.

"You'd use it before you shaved."

"I suppose there might be people who'd prefer to use it beforehand," I conceded.

"There will be people," he said darkly, and subsided.

Mrs. Miller came out to the barn after a while, bringing a bucket of soft drinks and ice, a couple of loaves of bread and ingredients for a variety of sandwiches. The parents had agreed to underwrite lunches at the barn and Betty Miller philosophically assumed the role of commissary officer. She paused only to say hello and to ask how we were progressing with our organization meeting.

I'd forgotten all about organization, and that, according to all the articles I had perused, is most important to such groups. It's standard practice for every member of the group to be a company officer. Of course a young boy who doesn't know any better, may wind up sales manager.

Over the sandwiches, then, I suggested nominating company officers, but they seemed not to be interested. Peter Cope waved it off by remarking that they'd each do what came naturally. On the other hand, they pondered at some length about a name for the organization, without reaching any conclusions, so we returned to the problem of what to make.

It was Mary, finally, who advanced the thought of kites. At first there was little enthusiasm, then Peter said, "You know, we could work up something new. Has anybody ever seen a kite made like a wind sock?"

Nobody had. Pete drew figures in the air with his hands. "How about the hole at the small end?"

"I'll make one tonight," said Doris, "and think about the small end. It'll work out all right."

I wished that the youngsters weren't starting out by inventing a new article to manufacture, and risking an almost certain disappointment, but to hold my guidance to the minimum, I said nothing, knowing that later I could help them redesign it along standard lines.

At supper I reviewed the day's happenings with Marjorie and tried to recall all of the ideas which had been propounded. Most of them were impractical, of course, for a group of children to attempt, but several of them appeared quite attractive.

Tommy, for example, wanted to put tooth powder into tablets that one would chew before brushing the teeth. He thought there should be two colors in the same bottle—orange for morning and blue for night, the blue ones designed to leave the mouth alkaline at bedtime.

Pete wanted to make a combination nail and wood screw. You'd drive it in with a hammer up to the threaded part, then send it home with a few turns of a screwdriver.

Hilary, reluctantly forsaking his ideas on detergents, suggested we make black plastic disks, like poker chips but thinner and as cheap as possible, to scatter on a snowy sidewalk where they would pick up extra heat from the sun and melt the snow more rapidly. Afterward one would sweep up and collect the disks.

Doris added to this that if you could make the disks light enough to float, they might be colored white and spread on the surface of a reservoir to reduce evaporation.

These latter ideas had made unknowing use of some basic physics, and I'm afraid I relapsed for a few minutes into the role of teacher and told them a little bit about the laws of radiation and absorption of heat.

"My," said Marjorie, "they're really smart boys and girls. Tommy Miller does sound like a born salesman. Somehow I don't think you're going to have to call in Mr. Wells."

I do feel just a little embarrassed about the kite, even now. The fact that it flew surprised me. That it flew so confoundedly well was humiliating. Four of them were at the barn when I arrived next morning; or rather on the rise of ground just beyond it, and the kite hung motionless and almost out of sight in the pale sky. I stood and watched for a moment, then they saw me.

"Hello, Mr. Henderson," Mary said, and proffered the cord which was wound on a fishing reel. I played the kite up and down for a few minutes, then reeled it in. It was, almost exactly, a wind sock, but the hole at the small end was shaped—by wire—into the general form of a kidney bean. It was beautifully made, and had a sort of professional look about it.

"It flies too well," Mary told Doris. "A kite ought to get caught in a tree sometimes."

"You're right," Doris agreed. "Let's see it." She gave the wire at the small end the slightest of twists. "There, it ought to swoop."

Sure enough, in the moderate breeze of that morning, the kite swooped and yawed to Mary's entire satisfaction. As we trailed back to the barn I asked Doris, "How did you know that flattening the lower edge of the hole would create instability?" She looked doubtful.

"Why, it would have to, wouldn't it? It changed the pattern of air pressures." She glanced at me quickly. "Of course, I tried a lot of different shapes while I was making it."

"Naturally," I said, and let it go at that. "Where's Tommy?"

"He stopped off at the bank," Pete Cope told me, "to borrow some money. We'll want to buy materials to make some of these kites."

"But I said yesterday that Mr. McCormack and I were going to advance some cash to get started."

"Oh sure, but don't you think it would be better to borrow from a bank? More businesslike?"

"Doubtless," I said, "but banks generally want some security." I would have gone on and explained matters further, except that Tommy walked in and handed me a pocket checkbook.

"I got two hundred and fifty," he volunteered, not without a hint of complacency in his voice. "It didn't take long, but they sure made it out a big deal. Half the guys in the bank had to be called in to listen to the proposition. The account's in your name, Mr. Henderson, and you'll have to make out the checks. And they want you to stop in at the bank and give them a specimen signature. Oh yes, and cosign the note."

My heart sank. I'd never had any dealings with banks except in the matter of mortgages, and bank people make me most uneasy. To say nothing of finding myself responsible for a two-hundred-and-fifty-dollar note—over two weeks salary. I made a mental vow to sign very few checks.

"So then I stopped by at Apex Stationers," Tommy went on, "and ordered some paper and envelopes. We hadn't picked a name yesterday, but I figured what's to lose, and picked one. Ridge Industries, how's that?" Everybody nodded.

"Just three lines on the letterhead," he explained. "Ridge Industries—Ridgeville—Montana."

I got my voice back and said, "Engraved, I trust."

"Well sure," he replied. "You can't afford to look chintzy."

My appetite was not at its best that evening, and Marjorie recognized that something was concerning me, but she asked no questions, and I only told her about the success of the kite, and the youngsters embarking on a shopping trip for paper, glue, and wood splints. There was no use in both of us worrying.

On Friday we all got down to work, and presently had a regular production line under way; stapling the wood splints, then wetting them with a resin solution and shaping them over a mandrel to stiffen, cutting the plastic film around a pattern, assembling and hanging the finished kites from an overhead beam until the cement had set. Pete Cope had located a big roll of red plastic film from somewhere, and it made a wonderful-looking kite. Happily, I didn't know what the film cost until the first kites were sold.

By Wednesday of the following week we had almost three hundred kites finished and packed into flat cardboard boxes, and frankly I didn't care if I never saw another. Tommy, who by mutual consent, was our authority on sales, didn't want to sell any until we had, as he put it, enough to meet the demand, but this quantity seemed to satisfy him. He said he would sell them the next week and Mary McCready, with a fine burst of confidence, asked him in all seriousness to be sure to hold out a dozen.

Three other things occurred that day, two of which I knew about immediately. Mary brought a portable typewriter from home and spent part of the afternoon banging away at what seemed to me, since I use two fingers only, a very creditable speed.

And Hilary brought in a bottle of his new detergent. It was a syrupy yellow liquid with a nice collar of suds. He'd been busy in his home laboratory after all, it seemed.

"What is it?" I asked. "You never told us."

Hilary grinned. "Lauryl benzyl phosphonic acid, dipotassium salt, in twenty-percent solution."

"Goodness," I protested, "it's been twenty-five years since my last course in chemistry. Perhaps if I saw the formula . . ."

He gave me a singularly adult smile and jotted down a scrawl of symbols and lines. It meant little to me.

"Is it good?"

For answer he seized the ice bucket, now empty of its soda bottles, trickled in a few drops from the bottle and swished the contents. Foam mounted to the rim and spilled over. "And that's our best grade of Ridgeville water," he pointed out. "Hardest in the country."

The third event of Wednesday came to my ears on Thursday morning.

I was a little late arriving at the barn, and was taken a bit aback to find the roadway leading to it rather full of parked automobiles, and the barn itself rather full of people, including two policemen. Our Ridgeville police are quite young men, but in uniform they still look ominous and I was relieved to see that they were laughing and evidently enjoying themselves.

"Well, now," I demanded, in my best classroom voice, "what is all this?"

"Are you Henderson?" the larger policeman asked.

"I am indeed," I said, and a flashbulb went off. A young lady grasped my arm.

"Oh please, Mr. Henderson, come outside where it's quieter and tell me all about it."

"Perhaps," I countered, "somebody should tell me."

"You mean you don't know, honestly? Oh, it's fabulous. Best story I've had for ages. It'll make the city papers." She led me around the corner of the barn to a spot of comparative quiet. "You didn't know that one of your junior whatsisnames poured detergent in the Memorial Fountain basin last night?"

I shook my head numbly.

"It was priceless. Just before rush hour. Suds built up in the basin and overflowed, and down the library steps and covered the whole street. And the funniest part was they kept right on coming. You couldn't imagine so much suds coming from that little pool of water. There was a three-block traffic jam and Harry got us some marvelous pictures—men rolling up their trousers to wade across the street. And this morning," she chortled, "somebody phoned in an anonymous tip to the police—of course it was the same boy who did it—Tommy—Miller?—and so here we are. And we just saw a demonstration of that fabulous kite and saw all those simply captivating mice."

"Mice?"

"Yes, of course. Who would ever have thought you could breed mice with those cute furry tails?"

Well, after a while things quieted down. They had to. The police left after sobering up long enough to give me a serious warning against letting such a thing happen again. Mr. Miller, who had come home to see what all the excitement was, went back to work and Mrs. Miller went back to the house and the reporter and photographer drifted off to file their story or whatever it is they do. Tommy was jubilant.

"Did you hear what she said? It'll make the city papers. I wish we had a thousand kites. Ten thousand. Oh boy, selling is fun. Hilary, when can you make some more of that stuff? And Doris, how many mice do you have?"

Those mice! I have always kept my enthusiasm for rodents within bounds, but I must admit they were charming little beasts, with tails as bushy as miniature squirrels.

"How many generations?" I asked Doris.

"Seventeen. No, eighteen, now. Want to see the genetic charts?"

I won't try to explain it as she did to me, but it was quite evident that the new mice were breeding true. Presently we asked Betty Miller to come back down to the barn for a conference. She listened and asked questions. As last she said, "Well, all right, if you promise me they can't get out of their cages. But heaven knows what you'll do when fall comes. They won't live in an unheated barn and you can't bring them into the house."

"We'll be out of the mouse business by then," Doris predicted. "Every pet shop in the country will have them and they'll be down to nothing apiece."

Doris was right, of course, in spite of our efforts to protect the market. Anyhow, that ushered in our cage-building phase, and for the next week—with a few interruptions—we built cages, hundreds of them, a good many for breeding, but mostly for shipping.

It was rather regrettable that, after the *Courier* gave us most of the third page, including photographs, we rarely had a day without a few visitors. Many of them wanted to buy mice or kites, but Tommy refused to sell any mice at retail and we soon had to disappoint those who wanted kites. The Supermarket took all we had—except a dozen—and at a dollar fifty each. Tommy's ideas of pricing rather frightened me, but he set the value of the mice at ten dollars a pair and got it without any arguments.

Our beautiful stationery arrived, and we had some invoice forms printed up in a hurry—not engraved, for a wonder.

It was on Tuesday—following the Thursday—that a lanky young man disentangled himself from his car and strolled into the barn. I looked up from the floor where I was tacking squares of screening onto wooden frames.

"Hi," he said. "You're Donald Henderson, right? My name is McCord—Jeff McCord—and I work in the Patent Section at the Commission's downtown office. My boss sent me over here, but if he hadn't, I think I'd have come anyway. What are you doing to get patent protection on Ridge Industries' new developments?"

I got my back unkinked and dusted off my knees. "Well, now," I said, "I've been wondering whether something shouldn't be done, but I know very little about such matters—"

"Exactly," he broke in. "We guessed that might be the case, and there are three patent men in our office who'd like to chip in and contribute some time. Partly for the kicks and partly because we think you may have some things worth protecting. How about it? You worry about the filing and final fees. That's sixty bucks per brainstorm. We'll worry about everything else."

"What's to lose," Tommy interjected.

And so we acquired a patent attorney, several of them, in fact.

The day that our application on the kite design went to Washington, Mary wrote a dozen toy manufacturers scattered from New York to Los Angeles, sent a kite to each one and offered to license the design. Result, one licensee with a thousand-dollar advance against next season's royalties.

It was a rainy morning about three weeks later that I arrived at the barn. Jeff McCord was there, and the whole team except Tommy. Jeff lowered his feet from the picnic table and said, "Hi."

"Hi, yourself," I told him. "You look pleased."

"I am," he replied, "in a cautious legal sense, of course. Hilary and I were just going over the situation on his phosphonate detergent. I've spent the last three nights studying the patent literature and a few standard texts touching on phosphonates. There are a zillion patents on synthetic detergents and a good round fifty on phosphonates, but it looks"—he held up a long admonitory hand—"it just looks as though we had a clear spot. If we do get protection, you've got a real salable property."

"That's fine, Mr. McCord," Hilary said, "but it's not very important."

"No?" Jeff tilted an inquiring eyebrow at me, and I handed him a small bottle. He opened and sniffed at it gingerly. "What gives?"

"Before-shave lotion," Hilary told him. "You've shaved this morning, but try some anyway."

Jeff looked momentarily dubious, then puddled some in his palm and moistened his jaw line. "Smells good," he noted, "and feels nice and cool. Now what?"

"Wipe your face." Jeff located a handkerchief and wiped, looked at the cloth, wiped again, and stared.

"What is it?"

"A whisker stiffener. It makes each hair brittle enough to break off right at the surface of your skin."

"So I perceive. What is it?"

"Oh, just a mixture of stuff. Cookbook chemistry. Cysteine thiolactone and a fat soluble magnesium compound."

"I see. Just a mixture of stuff. And do your whiskers grow back the next day?"

"Right on schedule," I said.

McCord unfolded his length and stood staring out into the rain. Presently he said, "Henderson, Hilary and I are heading for my office. We can work there better than here, and if we're going to break the hearts of the razor industry, there's no better time to start than now."

When they had driven off I turned and said, "Let's talk

awhile. We can always clean mouse cages later. Where's Tommy?"

"Oh, he stopped at the bank to get a loan."

"What on earth for? We have over six thousand in the account."

"Well," Peter said, looking a little embarrassed, "we were planning to buy a hydraulic press. You see, Doris put some embroidery on that scheme of mine for making ball bearings." He grabbed a sheet of paper. "Look, we make a roller bearing, this shape only it's a permanent magnet. Then you see—" And he was off.

"What did they do today, dear?" Marge asked as she refilled my coffee cup.

"Thanks," I said. "Let's see, it was a big day. We picked out a hydraulic press, Doris read us the first chapter of the book she's starting, and we found a place over a garage on Fourth Street that we can rent for winter quarters. Oh, yes, and Jeff is starting action to get the company incorporated."

"Winter quarters," Marge repeated. "You mean you're going to try to keep the group going after school starts?"

"Why not? The kids can sail through their courses without thinking about them, and actually they won't put in more than a few hours a week during the school year."

"Even so, it's child labor, isn't it?"

"Child labor nothing. They're the employers. Jeff McCord and I will be the only employees—just at first, anyway."

Marge choked on something. "Did you say you'd be an employee?"

"Sure," I told her. "They've offered me a small share of the company, and I'd be crazy to turn it down. After all, what's to lose?"

8

Cabin Boy

DAMON KNIGHT

Oh, what a double—or triple—life our Damon leads. I should say damon for he invariably eschews the capital.

If you were to meet him you might see why, for he is so gentle and quiet as he sits there that you would swear a capital letter was too noisy for him. He has a broad intellectual forehead, a small fine-boned jaw, a slight smile, and a general air of one in whose mouth butter would solidify and grow hard.

But then place him behind the typewriter and he becomes science fiction's most trenchant and merciless critic. With a hard, unsparing scalpel he exposes every trace of stupidity in the story on which he is operating. If you are yourself a writer you may tremble lest you be next, yet if you are a conscientious writer, you ought to hope you will be, for you are bound to learn from him.

Damon Knight—now president of the newly formed Science Fiction Writers of America—has never been guest of honor at one of the annual World Science Fiction Conventions. I wish he would be selected for the role. Not only does he deserve it but there would be the chance for a perfect parody of the great Cole Porter classic "Night and Day." I would be proud to lead a chorus beginning:

Damon Knight, you are the one . . .

If I myself were a critic of Damon's acidulous sort, I would never have the nerve to write stories. Damon is made of sterner stuff, however. He not only writes stories but writes them so well that I have never seen anyone feel tempted to turn Damon's own gun against him. He does not commit the crimes he castigates, so come, let him introduce you to a youngster radically different from any you have ever known, facing a most unearthly situation in outer space.

The cabin boy's name was unspeakable, and even its meaning would be difficult to convey in any human tongue. For convenience, we may as well call him Tommy Loy.

Please bear in mind that all these terms are approximations. Tommy was not exactly a cabin boy, and even the spaceship he served was not exactly a spaceship, nor was the Captain exactly a captain. But if you think of Tommy as a freckled, scowling, redhaired, willful, prank-playing, thoroughly abhorrent brat, and of the Captain as a crusty, ponderous man, you may be able to understand their relationship.

A word about Tommy will serve to explain why these approximations have to be made, and just how much they mean.

Tommy, to a human being, would have looked like a six-foot egg made of greenish gelatin. Suspended in this were certain dark or radiant shapes which were Tommy's nerve centers and digestive organs, and scattered about its surface were star-shaped and oval markings which were his sensory organs and gripping mechanisms—his "hands." At the lesser end was an orifice which expelled a stream of glowing vapor, Tommy's means of propulsion. It should be clear that if instead of saying, "Tommy ate his lunch," or, "Tommy said to the Captain—" we reported what really happened, some pretty complicated explanations would have to be made.

Similarly, the term "cabin boy" is used because it is the closest in human meaning. Some vocations, like seafaring, are so demanding and so complex that they simply cannot be taught in classrooms; they have to be lived. A cabin boy is one who is learning such a vocation and paying for his instruction by performing certain menial, degrading, and unimportant tasks.

That certainly describes Tommy, with one more similarity—the cabin boy of the sailing vessel was traditionally occupied after each whipping with preparing the mischief, or the stupidity, that earned him the next one.

Tommy, at the moment, had a whipping coming to him, and was fighting a delaying action. He knew he couldn't escape eventual punishment, but he planned, with a wholehearted determination, to hold it off as long as he could.

Floating alertly in one of the innumerable corridors of the ship, he watched as a dark wave sprang into being upon the glowing corridor wall and sped toward him. Instantly Tommy was moving away from it, and at the same rate of speed.

The wave rumbled: "Tommy! Tommy Loy! Where is that obscenity boy?"

The wave moved on, rumbling wordlessly, and Tommy moved with it. Ahead of him was another wave, and another beyond that, and it was the same throughout all the corridors of the ship. Abruptly the waves reversed their direction. So did Tommy, barely in time. The waves not only carried the Captain's orders, but scanned every corridor and compartment of the ten-mile ship. But as long as Tommy kept between the waves, the Captain could not see him.

It did not strike Tommy as odd that the Captain never

thought of keeping the scanning waves stationary and letting the search parties catch up to him. The Captain, like all the rest of the crew, was not very bright in comparison with Tommy. This was odd enough, but Tommy had long since given up trying to puzzle out the reason. It was part of his universe.

The trouble was that he could not keep this up forever, and he was being searched for by other lowly members of the crew. It took a long time to traverse each of those winding, interlaced passages, but it was a mathematical certainty that he would be caught eventually.

Tommy shuddered, and at the same time he squirmed with delight. He had interrupted the Old Man's sleep by a stench of a particularly noisome variety, one of which he had only lately found himself capable. The effect had been beautiful. In human terms, since Tommy's race communicated by odors, it was equivalent to setting off a firecracker beside a sleeper's ear.

Judging by the jerkiness of the scanning waves' motion, the Old Man was still unnerved.

"Tommy!" the waves rumbled. "Come out, you little piece of filth, or I'll smash you into a thousand separate stinks! By Spore, when I get hold of you—"

The corridor intersected another at this point, and Tommy seized his chance to duck into the new one. He had been working his way outward ever since his crime, knowing that the search parties would do the same. When he reached the outermost level of the ship, there would be a slight possibility of slipping back past the hunters—not much of a chance, but better than none.

He kept close to the wall. He was the smallest member of the crew—smaller than any of the other cabin boys, and less than half the size of an Ordinary; it was always possible that when he sighted one of the search party, he could get away before the crewman saw him. He was in a short connecting corridor now, but the scanning waves cycled endlessly, always turning back before he could escape into the next corridor. Tommy followed their movement patiently, while he listened to the torrent of abuse that poured from them. He snickered fragrantly to himself. When the Old Man was angry, everybody suffered. The ship would be stinking from stem to stern by now.

Eventually the Captain forgot himself and the waves flowed on around the next intersection. Tommy moved on. He was getting close to his goal by now; he could see a faint gleam of starshine up at the end of the corridor.

The next turn took him into it—and what Tommy saw through the semitransparent skin of the ship nearly made him falter and get caught. Not merely the fiery pinpoints of stars shone there, but a great, furious glow which could only mean that they were passing through a star system. It was the first time this had happened in Tommy's life, but of course it was nothing to the Captain, or even to most of the Ordinaries. Trust them, Tommy thought resentfully, to say nothing to him about it!

Now he knew he was glad he'd tossed that surprise at the Captain. If he hadn't, he wouldn't be here, and if he weren't here—

A waste capsule was bumping automatically along the corridor, heading for one of the exit pores in the hull. Tommy let it catch up to him, then englobed it, but it stretched him so tight that he could barely hold it. That was all to the good; the Captain wouldn't be likely to notice that anything had happened.

The hull was sealed, not to keep atmosphere inside, for there was none except by accident, but to prevent loss of liquid by evaporation. Metals and other mineral elements were replaceable; liquids and their constituents, in ordinary circumstances, were not.

Tommy rode the capsule to the exit sphincter, squeezed through, and instantly released it. Being polarized away from the ship's core, it shot into space and was lost. Tommy hugged the outer surface of the hull, and gazed at the astonishing panorama that surrounded him.

There was the enormous black half-globe of space—Tommy's sky, the only one he had ever known. It was sprinkled with the familiar yet always changing patterns of the stars. By themselves, these were marvels enough for a child whose normal universe was one of ninety-foot corridors and chambers measuring, at most, three times as much. But Tommy hardly noticed them. Down to his right, reflecting brilliantly from the long, gentle curve of the greenish hull, was a blazing yellow-white glory that he could hardly look at. A star, the first one he had ever seen close at hand. Off to the left was a tiny, milky-blue disk that could only be a planet.

Tommy let go a shout, for the sheer pleasure of its thin, hollow sound, or, if you prefer, smell. He watched the thin mist of particles spread lazily away from his body, faintly luminous against the jet blackness. He shivered a little, thickening his skin as much as he could. He could not stay long, he knew; he was radiating heat faster than he could absorb it from the sun on the ship's hull.

But he didn't want to go back inside, and not only because it meant being caught and punished. He didn't want to leave that great, dazzling jewel in the sky. For an instant he thought vaguely of the future time when he would be grown, the master of his own vessel, and could see the stars whenever he chose; but the picture was too far away to have any reality. Great Spore, that wouldn't happen for twenty thousand years!

Fifty yards away, an enormous dark spot on the hull, one of the ship's vision devices, swelled and darkened. Tommy looked up with interest. He could see nothing in that direction, but evidently the Captain had spotted something. Tommy watched and waited, growing colder every second, and after a long time he saw a new pinpoint of light spring into being. It grew steadily larger, turned fuzzy at one side, then became two linked dots, one hard and bright, the other misty.

Tommy looked down with sudden understanding, and saw that another wide area of the ship's hull was swollen and protruding. This one showed a pale color under the green and had a dark ring around it; it was a polarizer. The object he had seen must contain metal, and the Captain was bringing it in for fuel. Tommy hoped it was a big one; they had been short of metal ever since he could remember.

When he glanced up again, the object was much larger. He could see now that the bright part was hard and smooth, reflecting the light of the nearby sun. The misty part was a puzzler. It looked like a crewman's voice, seen against space—or the ion trail of a ship in motion. But was it possible for metal to be alive?

II

Leo Roget stared into the rear-view scanner and wiped beads of sweat from his brown, half-bald scalp. Flaming gas from the jets washed up toward him along the hull; he couldn't see much. But the huge dark void they were headed for was still there, and it was getting bigger. He glanced futilely at the control board. The throttle was on full. They were going to crash in a little more than two minutes, and there didn't seem to be a single thing he could do about it.

He looked at Frances McMenamin, strapped into the acceleration harness beside his own. She said, "Try cutting off the jets, why don't you?"

Roger was a short, muscular man with not very much straight black hair and sharp brown eyes. McMenamin was slender and ash blond, half an inch taller than he was, with one of those pale, exquisitely shaped faces that seem to be distributed equally among the very stupid and the very bright. Roget had never been perfectly sure which she was, although they had been companions for more than three years. That, in a way, was part of the reason they had taken this pretty wild trip; she had made Roget uneasy, and he wanted to break away, and at the same time he didn't. So he had fallen in with her idea of a trip to Mars—"to get off by ourselves and think"—and here, Roget thought, they were, not thinking particularly.

He said, "You want us to crash quicker?"

"How do you know we will?" she countered. "It's the only thing we haven't tried. Anyhow, we'd be able to see where we're going, and that's more than we can do now."

"All right," said Roget, "all *right*." She was perfectly capable of giving him six more reasons, each screwier than the last, and then turning out to be justified. He pulled the throttle back to zero, and the half-heard, half-felt roar of the jets died.

The ship jerked backward suddenly, yanking them against the couch straps, and then slowed.

Roget looked into the scanner again. They were approaching the huge object, whatever it was, at about the same rate as before. Maybe, he admitted unwillingly, a little slower. Damn the woman! How could she possibly have figured that one out in advance?

"And," McMenamin added reasonably, "we'll save fuel for the takeoff."

Roget scowled at her. "If there is a takeoff," he said. "Whatever is pulling us down there isn't doing it to show off. What do we do—tell them that was a very impressive trick and we enjoyed it, but we've got to be leaving now?"

"We'll find out what's doing it," said McMenamin, "and stop it if we can. If we can't, the fuel won't do us any good anyway."

That was, if not Frances' most exasperating trick, at least high on the list. She had a habit of introducing your own argument as if it were not only a telling point on her side, but something you had been too dense to see. Arguing with her was like swinging at someone who abruptly disappeared and then sandbagged you from behind.

Roget was fuming, but he said nothing. The greenish surface below was approaching more and more slowly, and now he felt a slight but definite tightening of the couch straps that could only mean deceleration. They were being maneuvered in for a landing as carefully and efficiently as if they were doing it themselves.

A few seconds later a green horizon line appeared in the direct-view ports, and they touched. Roget's and McMenamin's couches swung on their gimbals as the ship tilted slowly, bounced, and came to rest.

Frances reached inside the wide collar of her pressure suit to smooth a ruffle that had got crumpled between the volcanic swell of her bosom and the front of the transparent suit. Watching her, Roget felt a sudden irrational flow of affection and—as usually happened—a simultaneous notification that his body disagreed with his mind's opinion of her. She was nuts, but he couldn't do without her. This trip, it had been tacitly agreed, was to be a kind of final trial period. At the end of it, either they would split up or decide to make it permanent, and up to now Roget had been silently determined that it was going to be a split. Now he was just as sure that, providing they ever got to Mars or back to Earth, he was going to nail her for good.

He glanced at her face. She knew, all right, just as she'd known when he'd felt the other way. It should have irritated him, but he felt oddly pleased and comforted. He unstrapped himself, fastened down his helmet, and moved toward the airlock.

"Be careful," she said.

"Yeah." He looked at her. "Be back in a minute."

She smiled—not a big one for show, but the little, quiet kind that lit up her face. Roget grinned back and closed the airlock door behind him.

He stood on a pale-green, almost featureless surface that curved gently away in every direction. Where he stood, it was brilliantly lit by the sun, and his shadow was sharp and as black as space. About two thirds of the way to the horizon, looking across the short axis of the ship, the sunlight stopped with knife-edge sharpness, and he could make out the rest only as a ghostly reflection of starlight.

Their ship was lying on its side, with the pointed stern apparently sunk a few inches into the green surface of the alien ship. He took a cautious step in that direction, and nearly floated past it before he could catch himself. His boot magnets had failed to grip. The metal of this hull—if it was metal—must be something that contained no steel.

The green hull was shot through with other colors here, and it rose in a curious, almost rectangular mound. At the center, just at the tip of the Earth vessel's jets, there was a pale area; around that was a dark ring which lapped up over the side of the ship. He bent to examine it. It was in shadow, and he used his helmet light.

The light shone through the mottled green substance; he could see the skin of his own ship. It was pitted, corroding. As he watched, another pinpoint of corruption appeared on the shiny surface, and slowly grew.

Roget straightened up with an exclamation. His helmet phones asked, "What is it, Leo?"

He said, "Acid or something eating the hull. Wait a minute." He looked again at the pale and dark mottlings under the green surface. The center area was not attacking the ship's metal; that might be the muzzle of whatever instrument had been used to pull them down out of their orbit and hold them there. But if it was turned off now— He had to get the ship away from the dark ring that was destroying it. He couldn't fire the jets otherwise, because they were half-buried; he'd blow the tubes if he tried.

He said, "You still strapped in?"

"Yes."

"All right, hold on." He stepped back to the center of the little ship, braced his corrugated boot soles against the hard green surface, and shoved.

The ship rolled. But it rolled like a top, around the axis of its pointed end. The dark area gave way before it, as if it were jelly soft. The jets still pointed to the middle of the pale area, and the dark ring still lapped over them. Roget moved farther down and tried again, with the same result. The ship would move freely in every direction but the right one. The attracting power, clearly enough, was still on.

He straightened dejectedly and looked around. A few hundred yards away, he saw something he had noticed before, without attaching any significance to it: a six-foot egg, of some lighter, more translucent substance than the one on which it lay. He leaped toward it. It moved sluggishly away, trailing a cloud of luminous gas. A few seconds later he had it between his gloved hands. It squirmed, then ejected a thin spurt of vapor from its forward end. It was alive.

McMenamin's head was silhouetted in one of the forward ports. He said, "See this?"

"Yes! What is it?"

"One of the crew, I think. I'm going to bring it in. You work the airlock—it won't hold both of us at once."

". . . All right."

The huge egg crowded the cabin uncomfortably. It was pressed up against the rear wall, where it had rolled as soon as Frances had pulled it into the ship. The two humans stood at the other side of the room, against the control panel, and watched it.

"No features," said Roget, "unless you count those markings on the surface. This thing isn't from anywhere in the Solar System, Frances—it isn't even any order of evolution we ever heard of."

"I know," she said abstractedly. "Leo, is he wearing any protection against space that you can see?"

"No," said Roget. "That's *him,* not a spacesuit. Look, you can see halfway into him. But—"

Frances turned to look at him. "That's it," she said. "It means this is his natural element—space!"

Roget looked thoughtfully at the egg. "It makes sense," he said. "He's adapted for it, anyhow—ovoid, for a high volume-to-surface ratio. Tough outer shell. Moves by jet propulsion. It's hard to believe, because we've never run into a creature like him before, but I don't see why not. On Earth there are organisms, plants, that can live and reproduce in boiling water, and others that can stand near-zero temperatures."

"He's a plant too, you know," Frances put in.

Roget stared at her, then back at the egg. "That color, you mean? Chlorophyl. It could be."

"Must be," she corrected firmly. "How else would he live in a vacuum?" And then, distressedly, "Oh, what a smell!"

They looked at each other. It *had* been something monumental in the way of smells, though it had only lasted a fraction of a second. There had been a series of separate odors, all unfamiliar and all overpoweringly strong. At least a dozen of them, Roget thought; they had gone past too quickly to count.

"He did it before, outside, and I saw the vapor." He closed his helmet abruptly and motioned McMenamin to do the same. She frowned and shook her head. He opened his helmet again. "It might be poisonous!"

"I don't think so," said McMenamin. "Anyway, we've got to try something." She walked toward the green egg. It rolled away from her, and she went past it into the bedroom.

In a minute she reappeared, carrying an armload of plastic boxes and bottles. She came back to Roget and knelt on the floor, lining up the containers with their nipples toward the egg.

"What's this for?" Roget demanded. "Listen, we've got to figure some way of getting out of here. The ship's being eaten up—"

"Wait," said McMenamin. She reached down and squeezed three of the nipples quickly, one after the other. There was a tiny spray of face powder, then one of cologne (*Nuit Juvienne*), followed by a jet of good Scotch.

Then she waited. Roget was about to open his mouth when

another blast of unfamiliar odors came from the egg. This time there were only three: two sweet ones and one sharp.

McMenamin smiled. "I'm going to name him Stinky," she said. She pressed the nipples again, in a different order. Scotch, face powder, *Nuit Juvienne*. The egg replied: sharp, sweet, sweet.

She gave him the remaining combination, and he echoed it; then she put a record cylinder on the floor and squirted the face powder. She added another cylinder and squeezed the cologne. She went along the line that way, releasing a smell for each cylinder until there were ten. The egg had responded, recognizably in some cases, to each one. Then she took away seven of the cylinders and looked expectantly at the egg.

The egg released a sharp odor.

"If ever we tell anybody," said Roget in an awed tone, "that you taught a six-foot Easter egg to count to ten by selected flatulence—"

"Hush, fool," she said, "this is a tough one."

She lined up three cylinders, waited for the sharp odor, then added six more to make three rows of three. The egg obliged with a penetrating smell which was a good imitation of citron extract, Frances' number nine. He followed it immediately with another of his own rapid, complicated series of smells.

"He gets it," said McMenamin. "I think he just told us that three times three are nine." She stood up. "You go out first, Leo. I'll put him out after you and then follow. There's something more we've got to show him before we let him go."

Roget followed orders. When the egg came out and kept on going, he stepped in its path and held it back. Then he moved away, hoping the thing would get the idea that they weren't trying to force it, but wanted it to stay. The egg wobbled indecisively for a moment, and then stayed where it was. Frances came out the next minute, carrying one of the plastic boxes and a portable flashlight.

"My nicest powder," she said regretfully, "but it was the only thing I could find enough of." She clapped her gloved hands together sharply, with the box between them. It burst, and a haze of particles spread around them, glowing faintly in the sunlight.

The egg was still waiting, somehow giving the impression that it was watching them alertly. McMenamin flicked on the flashlight and pointed it at Roget. It made a clear, narrow path in the haze of dispersed particles. Then she turned it on herself, on the ship, and finally upward, toward the tiny blue disk that was Earth. She did it twice more, then stepped back toward the airlock, and Roget followed her.

They stood watching as Tommy scurried off across the hull, squeezed himself into it and disappeared.

"That was impressive," Roget said, "but I wonder just how much good it's going to do us."

"He knows we're alive, intelligent, friendly, and that we come from Earth," said McMenamin thoughtfully. "Or, anyhow, we did our best to tell him. That's all we can do. Maybe he won't want to help us; maybe he can't. But it's up to him now."

III

The mental state of Tommy, as he dived through the hull of the ship and into the nearest radial corridor, would be difficult to describe fully to any human being. He was the equivalent of a very small boy—that approximation still holds good—and he had the obvious reactions to novelty and adventure. But there was a good deal more. He had seen living, intelligent beings of an unfamiliar shape and substance, who lived in metal and had some connection with one of those enormous, enigmatic ships called planets, which no captain of his own race dared approach.

And yet Tommy *knew*, with all the weight of knowledge accumulated, codified, and transmitted over a span measured in billions of years, that there was no other intelligent race than his own in the entire universe, that metal, though life-giving, could not itself be alive, and that no living creature, having the ill luck to be spawned aboard a planet, could ever hope to escape so tremendous a gravitational field.

The final result of all this was that Tommy desperately wanted to go somewhere by himself and think. But he couldn't; he had to keep moving, in time with the scanning waves along the corridor, and he had to give all his mental energy to the problem of slipping past the search party.

The question was—how long had he been gone? If they had

reached the hull while he was inside the metal thing, they might have looked for him outside and concluded that he had somehow slipped past them, back to the center of the ship. In that case, they would probably be working their way back, and he had only to follow them to the axis and hide in a chamber as soon as they left it. But if they were still working outward, his chances of escape were almost nil. And now it seemed more important to escape than it had before.

There was one possibility which Tommy, who, in most circumstances, would try anything, hated to think about. Fuel lines—tubes carrying the rushing, radiant ion vapor that powered the ship—adjoined many of these corridors, and it was certain that if he dared to enter one, he would be perfectly safe from detection as long as he remained in it. But, for one thing, these lines radiated from the ship's axis and none of them would take him where he wanted to go. For another, they were the most dangerous places aboard ship. Older crew members sometimes entered them to make emergency repairs, but they got out as quickly as they could. Tommy did not know how long he could survive there; he had an unpleasant conviction that it would not be long.

Only a few yards up the corridor was the sealed sphincter which gave entrance to such a tube. Tommy looked at it indecisively as the motion of the scanning waves brought him nearer. He had still not made up his mind when he caught a flicker reflected around the curve of the corridor behind him.

Tommy squeezed himself closer to the wall and watched the other end of the corridor approach with agonizing slowness. If he could only get around that corner . . .

The flicker of motion was repeated, and then he saw a thin rind of green poke into view. There was no more time to consider entering the fuel line, no time to let the scanning waves' movement carry him around the corner. Tommy put on full speed, cutting across the next wave and down the cross corridor ahead.

Instantly the Captain's voice shouted from the wall: "Ah! Was that him, the dirty scut? After him, lads!"

Tommy glanced behind as he turned another corner, and his heart sank. It was no cabin boy who was behind him, or even an Ordinary, but a Third Mate—so huge that he filled nearly half the width of the corridor, and so powerful that Tommy, in comparison, was like a boy on a bicycle racing an express train.

He turned another corner, realizing in that instant that he was as good as caught: the new corridor ahead of him stretched straight and without a break for three hundred yards. As he flashed down it, the hulk of the Mate appeared around the bend behind. The Captain's voice bellowed, "Get the little essence of putrescence!"

The Mate was coming up with terrifying speed, and Tommy had time for only one last desperate spurt. Then the other body slammed with stunning force against his, and he was held fast.

As they coasted to a halt, the Captain's voice rumbled from the wall: "*That's* it, mister. Hold him where I can see him!"

The scanning areas were stationary now. The Mate moved Tommy forward until he was squarely in range of the nearest.

Tommy squirmed futilely. The Captain said, "*There's* our little jokester. It's a pure pleasure to see you again, Tommy. What—no witty remarks? Your humor all dried up?"

Tommy gasped, "Hope you enjoyed your nap, Captain."

"Very good," said the Captain with heavy sarcasm. "Oh, *very* entertaining, Tommy. Now would you have anything more to say, before I put the whips to you?"

Tommy was silent.

The Captain said to the Mate, "Nice work, mister. You'll get extra rations for this."

The Mate spoke for the first time, and Tommy recognized his high, affected voice. It was George Adkins—to choose a name only for identification purposes—who had recently spored and was so proud of the new life inside his body that there was no living with him. George said prissily, "Thank you, sir, I'm sure. Of course, I really shouldn't have exerted myself the way I just did, in my state."

"Well, you'll be compensated for it," the Captain said testily. "Now take the humorist down to Assembly Five. We'll have a little ceremony there."

"Yes, sir," said the Mate distantly. He moved off, shoving Tommy ahead of him, and dived into the first turning that led downward.

They moved along in silence for the better part of a mile, crossing from one lesser passage to another until they reached a main artery that led directly to the center of the ship. The scanning waves were still stationary, and they were moving so swiftly that there was no danger of being overheard. Tommy said politely, "You won't let them be too hard on me, will you, sir?"

The Mate did not reply for a moment. He had been baited by Tommy's mock courtesy before, and he was as wary as his limited intelligence allowed. Finally he said, "You'll get no more than what's coming to you, young Tom."

"Yes, sir. I know that, sir. I'm sorry I made you exert yourself, sir, in your condition and all."

"You should be," said the Mate stiffly, but his voice betrayed his pleasure. It was seldom enough that even a cabin boy showed a decent interest in the Mate's prospective parenthood. "They're moving about, you know," he added, unbending a little.

"Are they, sir? Oh, you must be careful of yourself, sir. How many are there, please, sir?"

"Twenty-eight," said the Mate, as he had on every possible occasion for the past two weeks. "Strong and healthy—so far."

"That's remarkable, sir!" cried Tommy. "Twenty-eight! If I might be so bold, sir, you ought to be careful of what you eat. Is the Captain going to give you your extra rations out of that mass he just brought in topside, sir?"

"I'm sure *I* don't know."

"Gosh!" exclaimed Tommy. "I wish I could be sure . . ."

He let the pause grow. Finally the Mate said querulously, "What do you mean? Is there anything wrong with the metal?"

"I don't really know, sir, but it isn't like any we ever had before. That is," Tommy added, "since I was spored, sir."

"Naturally," said the Mate. "*I've* eaten all kinds myself, you know."

"Yes, sir. But doesn't it usually come in ragged shapes, sir, and darkish?"

"Of course it does. Everybody knows that. Metal is nonliving, and only living things have regular shapes."

"Yes, sir. But I was topside, sir, while I was trying to get away, and I saw this metal. It's quite regular, except for some knobs at one end, sir, and it's as smooth as you are, sir, and shiny. If you'll forgive me, sir, it didn't look at all appetizing to me."

"Nonsense," said the Mate uncertainly. "Nonsense," he repeated, in a stronger tone. "You must have been mistaken. Metal can't be alive."

"That's just what I thought, sir," said Tommy excitedly. "But there are live things in this metal, sir. I saw them. And the metal wasn't just floating along the way it's supposed to, sir. I saw it when the Captain brought it down, and– But I'm afraid you'll think I'm lying, sir, if I tell you what it was doing."

"Well, what was it doing?"

"I swear I saw it, sir," Tommy went on. "The Captain will tell you the same thing, sir, if you ask him–he must have noticed."

"Sterilize it all, what *was* it doing?"

Tommy lowered his voice. "There was an ion trail shooting from it, sir. It was trying to get away!"

While the Mate was trying to absorb that, they reached the bottom of the corridor and entered the vast globular space of Assembly Five, lined with crewmen waiting to witness the punishment of Tommy Loy.

This was not going to be any fun at all, thought Tommy, but at least he had paid back the Third Mate in full measure. The Mate, for the moment, at any rate, was not taking any joy in his promised extra rations.

When it was over, Tommy huddled in a corner of the crew compartment where they had tossed him, bruised and smarting in every nerve, shaken by the beating he had undergone. The pain was still rolling through him in faint, uncontrollable waves, and he winced at each one, in spite of himself, as though it were the original blow.

In the back of his mind, the puzzle of the metal ship was still calling, but the other experience was too fresh, the remembered images too vivid.

The Captain had begun, as always, by reciting the Creed.

In the beginning was the Spore, and the Spore was lone.

(And the crew: *Praised be the Spore!*)

Next there was light, and the light was good. Yea, good for the Spore and the Spore's First Children.

(*Praised be they!*)

But the light grew evil in the days of the Spore's Second Children.

(Woe unto them!)

And the light cast them out. Yea, exiled were they, into the darkness and the Great Deep.

(Pity for the outcasts in the Great Deep!)

Tommy had mumbled his response with the rest of them, thinking rebellious thoughts. There was nothing evil about light; they lived by it still. What must have happened—the Captain himself admitted as much when he taught history and natural science classes—was that the earliest ancestors of the race, spawned in the flaming heart of the Galaxy, had grown too efficient for their own good.

They had specialized, more and more, in extracting energy from starlight and the random metal and other elements they encountered in space; and at last they absorbed, willy-nilly, more than they could use. So they had moved, gradually and naturally, over many generations, out from that intensely radiating region into the "Great Deep"—the universe of thinly scattered stars. And the process had continued, inevitably; as the level of available energy fell, their absorption of it grew more and more efficient.

Now, not only could they never return to their birthplace, but they could not even approach a single sun as closely as some planets did. Therefore the planets, and the stars themselves, were objects of fear. That was natural and sensible. But why did they have to continue this silly ritual, invented by some half-evolved, superstitious ancestor, of "outcasts" and "evil"?

The Captain finished:

Save us from the Death that lies in the Great Deep . . .

(The creeping Death that lies in the Great Deep!)

And keep our minds pure . . .

(As pure as the light in the days of the Spore, blessed be He!)

And our course straight . . .

(As straight as the light, brothers!)

That we may meet our lost brothers again in the Day of Reuniting.

(Speed that day!)

Then the pause, the silence that grew until it was like the

silence of the space. At last the Captain spoke again, pronouncing judgment against Tommy, ending:

"Let him be whipped!"

Tommy tensed himself, thickening his skin, drawing his body into the smallest possible compass. Two husky Ordinaries seized him and tossed him at a third. As Tommy floated across the room, the crewman pressed himself tightly against the wall, drawing power from it until he could contain no more. And as Tommy neared him, he discharged it in a crackling arc that filled Tommy's body with the pure essence of pain, and sent him hurtling across the chamber to the next shock—and the next —and the next—

Until the Captain boomed, "Enough!" and they had carried him out and left him here alone.

He heard the voices of crewmen as they drew their rations. One of them was grumbling about the taste, and another, sounding happily bloated, was telling him to shut up and eat, that metal was metal.

That would be the new metal, however much of it had been absorbed by now, mingled with the old in the reservoir. Tommy wondered briefly how much of it there was, and whether the alien ship—if it *was* a ship—could repair even a little damage to itself. But that assumed life in the metal and, in spite of what he had seen, Tommy couldn't believe in it. It seemed beyond question, though, that there were living things inside the metal; and when the metal was gone, how would they live?

Tommy imagined himself set adrift from the ship, alone in space, radiating more heat than his tiny volume could absorb. He shuddered.

He thought again of the problem that had obsessed him ever since he had seen the alien, five-pointed creatures in the metal ship. Intelligent life was supposed to be sacred. That was part of the Creed, and it was stated in a sloppy, poetic way like the rest of it, but it made a certain kind of sense. No crewman or Captain had the right to destroy another for his benefit, because the same heredity was in them all. They were all potentially the same, none better than another.

And you ate metal, because metal was nonliving and certainly not intelligent. But if that stopped being true?

Tommy felt he was missing something. Then he had it:

In the alien ship, trying to talk to the creatures that lived in metal, he had been scared almost scentless, but underneath the fright and the excitement he had felt wonderful. It had been, he realized suddenly, like the mystic completion that was supposed to come when all the straight lines met, in the "Day of Reuniting"—when all the far-flung ships, parted for all the billions of years of their flight, came together at last. It was talking to someone different from yourself.

He wanted to talk again to the aliens, teach them to form their uncouth sounds into words, learn from them . . . Vague images swirled in his mind. They were products of an utterly different line of evolution. Who knew what they might be able to teach him?

And now the dilemma took shape. If his own ship absorbed the metal of theirs, they would die; therefore he would have to make the Captain let them go. But if he somehow managed to set them free, they would leave and he would never see them again.

A petty officer looked into the cubicle and said, "All right, Loy, out of it. You're on garbage detail. You eat after you work, if there's anything left. Lively, now!"

Tommy moved thoughtfully out into the corridor, his pain almost forgotten. The philosophical problems presented by the alien ship, too, having no apparent solution, were receding from his mind. A new thought was taking their place, one that made him glow inside with the pure rapture of the devoted practical jokester.

The whipping he was certainly going to get—and, so soon after the last offense, it would be a beauty—scarcely entered his mind.

IV

Roget climbed in, opening his helmet, and sat down warily in the acceleration couch. He didn't look at the woman.

McMenamin said quietly, "Bad?"

"Not good. The outer skin's gone all across that area, and it's eating into the lead sheathing. The tubes are holding up pretty well, but they'll be next."

"We've done as much as we can by rolling the ship around?"

"Just about. I'll keep at it, but I don't see how it can be more than a few hours before the tubes go. Then we're cooked, whatever your fragrant little friend does."

He stood up abruptly and climbed over the slanting wall which was now their floor, to peer out the direct-view port. He swore slowly and bitterly. "You try the radio again while I was out?" he asked.

"Yes." She did not bother to add that there had been no response. Here, almost halfway between the orbits of Earth and Mars, they were hopelessly out of touch. A ship as small as theirs couldn't carry equipment enough to bridge the distance.

Roget turned around, said, "By God," and then clenched his jaw and strode out of the room. McMenamin heard him walk through the bedroom and clatter around in the storage compartment behind.

In a few moments he was back with a welding torch in his hand. "Should have thought of this before," he said. "I don't know what'll happen if I cut into that hull—damn thing may explode, for all I know—but it's better than sitting doing nothing." He put his helmet down with a bang and his voice came tinnily in her helmet receiver. "Be back in a minute."

"Be careful," McMenamin said again.

Roget closed the outer lock door behind him and looked at the ravished hull of the ship. The metal had been eaten away in a broad band all around the ship, just above the tail, as if a child had bitten around the small end of a pear. In places the clustered rocket tubes showed through like gnawed bones. He felt a renewed surge of anger, with fear deep under it.

A hundred years ago, he reminded himself, the earliest space voyagers had encountered situations as bad as this one, maybe worse. But Roget was a city man, bred for city virtues. He didn't, he decided, know quite how to feel or act. What were you supposed to do when you were about to die, fifteen million miles from home? Try to calm McMenamin—who was dangerously calm already—or show your true nobility by making one of those death-bed speeches you read in the popular histories? What about suggesting a little suicide pact? There was nothing in the ship that would give them a cleaner death than the one ahead of them. About all he could do would be to stab Frances, then himself, with a screwdriver.

Her voice said in the earphones, "You all right?"

He said, "Sure. Just going to try it." He lowered himself to the green surface, careful not to let his knees touch the dark, corrosive area. The torch was a small, easily manageable tool. He pointed the snout at the dark area where it lapped up over the hull, turned the switch on and pressed the button. Flame leaped out, washing over the dark surface. Roget felt the heat through his suit. He turned off the torch to see what effect it had had.

There was a deep, charred pit in the dark stuff, and it seemed to him that it had pulled back a little from the area it was attacking. It was more than he had expected. Encouraged, he tried again.

There was a sudden tremor under him and he leaped nervously to his feet, just in time to avoid the corrosive wave as it rolled under him. For a moment he was only conscious of the thick metal of his boot soles and the thinness of the fabric that covered his knees; then, as he was about to step back out of the way, he realized that it was not only the dark ring that had expanded, that was still expanding.

He moved jerkily—too late—as the pale center area swept toward and under him. Then he felt as if he had been struck by a mighty hammer.

His ears rang, and there was a mist in front of his eyes. He blinked, tried to raise an arm. It seemed to be stuck fast at the wrist and elbow. Panicked, he tried to push himself away and couldn't. As his vision cleared, he saw that he was spread-eagled on the pale disk that had spread out under him. The metal collars of his wrist and elbow joints, all the metal parts of his suit, were held immovably. The torch lay a few inches away from his right hand.

For a few moments, incredulously, Roget still tried to move. Then he stopped and lay in the prison of his suit, looking at the greenish cream surface under his helmet.

Frances' voice said abruptly, "Leo, is anything wrong?"

Roget felt an instant relief that left him shaken and weak. His forehead was cold. He said after a moment, "Pulled a damn fool trick, Frances. Come out and help me if you can."

He heard a click as her helmet went down. He added anxiously, "But don't come near the pale part, or you'll get caught too."

After a while she said, "Darling, I can't think of anything to do."

Roget was feeling calmer, somehow not much afraid any more. He wondered how much oxygen was left in his suit. Not more than an hour, he thought. He said, "I know. I can't either."

Later he called, "Frances?"

"Yes?"

"Roll the ship once in a while, will you? Might get through to the wiring or something, otherwise."

". . . All right."

After that, they didn't talk. There was a great deal to be said, but it was too late to say it.

V

Tommy was on garbage detail with nine other unfortunates. It was a messy, hard, unpleasant business, fit only for a cabin boy—collecting waste from the compartment and corridor receptacles and pressing it into standard capsule shapes, then hauling it to the nearest polarizer. But Tommy, under the suspicious eye of the petty officer in charge, worked with an apparent total absorption until they had cleaned out their section of the six inmost levels and were well into the seventh.

This was the best strategic place for Tommy's departure, since it was about midway from axis to hull, and the field of operations of any pursuit was correspondingly broadened. Also, the volume in which they labored had expanded wedgewise as they climbed, and the petty officer, though still determined to watch Tommy, could no longer keep him constantly in view.

Tommy saw the officer disappear around the curve of the corridor, and kept on working busily. He was still at it, with every appearance of innocence and industry, when the officer abruptly popped into sight again about three seconds later.

The officer stared at him with baffled disapproval and said unreasonably, "Come on, come on, Loy. Don't slack."

"Right," said Tommy, and scurried faster.

A moment later Third Mate Adkins hove majestically into view. The petty officer turned respectfully to face him.

"Keeping young Tom well occupied, I see," said the Mate.

"Yes, sir," said the officer. "Appears to be a reformed character, now, sir. Must have learned a lesson, one way or another."

"Ha!" said the Mate. "Very good. Oh, Loy, you might be interested in this—the Captain himself has told me that the new metal is perfectly all right. Unusually rich, in fact. I've had my first ration already—very good it was, too—and I'm going to get my extras in half an hour or so. Well, good appetite, all." And, while the lesser crewmen clustered against the walls to give him room, he moved haughtily off down the corridor.

Tommy kept on working as fast as he could. He was draining energy he might need later, but it was necessary to quiet the petty officer's suspicions entirely, in order to give himself a decent start. In addition, his artist's soul demanded it. Tommy, in his own way, was a perfectionist.

Third Mate Adkins was due to get his extras in about half an hour, and if Tommy knew the Captain's habits, the Captain would be taking his first meal from the newly replenished reservoir at about the same time. That set the deadline. Before the half hour was up, Tommy would have to cut off the flow of the new metal, so that stomachs which had been gurgling in anticipation would remain desolately void until the next windfall.

The Mate, in spite of his hypochondria, was a glutton. With any luck, this would make him bitter for a month. And the Old Man— But it was better not to dwell on that.

The petty officer hung around irresolutely for another ten minutes, then dashed off down the corridor to attend to the rest of his detail. Without wasting a moment, Tommy dropped the capsule he had just collected and shot away in the other direction.

The rest of the cabin boys, as fearful of Tommy as they were of constituted authority, would not dare to raise an outcry until they spotted the officer coming back. The officer, because of the time he had wasted in watching Tommy, would have to administer a thorough lecture on slackness to the rest of the detail before he returned.

Tommy had calculated his probable margin to a nicety, and it was enough, barring accidents, to get him safely away. Nevertheless, he turned and twisted from one system of corridors to another, carefully confusing his trail before he set himself to put as much vertical distance behind him as he could.

This part of the game had to be accomplished in a fury of action, for he was free to move in the corridors only until the Captain was informed that he was loose again. After that, he had to play hounds and hares with the moving strips through which the Captain could see him.

When the time he had estimated was three quarters gone, Tommy slowed and came to a halt. He inspected the corridor wall minutely and found the almost imperceptible trace that showed where the scanning wave nearest him had stopped it. He jockeyed his body clear of it, and then waited. He still had a good distance to cover before he dared play his trump, but it was not safe to move now; he had to wait for the Captain's move.

It came soon enough: the scanning waves erupted into simultaneous motion and anger. "Tommy!" they bellowed. "Tommy Loy! Come back, you unmentionable excrescence, or by Spore you'll regret it! Tommy!"

Moving between waves, Tommy waited patiently until their motion carried him from one corridor to another. The Captain's control over the waves was not complete: in some corridors they moved two steps upward for one down, in others the reverse. When he got into a downward corridor, Tommy scrambled out of it again as soon as he could and started over.

Gradually, with many false starts, he worked his way up to the thirteenth level, one level short of the hull.

Now came the hard part. This time he had to enter the fuel lines, not only for sure escape, but to gather the force he needed. And for the first time in his life, Tommy hesitated before something that he had set himself to do.

Death was a phenomenon that normally touched each member of Tommy's race only once—only Captains died, and they died alone. For lesser members of the crew, there was almost no mortal danger; the ship protected them. But Tommy knew what death was, and as the sealed entrance to the fuel line swung into view, he knew that he faced it.

He made himself small, as he had under the lash. He broke the seal. Quickly, before the following wave could catch him, he thrust himself through the sphincter.

The blast of ions gripped him, flung him forward, hurting him like a hundred whips. Desperately he held himself together, thickening his insulating shell against that deadly flux of energy; but still his body absorbed it, till he felt a horrid fullness. The walls of the tube fled past him, barely perceptible in the rush of glowing haze. Tommy held in that growing tautness with his last strength, meanwhile looking for an exit. He neither knew nor cared whether he had reached his goal; he had to get out or die.

He saw a dim oval on the wall ahead, hurled himself at it, clung, and forced his body through.

He was in a horizontal corridor, just under the hull. He drank the blessed coolness of it for an instant, before moving to the nearest sphincter. Then he was out, under the velvet-black sky and the diamond blaze of stars.

He looked around. The pain was fading now; he felt only an atrocious bloatedness that tightened his skin and made all his movements halting. Forward of him, up the long shallow curve of the hull, he could see the alien ship, and the two five-pointed creatures beside it. Carefully, keeping a few feet between himself and the hull, he headed toward it.

One of the creatures was sprawled flat on the polarizer that had brought its ship down. The other, standing beside it, turned as Tommy came near, and two of its upper three points moved in an insane fashion that made Tommy feel ill. He looked away quickly and moved past them, till he was directly over the center of the polarizer and only a few inches away. Then, with a sob of relief, he released the energy his body had stored. In one thick, white bolt, it sparked to the polarizer's center.

Shaken and spent, Tommy floated upward and surveyed what he had done. The muzzle of the polarizer was contracting, puckering at the center, the dark corrosive ring following it in. So much energy, applied in one jolt, must have shorted and paralyzed it all the way back to the ship's nerve center. The Captain, Tommy thought wryly, would be jumping now!

And he wasn't done yet. Tommy took one last look at the aliens and their ship. The sprawled one was up now, and the two of them had their upper points twined around each other in a nauseating fashion. Then they parted suddenly, and, facing

Tommy, wiggled their free points. Tommy moved purposefully off across the width of the ship, heading for the three heavy-duty polarizers.

He had to go in again through that hell not once more, but twice. Though his nerves shrank from the necessity, there was no way of avoiding it. For the ship could not alter its course, except by allowing itself to be attracted by a sun or other large body—which was unthinkable—or it could rotate at the Captain's will. The aliens were free now, but the Captain had only to spin ship in order to snare them again.

Four miles away, Tommy found the second polarizer. He backed away a carefully calculated distance before he re-entered the hull. At least he could know in advance how far he had to go—and he knew now, too, that the energy he had stored the first time had been adequate twice over. He rested a few moments; then, like a diver plunging into a torrent, he thrust himself into the fuel line.

He came out again, shuddering with pain, and pushed himself through the exit. He felt as bloated as he had before. The charge of energy was not as great, but Tommy knew that he was weakening. This time, when he discharged over the polarizer and watched it contract into a tiny, puckered mass, he felt as if he could never move again, let alone expose himself once more to that tunnel of flame.

The stars, he realized dully, were moving in slow, ponderous arcs over his head. The Captain was spinning ship. Tommy sank to the hull and lay motionless, watching half-attentively for a sight of the alien ship.

There it was, a bright dot haloed by the flame of its exhaust. It swung around slowly, gradually, with the rest of the firmament, growing smaller slowly.

"He'll get them before they're out of range," Tommy thought. He watched as the bright dot climbed overhead, began to fall on the other side.

The Captain had one polarizer left. It would be enough.

Wearily Tommy rose and followed the bright star. It was not a joke any longer. He would willingly have gone inside to the bright, warm, familiar corridors that led downward to safety and deserved punishment. But somehow he could not bear to think of those fascinating creatures—those wonderful playthings—going to fill the Captain's fat belly.

Tommy followed the ship until he could see the pale gleam of the functioning polarizer. Then he crawled through the hull once more, and again he found a sealed entrance to the fuel tube. He did not let himself think about it. His mind was numb already, and he pushed himself through uncaring, as condemned criminals often go carelessly to execution.

This time it was worse than ever before; he had not dreamed that it could be so bad. His vision dimmed and he could barely see the exit, or feel its pressure, when he dragged himself out. Lurching drunkenly, he passed a scanning wave on his way to the hull sphincter, and heard the Captain's voice explode.

Outside, ragged black patches obscured his vision of the stars. The pressure inside him pressed painfully outward, again and again, and each time he held it back. Then he felt rather than saw that he was over the pale disk, and as he let go the bolt he lost consciousness.

When his vision cleared, the alien ship was still above him, alarmingly close. The Captain must have had it almost reeled in again, he thought, when he had let go that last charge.

Flaming, it receded into the Great Deep, and he watched it go until it shrank beyond his vision to follow.

He felt a great peace and a great weariness. The tiny blue disk that was a planet had moved its apparent position a little nearer its star. The aliens were going back there, to their unimaginable home, and Tommy's ship was forging onward into new depths of darkness—toward the edge of the Galaxy and the greatest Deep.

He moved to the nearest sphincter as the cold bit at him. His spirits lifted suddenly as he thought of those three stabs of energy, equally spaced around the twelve-mile perimeter of the ship. The Captain would be utterly speechless with rage, he thought, like an aged martinet who had had his hands painfully slapped by a small boy.

For, as we warned you, the Captain was not precisely a captain, nor the ship precisely a ship. Ship and Captain were one and the same, hive and queen bee, castle and lord.

In effect, Tommy had circumnavigated the skipper.

9

The Little Terror

WILL F. JENKINS

Here's the giant sequoia of the science fiction world, the hardy perennial, the man to whom mere decades mean nothing.

If sheer longevity is to be considered, Will F. Jenkins is the real thing. Under the pseudonym of Murray Leinster, he has been writing science fiction since before I could read. Indeed, he was writing science fiction before I was born, and I am no longer in my very earliest youth.

This wouldn't be so remarkable in itself if it weren't for the fact that he is still actively writing, still winning awards, still establishing himself as a big name in the field not on the basis of past performance but on that of current deeds.

Nor is Will so advanced in age that he has lost his sense of healthy respect for children.

Or do we all have a kind of respect for them? And fear, too?

Maybe it dates back to the time that a young brother or sister was added to the family and promptly took over. With nothing but a squally red face and a set of unbelievably messy habits, he or she moved in firmly and left big brother and sister resentfully out in the cold.

Nor could an only child escape, if he were a boy. The time would come when the idol of his life, the one and only girl, the angel he had married, would have a precious little bundle of joy, and from that moment on, he, the stalwart husband, would be consigned to play a meager second fiddle.

Of course, children are little terrors, but let Will Jenkins introduce you to one who was a particular little terror.

There was no crashing roll of thunder when the principles of psychological acosmistic idealism became practicalities in the world inhabited by Nancy. Her mother had no twinge of uneasiness, and her father was reading his newspaper. There was no breathless hush over the earth at the bloodcurdling instant, though possibly Bishop Berkeley (1685–1753), up in heaven, was pleasantly interested. Joe Holt, who was a practicing psychiatrist and might be presumed to have a feeling for such things, hadn't the trace of an intuition of it. The skies did not darken suddenly, nor were there deep rumblings underground. There was not even an unnatural gray twilight in which birds chirped faintly and cattle affrightedly rolled their eyes. There was no sign whatever that the most alarming moment in history was at hand. But still . . .

Nancy went to the gate with her grandfather. She was six and he was sixty, and they were very congenial. Nancy skipped, because she never walked when she could skip or, preferably, run. It was nearing dusk, but there was still a ruddy sunshine in the air, yet the sky was perceptibly darkening.

At the gate Nancy permitted her grandfather to kiss her good-bye, in the benign, smug condescension of little girls who know they are irresistible.

Then she said, "Make a penny go away, Granddaddy."

Her grandfather obediently took a copper penny from his pocket. He put it between his thumb and middle finger and offered it gravely for Nancy's inspection. She held her breath. Her grandfather snapped his fingers. The penny vanished.

Nancy beamed. "Do it again, Granddaddy!"

Her grandfather prepared to repeat. Nancy put her eyes within inches of the coin. She watched with rapt fascination.

The penny vanished a second time.

"It's real magic?" asked Nancy hopefully. She was beginning to discover that one could not count on fairy godmothers—not confidently, at any rate—in moments of despair. But still she hoped.

"It's real magic," agreed her grandfather.

"Show me how!" begged Nancy. "Please!"

Her grandfather whispered confidentially in her ear, "I say 'Oogledeboo' and it vanishes. Can you say that?"

Nancy whispered, "Oogledeboo."

"Splendid!" said her grandfather. He straightened up. "Now you say 'Oogledeboo' at this penny, and see what happens!" He held the penny as before, between thumb and middle finger.

Nancy giggled at it. She said, "Oogledeboo!"

Her grandfather's fingers snapped. The penny vanished.

Nancy beamed. "Again, Granddaddy?"

"Once more," conceded her grandfather. He proffered the penny. It was the same one, but Nancy did not reflect upon that. He took it in his fingers. Her eyes sparkled. She said, "Oogledeboo!"

The penny vanished. Her grandfather looked slightly surprised. But it was natural. He had never heard of Bishop Berkeley's dictum that *esse* is *percipi,* nor drawn inferences from the statement. However, he beamed at Nancy.

"Now I have to go, Nancy. Good night."

Nancy waved cheerfully as he walked down the street. When he was out of sight, she skipped back to where she had been playing. She did not notice that her grandfather was shaking his coat sleeve absently, as if to make something come out of it—something that did not come.

Nancy settled down placidly to play alone. There was a caterpillar on the doll she had neglected for her grandfather. Nancy regarded it with disfavor. She said sternly, "Oogledeboo!"

The caterpillar vanished. Nancy played with her doll. The sunset proceeded. Twilight fell. Nancy's mother called her, and she went in cheerfully, dragging the doll by one arm. She ate her supper with excellent appetite and beamed at her father and mother. There was only one alarming incident, and it happened to pass unnoticed. Nancy did not want to finish her milk. Her mother said firmly that she must. Then the telephone rang, and her mother got up to answer it.

Nancy looked confidently at the milk in her glass and said, "Oogledeboo."

The milk vanished.

Nancy went happily to bed later, after kissing her father and mother with extravagant affection. She went dreamlessly and placidly to sleep. She slept blissfully all night long.

All was serene through all the cosmos. There was no hint of the appalling thing that had happened. Nobody cringed in nameless horror. Nobody trembled in justified apprehension. Nobody, it appears, happened to be thinking of the Right Reverend George Berkeley, of the Anglican Church, who wrote books of philosophy and died in 1753.

Nancy woke next morning in her customary ebullient mood. She sang lustily as she was dressed, and there was no hint of disturbance until breakfast was served. Then there was a slight collision of wills over Nancy's reluctance to eat her cereal. But just then the milkman came to collect, and her mother went to pay him. When her mother came back, the cereal bowl was quite empty. Nancy's mother praised her warmly. Nancy giggled.

It was a charming morning. Nancy, scrubbed to radiance and wearing a playsuit of healthful brevity, went out to play in her sand box behind the house. She sang as she played. She was a delightfully happy child. Presently Charles, the little boy next door, came over to play with her. She greeted him with that cordial suspicion with which little girls regard little boys. He stepped on a sand house she had decorated with small stray sticks and cherished bottle caps. She scolded.

"Huh!" said Charles scornfully. "That's no fun! Let's play going to the moon. Let's fight the cat men. Rnnnnnnnh! Bang-bang!"

Nancy demurred.

"Let's play spaceship," insisted Charles. He began to hop excitedly. He shouted, "Whoooooooom! Three gravs! Four! Turn on the stern rockets! Whoooooooooooom! There come the space pirates! Warm up the disintegrators! Shoot the space warp! Bang! Bang! Rnnnnnnnnnnh! Bang!"

He rushed about madly, fighting a splendid space battle with space pirates from the rings of Saturn, while Nancy placidly practiced interior decorating in her sandpile. She set a wilted buttercup on a dab of sand which to her represented a sideboard—undoubtedly Sheraton. She reflectively arranged another dab of sand into a luxurious sofa. She began to smooth out wall-to-wall carpeting, with the intent to add a grandfather's clock next to her sandpile scheme for gracious living.

Charles got into difficulties. A fleet of black spaceships from Sirius winked into existence from the fourth dimension over by the back-porch steps. They sped toward him, disintegrator rays flaming. He flashed into faster-than-light attack, throwing out atomic bombs and with tractor and pressor beams busy. Then came a despairing call from an Earth passenger spaceliner under attack by pirates near the hydrangea bush.

"Whoooooooom!" shouted Charles ferociously. "Coming, Earthship, with all jets firing! Rnnnnnnnnh! Take that! And that! Bang! Bang! Here's an H-bomb for you! Boom!"

Disaster struck. Charles, rushing to the defense of the helpless passenger craft, cut across the sandpile. One sandaled foot landed in the kitchen of Nancy's ranch-type sandhouse. Kitchen sink, dishwasher, and breakfast nook—they were marked by rather wobbly lines of pebbles—were obliterated as if by collision with a giant meteor in space. Sand sprayed on Nancy.

"Bang, bang!" roared Charles in his high treble. "Rnnnnnnnh! Take that, you old pirates! Calling Earth! Space-patrol ship reporting pirates wiped out! I'm taking off for Pluto!"

Nancy trembled with indignation. She said sternly, "You go home!"

"Huh?" said Charles. He stopped short. "I'm Captain Space! I've got to fight space pirates and things, haven't I?"

"You go home!" said Nancy sternly. "You stepped on my house! You go home or I'll say something at you!"

If she had threatened to tell her mother on him, it might have been effective. But this threat had no meaning to Charles. He shouted. "Whoooooom! Taking off for Pluto! Invaders from space! Coming, Earth garrison! Hold on, I'm coming with all jets firing! Whooooom!"

He started for Pluto. Unfortunately it appeared that Pluto lay somewhere in the general direction of a yellow tea-rose bush at the edge of the lawn. Charles's orbit would coincide with the sandpile again.

Nancy said vengefully, "Oogledeboo!"

Charles vanished.

Silence fell, and Nancy returned to the building of a sandpile ranchhouse. Presently she sang happily as she worked. Presently, again, she went into the house and asked for cookies. Having skipped her breakfast cereal, she was hungry.

Her mother said, "Where's Charles? Didn't I hear him playing with you?"

Nancy bit into a cooky and said placidly, "I said 'Oogledeboo' at him and he went away."

Nancy's mother smiled absently and went about what she thought were more important affairs. Which was a mistake. There were no more important affairs. According to the principles laid down by Bishop Berkeley between 1685 and 1753, things exist because a mind thinks of them as existing. Nancy had acquired the ability to think confidently of things as ceasing to exist—a gift no adult can acquire. So—by a natural extrapolation of Bishop Berkeley's principle—when she thought of something as ceasing to exist, it did. All of us have wished for such a talent at some time or another, but Nancy had it.

When she was at lunch, the voice of Charles's mother could be heard, calling him. He did not answer, and presently she was at the door. Nancy had arrived at the custard-with-strawberry-jam stage of her lunch then, and she worked zestfully with a spoon. Her mother went to confer with Charles's mother about his whereabouts.

"Why, no," Nancy heard her say. "He was playing with Nancy, but he left." She called, "Nancy! Do you know where Charles went?"

"No, Mother-r!" Nancy sang out happily. She worked further on the custard. She was absorbed.

There was talk at the door. Nancy got some strawberry jam on the large napkin her mother spread over her at mealtime. She was enjoyably licking it off when her mother returned.

"Charles's mother is worried," said Nancy's mother. She frowned a little. "He doesn't usually wander away. You're sure you didn't notice which way he went?" Nancy shook her head. "He didn't go with anybody?" her mother asked uneasily.

Nancy got a big spoonful of custard. "No," she said placidly. "I said 'Oogledeboo' at him and he went away."

Her mother did not inquire further. But she looked unhappy. A parent of a small child always shares the anguish of another parent when a small child can't be found. But it didn't occur to Nancy's mother that she might have heard a complete and accurate description of Charles's disappearance.

Immediately after lunch Nancy's mother dressed her up to go downtown. There was to be a parade, and Nancy's mother was making the sacrifice of an afternoon to Nancy's pleasure. Of course Nancy loathed being dragged through stores, but since her mother was devoting an entire afternoon to her, it was only reasonable that they should start early, to do some shopping, and do more shopping later. This is what is called thinking only of one's children.

Nancy had no forebodings. She adored being dressed up, and wriggled with pleasure as her mother attired her in a very frilly dress, a very frilly hat, a smart little coat, and tiny white gloves which to Nancy were the ultimate of bliss. She sang and paraded before a mirror as her mother prepared for the outing.

She sang, also, as her mother drove downtown. When the traffic grew thick and they stopped at traffic lights, Nancy continued to sing lustily and without self-consciousness. People looked at her and smiled, thinking of innocent and happy childhood.

There were mobs in every store. Other self-sacrificing mothers were out to show their children the parade. They constituted an outrageous crush by a ladies'-purse counter. A fat woman jammed Nancy against a counter. She was enraged. Somebody protested, and the fat woman turned indignantly, and in pivoting, that protruding part of her body which was at the height of Nancy's six-year-old head sent Nancy reeling.

Nancy said wrathfully, "Oogledeboo!"

There was no fat woman.

Somebody screamed in a stifled fashion. But nobody believed it. There was a surging of bodies to fill the space where a fat woman had been, and Nancy was banged again and wailed, and grabbed her mother hysterically by the legs.

Her mother completed the purchase of a handbag and harassedly got Nancy out of the crowd. Nancy's frilly hat was dangling and she was very unhappy.

"There, darling!" said her mother penitently. "I shouldn't have brought you into such a crowded place! We'll go upstairs where there won't be so many people."

They got into an elevator. Then a mob charged it. A horde of women resolutely thrust and pushed and shoved, while small children howled. Women are less than ladylike when there are no men around. The elevator operator tried to stem the flood, to no avail.

Nancy was crushed ruthlessly. She became terrified. She gasped, "Oogledeboo!"

There were only five people in the elevator. There was not even a crowd trying to push in.

Nancy's mother trembled for a considerable time after that. Of course it could not possibly be true. Even the elevator operator merely stammered unintelligibly when a floorwalker questioned him. There was nothing to tell. The elevator had been crowded, and suddenly it wasn't. There had been no outcry. The crowd hadn't even visibly faded. It just was—and then it wasn't. So the elevator operator, completely overwrought, was relieved of duty and the floorwalker apologized to the few passengers remaining. They were all remarkably pale, and they all went quickly out of the store. But of course they didn't believe it either. Not even Nancy's mother.

But Nancy felt much better. More confident. Now, she knew placidly, she could always get room around her if people pushed. Her mother drank a cup of tea in the nearest tea room, and tried tremblingly to remember the psychiatric meaning of the delusion that people vanished before one's eyes. But while her mother trembled, Nancy ate a small plate of vanilla ice cream, with relish.

Nancy's mother really wanted to go straight home then. Already she had made up her mind to ask Joe Holt about the experience. He was the only psychiatrist she knew personally, but he and his wife were fairly close friends. She could mention it in an offhand manner, perhaps. But Nancy had been promised the parade. So they saw it.

It began appropriately with motorcycle policemen, at whom Nancy waved enthusiastically. Her mother had been able to get a place at the very curb, so nothing would interfere with Nancy's view. There came a high school band, with drum majorettes strutting in costumes which would have caused their great-grandmothers to die of heart failure. There came a cadet corps. And then the floats.

Nancy was thrilled by a float in the shape of a swan, decorated by young girls in tinsel dresses and fixed smiles. There was a float showing embarrassed Boy Scouts about a campfire. A float resembling a battleship. A Girl Scout float.

There came a traveling squealing down the street. Children's shrill voices shrieked and shouted. Nancy squirmed to look. Her mother held her tightly. But Nancy's mother was thinking desperately that she'd never expected to call on Joe Holt professionally, but, after all, he was a psychiatrist and he played golf with—

Nancy squealed in pure excitement. Her mother looked numbly at the float which caused all the high-pitched tumult. It represented a dragon. It was a very ambitious job. The body of the beast completely hid the truck on which it was built, and a long and ungainly hooped-canvas tail trailed three car-lengths behind. But it was what went on before that caused the excitement.

The dragon had a twenty-foot movable neck of hooped canvas

painted red, with a five-foot head at the end of it. The head had short, blunt horns. It had eyes the size of saucers, and an expression of imbecilic amiability, and smoke came lavishly out of its nostrils. And its head moved from side to side on the movable neck, and it turned coquettishly and seemed to gaze at the spectators wherever it turned with an admirable look of benign imbecility.

Children squealed and shrieked and cheered as the dragon proceeded down the main street. Those at whom it seemed to look shrank back in delighted terror. Those from whom it looked away yelled in sheer excitement.

Nancy trembled in delicious thrill. She jumped up and down. She squealed.

Opposite her, the long, articulated neck swung in her direction. The dragon's head turned toward her. It seemed to look directly at her, in a sort of wall-eyed cordiality. Smoke welled from its nostrils. It swung still closer, as if to take an even closer and even more admiring look.

Nancy said zestfully, "Oogledeboo!"

A smoke pot fell to the pavement and smashed. It scattered strangling, smoldering stuff over five yards of asphalt. A man fell with a clank, landing astride the hood of a battered motor truck which had been hidden by the dragon's body. His expression was that of stunned bewilderment, and he stared at his hands. They had held ropes by which he moved the dragon's neck and head. Now they were empty. There were four men in their undershirts, riding in the truck, and they regarded their public incredulously, because there was no longer a dragon to hide them.

There was, though, an impressive smoldering conflagration on the street. It called for fire engines. They came.

Nancy's mother was in a chaotic state of mind when she managed to fight her way, with Nancy, to where her car was parked. Her expression tended to be on the wild-eyed side, but she got Nancy into the car and herself behind the wheel. Then she doubted frenziedly whether she was in a fit state to drive. She started off, finally, on the dubious premise that somebody who is really crazy never suspects it.

They were late getting home, and Nancy's father was beginning to be worried. He'd been informed of the disappearance of Charles, next door, and of the feverish hunt for him by police and all the neighbors.

He was relieved when Nancy and her mother turned up, but Nancy's mother got out of the car and said tautly, "Get Joe Holt to come here at once." Nancy's mother spoke in the level, tense tone of one who is likely to scream in another split second. "He's a psychiatrist. I have to see a psychiatrist. Everything's happened today! Charles disappeared. An elevatorful of people vanished before my eyes, and a dragon faded to nothingness while I was looking at it. Things like that don't happen! I'm going crazy, but maybe Joe Holt can do something! Get him, quick!"

Then she collapsed, blubbering. She was thinking of Nancy. Already she envisioned a broken home, herself a madwoman and divorced, Nancy's father remarried to someone who would be cruel to Nancy, and Nancy haunted by the specter of madness looming ever before her. Nancy's mother did not worry about her husband. Perhaps that was significant.

But Nancy's father knew when not to try to be reasonable. Also, he was frightened. He grabbed the telephone and spoke with such desperate urgency that in five minutes Joe Holt, that rising young psychiatrist, had got into his car, raced the necessary five blocks, and was looking anxiously at Nancy's mother, in his houseslippers and without a necktie.

"What the hell?" asked Joe Holt unprofessionally.

Nobody noticed Nancy. Her mother began to tell her wholly incredible story. Her tone was pure desperation. She suddenly remembered the fat woman. She told about it, shrilly.

Nancy said reassuringly, "But that was all right, Mother-r! I said 'Oogledeboo' at her!"

Her mother paid no heed. Nancy's father moved to take her out of the room. She clung convulsively to her mother, and her mother to her. Nancy's father was in an unenviable spot for a moment, there.

"Don't take her away!" panted her mother despairingly. "Not yet! Wait! . . . And five minutes later an elevatorful of people vanished before my eyes!"

She sobbed suddenly. Nancy's father ran his hands through his hair.

Nancy's voice said consolingly, "But Mother-r, they were

crowding us! That's why I said 'Oogledeboo' at them. Like Charles was bothering me and I said 'Oogledeboo' at him and made him go away."

Her mother's whole body jerked. She stared at Nancy. And then her anguished face smoothed out suddenly. She said in a quiet and interested tone, "Did you, darling?" But she turned tragic eyes upon Joe Holt. "You see, Joe? Listen to her! The things that've happened have turned her little brain too! Don't bother about me, Joe! Do something for Nancy!"

Joe breathed a small sigh of professional relief. All this business was completely bewildering, but he did know that sometimes a woman will do anything for her child—even stay sane, if necessary.

So he said cheerfully to Nancy, "So you made things go away? That's interesting, Nancy. Tell us about it."

Nancy beamed at him. She liked people. They found her irresistible. So she told how her granddaddy had told her how to do magic. One said "Oogledeboo" at things and they went away.

"I said it to the penny," she finished happily, "and to a caterpillar on my doll, and my milk last night, and my cereal this morning, and Charles, and a fat woman, and the people in the elevator, and the dragon. It's easy," she finished generously. "Want me to show you?"

Her mother gasped. But Joe Holt noticed that she wasn't thinking of herself any longer but of Nancy. And as a practical matter, nobody is neurotic who sincerely cares about anybody else. Joe didn't understand anything, but he began to have hope.

"Why, yes, Nancy!" he said blithely. "Make this—h'm—this vase of flowers go away, will you?"

Nancy's mother said involuntarily, "That's my best vase." But then she said calmly, "Yes, darling, make that go away."

So Nancy, blithe and beaming and six years old, looked at her mother's most-prized almost-Ming vase and said happily, "Oogledeboo."

And of course the vase went away.

It was two o'clock in the morning and raining heavily when they got Nancy's grandfather out of bed to answer the bell. Then Nancy's father and Joe Holt crowded inside the door to talk desperately to him with rain-wet, disheveled faces. He stared.

"You've got to come to the house, sir!" said Nancy's father feverishly. "Nancy's got a psychological acosmistic idea from you, and it's got to be cured!"

Joe Holt said reprovingly, if harassedly, "Not idea. Ability. It's a psychokinetic ability."

Nancy's grandfather said in a rising tone, "Nancy's sick? Sick? And you talk? Come on!"

He grabbed an overcoat and flung out of the house, pulling the coat on over his pajamas. Rain poured down. Lightning glinted on it as it fell. They piled into Joe's convertible and he started it off at frantic speed.

Nancy's grandfather snapped, "How's she sick? When did it start?"

"She says 'Oogledeboo' at things!" panted Nancy's father. "And they vanish! We've got her to bed now, but she's got to be cured! Think what she may do next! She says 'Oogledeboo'!"

Nancy's grandfather barked, "Oogledeboo? What's the matter with saying 'Oogledeboo'? I say 'Oogledeboo' if I feel like it! I taught her to say it!"

"That's just it," said Joe Holt, swallowing. He turned to gesticulate. "You showed her that a penny vanished when she said it. She believed it! It's—idealistic immaterialism! . . . Oops!"

He yanked at the wheel and pulled the car out of skid as it headed for a telephone pole aglitter with wetness.

"It was Bishop Berkeley," panted Nancy's father. "Joe just showed me! In a book! Bishop Berkeley said that matter cannot exist without mind. A mind has to perceive something in order for it to exist. It's been a big argument for years. Locke, Hume, Kant, Hegel and all the rest."

The car plunged through a black puddle on the pavement, pockmarked with falling rain under an arc light. Sheets of water, like shining wings, rose on either side of the car.

"*Esse*," said Joe Holt, gulping, "is *percipi*. If a thing isn't perceived by some mind somewhere, it isn't. But when we know something is, we have to let it go at that. Nancy doesn't. You fixed it so she doesn't. When she says 'Oogledeboo' at something, she's able to think of it as ceasing to exist. So it does cease to exist. Nobody else in the world, thank God, can do that! But Nancy can!"

In the racing, leaking car, Nancy's grandfather stared suspiciously at the water-soaked and nerve-racked individuals beside him. His pajama collar rose out of his overcoat. His white hair bristled.

"And you're telling me Nancy's sick!" he roared. "You two lunatics!"

They babbled further details. Preposterous details. They explained what he had to do. Then suddenly Joe Holt swung into the driveway of the house Nancy lived in. As if on signal, the rain stopped. The two younger men piled out of the car and raced into the house. Nancy's grandfather plodded after them. He entered to hear the chattered query, "She's—still asleep?"

"Yes, the darling!" said Nancy's mother in a warm, throaty voice. She hugged Nancy's grandfather. "Daddy! I'm so glad—"

The living room looked like a shambles. The piano was gone. The almost-Ming vase—of course. The picture over the mantel. Two chairs. A scatter rug.

"We experimented!" babbled Joe Holt desperately. "She made the vase vanish. We couldn't believe it. So she said 'Oogledeboo' at the piano. It wasn't there. The picture over the fireplace! It got to be a happy game! She stood there beaming and saying 'Oogledeboo.' She looked at me once—" He shuddered violently.

Nancy's grandfather could not believe. Naturally! But Nancy's mother pleaded with him. The three of them—Nancy's parents and the psychiatrist—argued hysterically. Their voices rose.

Then there was a delighted giggle from the doorway. Nancy stood there, smiling brightly at her grandfather. She wore her very favorite blue pajamas with Mickey Mouse figures printed on them.

She was sleepy-eyed, but very glad to see her grandfather.

"Hello, Granddaddy!" she said happily. "You waked me up. I can do magic like you told me. Want to see?"

Her grandfather gulped suddenly. He had a moment of dreadful doubt. His daughter had turned wholly pale. Nancy's father was speechless. Joe Holt wrung his hands.

"Wait, now," said Nancy's grandfather shakily. "Just try it on a little thing, Nancy. Just a little thing."

With the sure instinct of a grandfather, he remembered that his overcoat was wet. He put it down on a remaining chair before he took Nancy in his arms. Stout elderly man and beaming six-year-old, they made a pleasant picture in their pajamas.

"There, there," said Nancy's grandfather fondly.

"Su-su-suppose," said Joe Holt, "you make your granddaddy's overcoat go away, Nancy?"

Nancy giggled. Her soft, happy voice pronounced the fateful syllables. Her grandfather's overcoat abruptly was not. Her grandfather sat down suddenly. Nancy slipped from his arms to his knee.

She said benignly, "Are you cold, Granddaddy? You're shivering!"

Nancy's grandfather swallowed loudly. Then he said with infinite care, "Why, yes, Nancy. I am cold. I shouldn't have taken off my overcoat. I need it back. Will you get it back for me, Nancy?"

Nancy said fondly, "But I don't know how, Granddaddy!"

"Why—er—you say 'Oogledeboo' backwards, Nancy. But you have to say it. You made my overcoat go away, so you have to make it come back. 'Oogledeboo' backwards is—ah—is—"

"'Oobedelgoo,'" said Nancy's father hoarsely. "'Oogledeboo' spelled backwards is 'Oobedelgoo.' Oobedelgoo!"

Nancy considered, and snuggled against her grandfather. "You say it, Granddaddy!"

"It's no good when I say it," said her grandfather, with false heartiness. "See? Oobedelgoo! But it will work for you! And now— Wait a moment, Nancy! When you say it, don't say it at just my overcoat. You say it at all the things you said 'Oogledeboo' at, all at the same time, and they'll all come back at once. Won't that be nice?"

"No," said Nancy. "Charles bothers me."

Joe Holt moaned.

Nancy's mother said softly, "But he won't anymore, darling! Just say 'Oobe—Oobedelgoo' nicely, darling, for mother, at all the things you said the other word to!"

Nancy considered again. Her mother stroked her hand. And

presently Nancy said, without enthusiasm, without verve, but with a sort of resigned acquiescence, "Oobedelgoo."

The almost-Ming vase came back, and her grandfather's overcoat, and the piano, and the picture over the mantelpiece and a scatter rug, and two chairs. Out on the lawn there was suddenly the howling wail of a scared small boy, "Wa-a-a-ah!" That was Charles, who found himself suddenly in the dark on a rain-wet lawn. He howled. Those in Nancy's house heard doors open next door and shrieks of joy. Nancy's mother closed her eyes and imagined other screams: a fat woman suddenly finding herself alone in the ladies'-purse department of a closed-up department store, an elevatorful of people finding themselves parked in the cellar of the same store, to wait for morning. The nightwatchman of that store would have a busy half hour.

The policeman who suddenly found a dragon in the middle of the street would be upset too, as would the hard-working detectives now busily hunting for a small boy who would insist frantically that he hadn't been anywhere. And he hadn't. He'd been nowhere.

Even a caterpillar, which had been crawling on Nancy's doll until she said "Oogledeboo" at it, would have a difficult time finding a proper place to hide from the rain. It happened to be a diurnal caterpillar, not used to being out at night.

Then Nancy's grandfather spoke with very great care and painstaking charm.

"I forgot to tell you, Nancy," he said with seeming ruefulness, "that now you've said 'Oobedelgoo,' saying 'Oogledeboo' won't work for you any longer. That's why I can't work that magic anymore myself. But you won't mind things not going away when you say 'Oogledeboo,' will you?"

"Won't they?" asked Nancy disappointedly. She said loudly, "Oogledeboo!"

Her father and mother and Joe Holt jumped a foot.

But nothing happened. The four grownups sat still, weak with relief. Nancy cuddled against her grandfather. She sighed. Presently her eyelids drooped sleepily.

There had been no rolling of thunder or flashing of lightning, or earthquakes when the most bloodcurdling instant in history began. But, now that everything was all over, there was a blinding flash of lightning and a reverberating roar of thunder, and the rain began to pour down again.

10

Gilead

ZENNA HENDERSON

I suppose we have all wished we could have special powers. As children, of course, but as adults, too, I'll bet.

Lives there a man so immune to fury and frustration that he hasn't savored, at least once in a while, the secret joy of imagining he could kill by merely pointing his finger? Oh, the pleasure of secretly selecting one's victims.

Or, in less bloodthirsty mood, who has not wanted to fly?

When I was young in years and could not drop off to sleep at once, I sometimes varied my amusements from daydreaming to practicing the art of flight. The practice went as follows: I would stare hard at the ceiling while lying flat on my back and say to myself, "I'm rising! I'm rising! I'm rising!"

My theory was that if I concentrated hard enough and tried hard enough and believed *hard enough, I would slowly rise from the mattress.*

Alas, I never did, not the merest fraction of an inch. I suppose I never managed to believe quite hard enough after all.

But wouldn't it be nice if we had all sorts of wild abilities? Failing that, isn't it pleasurable to share such abilities with characters in science fiction?

Meet Zenna Henderson's "People" then. In a series of tales—of which "Gilead" is merely one—she has told of the adventures of the natives of a dying planet who have escaped to Earth and who find themselves faced with a double problem: maintaining their separate identity and racial heritage, and—frustratingly enough—hiding their odd powers from ordinary Earthmen, whom, except for those powers, they very closely resemble.

I don't know when it was that I found out that our family was different from other families. There was nothing to point it out. We lived in a house very like the other houses in Socorro. Our pasture lot sloped down just like the rest through arrowweed and mesquite trees to the sometime Rio Gordo that looped around town. And on occasion our cow bawled just as loudly across the river at the Jacobses' bull as all the other cows in all the other pasture lots. And I spent as many lazy days as any other boy in Socorro lying on my back in the thin shade of the mesquites, chewing on the beans when work was waiting somewhere. It never occurred to me to wonder if we were different.

I suppose my first realization came soon after I started to

school and fell in love—with the girl with the longest pigtails and the widest gap in her front teeth of all the girls in my room. I think she was seven to my six.

My girl and I had wandered down behind the school woodshed, under the cottonwoods, to eat our lunch together, ignoring the chanted "Peter's got a gir-ul! Peter's got a gir-ul!" and the whittling fingers that shamed me for showing my love. We ate our sandwiches and pickles and then lay back, arms doubled under our heads, and blinked at the bright sky while we tried to keep the crumbs from our cupcakes from falling into our ears. I was so full of lunch, contentment and love that I suddenly felt I just had to do something spectacular for my ladylove. I sat up, electrified by a great idea and by the knowledge that I could carry it out.

"Hey! Did you know that I can fly?" I scrambled to my feet, leaving my love sitting gape-mouthed in the grass.

"You can't neither fly! Don't be crazy!"

"I can too fly!"

"You can not neither!"

"I can so! You just watch!" And lifting my arms I swooped up to the roof of the shed. I leaned over the edge and said, "See there? I can, too!"

"I'll tell teacher on you!" she gasped, wide-eyed, staring up at me. "You ain't supposed to climb up on the shed."

"Oh, poof," I said, "I didn't climb. Come on, you fly up too. Here, I'll help you."

And I slid down the air to the ground. I put my arms around my love and lifted. She screamed and wrenched away from me and fled shrieking back to the schoolhouse. Somewhat taken aback by her desertion, I gathered up the remains of my cake and hers and was perched comfortably on the ridgepole of the shed, enjoying the last crumbs, when teacher arrived with half the school trailing behind her.

"Peter Merrill! How many times have you been told not to climb things at school?"

I peered down at her, noting with interest that the spit curls on her cheeks had been jarred loose by her hurry and agitation and one of them was straightening out, contrasting oddly with the rest of her shingled bob.

"Hang on tight until Stanley gets the ladder!"

"I can get down," I said, scrambling off the ridgepole. "It's easy."

"Peter!" teacher shrieked. "Stay where you are!"

So I did, wondering at all the fuss.

By the time they got me down and teacher yanked me by one arm back up to the schoolhouse I was bawling at the top of my voice, outraged and indignant because no one would believe me, even my girl denying obstinately the evidence of her own eyes. Teacher, annoyed at my persistence, said over and over, "Don't be silly, Peter. You can't fly. Nobody can fly. Where are your wings?"

"I don't need wings," I bellowed. "People don't need wings. I ain't a bird!"

"Then you can't fly. Only things with wings can fly."

So I alternately cried and kicked the schoolhouse steps for the rest of the noon hour, and then I began to worry for fear teacher would tattle to Dad. After all I had been on forbidden territory, no matter how I got there.

As it turned out she didn't tell Dad, but that night after I was put to bed I suddenly felt an all-gone feeling inside me. Maybe I *couldn't* fly. Maybe teacher was right. I sneaked out of bed and cautiously flew up to the top of the dresser and back. Then I pulled the covers up tight under my chin and whispered to myself, "I can so fly," and sighed heavily. Just another fun stuff that grownups didn't allow, like having cake for breakfast or driving the tractor or borrowing the cow for an Indian-pony-on-a-warpath.

And that was all of that incident except that when teacher met Mother and me at the store that Saturday she ruffled my hair and said, "How's my little bird?" Then she laughed and said to Mother, "He thinks he can fly!"

I saw Mother's fingers tighten whitely on her purse, and she looked down at me with all the laughter gone from her eyes. I was overflooded with incredulous surprise mixed with fear and dread that made me want to cry, even though I knew it was Mother's emotions and not my own that I was feeling.

Mostly Mother had laughing eyes. She was the laughingest mother in Socorro. She carried happiness inside her as if it were a bouquet of flowers and she gave part of it to everyone she met. Most of the other mothers seemed to have hardly enough to go around to their own families. And yet there were other times, like at the store, when laughter fled and fear showed through—and an odd wariness. Other times she made me think of a caged bird, pressing against the bars. Like one night I remember vividly.

Mother stood at the window in her ankle-length flannel nightgown, her long dark hair lifting softly in the draft from the rattling window frames. A high wind was blowing in from a spectacular thunderstorm in the Huachucas. I had been awakened by the rising crescendo and was huddled on the sofa wondering if I was scared or excited as the house shook with the constant thunder. Dad was sitting with the newspaper in his lap.

Mother spoke softly, but her voice came clearly through the tumult.

"Have you ever wondered what it would be like to be up there in the middle of the storm with clouds under your feet and over your head and lightning lacing around you like hot golden rivers?"

Dad rattled his paper. "Sounds uncomfortable," he said.

But I sat there and hugged the words to me in wonder. I knew! *I remembered!* "'And the rain like icy silver hair lashing across your lifted face,'" I recited as though it were a loved lesson.

Mother whirled from the window and stared at me. Dad's eyes were on me, dark and troubled.

"How do you know?" he asked.

I ducked my head in confusion. "I don't know," I muttered.

Mother pressed her hands together, hard, her bowed head swinging the curtains of her hair forward over her shadowy face. "He knows because I know. I know because my mother knew. She knew because our People used to—" Her voice broke. "Those were her words—"

She stopped and turned back to the window, leaning her arm against the frame, her face pressed to it, like a child in tears.

"Oh, Bruce, I'm sorry!"

I stared, round-eyed in amazement, trying to keep tears from coming to my eyes as I fought against Mother's desolation and sorrow.

Dad went to Mother and turned her gently into his arms. He looked over her head at me. "Better run on back to bed, Peter. The worst is over."

I trailed off reluctantly, my mind filled with wonder. Just before I shut my door I stopped and listened.

"I've never said a word to him, honest." Mother's voice quivered. "Oh, Bruce, I try so hard, but sometimes—oh sometimes!"

"I know, Eve. And you've done a wonderful job of it. I know it's hard on you, but we've talked it out so many times. It's the only way, honey."

"Yes," Mother said. "It's the only way, but—oh, be my strength, Bruce! Bless the Power for giving me you!"

I shut my door softly and huddled in the dark in the middle of my bed until I felt Mother's anguish smooth out to loving warmness again. Then for no good reason I flew solemnly to the top of the dresser and back, crawled into bed and relaxed. And remembered. Remembered the hot golden rivers, the clouds over and under and the wild winds that buffeted like foam-frosted waves. But with all the sweet remembering was the reminder, *You can't because you're only eight. You're only eight. You'll have to wait.*

And then Bethie was born, almost in time for my ninth birthday. I remember peeking over the edge of the bassinet at the miracle of tiny fingers and spun-sugar hair. Bethie, my little sister. Bethie, who was whispered about and stared at when Mother let her go to school, though mostly she kept her home even after she was old enough. Because Bethie was different—too.

When Bethie was a month old I smashed my finger in the bedroom door. I cried for a quarter of an hour, but Bethie sobbed on and on until the last pain left my finger.

When Bethie was six months old our little terrier, Glib, got caught in a gopher trap. He dragged himself, yelping, back to the house dangling the trap. Bethie screamed until Glib fell asleep over his bandaged paw.

Dad had acute appendicitis when Bethie was two, but it was Bethie who had to be given a sedative until we could get Dad to the hospital.

One night Dad and Mother stood over Bethie as she slept restlessly under sedatives. Mr. Tyree-next-door had been cutting wood and his axe slipped. He lost a big toe and a pint or so of blood, but as Doctor Dueff skidded to a stop on our street it was into our house that he rushed first and then to Mr. Tyree next-door who lay with his foot swathed and propped up on a chair, his hands pressed to his ears to shut out Bethie's screams.

"What can we do, Eve?" Dad asked. "What does the doctor say?"

"Nothing. They can do nothing for her. He hopes she will outgrow it. He doesn't understand it. He doesn't know that she—"

"What's the matter? What makes her like this?" Dad asked despairingly.

Mother winced. "She's a Sensitive. Among my People there were such—but not so young. Their perception made it possible for them to help sufferers. Bethie has only half the Gift. She has no control."

"Because of me?" Dad's voice was ragged.

Mother look at him with steady loving eyes. "Because of us, Bruce. It was the chance we took. We pushed our luck after Peter."

So there we were, the two of us—different—but different in our differences. For me it was mostly fun, but not for Bethie.

We had to be careful for Bethie. She tried school at first, but skinned knees and rough rassling and aching teeth and bumped heads and the janitor's Monday hangover sent her home exhausted and shaking the first day, with hysteria hanging on the flick of an eyelash. So Bethie read for Mother and learned her numbers and leaned wistfully over the gate as the other children went by.

It wasn't long after Bethie's first day in school that I found a practical use for my difference. Dad sent me out to the woodshed to stack a cord of mesquite that Delfino dumped into our back yard from his old wood wagon. I had a date to explore an old fluorspar mine with some other guys and bitterly resented being sidetracked. I slouched out to the woodpile and stood, hands in pockets, kicking the heavy rough stove lengths. Finally I carried in one armload, grunting under the weight, and afterward sucking the round of my thumb where the sliding wood had peeled me. I hunkered down on my heels and stared as I sucked. Suddenly something prickled inside my brain. If I could fly why couldn't I make the wood fly? *And I knew I could!* I leaned forward and flipped a finger under half a dozen sticks, concentrating as I did so. They lifted into the air and hovered. I pushed them into the shed, guided them to where I wanted them and distributed them like dealing a pack of cards. It didn't take me long to figure out the maximum load, and I had all the wood stacked in a wonderfully short time.

I whistled into the house for my flashlight. The mine was spooky and dark, and I was the only one of the gang with a flashlight.

"I told you to stack the wood." Dad looked up from his milk records.

"I did," I said, grinning.

"Cut the kidding," Dad grunted. "You couldn't be done already."

"I am, though," I said triumphantly. "I found a new way to do it. You see—" I stopped, frozen by Dad's look.

"We don't need any new ways around here," he said evenly. "Go back out there until you've had time to stack the wood right!"

"It *is* stacked," I protested. "And the kids are waiting for me!"

"I'm not arguing, son," said Dad, white-faced. "Go back out to the shed."

I went back out to the shed—past Mother, who had come in from the kitchen and whose hand half went out to me. I sat in the shed fuming for a long time, stubbornly set that I wouldn't leave till Dad told me to.

Then I got to thinking. Dad wasn't usually unreasonable like this. Maybe I'd done something wrong. Maybe it was bad to stack wood like that. Maybe—my thoughts wavered as I remembered whispers I'd overheard about Bethie. Maybe it—it was a crazy thing to do—an insane thing.

I huddled close upon myself as I considered it. Crazy means not doing like other people. Crazy means doing things ordinary people don't do. Maybe that's why Dad made such a fuss. Maybe I'd done an insane thing! I stared at the ground, lost in bewilderment. What *was* different about our family? And for the first time I was able to isolate and recognize the feeling I must have had for a long time—the feeling of being on the outside looking in—the feeling of apartness. With this recognition came a wariness, a need for concealment. If something was wrong no one else must know—I must not betray . . .

Then Mother was standing beside me. "Dad says you may go now," she said, sitting down on my log.

"Peter—" She looked at me unhappily. "Dad's doing what is best. All I can say is: remember that whatever you do, wherever you live, different is dead. You have to conform or—or die. But Peter, don't be ashamed. Don't ever be ashamed!" Then swiftly her hands were on my shoulders and her lips brushed my ear. "Be different!" she whispered. "Be as different as you can. But don't let anyone see—don't let anyone know!" And she was gone up the back steps, into the kitchen.

As I grew further into adolescence I seemed to grow further and further away from kids my age. I couldn't seem to get much of a kick out of what they considered fun. So it was that with increasing frequency in the years that followed I took Mother's whispered advice, never asking for explanations I knew she wouldn't give. The wood incident had opened up a whole vista of possibilities—no telling what I might be able to do—so I got in the habit of going down to the foot of our pasture lot. There, screened by the brush and greasewood, I tried all sorts of experiments, never knowing whether they would work or not. I sweated plenty over some that didn't work—and some that did.

I found that I could snap my fingers and bring things to me, or send them short distances from me without bothering to touch them as I had the wood. I roosted regularly in the tops of the tall cottonwoods, swan-diving ecstatically down to the ground, warily, after I got too ecstatic once and crashlanded on my nose and chin. By headaching concentration that left me dizzy, I even set a small campfire ablaze. Then blistered and charred both hands unmercifully by confidently scooping up the crackling fire.

Then I guess I got careless about checking for onlookers because some nasty talk got started. Bub Jacobs whispered around that I was "doing things" all alone down in the brush. His sly grimace as he whispered made the "doing things" any nasty perversion the listeners' imaginations could conjure up, and the "alone" damned me on the spot. I learned bitterly then what Mother had told me. Different is dead -and one death is never enough. You die and die and die.

Then one day I caught Bub cutting across the foot of our wood lot. He saw me coming and hit for tall timber, already smarting under what he knew he'd get if I caught him. I started full speed after him, then plowed to a stop. Why waste effort? If I could do it to the wood I could do it to a blockhead like Bub.

He let out a scream of pure terror as the ground dropped out from under him. His scream flatted and strangled into silence as he struggled in mid-air, convulsed with fear of falling and the terrible thing that was happening to him. And I stood and laughed at him, feeling myself a giant towering above stupid dopes like Bub.

Sharply, before he passed out, I felt his terror, and an echo of his scream rose in my throat. I slumped down in the dirt, sick with sudden realization, knowing with a knowledge that went beyond ordinary experience that I had done something terribly wrong, that I had prostituted whatever powers I possessed by using them to terrorize unjustly.

I knelt and looked up at Bub, crumpled in the air, higher than my head, higher than my reach, and swallowed painfully as I realized that I had no idea how to get him down. He wasn't a stick of wood to be snapped to the ground. He wasn't me, to dive down through the air. I hadn't the remotest idea how to get a human down.

Half dazed, I crawled over to a shaft of sunlight that slit the cottonwood branches overhead and felt it rush through my fingers like something to be lifted- and twisted—and fashioned and *used! Used on Bub!* But how? *How?* I clenched my fist in the flood of light, my mind beating against another door that needed only a word or look or gesture to open, but I couldn't say it, or look it, or make it.

I stood up and took a deep breath. I jumped, batting at Bub's heels that dangled a little lower than the rest of him. I missed. Again I jumped and the tip of one finger flicked his heel and he moved sluggishly in the air. Then I swiped the back of my hand across my sweaty forehead and laughed—laughed at my stupid self.

Cautiously, because I hadn't done much hovering, mostly just up and down, I lifted myself up level with Bub. I put my hands on him and pushed down hard. He didn't move. I tugged him up and he rose with me. I drifted slowly and deliberately away from him and pondered. Then I got on the other side of him and pushed him toward the branches of the cottonwood. His head was beginning to toss and his lips moved with returning consciousness. He drifted through the air like a waterlogged stump, but he moved and I draped him carefully over a big limb near the top of the tree, anchoring his arms and legs as securely as I could. By the time his eyes opened and he clutched frenziedly for support I was standing down at the foot of the tree, yelling up at him.

"Hang on, Bub! I'll go get someone to help you down!"

So for the next week or so people forgot me, and Bub squirmed under "Who treed you, feller?" and "How's the weather up there?" and "Get a ladder, Bub, get a ladder!"

Even with worries like that it was mostly fun for me. Why couldn't it be like that for Bethie? Why couldn't I give her part of my fun and take part of her pain?

Then Dad died, swept out of life by our Rio Gordo as he tried to rescue a fool Easterner who had camped on the bone-dry white sands of the river bottom in cloudburst weather. Somehow it seemed impossible to think of Mother by herself. It had always been Mother and Dad. Not just two parents but Mother-and-Dad, a single entity. And now our thoughts must limp to Mother-and, Mother-and. And Mother—well, half of her was gone.

After the funeral Mother and Bethie and I sat in our front room, looking at the floor. Bethie was clenching her teeth against the stabbing pain of Mother's fingernails gouging Mother's palms.

I unfolded the clenched hands gently and Bethie relaxed. "Mother," I said softly, "I can take care of us. I have my part-time job at the plant. Don't worry. I'll take care of us."

I knew what a trivial thing I was offering to her anguish, but I had to do something to break through to her.

"Thank you, Peter," Mother said, rousing a little. "I know you will—" She bowed her head and pressed both hands to her dry eyes with restrained desperation. "Oh, Peter, Peter! I'm enough of this world now to find death a despair and desolation instead of the solemnly sweet calling it is. Help me, help me!" Her breath labored in her throat and she groped blindly for my hand.

"If I can, Mother," I said, taking one hand as Bethie took the other. "Then help me remember. Remember with me."

And behind my closed eyes I remembered. Unhampered flight through a starry night, a flight of a thousand happy people like birds in the sky, rushing to meet the dawn—the dawn of the Festival. I could smell the flowers that garlanded the women and feel the quiet exultation that went with the Festival dawn. Then the leader sounded the magnificent opening notes of the Festival song as he caught the first glimpse of the rising sun over the heavily wooded hills. A thousand voices took up the song. A thousand hands lifted in the Sign . . .

I opened my eyes to find my own fingers lifted to trace a sign I did not know. My own throat throbbed to a note I had never sung. I took a deep breath and glanced over at Bethie. She met my eyes and shook her head sadly. She hadn't seen. Mother sat quietly, eyes closed, her face cleared and calmed.

"What was it, Mother?" I whispered.

"The Festival," she said softly. "For all those who had been called during the year. For your father, Peter and Bethie. We remembered it for your father."

"Where was it?" I asked. "Where in the world—?"

"Not in this—" Mother's eyes flicked open. "It doesn't matter, Peter. You are of this world. There is no other for you."

"Mother," Bethie's voice was a hesitant murmur, "what do you mean, 'remember'?"

Mother looked at her and tears welled into her dry burned-out eyes.

"Oh, Bethie, Bethie, all the burdens and none of the blessings! I'm sorry, Bethie, I'm sorry." And she fled down the hall to her room.

Bethie stood close against my side as we looked after Mother.

"Peter," she murmured, "what did Mother mean, 'none of the blessings'?"

"I don't know," I said.

"I'll bet it's because I can't fly like you."

"Fly!" My startled eyes went to hers. "How do you know?"

"I know lots of things," she whispered. "But mostly I know we're different. Other people aren't like us. Peter, what made us different?"

"Mother?" I whispered. "Mother?"

"I guess so," Bethie murmured. "But how come?"

We fell silent and then Bethie went to the window where the late sun haloed her silvery blond hair in fire.

"I can do things too," she whispered. "Look."

She reached out and took a handful of sun, the same sort of golden sun-slant that had flowed so heavily through my fingers under the cottonwoods while Bub dangled above me. With flashing fingers she fashioned the sun into an intricate glowing pattern. "But what's it for," she murmured, "except for pretty?"

"I know," I said, looking at my answer for lowering Bub. "I know, Bethie." And I took the pattern from her. It strained between my fingers and flowed into darkness.

The years that followed were casual uneventful years. I finished high school, but college was out of the question. I went to work in the plant that provided work for most of the employables in Socorro.

Mother built up quite a reputation as a midwife—a very necessary calling in a community which took literally the injunction to multiply and replenish the earth and which lay exactly seventy-five miles from a hospital, no matter which way you turned when you got to the highway.

Bethie was in her teens and with Mother's help was learning to control her visible reactions to the pain of others, but I knew she still suffered as much as, if not more than, she had when she was smaller. But she was able to go to school most of the time now and was becoming fairly popular in spite of her quietness.

So all in all we were getting along quite comfortably and quite ordinarily except—well, I always felt as though I were waiting for something to happen or for someone to come.

And Bethie must have, too, because she actually watched and listened—especially after a particularly bad spell. And even Mother. Sometimes as we sat on the porch in the long evenings she would cock her head and listen intently, her rocking chair still. But when we asked what she heard she'd sigh and say, "Nothing. Just the night." And her chair would rock again.

Of course I still indulged my differences. Not with the white fire of possible discovery that they had kindled when I first began, but more like the feeding of a small flame just "for pretty." I went farther afield now for my "holidays," but Bethie went with me. She got a big kick out of our excursions, especially after I found that I could carry her when I flew, and most especially after we found, by means of a heart-stopping accident, that though she couldn't go up she could control her going down. After that it was her pleasure to have me carry her up as far as I could and she would come down, sometimes taking an hour to make the descent, often weaving about her the intricate splendor of her sunshine patterns.

It was a rustling russet day in October when our world ended—again. We talked and laughed over the breakfast table, teasing Bethie about her date the night before. Color was high in her usually pale cheeks, and, with all the laughter and brightness the tingle of fall, everything just felt good.

But between one joke and another the laughter drained out of Bethie's face and the pinched set look came to her lips.

"Mother!" she whispered, and then she relaxed.

"Already?" asked Mother, rising and finishing her coffee as I went to get her coat. "I had a hunch today would be the day. Reena would ride that jeep up Peppersauce Canyon this close to her time."

I helped her on with her coat and hugged her tight.

"Bless-a-mama," I said, "when are you going to retire and let someone else snatch the fall and spring crops of kids?"

"When I snatch a grandchild or so for myself," she said, joking, but I felt her sadness. "Besides she's going to name this one Peter—or Bethie, as the case may be." She reached for her little black bag and looked at Bethie. "No more yet?"

Bethie smiled. "No," she murmured.

"Then I've got plenty of time. Peter, you'd better take Bethie for a holiday. Reena takes her own sweet time and being just across the road makes it bad on Bethie."

"Okay, Mother," I said. "We planned one anyway, but we hoped this time you'd go with us."

Mother looked at me, hesitated and turned aside. "I—I might sometime."

"Mother! Really?" This was the first hesitation from Mother in all the times we'd asked her.

"Well, you've asked me so many times and I've been wondering. Wondering if it's fair to deny our birthright. After all there's nothing wrong in being of the People."

"What people, Mother?" I pressed. "*Where* are you from? Why *can*—?"

"Some other time, son," Mother said. "Maybe soon. These last few months I've begun to sense—yes, it wouldn't hurt you to know even if nothing could ever come of it; and perhaps soon something *can* come, and you will have to know. But no," she chided as we clung to her. "There's no time now. Reena might fool us after all and produce before I get there. You kids scoot, now!"

We looked back as the pickup roared across the highway and headed for Mendigo's Peak. Mother answered our wave and went in the gate of Reena's yard, where Dalt, in spite of this being their sixth, was running like an anxious puppy dog from Mother to the porch and back again.

It was a day of perfection for us. The relaxation of flight for me, the delight of hovering for Bethie, the frosted glory of the burning-blue sky, the russet and gold of grasslands stretching for endless miles down from the snow-flecked blue and gold Mendigo.

At lunchtime we lolled in the pleasant warmth of our favorite baby box canyon that held the sun and shut out the wind. After we ate we played our favorite game, Remembering. It began with my clearing my mind so that it lay as quiet as a hidden pool of water, as receptive as the pool to every pattern the slightest breeze might start quivering across its surface. Then the memories would come—strange un-Earthlike memories that were like those Mother and I had had when Dad died. Bethie could not remember with me, but she seemed to catch the memories from me almost before the words could form in my mouth.

So this last lovely "holiday" we remembered again our favorite. We walked the darkly gleaming waters of a mountain lake, curling our toes in the liquid coolness, loving the tilt and sway of the waves beneath our feet, feeling around us from shore and sky a dear familiarity that was stronger than any Earth ties we had yet formed.

Before we knew it the long lazy afternoon had fled and we shivered in the sudden chill as the sun dropped westward, nearing the peaks of the Huachucas. We packed the remains of our picnic in the basket, and I turned to Bethie, to lift her and carry her back to the pickup.

She was smiling her soft little secret smile.

"Look, Peter," she murmured. And flicking her fingers over her head she shook out a cloud of snowflakes, gigantic whirling tumbling snowflakes that clung feather-soft to her pale hair and melted, glistening, across her warm cheeks and mischievous smile.

"Early winter, Peter!" she said.

"Early winter, punkin!" I cried and snatching her up, boosted her out of the little canyon and jumped over her, clearing the boulders she had to scramble over. "For that you walk, young lady!"

But she almost beat me to the car anyway. For one who couldn't fly she was learning to run awfully light.

Twilight had fallen before we got back to the highway. We could see the headlights of the scurrying cars that seldom even slowed down for Socorro. "So this is Socorro, wasn't it?" was the way most traffic went through.

We had topped the last rise before the highway when Bethie screamed. I almost lost control of the car on the rutty road. She screamed again, a wild tortured cry as she folded in on herself.

"Bethie!" I called, trying to get through to her. "What is it? Where is it? Where can I take you?"

But her third scream broke off short and she slid limply to the floor. I was terrified. She hadn't reacted like this in years. She had never fainted like this before. Could it be that Reena hadn't had her child yet? That she was in such agony—but even when Mrs. Allbeg had died in childbirth Bethie hadn't—

I lifted Bethie to the seat and drove wildly homeward, praying that Mother would be—

And then I saw it. In front of our house. The big car skewed across the road. The kneeling cluster of people on the pavement.

The next thing I knew I was kneeling too, beside Dr. Dueff, clutching the edge of the blanket that mercifully covered Mother from chin to toes. I lifted a trembling hand to the dark trickle of blood that threaded crookedly down from her forehead.

"Mother," I whispered. "Mother!"

Her eyelids fluttered and she looked up blindly. "Peter." I could hardly hear her. "Peter, where's Bethie?"

"She's fainted. She's in the car—" I faltered. "Oh, Mother!"

"Tell the doctor to go to Bethie."

"But, Mother!" I cried. "You—"

"I am not called yet. Go to Bethie."

We knelt by her bedside, Bethie and I. The doctor was gone. There was no use trying to get Mother to a hospital. Just moving her indoors had started a dark oozing from the corner of her mouth. The neighbors were all gone except Gramma Reuther who always came to troubled homes and had folded the hands of the dead in Socorro from the founding of the town. She sat now in the front room holding her worn Bible in quiet hands, after all these years no longer needing to look up the passages of comfort and assurance.

The doctor had quieted the pain for Mother and had urged sleep upon Bethie, not knowing how long the easing would last, but Bethie wouldn't take it.

Suddenly Mother's eyes were open.

"I married your father," she said clearly, as though continuing a conversation. "We loved each other so, and they were all dead—all my People. Of course I told him first, and oh, Peter! He believed me! After all that time of having to guard every word and every move I had someone to talk to—someone to believe me. I told him all about the People and lifted myself and then I lifted the car and turned it in mid-air above the highway—just for fun. It pleased him a lot but it made him thoughtful and later he said, 'You know, honey, your world and ours took different turns way back there. We turned to gadgets. You turned to the Power.'"

Her eyes smiled. "He got so he knew when I was lonesome for the Home. Once he said, 'Homesick, honey? So am I. For what this world could have been. Or maybe—God willing—what it may become.'

"Your father was the other half of me." Her eyes closed, and in the silence her breath became audible, a harsh straining sound. Bethie crouched with both hands pressed to her chest, her face dead white in the shadows.

"We discussed it and discussed it," Mother cried. "But we had to decide as we did. We thought I was the last of the People. I had to forget the Home and be of Earth. You children had to be of Earth, too, even if— That's why he was so stern with you, Peter. Why he didn't want you to—experiment. He was afraid you'd do too much around other people if you found out—" She stopped and lay panting. "Different is dead," she whispered, and lay scarcely breathing for a moment.

"I knew the Home." Her voice was heavy with sorrow. "I remember the Home. Not just because my People remembered it but because I saw it. I was born there. It's gone now. Gone forever. There is no Home. Only a band of dust between the stars!" Her face twisted with grief and Bethie echoed her cry of pain.

Then Mother's face cleared and her eyes opened. She half propped herself up in her bed.

"You have the Home, too. You and Bethie. You will have it always. And your children after you. Remember, Peter? Remember?"

Then her head tilted attentively and she gave a laughing sob. "Oh, Peter! Oh, Bethie! Did you hear it? I've been called! I've been called!" Her hand lifted in the Sign and her lips moved tenderly.

"Mother!" I cried fearfully. "What do you mean? Lie down. Please lie down!" I pressed her back against the pillows.

"I've been called back to the Presence. My years are finished. My days are totaled."

"But Mother," I blubbered like a child, "what will we do without you?"

"Listen!" Mother whispered rapidly, one hand pressed to my hair. "You must find the rest. You must go right away. They can help Bethie. They can help you, Peter. As long as you are separated from them you are not complete. I have felt them calling the last year or so, and now that I am on the way to the Presence I can hear them clearer, and clearer." She paused and held her breath. "There is a canyon—north. The ship crashed there, after our life slips—here, Peter, give me your hand." She reached urgently toward me and I cradled her hand in mine.

And I saw half the state spread out below me like a giant map. I saw the wrinkled folds of the mountains, the deceptively smooth roll of the desert up to the jagged slopes. I saw the blur of timber blunting the hills and I saw the angular writhing of the narrow road through the passes. Then I felt a sharp pleasurable twinge, like the one you feel when seeing home after being away a long time.

"There!" Mother whispered as the panorama faded. "I wish I could have known before. It's been lonely—

"But you, Peter," she said strongly. "You and Bethie must go to them."

"Why should we, Mother?" I cried in desperation. "What are they to us or we to them that we should leave Socorro and go among strangers?"

Mother pulled herself up in bed, her eyes intent on my face. She wavered a moment and then Bethie was crouched behind her, steadying her back.

"They are not strangers," she said clearly and slowly. "They are the People. We shared the ship with them during the Crossing. They were with us when we were out in the middle of emptiness with only the fading of stars behind and the brightening before to tell us we were moving. They, with us, looked at all the bright frosting of stars across the blackness, wondering if on one of them we would find a welcome.

"You are woven of their fabric. Even though your father was not of the People—"

Her voice died, her face changed. Bethie moved from in back of her and lowered her gently. Mother clasped her hands and sighed.

"It's a lonely business," she whispered. "No one can go with you. Even with them waiting it's lonely."

In the silence that followed we heard Gramma Reuther rocking quietly in the front room. Bethie sat on the floor beside me, her cheeks flushed, her eyes wide with a strange dark awe.

"Peter, it didn't hurt. It didn't hurt at all. It—healed!"

But we didn't go. How could we leave my job and our home and go off to—where? Looking for—whom? Because—why? It was mostly me, I guess, but I couldn't quite believe what Mother had told us. After all she hadn't said anything definite. We were probably reading meaning where it didn't exist. Bethie returned again and again to the puzzle of Mother and what she had meant, but we didn't go.

And Bethie got paler and thinner, and it was nearly a year later that I came home to find her curled into an impossibly tight ball on her bed, her eyes tight shut, snatching at breath that came out again in sharp moans.

I nearly went crazy before I at last got through to her and uncurled her enough to get hold of one of her hands. Finally, though, she opened dull dazed eyes and looked past me.

"Like a dam, Peter," she gasped. "It all comes in. It should —it should! I was born to—" I wiped the cold sweat from her forehead. "But it just piles up and piles up. It's supposed to go somewhere. I'm supposed to do something! Peter, Peter, Peter!" She twisted on the bed, her distorted face pushing into the pillow.

"What does, Bethie?" I asked, turning her face to mine. "What does?"

"Glib's foot and Dad's side and Mr. Tyree-next-door's toe—" and her voice faded down through the litany of years of agony.

"I'll go get Dr. Dueff," I said hopelessly.

"No." She turned her face away. "Why build the dam higher? Let it break. Oh, soon, soon!"

"Bethie, don't talk like that," I said, feeling inside me my terrible aloneness that only Bethie could fend off now that Mother was gone. "We'll find something—some way—"

"Mother could help," she gasped. "A little. But she's gone. And now I'm picking up mental pain too! Reena's afraid she's got cancer. Oh, Peter, Peter!" Her voice strained to a whisper. "Let me die! Help me die!"

Both of us were shocked to silence by her words. Help her die? I leaned against her hand. Go back into the Presence with the weight of unfinished years dragging at our feet? For if she went I went too.

Then my eyes flew open and I stared at Bethie's hand. What Presence? Whose ethics and mores were talking in my mind?

And so I had to decide. I talked Bethie into a sleeping pill and sat by her even after she was asleep. And as I sat there all the past years wound through my head. The way it must have been for Bethie all this time and I hadn't let myself know.

Just before dawn I woke Bethie. We packed and went. I left a note on the kitchen table for Dr. Dueff saying only that we were going to look for help for Bethie and would he ask Reena to see to the house. And thanks.

I slowed the pickup over to the side of the junction and slammed the brakes on.

"Okay," I said hopelessly. "You choose which way this time. Or shall we toss for it? Heads straight up, tails straight down! I can't tell where to go, Bethie. I had only that one little glimpse that Mother gave me of this country. There's a million canyons and a million side roads. We were fools to leave Socorro. After all we have nothing to go on but what Mother said. It might have been delirium."

"No," Bethie murmured. "It can't be. It's got to be real."

"But, Bethie," I said, leaning my weary head on the steering wheel, "you know how much I want it to be true, not only for you but for myself too. But look. What do we have to assume if Mother was right? First, that space travel is possible—was possible nearly fifty years ago. Second, that Mother and her People came here from another planet. Third, that we are, bluntly speaking, half-breeds, a cross between Earth and heaven knows what world. Fourth, that there's a chance—in ten million—of our finding the other People who came at the same time Mother did, presupposing that any of them survived the Crossing.

"Why, any one of these premises would brand us as crazy crackpots to any normal person. No, we're building too much on a dream and a hope. Let's go back, Bethie. We've got just enough gas money along to make it. Let's give it up."

"And go back to what?" Bethie asked, her face pinched. "No, Peter. Here."

I looked up as she handed me one of her sunlight patterns, a handful of brilliance that twisted briefly in my fingers before it flickered out.

"Is that Earth?" she asked quietly. "How many of our friends can fly? How many–" she hesitated, "how many can Remember?"

"Remember!" I said slowly, and then I whacked the steering wheel with my fist. "Oh, Bethie, of all the stupid–! Why, it's Bub all over again!"

I kicked the pickup into life and turned on the first faint desert trail beyond the junction. I pulled off even that suggestion of a trail and headed across the nearly naked desert toward a clump of ironwood, mesquite, and catclaw that marked a sand wash against the foothills. With the westering sun making shadow lace through the thin foliage we made camp.

I lay on my back in the wash and looked deep into the arch of the desert sky. The trees made a typical desert pattern of warmth and coolness on me, warm in the sun, cool in the shadow, as I let my mind clear smoother, smoother, until the soft intake of Bethie's breath as she sat beside me sent a bright ripple across it.

And I remembered. But only Mother-and-Dad and the little campfire I had gathered up, and Glib with the trap on his foot and Bethie curled, face to knees on the bed, and the thin crying sound of her labored breath.

I blinked at the sky. I *had* to Remember. I just had to. I shut my eyes and concentrated and concentrated, until I was exhausted. Nothing came now, not even a hint of memory. In despair I relaxed, limp against the chilling sand. And all at once unaccustomed gears shifted and slipped into place in my mind and there I was, just as I had been, hovering over the life-sized map.

Slowly and painfully I located Socorro and the thin thread that marked the Rio Gordo. I followed it and lost it and followed it again, the finger of my attention pressing close. Then I located Vulcan Springs Valley and traced its broad rolling to the upsweep of the desert, to the Sierra Cobreña Mountains. It was an eerie sensation to look down on the infinitesimal groove that must be where I was lying now. Then I handspanned my thinking around our camp spot. Nothing. I probed farther north, and east, and north again. I drew a deep breath and exhaled it shakily. There it was. The Home twinge. The call of familiarity.

I read it off to Bethie. The high thrust of a mountain that pushed up baldly past its timber, the huge tailings dump across the range from the mountain. The casual wreathing of smoke from what must be a logging town, all forming sides of a slender triangle. Somewhere in this area was the place.

I opened my eyes to find Bethie in tears.

"Why, Bethie!" I said. "What's wrong? Aren't you glad--?"

Bethie tried to smile but her lips quivered. She hid her face in the crook of her elbow and whispered. "I saw, too! Oh, Peter, this time I saw, too!"

We got out the road map and by the fading afternoon light we tried to translate our rememberings. As nearly as we could figure out we should head for a place way off the highway called Kerry Canyon. It was apparently the only inhabited spot anywhere near the big bald mountain. I looked at the little black dot in the kink in the third-rate road and wondered if it would turn out to be a period to all our hopes or the point for the beginning of new lives for the two of us. Life and sanity for Bethie, and for me . . . In a sudden spasm of emotion I crumpled the map in my hand. I felt blindly that in all my life I had never known anyone but Mother and Dad and Bethie. That I was a ghost walking the world. If only I could see even one other person that felt like our kind! Just to know that Bethie and I weren't all alone with our unearthly heritage!

I smoothed out the map and folded it again. Night was on us and the wind was cold. We shivered as we scurried around looking for wood for our campfire.

Kerry Canyon was one business street, two service stations, two saloons, two stores, two churches, and a handful of houses flung at random over the hillsides that sloped down to an area that looked too small to accommodate the road. A creek which was now thinned to an intermittent trickle that loitered along, waited for the fall rains to begin. A sudden speckling across our windshield suggested it hadn't long to wait.

We rattled over the old bridge and half through the town. The road swung up sharply over a rusty single-line railroad and turned left, shying away from the bluff that was hollowed just enough to accommodate one of the service stations.

We pulled into the station. The uniformed attendant came alongside.

"We just want some information," I said, conscious of the thinness of my billfold. We had picked up our last tankful of gas before plunging into the maze of canyons between the main highway and here. Our stopping place would have to be soon whether we found the People or not.

"Sure! Sure! Glad to oblige." The attendant pushed his cap back from his forehead. "How can I help you?"

I hesitated, trying to gather my thoughts and words—and some of the hope that had jolted out of me since we had left the junction.

"We're trying to locate some—friends—of ours. We were told they lived out the other side of here, out by Baldy. Is there anyone—?"

"Friends of *them* people?" he asked in astonishment. "Well, say, now, that's interesting! You're the first I ever had come asking after them."

I felt Bethie's arm trembling against mine. Then there *was* something beyond Kerry Canyon!

"How come? What's wrong with them?"

"Why, nothing, Mac, nothing. Matter of fact they're dern nice people. Trade here a lot. Come in to church and the dances."

"Dances?" I glanced around the steep sloping hills.

"Sure. We ain't as dead as we look." The attendant grinned. "Come Saturday night we're quite a town. Lots of ranches around these hills. Course, not much out Cougar Canyon way. That's where your friends live, didn't you say?"

"Yeah. Out by Baldy."

"Well, nobody else lives out that way." He hesitated. "Hey, there's something I'd like to ask."

"Sure. Like what?"

"Well, them people pretty much keep themselves to themselves. I don't mean they're stuck-up or anything, but—well, I've always wondered. Where they from? One of them overrun countries in Europe? They're foreigners, ain't they? And seems like most of what Europe exports any more is DP's. Are them people some?"

"Well, yes, you might call them that. Why?"

"Well, they talk just as good as anybody and it must have been a war a long time ago because they've been around since my Dad's time, but they just—feel different." He caught his upper lip between his teeth reflectively. "Good different. Real nice different." He grinned again. "Wouldn't mind shining up to some of them gals myself. Don't get no encouragement, though.

"Anyway, keep on this road. It's easy. No other road going that way. Jackass Flat will beat the tar outa your tires, but you'll probably make it, less'n comes up a heavy rain. Then you'll skate over half the county and most likely end up in a ditch. Slickest mud in the world. Colder'n hell—beg pardon, lady—out there on the flat when the wind starts blowing. Better bundle up."

"Thanks, fella," I said. "Thanks a lot. Think we'll make it before dark?"

"Oh, sure. 'Tain't so awful far but the road's lousy. Oughta make it in two-three hours, less'n like I said, comes up a heavy rain."

We knew when we hit Jackass Flat. It was like dropping off the edge. If we had thought the road to Kerry Canyon was bad we revised our opinions, but fast. In the first place it was choose your own ruts. Then the tracks were deep sunk in heavy clay generously mixed with sharp splintery shale and rocks as big as your two fists that were like a gigantic gravel as far as we could see across the lifeless expanse of the flat.

But to make it worse, the ruts I chose kept ending abruptly as though the cars that had made them had either backed away from the job or jumped over. Jumped over! I drove, in and out of ruts, so wrapped up in surmises that I hardly noticed the rough going until a cry from Bethie aroused me.

"Stop the car!" she cried. "Oh, Peter! Stop the car!"

I braked so fast that the pickup swerved wildly, mounted the side of a rut, lurched and settled sickeningly down on the back tire which sighed itself flatly into the rising wind.

"What on earth!" I yelped, as near to being mad at Bethie as I'd ever been in my life. "What was that for?"

Bethie, white-faced, was emerging from the army blanket she had huddled in against the cold. "It just came to me. Peter, supposing they don't want us?"

"Don't want us? What do you mean?" I growled, wondering if that lace doily I called my spare tire would be worth the trouble of putting it on.

"We never thought. It didn't even occur to us. Peter, we—we don't belong. We won't be like them. We're partly of Earth—as much as we are of wherever else. Supposing they reject us? Supposing they think we're undesirable—?" Bethie turned her face away. "Maybe we don't belong anywhere, Peter, not anywhere at all."

I felt a chill sweep over me that was not of the weather. We had assumed so blithely that we would be welcome. But how did we know? Maybe they *wouldn't* want us. We weren't of the People. We weren't of Earth. Maybe we didn't belong—not anywhere.

"Sure they'll want us," I forced out heartily. Then my eyes wavered away from Bethie's and I said defensively, "Mother said they would help us. She said we were woven of the same fabric—"

"But maybe the warp will only accept genuine woof. Mother couldn't know. There weren't any—half-breeds—when she was separated from them. Maybe our Earth blood will mark us—"

"There's nothing wrong with Earth blood," I said defiantly. "Besides, like you said, what would there be for you if we went back?"

She pressed her clenched fists against her cheeks, her eyes wide and vacant. "Maybe," she muttered, "maybe if I'd just go on and go completely insane it wouldn't hurt so terribly much. It might even feel good."

"Bethie!" my voice jerked her physically. "Cut out that talk right now! We're going on. The only way we can judge the People is by Mother. She would never reject us or any others like us. And that fellow back there said they were good people."

I opened the door. "You better try to get some kinks out of your legs while I change the tire. By the looks of the sky we'll be doing some skating before we get to Cougar Canyon."

But for all my brave words it wasn't just for the tire that I knelt beside the car, and it wasn't only the sound of the lug wrench that the wind carried up into the darkening sky.

I squinted through the streaming windshield, trying to make out the road through the downpour that fought our windshield wiper to a standstill. What few glimpses I caught of the road showed a deceptively smooth-looking chocolate river, but we alternately shook like a giant maraca, pushed out sheets of water like a speedboat, or slithered aimlessly and terrifyingly across sudden mud flats that often left us yards off the road. Then we'd creep cautiously back until the soggy squelch of our tires told us we were in the flooded ruts again.

Then all at once it wasn't there. The road, I mean. It stretched a few yards ahead of us and then just flowed over the edge, into the rain, into nothingness.

"It couldn't go there," Bethie murmured incredulously. "It can't just drop off like that."

"Well, I'm certainly not dropping off with it, sight unseen," I said, huddling deeper into my army blanket. My jacket was packed in back and I hadn't bothered to dig it out. I hunched my shoulders to bring the blanket up over my head. "I'm going to take a look first."

I slid out into the solid wall of rain that hissed and splashed around me on the flooded flat. I was soaked to the knees and mudcoated to the shins before I slithered to the drop-off. The trail—call that a road?—tipped over the edge of the canyon and turned abruptly to the right, then lost itself along a shrub-grown ledge that sloped downward even as it paralleled the rim of the canyon. If I could get the pickup over the rim and onto the trail it wouldn't be so bad. But— I peered over the drop-off at the turn. The bottom was lost in shadows and rain. I shuddered.

Then quickly, before I could lose my nerve, I squelched back to the car.

"Pray, Bethie. Here we go."

There was the suck and slosh of our turning tires, the awful moment when we hung on the brink. Then the turn. And there we were, poised over nothing, with our rear end slewing outward.

The sudden tongue-biting jolt as we finally landed, right side up, pointing the right way on the narrow trail, jarred the cold sweat on my face so it rolled down with the rain.

I pulled over at the first wide spot in the road and stopped the car. We sat in the silence, listening to the rain. I felt as though something infinitely precious were lying just before me. Bethie's hand crept into mine and I knew she was feeling it, too. But suddenly Bethie's hand was snatched from mine and she was pounding with both fists against my shoulder in most un-Bethie-like violence.

"I can't stand it, Peter!" she cried hoarsely, emotion choking her voice. "Let's go back before we find out any more. If they should send us away! Oh, Peter! Let's go before they find us! Then we'll still have our dream. We can pretend that someday we'll come back. We can never dream again, never hope again!" She hid her face in her hands. "I'll manage somehow. I'd rather go away, hoping, than run the risk of being rejected by them."

"Not me," I said, starting the motor. "We have as much chance of a welcome as we do of being kicked out. And if they can help you— Say, what's the matter with you today? I'm supposed to be the doubting one, remember? You're the mustard seed of this outfit!" I grinned at her, but my heart sank at the drawn white misery of her face. She almost managed a smile.

The trail led steadily downward, lapping back on itself as it worked back and forth along the canyon wall, sometimes steep, sometimes almost level. The farther we went the more rested I felt, as though I were shutting doors behind or opening them before me.

Then came one of the casual miracles of mountain country. The clouds suddenly opened and the late sun broke through. There, almost frighteningly, a huge mountain pushed out of the featureless gray distance. In the flooding light the towering slopes seemed to move, stepping closer to us as we watched. The rain still fell, but now in glittering silver-beaded curtains; and one vivid end of a rainbow splashed color recklessly over trees and rocks and a corner of the sky.

I didn't watch the road. I watched the splendor and glory spread out around us. So when, at Bethie's scream, I snatched back to my driving all I took down into the roaring splintering darkness was the thought of Bethie and the sight of the other car, slanting down from the bobbing top branches of a tree, seconds before it plowed into us broadside, a yard above the road.

I thought I was dead. I was afraid to open my eyes because I could feel the rain making little puddles over my closed lids. And then I breathed. I was alive, all right. A knife jabbed itself up and down the left side of my chest and twisted itself viciously with each reluctant breath I drew.

Then I heard a voice.

"Thank the Power they aren't hurt too badly. But, oh, Valancy! What will Father say?" The voice was young and scared.

"You've known him longer than I have," another girl-voice answered. "You should have some idea."

"I never had a wreck before, not even when I was driving instead of lifting."

"I have a hunch that you'll be grounded for quite a spell," the second voice replied. "But that isn't what's worrying me, Karen. Why didn't we know they were coming? We always can sense Outsiders. We should have known—"

"Q. E. D. then," said the Karen-voice.

"'Q. E. D.'?"

"Yes. If we didn't sense them, then they're not Outsiders—" There was the sound of a caught breath and then, "Oh, what I said, Valancy! You don't suppose!" I felt a movement close to me and heard the soft sound of breathing. "Can it really be two more of us? Oh, Valancy, they must be second generation—they're about our age. How did they find us? Which of our Lost Ones were their parents?"

Valancy sounded amused. "Those are questions they're certainly in no condition to answer right now, Karen. We'd better figure out what to do. Look, the girl is coming to."

I was snapped out of my detached eavesdropping by a moan beside me. I started to sit up. "Bethie—" I began, and all the knives twisted through my lungs. Bethie's scream followed my gasp.

My eyes were open now, but good, and my leg was an agonized burning ache down at the far end of my consciousness. I gritted my teeth but Bethie moaned again.

"Help her, help her!" I pleaded to the two fuzzy figures leaning over us as I tried to hold my breath to stop the jabbing.

"But she's hardly hurt," Karen cried. "A bump on her head. Some cuts."

With an effort I focused on a luminous clear face—Valancy's—whose deep eyes bent close above me. I locked the rain from my lips and blurted foolishly, "You're not even wet in all this rain!" A look of consternation swept over her face. There was a pause as she looked at me intently and then said, "Their shields aren't activated, Karen. We'd better extend ours."

"Okay, Valancy." And the annoying sibilant wetness of the rain stopped.

"How's the girl?"

"It must be shock or maybe internal—"

I started to turn to see, but Bethie's sobbing cry pushed me flat again.

"Help her," I gasped, grabbing wildly in my memory for Mother's words. "She's a—a Sensitive!"

"A Sensitive?" The two exchanged looks. "Then why doesn't she—?" Valancy started to say something, then turned swiftly. I crooked my arm over my eyes as I listened.

"Honey—Bethie—hear me!" The voice was warm but authoritative. "I'm going to help you. I'll show you how, Bethie."

There was a silence. A warm hand clasped mine and Karen squatted close beside me.

"She's sorting her," she whispered. "Going into her mind. To teach her control. It's so simple. How could it happen that she doesn't know?"

I heard a soft wondering "Oh!" from Bethie, followed by a breathless "Oh, thank you, Valancy, thank you!"

I heaved myself up onto my elbow, fire streaking me from head to foot, and peered over at Bethie. She was looking at me, and her quiet face was happier than smiles could ever make it. We stared for the space of two relieved tears, then she said softly, "Tell them now, Peter. We can't go any farther until you tell them."

I lay back again, blinking at the sky where the scattered raindrops were still falling, though none of them reached us. Karen's hand was warm on mine and I felt a shiver of reluctance. If they sent us away . . . ! But then they couldn't take back what they had given to Bethie, even if— I shut my eyes and blurted it out as bluntly as possible.

"We aren't of the People—not entirely. Father was not of the People. We're half-breeds."

There was a startled silence.

"You mean your mother married an Outsider?" Valancy's voice was filled with astonishment. "That you and Bethie are—?"

"Yes she did and yes we are!" I retorted. "And Dad was the best—" My belligerence ran thinly out across the sharp edge of my pain. "They're both dead now. Mother sent us to you."

"But Bethie is a Sensitive . . ." Valancy's voice was thoughtful.

"Yes, and I can fly and make things travel in the air and I've even made fire. But Dad—" I hid my face and let it twist with the increasing agony.

"Then we *can!*" I couldn't read the emotion in Valancy's voice. "Then the People and Outsiders— But it's unbelievable that you . . ." Her voice died.

In the silence that followed, Bethie's voice came fearful and tremulous, "Are you going to send us away?" My heart twisted to the ache in her voice.

"Send you away! Oh, my people, my people! Of course not! As if there were any question!" Valancy's arm went tightly around Bethie, and Karen's hand closed warmly on mine. The tension that had been a hard twisted knot inside me dissolved, and Bethie and I were home.

Then Valancy became very brisk.

"Bethie, what's wrong with Peter?"

Bethie was astonished. "How did you know his name?" Then she smiled. "Of course. When you were sorting me!" She touched me lightly along my sides, along my legs. "Four of his ribs are hurt. His left leg is broken. That's about all. Shall I control him?"

"Yes," Valancy said. "I'll help."

And the pain was gone, put to sleep under the persuasive warmth that came to me as Bethie and Valancy came softly into my mind.

"Good," Valancy said. "We're pleased to welcome a Sensitive. Karen and I know a little of their function because we are Sorters. But we have no full-fledged Sensitive in our Group now."

She turned to me. "You said you know the inanimate lift?"

"I don't know," I said. "I don't know the words for lots of things."

"You'll have to relax completely. We don't usually use it on people. But if you let go all over we can manage."

They wrapped me warmly in our blankets and lightly, a hand under my shoulders and under my heels, lifted me carrying-high and sped with me through the trees, Bethie trailing from Valancy's free hand.

Before we reached the yard the door flew open and warm yellow light spilled out into the dusk. The girls paused on the porch and shifted me to the waiting touch of two men. In the wordless pause before the babble of question and explanation I felt Bethie beside me draw a deep wondering breath and merge like a raindrop in a river into the People around us.

But even as the lights went out for me again, and I felt myself slide down into comfort and hunger-fed belongingness, somewhere deep inside of me was a core of something that couldn't quite—no, *wouldn't* quite dissolve—wouldn't yet yield itself completely to the People.

11

The Menace from Earth

ROBERT A. HEINLEIN

During World War II, Bob Heinlein and I did time together at the U. S. Navy Yard in Philadelphia. At noon we would cross the burning desert to eat in the cafeteria along with several other kindred souls.

For a while I amused myself each lunch hour by berating the food and discoursing eloquently on its manifold insufficiencies. Bob eventually grew tired of this and issued a ukase. Every time I complained about the food I must pay a nickel fine. The rest of the table agreed. I pleaded for mercy and I was given one way out. If I could ever find a way of complaining about the food that was truly novel and ingenious I would be let off the hook and given my freedom.

For months I tried, twisting and turning in every possible way, and always I failed. "Nickel fine," everyone would chorus. I tried indirection. One time, I remember, I looked up innocently from my filet of sole and said, "Is there such a thing as tough fish?"

"Nickel fine!" yelled everyone.

I objected that I hadn't complained, I had only asked; *but no one listened. They were obdurate. In the months this lasted, I must have lost five dollars in nickels and, I tell you frankly, I was growing desperate.*

Finally, a newcomer joined our table and somehow the boys had neglected to tell him of the situation. He had scarcely eaten a mouthful before he said in disgust, "Boy, this is rotten food."

At which I leaped to my feet, raised one hand, and said loudly, "I disagree with every word this man has said, but I will defend to my death his right to say it." And the fine system was rescinded forever.

Those were great times with Bob and the others, but more fun than even Bob himself are Bob's stories. He is the acknowledged master of us all, for when he visualizes a future society, he sees it with all its details, down to the shoelaces.

Come, then, and let Robert Heinlein show you what it's like to fly—really fly—not by means of a strange talent but by a thoroughly possible, and delightful, technical development. All you need for the purpose is to be on the moon.

My name is Holly Jones and I'm fifteen. I'm very intelligent but it doesn't show, because I look like an underdone angel. Insipid.

I was born right here in Luna City, which seems to surprise Earthside types. Actually, I'm third generation; my grandparents pioneered in Site One, where the Memorial is. I live with my parents in Artemis Apartments, the new co-op in Pressure Five, eight hundred feet down near City Hall. But I'm not there much; I'm too busy.

Mornings I attend Tech High and afternoons I study or go flying with Jeff Hardesty—he's my partner—or whenever a tourist ship is in I guide groundhogs. This day the *Gripsholm* grounded at noon so I went straight from school to American Express.

The first gaggle of tourists was trickling in from Quarantine but I didn't push forward as Mr. Dorcas, the manager, knows I'm the best. Guiding is just temporary (I'm really a spaceship designer), but if you're doing a job you ought to do it well.

Mr. Dorcas spotted me. "Holly! Here, please. Miss Brentwood, Holly Jones will be your guide."

"'Holly,'" she repeated. "What a quaint name. Are you really a guide, dear?"

I'm tolerant of groundhogs—some of my best friends are from Earth. As Daddy says, being born on Luna is luck, not judgment, and most people Earthside are stuck there. After all, Jesus and Gautama Buddha and Dr. Einstein were all groundhogs.

But they can be irritating. If high school kids weren't guides, whom could they hire? "My license says so," I said briskly and looked her over the way she was looking me over.

Her face was sort of familiar and I thought perhaps I had seen her picture in those society things you see in Earthside magazines—one of the rich playgirls we get too many of. She was almost loathsomely lovely . . . nylon skin, soft, wavy, silver-blond hair, basic specs about 35-24-34 and enough this and that to make me feel like a matchstick drawing, a low intimate voice and everything necessary to make plainer females think about pacts with the Devil. But I did not feel apprehensive; she was a groundhog and groundhogs don't count.

"All city guides are girls," Mr. Dorcas explained. "Holly is very competent."

"Oh, I'm sure," she answered quickly and went into tourist routine number one: surprise that a guide was needed just to find her hotel, amazement at no taxicabs, same for no porters, and raised eyebrows at the prospect of two girls walking alone through "an underground city."

Mr. Dorcas was patient, ending with: "Miss Brentwood, Luna City is the only metropolis in the Solar System where a woman is really safe—no dark alleys, no deserted neighborhoods, no criminal element."

I didn't listen; I just held out my tariff card for Mr. Dorcas to stamp and picked up her bags. Guides shouldn't carry bags and most tourists are delighted to experience the fact that their thirty-pound allowance weighs only five pounds. But I wanted to get her moving.

We were in the tunnel outside and me with a foot on the slidebelt when she stopped. "I forgot! I want a city map."

"None available."

"Really?"

"There's only one. That's why you need a guide."

"But why don't they supply them? Or would that throw you guides out of work?"

See? "You think guiding is makework? Miss Brentwood, labor is so scarce they'd hire monkeys if they could."

"Then why not print maps?"

"Because Luna City isn't flat like—" I almost said, "groundhog cities," but I caught myself.

"—like Earthside cities," I went on. "All you saw from space was the meteor shield. Underneath it spreads out and goes down for miles in a dozen pressure zones."

"Yes, I know, but why not a map for each level?"

Groundhogs always say, "Yes, I know, but—"

"I can show you the one city map. It's a stereo tank twenty feet high and even so all you see clearly are big things like the Hall of the Mountain King and hydroponics farms and the Bats' Cave."

" 'The Bats' Cave,' " she repeated. "That's where they fly, isn't it?"

"Yes, that's where we fly."

"Oh, I want to see it!"

"Okay. It first . . . or the city map?"

She decided to go to her hotel first. The regular route to the Zurich is to slide up and west through Gray's Tunnel past the Martian Embassy, get off at the Mormon Temple, and take a pressure lock down to Diana Boulevard. But I know all the shortcuts; we got off at Macy-Gimbel Upper to go down their personnel hoist. I thought she would enjoy it.

But when I told her to grab a hand grip as it dropped past her, she peered down the shaft and edged back. "You're joking."

I was about to take her back the regular way when a neighbor of ours came down the hoist. I said, "Hello, Mrs. Greenberg," and she called back, "Hi, Holly. How are your folks?"

Susie Greenberg is more than plump. She was hanging by one hand with young David tucked in her other arm and holding the *Daily Lunatic,* reading as she dropped. Miss Brentwood stared, bit her lip, and said, "How do I do it?"

I said, "Oh, use both hands; I'll take the bags." I tied the handles together with my hanky and went first.

She was shaking when we got to the bottom. "Goodness, Holly, how do you stand it? Don't you get homesick?"

Tourist question number six . . . I said, "I've been to Earth," and let it drop. Two years ago Mother made me visit my aunt in Omaha and I was *miserable*—hot and cold and dirty and beset by creepy-crawlies. I weighed a ton and I ached and my aunt was always chivvying me to go outdoors and exercise when all I wanted was to crawl into a tub and be quietly wretched. And I had hay fever. Probably you've never heard of hay fever —you don't die but you wish you could.

I was supposed to go to a girls' boarding school but I phoned Daddy and told him I was desperate and he let me come home. What groundhogs can't understand is that *they* live in savagery. But groundhogs are groundhogs and loonies are loonies and never the twain shall meet.

Like all the best hotels the Zurich is in Pressure One on the west side so that it can have a view of Earth. I helped Miss Brentwood register with the roboclerk and found her room; it had its own port. She went straight to it, began staring at Earth and going *ohh!* and *ahh!*

I glanced past her and saw that it was a few minutes past thirteen; sunset sliced straight down the tip of India—early enough to snag another client. "Will that be all, Miss Brentwood?"

Instead of answering she said in an awed voice, "Holly. isn't that the most beautiful sight you ever saw?"

"It's nice," I agreed. The view on that side is monotonous except for earth hanging in the sky—but Earth is what tourists always look at even though they've just left it. Still, Earth is pretty. The changing weather is interesting if you don't have to be in it. Did you ever endure a summer in Omaha?

"It's gorgeous," she whispered.

"Sure," I agreed. "Do you want to go somewhere? Or will you sign my card?"

"What? Excuse me, I was daydreaming. No, not right now —yes, I do! Holly, I want to go out *there!* I must! Is there time? How much longer will it be light?"

"Huh? It's two days to sunset."

She looked startled. "How quaint. Holly, can you get us spacesuits? I've got to go outside."

I didn't wince—I'm used to tourist talk. I suppose a pressure suit looked like a spacesuit to them. I simply said, "We girls aren't licensed outside. But I can phone a friend."

Jeff Hardesty is my partner in spaceship designing, so I throw business his way. Jeff is eighteen and already in Goddard Institute, but I'm pushing hard to catch up so that we can set up offices for our firm: "Jones & Hardesty, Spaceship Engineers." I'm very bright in mathematics, which is everything in space engineering, so I'll get my degree pretty fast. Meanwhile we design ships anyhow.

I didn't tell Miss Brentwood this, as tourists think that a girl my age can't possibly be a spaceship designer.

Jeff has arranged his classes to let him guide on Tuesdays and Thursdays; he waits at West City Lock and studies between clients. I reached him on the lockmaster's phone. Jeff grinned and said, "Hi, Scale Model."

"Hi, Penalty Weight. Free to take a client?"

"Well, I was supposed to guide a family party, but they're late."

"Cancel them. Miss Brentwood . . . step into pickup, please. This is Mr. Hardesty."

Jeff's eyes widened and I felt uneasy. But it did not occur to me that Jeff could be attracted by a *groundhog* . . . even though it is conceded that men are robot slaves of their body chemistry in such matters. I knew she was exceptionally decorative, but it was unthinkable that Jeff could be captivated by any groundhog, no matter how well designed. They don't speak our language!

I am not romantic about Jeff; we are simply partners. But anything that affects Jones & Hardesty affects me.

When we joined him at West Lock he almost stepped on his tongue in a disgusting display of adolescent rut. I was ashamed of him and, for the first time, apprehensive. Why are males so childish?

Miss Brentwood didn't seem to mind his behavior. Jeff is a big hulk; suited up for outside he looks like a Frost Giant from *Das Rheingold*; she smiled up at him and thanked him for changing his schedule. He looked even sillier and told her it was a pleasure.

I keep my pressure suit at West Lock so that when I switch a client to Jeff he can invite me to come along for the walk. This time he hardly spoke to me after that platinum menace was in sight. But I helped her pick out a suit and took her into the dressing room and fitted it. Those rental suits take careful adjusting or they will pinch you in tender places once out in vacuum . . . besides those things about them that one girl ought to explain to another.

When I came out with her, not wearing my own, Jeff didn't even ask why I hadn't suited up—he took her arm and started toward the lock. I had to butt in to get her to sign my tariff card.

The days that followed were the longest in my life. I saw Jeff only once . . . on the slidebelt in Diana Boulevard, going the other way. She was with him.

Though I saw him but once, I knew what was going on. He was cutting classes and three nights running he took her to the Earthview Room of the Duncan Hines. None of my business!—I hope she had more luck teaching him to dance than I had. Jeff is a free citizen and if he wanted to make an utter fool of himself neglecting school and losing sleep over an upholstered groundhog that was his business.

But he should not have neglected the firm's business!

Jones & Hardesty had a tremendous backlog because we were designing Starship *Prometheus*. This project we had been slaving over for a year, flying not more than twice a week in order to devote time to it—and that's a sacrifice.

Of course you can't build a starship today, because of the powerplant. But Daddy thinks that there will soon be a technological break-through and mass-conversion powerplants will be built—which means starships. Daddy ought to know—he's Luna Chief Engineer for Space Lanes and Fermi Lecturer at Goddard Institute. So Jeff and I are designing a self-supporting interstellar ship on that assumption: quarters, auxiliaries, surgery, labs—everything.

Daddy thinks it's just practice but Mother knows better—Mother is a mathematical chemist for General Synthetics of Luna and is nearly as smart as I am. She realizes that Jones & Hardesty plans to be ready with a finished proposal while other designers are still floundering.

Which was why I was furious with Jeff for wasting time over this creature. We had been working every possible chance. Jeff would show up after dinner, we would finish our homework, then get down to real work, the *Prometheus* . . . checking each other's computations, fighting bitterly over details, and having a wonderful time. But the very day I introduced him to Ariel Brentwood, he failed to appear. I had finished my lessons and was wondering whether to start or wait for him—we were making a radical change in powerplant shielding—when his mother phoned me. "Jeff asked me to call you, dear. He's having dinner with a tourist client and can't come over."

Mrs. Hardesty was watching me so I looked puzzled and said, "Jeff thought I was expecting him? He has his dates mixed." I don't think she believed me; she agreed too quickly.

All that week I was slowly convinced against my will that Jones & Hardesty was being liquidated. Jeff didn't break any more dates—how can you break a date that hasn't been made?—but we always went flying Thursday afternoons unless one of us was guiding. He didn't call. Oh, I know where he was; he took her iceskating in Fingal's Cave.

I stayed home and worked on the *Prometheus,* recalculating masses and moment arms for hydroponics and stores on the basis of the shielding change. But I made mistakes and twice I had to look up logarithms instead of remembering . . . I was so used to wrangling with Jeff over everything that I just couldn't function.

Presently I looked at the name plate of the sheet I was revising. "Jones & Hardesty" it read, like all the rest. I said to myself, "Holly Jones, quit bluffing; this may be The End. You knew that someday Jeff would fall for somebody."

"Of course . . . but not a *groundhog.*"

"But he *did.* What kind of an engineer are you if you can't face facts? She's beautiful and rich—she'll get her father to give him a job Earthside. You hear me? *Earthside!* So you look for another partner . . . or go into business on your own."

I erased "Jones & Hardesty" and lettered "Jones & Company" and stared at it. Then I started to erase that too—but it smeared; I had dripped a tear on it. Which was ridiculous!

The following Tuesday both Daddy and Mother were home for lunch, which was unusual, as Daddy lunches at the spaceport. Now Daddy can't even see you unless you're a spaceship but that day he picked to notice that I had dialed only a salad and hadn't finished it. "That plate is about eight hundred calories short," he said, peering at it. "You can't boost without fuel—aren't you well?"

"Quite well, thank you," I answered with dignity.

"Mmm . . . now that I think back, you've been moping for several days. Maybe you need a checkup." He looked at Mother.

"I do not either need a checkup!" I had *not* been moping—doesn't a woman have a right not to chatter?

But I hate to have doctors poking at me so I added, "It happens I'm eating lightly because I'm going flying this afternoon. But if you insist, I'll order pot roast and potatoes and sleep instead!"

"Easy, punkin," he answered gently. "I didn't mean to intrude. Get yourself a snack when you're through . . . and say hello to Jeff for me."

I simply answered, "Okay," and asked to be excused; I was humiliated by the assumption that I couldn't fly without Mr. Jefferson Hardesty but did not wish to discuss it.

Daddy called after me, "Don't be late for dinner," and Mother said, "Now, Jacob—" and to me, "Fly until you're tired, dear; you haven't been getting much exercise. I'll leave your dinner in the warmer. Anything you'd like?"

"No, whatever you dial for yourself." I just wasn't interested in food, which isn't like me. As I headed for Bats' Cave I wondered if I had caught something. But my cheeks didn't feel warm and my stomach wasn't upset even if I wasn't hungry.

Then I had a horrible thought. Could it be that I was jealous? *Me?*

It was unthinkable. I am not romantic; I am a career woman. Jeff had been my partner and pal, and under my guidance he could have become a great spaceship designer, but our relationship was straightforward . . . a mutual respect for each other's abilities, with never any of that lovey-dovey stuff. A career woman can't afford such things—why look at all the professional time Mother had lost over having me!

No, I couldn't be jealous; I was simply worried sick because my partner had become involved with a groundhog. Jeff isn't bright about women and, besides, he's never been to Earth and has illusions about it. If she lured him Earthside, Jones & Hardesty was finished.

And somehow, "Jones & Company" wasn't a substitute: the *Prometheus* might never be built.

I was at Bats' Cave when I reached this dismal conclusion. I didn't feel like flying but I went to the locker room and got my wings anyhow.

Most of the stuff written about Bats' Cave gives a wrong impression. It's the air storage tank for the city, just like all the colonies have—the place where the scavenger pumps, deep down, deliver the air until it's needed. We just happen to be lucky enough to have one big enough to fly in. But it never was built, or anything like that; it's just a big volcanic bubble, two miles across, and if it had broken through, way back when, it would have been a crater.

Tourists sometimes pity us loonies because we have no chance to swim. Well, I tried it in Omaha and got water up my nose and scared myself silly. Water is for drinking, not playing in; I'll take flying. I've heard groundhogs say, oh yes, they had "flown" many times. But that's not *flying*. I did what they talk about, between White Sands and Omaha. I felt awful and got sick. Those things aren't safe.

I left my shoes and skirt in the locker room and slipped my tail surfaces on my feet, then zipped into my wings and got someone to tighten the shoulder straps. My wings aren't ready-made condors; they are Storer-Gulls, custom-made for my weight distribution and dimensions. I've cost Daddy a pretty penny in wings, outgrowing them so often, but these latest I bought myself with guide fees.

They're lovely!—titanalloy struts as light and strong as bird bones, tension-compensated wrist-pinion and shoulder joints, natural action in the alula slots, and automatic flap action in stalling. The wing skeleton is dressed in styrene feather-foils with individual quilling of scapulars and primaries. They almost fly themselves.

I folded my wings and went into the lock. While it was cycling I opened my left wing and thumbed the alula control—I had noticed a tendency to sideslip the last time I was airborne. But the alula opened properly and I decided I must have been overcontrolling, easy to do with Storer-Gulls; they're extremely maneuverable. Then the door showed green and I folded the wing and hurried out, while glancing at the barometer. Seventeen pounds—two more than Earth sea-level and nearly twice what we use in the city; even an ostrich could fly in that. I perked up and felt sorry for all groundhogs, tied down by six times proper weight, who never, never, *never* could fly.

Not even I could, on Earth. My wing loading is less than a pound per square foot, as wings and all I weigh less than twenty pounds. Earthside that would be over a hundred pounds and I could flap forever and never get off the ground.

I felt so good that I forgot about Jeff and his weakness. I spread my wings, ran a few steps, warped for lift and grabbed air—lifted my feet and was airborne.

I sculled gently and let myself glide toward the air intake at the middle of the floor—the Baby's Ladder, we call it, because you can ride the updraft clear to the roof, half a mile above, and never move a wing. When I felt it I leaned right, spoiling with right primaries, corrected, and settled in a counterclockwise soaring glide and let it carry me toward the roof.

A couple of hundred feet up, I looked around. The cave was almost empty, not more than two hundred in the air and half that number perched or on the ground—room enough for didoes. So as soon as I was up five hundred feet I leaned out of the updraft and began to beat. Gliding is no effort but flying is as hard work as you care to make it. In gliding I support a mere ten pounds on each arm—shucks, on Earth you work harder than that lying in bed. The lift that keeps you in the air doesn't take any work; you get it free from the shape of your wings just as long as there is air pouring past them.

Even without an updraft all a level glide takes is gentle sculling with your fingertips to maintain airspeed; a feeble old lady could do it. The lift comes from differential air pressures but you don't have to understand it; you just scull a little and the air supports you, as if you were lying in an utterly perfect bed. Sculling keeps you moving forward just like sculling a rowboat . . . or so I'm told; I've never been in a rowboat. I had a chance to in Nebraska but I'm not that foolhardy.

But when you're really flying, you scull with forearms as well as hands and add power with your shoulder muscles. Instead of only the outer quills of your primaries changing pitch (as in gliding), now your primaries and secondaries clear back to the joint warp sharply on each downbeat and recovery; they no longer lift, they force you forward—while your weight is carried by your scapulars, up under your armpits.

So you fly faster, or climb, or both, through controlling the angle of attack with your feet—with the tail surfaces you wear on your feet, I mean.

Oh dear, this sounds complicated and isn't—you just *do* it. You fly exactly as a bird flies. Baby birds can learn it and they aren't very bright. Anyhow, it's easy as breathing after you learn . . . and more fun than you can imagine!

I climbed to the roof with powerful beats, increasing my angle of attack and slotting my alulae for lift without burble —climbing at an angle that would stall most fliers. I'm little but it's all muscle and I've been flying since I was six. Once up there I glided and looked around. Down at the floor near the south wall tourists were trying glide wings—if you call those things "wings." Along the west wall the visitors' gallery was loaded with goggling tourists. I wondered if Jeff and his Circe character were there and decided to go down and find out.

So I went into a steep dive and swooped toward the gallery, leveled off and flew very fast along it. I didn't spot Jeff and his groundhoggess but I wasn't watching where I was going and overtook another flier, almost collided. I glimpsed him just in time to stall and drop under, and fell fifty feet before I got control. Neither of us was in danger as the gallery is two hundred feet up, but I looked silly and it was my own fault; I had violated a safety rule.

There aren't many rules but they are necessary; the first is that orange wings always have the right of way—they're beginners. This flier did not have orange wings but I was overtaking. The flier underneath—or being overtaken—or nearer the wall—or turning counterclockwise, in that order, has the right of way.

I felt foolish and wondered who had seen me, so I went all the way back up, made sure I had clear air, then stooped like a hawk toward the gallery, spilling wings, lifting tail, and letting myself fall like a rock.

I completed my stoop in front of the gallery, lowering and spreading my tail so hard I could feel leg muscles knot and grabbing air with both wings, alulae slotted. I pulled level in an extremely fast glide along the gallery. I could see their eyes pop and thought smugly, "There! That'll show 'em!"

When darn if somebody didn't stoop on *me!* The blast from a flier braking right over me almost knocked me out of control. I grabbed air and stopped a sideslip, used some shipyard words and looked around to see who had blitzed me. I knew the black-and-gold wing pattern—Mary Muhlenburg, my best girl friend. She swung toward me, pivoting on a wingtip. "Hi, Holly! Scared you, didn't I?"

"You did not! You better be careful; the flightmaster'll ground you for a month."

"Slim chance! He's down for coffee."

I flew away, still annoyed, and started to climb. Mary called after me, but I ignored her, thinking, "Mary my girl, I'm going to get over you and fly you right out of the air."

This was a foolish thought as Mary flies every day and has shoulders and pectoral muscles like Mrs. Hercules. By the time she caught up with me I had cooled off and we flew side by side, still climbing. "Perch?" she called out.

"Perch," I agreed. Mary has lovely gossip and I could use a breather. We turned toward our usual perch, a ceiling brace for flood lamps—it isn't supposed to be a perch but the flightmaster hardly ever comes up there.

Mary flew in ahead of me, braked and stalled dead to a perfect landing. I skidded a little but Mary stuck out a wing and steadied me. It isn't easy to come into a perch, especially when you have to approach level. Two years ago a boy who had just graduated from orange wings tried it . . . knocked off his left alula and primaries on a strut—went fluttering and spinning down two thousand feet and crashed. He could have saved himself—you can come in safely with a badly damaged wing if you spill air with the other and accept the steeper glide, then stall as you land. But this poor kid didn't know how; he broke his neck, dead as Icarus. I haven't used that perch since.

We folded our wings and Mary sidled over. "Jeff is looking for you," she said with a sly grin.

My insides jumped but I answered coolly "So? I didn't know he was here."

"Sure. Down there," she added, pointing with her left wing. "Spot him?"

Jeff wears striped red and silver, but she was pointing at the tourist glide slope, a mile away. "No."

"He's there all right." She looked at me sidewise. "But I wouldn't look him up if I were you."

"Why not? Or for that matter, why should I?" Mary can be exasperating.

"Huh? You always run when he whistles. But he has that Earthside siren in tow again today; you might find it embarrassing."

"Mary, whatever are you talking about?"

"Huh? Don't kid me, Holly Jones; you know what I mean."

"I'm sure I don't," I answered with cold dignity.

"Humph! Then you're the only person in Luna City who doesn't. Everybody knows you're crazy about Jeff; everybody knows she's cut you out . . . and that you are simply simmering with jealousy."

Mary is my dearest friend but someday I'm going to skin her for a rug. "Mary, that's preposterously ridiculous! How can you even think such a thing?"

"Look, darling, you don't have to pretend. I'm for you." She patted my shoulders with her secondaries.

So I pushed her over backwards. She fell a hundred feet, straightened out, circled and climbed, and came in beside me, still grinning. It gave me time to decide what to say.

"Mary Muhlenburg, in the first place I am not crazy about

anyone, least of all Jeff Hardesty. He and I are simply friends. So it's utterly nonsensical to talk about me being 'jealous.' In the second place Miss Brentwood is a lady and doesn't go around 'cutting out' anyone, least of all me. In the third place she is simply a tourist Jeff is guiding—business, nothing more."

"Sure, sure," Mary agreed placidly. "I was wrong. Still—" She shrugged her wings and shut up.

"'Still' what? Mary, don't be mealy-mouthed."

"Mmm . . . I was wondering how you knew I was talking about Ariel Brentwood—since there isn't anything to it."

"Why, you mentioned her name."

"I did not."

I thought frantically. "Uh, maybe not. But it's perfectly simple. Miss Brentwood is a client I turned over to Jeff myself, so I assumed that she must be the tourist you meant."

"So? I don't recall even saying she was a tourist. But since she is just a tourist you two are splitting, why aren't you doing the inside guiding while Jeff sticks to outside work? I thought you guides had an agreement?"

"Huh? If he has been guiding her inside the city, I'm not aware of it—"

"You're the only one who isn't."

"—and I'm not interested; that's up to the grievance committee. But Jeff wouldn't take a fee for inside guiding in any case."

"Oh, sure!—not one he could *bank*. Well, Holly, seeing I was wrong, why don't you give him a hand with her? She wants to learn to glide."

Butting in on that pair was farthest from my mind. "If Mr. Hardesty wants my help, he will ask me. In the meantime I shall mind my own business . . . a practice I recommend to you!"

"Relax, shipmate," she answered, unruffled. "I was doing you a favor."

"Thank you, I don't need one."

"So I'll be on my way—got to practice for the gymkhana." She leaned forward and dropped off. But she didn't practice aerobatics; she dived straight for the tourist slope.

I watched her out of sight, then sneaked my left hand out the hand slit and got at my hanky—awkward when you are wearing wings but the floodlights had made my eyes water. I wiped them and blew my nose and put my hanky away and wiggled my hand back into place, then checked everything, thumbs, toes, and fingers, preparatory to dropping off.

But I didn't. I just sat there, wings drooping, and thought. I had to admit that Mary was partly right; Jeff's head was turned completely . . . over a *groundhog*. So sooner or later he would go Earthside and Jones & Hardesty was finished.

Then I reminded myself that I had been planning to be a spaceship designer like Daddy long before Jeff and I teamed up. I wasn't dependent on anyone; I could stand alone, like Joan of Arc, or Lise Meitner.

I felt better . . . a cold, stern pride, like Lucifer in *Paradise Lost*.

I recognized the red and silver of Jeff's wings while he was far off and I thought about slipping quietly away. But Jeff can overtake me if he tries, so I decided, "Holly, don't be a fool! You've no reason to run . . . just be coolly polite."

He landed by me but didn't sidle up. "Hi, Decimal Point."

"Hi, Zero. Uh, stolen much lately?"

"Just the City Bank but they made me put it back." He frowned and added, "Holly, are you mad at me?"

"Why, Jeff, whatever gave you such a silly notion?"

"Uh . . . something Mary the Mouth said."

"Her? Don't pay any attention to what *she* says. Half of it's always wrong and she doesn't mean the rest."

"Yeah, a short circuit between her ears. Then you aren't mad?"

"Of *course* not. Why should I be?"

"No reason I know of. I haven't been around to work on the ship for a few days . . . but I've been awfully busy."

"Think nothing of it. I've been terribly busy myself."

"Uh, that's fine. Look, Test Sample, do me a favor. Help me out with a friend—a client, that is—well, she's a friend, too. She wants to learn to use glide wings."

I pretended to consider it. "Anyone I know?"

"Oh, yes. Fact is, you introduced us. Ariel Brentwood."

"'Brentwood'? Jeff, there are so many tourists. Let me think. Tall girl? Blonde? Extremely pretty?"

He grinned like a goof and I almost pushed him off. "That's Ariel!"

"I recall her . . . she expected me to carry her bags. But you don't need help, Jeff. She seemed very clever. Good sense of balance."

"Oh, yes, sure, all of that. Well, the fact is, I want you two to know each other. She's . . . well, she's just wonderful, Holly. A real person all the way through. You'll love her when you know her better. Uh . . . this seemed like a good chance."

I felt dizzy. "Why, that's very thoughtful, Jeff, but I doubt if she wants to know me better. I'm just a servant she hired—you know groundhogs."

"But she's not at all like the ordinary groundhog. And she does want to know you better—she *told* me so!"

After you told her to think so! I muttered. But I had talked myself into a corner. If I had not been hampered by polite upbringing I would have said, "On your way, vacuum skull! I'm not interested in your groundhog girl friends"—but what I did say was, "Okay, Jeff," then gathered the fox to my bosom and dropped off into a glide.

So I taught Ariel Brentwood to "fly." Look, those so-called wings they let tourists wear have fifty square feet of lift surface, no controls except warp in the primaries, a built-in dihedral to make them stable as a table, and a few meaningless degrees of hinging to let the wearer think that he is "flying" by waving his arms. The tail is rigid, and canted so that if you stall (almost impossible) you land on your feet. All a tourist does is run a few yards, lift up his feet (he can't avoid it) and slide down a blanket of air. Then he can tell his grandchildren how he flew, really *flew*, "just like a bird."

An ape could learn to "fly" that much.

I put myself to the humiliation of strapping on a set of the silly things and had Ariel watch while I swung into the Baby's Ladder and let it carry me up a hundred feet to show her that you really and truly could "fly" with them. Then I thankfully got rid of them, strapped her into a larger set, and put on my beautiful Storer-Gulls. I had chased Jeff away (two instructors is too many), but when he saw her wing up, he swooped down and landed by us.

I looked up. "You again."

"Hello, Ariel. Hi, Blip. Say, you've got her shoulder straps too tight."

"Tut, tut," I said. "One coach at a time, remember? If you want to help, shuck those gaudy fins and put on some gliders . . . then I'll use you to show how not to. Otherwise get above two hundred feet and stay there; we don't need any dining-lounge pilots."

Jeff pouted like a brat but Ariel backed me up. "Do what teacher says, Jeff. That's a good boy."

He wouldn't put on gliders but he didn't stay clear, either. He circled around us, watching, and got bawled out by the flightmaster for cluttering the tourist area.

I admit Ariel was a good pupil. She didn't even get sore when I suggested that she was rather mature across the hips to balance well; she just said that she had noticed that I had the slimmest behind around there and she envied me. So I quit trying to get her goat, and found myself almost liking her as long as I kept my mind firmly on teaching. She tried hard and learned fast—good reflexes and (despite my dirty crack) good balance. I remarked on it and she admitted diffidently that she had had ballet training.

About mid-afternoon she said, "Could I possibly try real wings?"

"Huh? Gee, Ariel, I don't think so."

"Why not?"

There she had me. She had already done all that could be done with those atrocious gliders. If she was to learn more, she had to have real wings. "Ariel, it's dangerous. It's not what you've been doing, believe me. You might get hurt, even killed."

"Would you be held responsible?"

"No. You signed a release when you came in."

"Then I'd like to try it."

I bit my lip. If she had cracked up without my help, I wouldn't have shed a tear—but to let her do something too dangerous while she was my pupil . . . well, it smacked of David and Uriah. "Ariel, I can't stop you . . . but I should put my wings away and not have anything to do with it."

It was her turn to bite her lip. "If you feel that way, I can't ask you to coach me. But I still want to. Perhaps Jeff will help me."

"He probably will," I blurted out, "if he is as big a fool as I think he is!"

Her company face slipped but she didn't say anything because just then Jeff stalled in beside us. "What's the discussion?"

We both tried to tell him and confused him for he got the idea I had suggested it, and started bawling me out. Was I crazy? Was I trying to get Ariel hurt? Didn't I have any sense?

"*Shut up!*" I yelled, then added quietly but firmly, "Jefferson Hardesty, you wanted me to teach your girl friend, so I agreed. But don't butt in and don't think you can get away with talking to me like that. Now beat it! Take wing. Grab air!"

He swelled up and said slowly, "I absolutely forbid it."

Silence for five long counts. Then Ariel said quietly, "Come, Holly. Let's get me some wings."

"Right, Ariel."

But they don't rent real wings. Fliers have their own; they have to. However, there are second-hand ones for sale because kids outgrow them, or people shift to custom-made ones, or something. I found Mr. Schultz who keeps the key, and said that Ariel was thinking of buying but I wouldn't let her without a tryout. After picking over forty-odd pairs I found a set which Johnny Queveras had outgrown but which I knew were all right. Nevertheless I inspected them carefully. I could hardly reach the finger controls but they fitted Ariel.

While I was helping her into the tail surfaces I said, "Ariel? This is still a bad idea."

"I know. But we can't let men think they own us."

"I suppose not."

"They do own us, of course. But we shouldn't let them know it." She was feeling out the tail controls. "The big toes spread them?"

"Yes. But don't do it. Just keep your feet together and toes pointed. Look, Ariel, you really aren't ready. Today all you will do is glide, just as you've been doing. Promise?"

She looked me in the eye. "I'll do exactly what you say . . . not even take wing unless you okay it."

"Okay. Ready?"

"I'm ready."

"All right. Wups! I goofed. They aren't orange."

"Does it matter?"

"It sure does." There followed a weary argument because Mr. Schultz didn't want to spray them orange for a tryout. Ariel settled it by buying them, then we had to wait a bit while the solvent dried.

We went back to the tourist slope and I let her glide, cautioning her to hold both alulae open with her thumbs for more lift at slow speeds, while barely sculling with her fingers. She did fine, and stumbled in landing only once. Jeff stuck around, cutting figure eights above us, but we ignored him. Presently I taught her to turn in a wide, gentle bank—you can turn those awful glider things but it takes skill; they're only meant for straight glide.

Finally I landed by her and said, "Had enough?"

"I'll never have enough! But I'll unwing if you say."

"Tired?"

"No." She glanced over her wing at the Baby's Ladder; a dozen fliers were going up it, wings motionless, soaring lazily. "I wish I could do that just once. It must be heaven."

I chewed it over. "Actually, the higher you are, the safer you are."

"Then why not?"

"Mmm . . . safer *provided* you know what you're doing. Going up that draft is just gliding like you've been doing. You lie still and let it lift you half a mile high. Then you come down the same way, circling the wall in a gentle glide. But you're going to be tempted to do something you don't understand yet—flap your wings, or cut some caper."

She shook her head solemnly. "I won't do anything you haven't taught me."

I was still worried. "Look, it's only half a mile up but you cover five miles getting there and more getting down. Half an hour at least. Will your arms take it?"

"I'm sure they will."

"Well . . . you can start down anytime; you don't have to go all the way. Flex your arms a little now and then, so they won't cramp. Just don't flap your wings."

"I won't."

"Okay." I spread my wings. "Follow me."

I led her into the updraft, leaned gently right, then back left to start the counterclockwise climb, all the while sculling very slowly so that she could keep up. Once we were in the groove I called out, "Steady as you are!" and cut out suddenly, climbed and took station thirty feet over and behind her. "Ariel?"

"Yes, Holly?"

"I'll stay over you. Don't crane your neck; you don't have to watch me, I have to watch you. You're doing fine."

"I feel fine!"

"Wiggle a little. Don't stiffen up. It's a long way to the roof. You can scull harder if you want to."

"Aye aye, Cap'n!"

"Not tired?"

"Heavens, no! Girl, I'm living!" She giggled. "And mama said I'd never be an angel!"

I didn't answer because red-and-silver wings came charging at me, braked suddenly and settled into the circle between me and Ariel. Jeff's face was almost as red as his wings. "What the devil do you think you are doing?"

"Orange wings!" I yelled. "Keep clear!"

"Get down out of here! Both of you!"

"Get out from between me and my pupil. You know the rules."

"Ariel!" Jeff shouted. "Lean out of the circle and glide down. I'll stay with you."

"Jeff Hardesty," I said savagely, "I give you three seconds to get out from between us—then I'm going to report you for violation of Rule One. For the third time—*Orange Wings!*"

Jeff growled something, dipped his right wing and dropped out of formation. The idiot sideslipped within five feet of Ariel's wingtip. I should have reported him for that; all the room you can give a beginner is none too much.

I said, "Okay, Ariel?"

"Okay, Holly. I'm sorry Jeff is angry."

"He'll get over it. Tell me if you feel tired."

"I'm not. I want to go all the way up. How high are we?"

"Four hundred feet, maybe."

Jeff flew below us a while, then climbed and flew over us . . . probably for the same reason I did: to see better. It suited me to have two of us watching her as long as he didn't interfere; I was beginning to fret that Ariel might not realize that the way down was going to be as long and tiring as the way up. I was hoping she would cry uncle. I knew I could glide until forced down by starvation. But a beginner gets tense.

Jeff stayed generally over us, sweeping back and forth—he's too active to glide very long—while Ariel and I continued to soar, winding slowly up toward the roof. It finally occurred to me when we were about halfway up that I could cry uncle myself; I didn't have to wait for Ariel to weaken. So I called out, "Ariel? Tired now?"

"No."

"Well, I am. Could we go down, please?"

She didn't argue, she just said, "All right. What am I to do?"

"Lean right and get out of the circle." I intended to have her move out five or six hundred feet, get into the return down draft, and circle the cave down instead of up. I glanced up, looking for Jeff. I finally spotted him some distance away and much higher but coming toward us. I called out, "Jeff! See you on the ground." He might not have heard me but he would see if he didn't hear; I glanced back at Ariel.

I couldn't find her.

Then I saw her, a hundred feet below—flailing her wings and falling, out of control.

I didn't know how it happened. Maybe she leaned too far, went into a sideslip and started to struggle. But I didn't try to figure it out; I was simply filled with horror. I seemed to hang there frozen for an hour while I watched her.

But the fact appears to be that I screamed "*Jeff!*" and broke into a stoop.

But I didn't seem to fall, couldn't overtake her. I spilled my wings completely—but couldn't manage to fall; she was as far away as ever.

You do start slowly, of course; our low gravity is the only thing that makes human flying possible. Even a stone falls a scant three feet in the first second. But that first second seemed endless.

Then I knew I was falling. I could feel rushing air—but I still didn't seem to close on her. Her struggles must have slowed her somewhat, while I was in an intentional stoop, wings spilled and raised over my head, falling as fast as possible. I had a wild notion that if I could pull even with her, I could shout sense into her head, get her to dive, then straighten out in a glide. But I couldn't *reach* her.

This nightmare dragged on for hours.

Actually we didn't have room to fall for more than twenty seconds; that's all it takes to stoop a thousand feet. But twenty seconds can be horribly long . . . long enough to regret every foolish thing I had ever done or said, long enough to say a prayer for us both . . . and to say good-bye to Jeff in my heart. Long enough to see the floor rushing toward us and knew that we were both going to crash if I didn't overtake her mighty quick.

I glanced up and Jeff was stooping right over us but a long way up. I looked down at once . . . and I was overtaking her . . . I was passing her—*I was under her!*

Then I was braking with everything I had, almost pulling my wings off. I grabbed air, held it, and started to beat without ever going to level flight. I beat once, twice, three times . . . and hit her from below, jarring us both.

Then the floor hit us.

I felt feeble and dreamily contented. I was on my back in a dim room. I think Mother was with me and I know Daddy was. My nose itched and I tried to scratch it, but my arms wouldn't work. I fell asleep again.

I woke up hungry and wide awake. I was in a hospital bed and my arms still wouldn't work, which wasn't surprising as they were both in casts. A nurse came in with a tray. "Hungry?" she asked.

"Starved," I admitted.

"We'll fix that." She started feeding me like a baby.

I dodged the third spoonful and demanded. "What happened to my arms?"

"Hush," she said and gagged me with a spoon.

But a nice doctor came in later and answered my question. "Nothing much. Three simple fractures. At your age you'll heal in no time. But we like your company so I'm holding you for observation of possible internal injury."

"I'm not hurt inside," I told him. "At least, I don't hurt."

"I told you it was just an excuse."

"Uh, Doctor?"

"Well?"

"Will I be able to fly again?" I waited, scared.

"Certainly. I've seen men hurt worse get up and go three rounds."

"Oh. Well, thanks. Doctor? What happened to the other girl? Is she . . . did she . . . ?"

"Brentwood? She's here."

"She's right here," Ariel agreed from the door. "May I come in?"

My jaw dropped, then I said, "Yeah. Sure. Come in."

The doctor said, "Don't stay long," and left. I said, "Well, sit down."

"Thanks." She hopped instead of walked and I saw that one foot was bandaged. She got on the end of the bed.

"You hurt your foot."

She shrugged. "Nothing. A sprain and a torn ligament. Two cracked ribs. But I would have been dead. You know why I'm not?"

I didn't answer. She touched one of my casts. "That's why. You broke my fall and I landed on top of you. You saved my life and I broke both your arms."

"You don't have to thank me. I would have done it for anybody."

"I believe you and I wasn't thanking you. You can't thank a person for saving your life. I just wanted to make sure you knew that I knew it."

I didn't have an answer so I said, "Where's Jeff? Is he all right?"

"He'll be along soon. Jeff's not hurt . . . though I'm surprised he didn't break both ankles. He stalled in beside us so hard that he should have. But Holly . . . Holly my very dear . . . I slipped in so that you and I could talk about him before he got here."

I changed the subject quickly. Whatever they had given me made me feel dreamy and good, but not beyond being embarrassed. "Ariel, what happened? You were getting along fine—then suddenly you were in trouble."

She looked sheepish. "My own fault. You said we were going down, so I looked down. Really looked, I mean. Before that, all my thoughts had been about climbing clear to the roof; I hadn't thought about how far down the floor was. Then I looked down . . . and got dizzy and panicky and went all to pieces." She shrugged. "You were right. I wasn't ready."

I thought about it and nodded. "I see. But don't worry—when my arms are well, I'll take you up again."

She touched my foot. "Dear Holly. But I won't be flying again; I'm going back where I belong."

"Earthside?"

"Yes. I'm taking the *Billy Mitchell* on Wednesday."

"Oh. I'm sorry."

She frowned slightly. "Are you? Holly, you don't like me, do you?"

I was startled silly. What can you say? Especially when it's true. "Well," I said slowly, "I don't dislike you. I just don't know you very well."

She nodded. "And I don't know you very well . . . even though I got to know you a lot better in a very few seconds. But Holly . . . listen, please, and don't get angry. It's about Jeff. He hasn't treated you very well the last few days—while I've been here, I mean. But don't be angry with him. I'm leaving and everything will be the same."

That ripped it open and I couldn't ignore it, because if I did, she would assume all sorts of things that weren't so. So I had to explain . . . about me being a career woman . . . how, if I had seemed upset, it was simply distress at breaking up the firm of Jones & Hardesty before it even finished its first starship . . . how I was *not* in love with Jeff but simply valued him as a friend and associate . . . but if Jones & Hardesty couldn't carry on, then Jones & Company would. "So you see, Ariel, it isn't necessary for you to give up Jeff. If you feel you owe me something, just forget it. It isn't necessary."

She blinked and I saw with amazement that she was holding back tears. "Holly, Holly . . . you don't understand at all."

"I understand all right. I'm not a child."

"No, you're a grown woman . . . but you haven't found it out." She held up a finger. "One—Jeff doesn't love me."

"I don't believe it."

"Two . . . I don't love him."

"I don't believe that, either."

"Three . . . you say you don't love him—but we'll take that up when we come to it. Holly, am I beautiful?"

Changing the subject is a female trait but I'll never learn to do it that fast. "Huh?"

"I said, 'Am I beautiful?'"

"You know darn well you are!"

"Yes. I can sing a bit and dance, but I would get few parts if I were not, because I'm no better than a third-rate actress. So I have to be beautiful. How old am I?"

I managed not to boggle. "Huh? Older than Jeff thinks you are. Twenty-one, at least. Maybe twenty-two."

She sighed. "Holly, I'm old enough to be your mother."

"Huh? I don't believe that either."

"I'm glad it doesn't show. But that's why, though Jeff is a dear, there never was a chance that I could fall in love with him. But how I feel about him doesn't matter; the important thing is that *he* loves *you*."

"*What?* That's the silliest thing you've said yet! Oh, he *likes* me—or did. But that's all." I gulped. "And it's all I want. Why, you should hear the way he talks to me."

"I have. But boys that age can't say what they mean; they get embarrassed."

"But—"

"Wait, Holly. I saw something you didn't because you were knocked cold. When you and I bumped, do you know what happened?"

"Uh, no."

"Jeff arrived like an avenging angel, a split second behind us. He was ripping his wings off as he hit, getting his arms free. He didn't even look at me. He just stepped across me and picked you up and cradled you in his arms, all the while bawling his eyes out."

"He *did?*"

"He did."

I mulled it over. Maybe the big lunk did kind of like me, after all.

Ariel went on, "So you see, Holly, even if you don't love him, you must be very gentle with him, because he loves you and you can hurt him terribly."

I tried to think. Romance was still something that a career woman should shun . . . but if Jeff really did feel that way—well . . . would it be compromising my ideals to marry him just to keep him happy? To keep the firm together? Eventually, that is?

But if I did, it wouldn't be Jones & Hardesty; it would be Hardesty & Hardesty.

Ariel was still talking: "—you might even fall in love with him. It does happen, hon, and if it did, you'd be sorry if you had chased him away. Some other girl would grab him; he's awfully nice."

"But—" I shut up for I heard Jeff's step—I can always tell it. He stopped in the door and looked at us, frowning.

"Hi, Ariel."

"Hi, Jeff."

"Hi, Fraction." He looked me over. "My, but you're a mess."

"You aren't pretty yourself. I hear you have flat feet."

"Permanently. How do you brush your teeth with those things on your arms?"

"I don't."

Ariel slid off the bed, balanced on one foot. "Must run. See you later, kids."

"So long, Ariel."

"Good-bye, Ariel. Uh . . . thanks."

Jeff closed the door after she hopped away, came to the bed and said gruffly, "Hold still."

Then he put his arms around me and kissed me.

Well, I couldn't stop him, could I? With both arms broken?

Besides it was consonant with the new policy for the firm. I was startled speechless because Jeff never kisses me, except birthday kisses, which don't count. But I tried to kiss back and show that I appreciated it.

I don't know what the stuff was they had been giving me but my ears began to ring and I felt dizzy again.

Then he was leaning over me. "Runt," he said mournfully, "you sure give me a lot of grief."

"You're no bargain yourself, flathead," I answered with dignity.

"I suppose not." He looked me over sadly. "What are you crying for?"

I didn't know that I had been. Then I remembered why. "Oh, Jeff—I busted my pretty wings!"

"We'll get you more. Uh, brace yourself. I'm going to do it again."

"All right." He did.

I suppose Hardesty & Hardesty has more rhythm than Jones & Hardesty.

It really sounds better.

12

The Wayward Cravat

GERTRUDE FRIEDBERG

After graduating from high school I attended Seth Low Junior College, a now forgotten undergraduate branch of Columbia University. (It ended as an active part of the university the year after I entered, but I don't believe there was any connection.)

Shortly after the beginning of the year, the Dean called me into his office. I entered in ill-concealed panic. To be sure, I expected sooner or later to be up before the Dean for something, but so soon? I had not yet had a chance, after all, to commit a single unforgivable crime.

As I stood before him quaking, the Dean regarded me solemnly, whipped out a toothed instrument and neatly combed my hair. That was all! He never said a word. When I left and consulted a mirror, I found, to my amazement, that I had a forehead.

In my own defense, I must state that I was a kind of premature college student and only fifteen at the time. I might also say, looking at the college students of today, that I was merely a premature towsle-head.

Nevertheless the fact remains that some boys live in a world of their own, which parents do not know how to enter. Even those parents who in their own time inhabited such a world seem helpless. (I happen to know this, but never mind how.)

Let Gertrude Friedberg, then, introduce you to such a boy in such a world.

"What are those on your feet?" asked Mrs. Hamilcar.

William was at the piano. He looked down and examined his feet apprehensively, not because he expected to find anything but slippers there, but because the sly hollowness of his mother's tone intimated that some principle or condition was at stake of which he felt quite ignorant.

"Slippers," he said carefully.

"Hah!" said Mrs. Hamilcar, her voice rising half a tone with a lift of triumph. "I never saw them on you before."

William looked down again. The slippers looked new, but then he may never have looked at them before.

"They fit fine," he said tentatively.

"Where did you find them?"

"In my closet."

He seemed sure of this and rather pleased that he knew where he had gotten them.

"And how on earth did they get there?"

Now he looked completely confused. Had he taken them from

the house in which he had spent the weekend? Had one of his numerous aunts handed them to him only the night before and had he completely forgotten the incident, the aunt, and the debt of gratitude? Had he picked them up off a counter and stuck them between the covers of his book to keep the page? These and countless other horrible manifestations of his inattention raced guiltily through his mind as he looked at his mother with perplexed apology in his soft brown eyes.

"Look, Mother," prompted Mrs. Hamilcar, "new slippers! You must have bought them for me. Thank you very much, Mother."

He smiled sheepishly and with relief that that was all.

"It isn't that I'm ungrateful," he said.

"Oh, I know you're not ungrateful. I only wanted you to realize that an event like strange slippers must have a reasonable cause, like somebody's earnest activity."

"It's just that my world is so filled with unfathomable events that one more is hardly to be wondered about."

Mrs. Hamilcar knew very well what he meant. What with the mysterious materialization in his unwilling custody of all manner of unfamiliar articles, the occult disappearance of people and things from before his very eyes, the willful tricks of time, and the jocular displacements of his body in space or of the scene about his body, William indeed led a life in which the usual logical sequence of cause and effect seemed often distorted.

This was not the first time, for example, that new clothing had appeared in his closet, as if generated spontaneously by the hangers in it. Even when he had been present himself at the actual acquisition, it would be some time before he would realize that a strange new furnishing was his. After a shopping expedition he would come in to breakfast and ask his mother, "Has anybody slept over here lately?"

"You had your friend, Grover, here a month ago."

"Well," he would say, clearly exhilarated to have been so observant, "I'm afraid my friend Grover has left a brand new jacket in my closet. How do you like that for carelessness!" And he would marshal the sliced bananas and milk for his Wheaties with a great show of knowing where everything was.

It was because of this tendency that Mrs. Hamilcar found

herself at last permitting him to buy the same tan gabardine topcoat every time that one was needed. Once, for variety, Mrs. Hamilcar had been foolhardy enough to urge upon him a navy gabardine. He had even seemed to choose it himself, because he had turned about several times to observe various angles in the store mirror. Later, Mrs. Hamilcar was obliged to recognize that whatever it was he had been measuring in the mirror, whether angles of reflection or the parabolic curve made by the shadow of a chandelier, it certainly had not been the coat. The very first time he wore it to dinner at a friend's house he came home without it.

"Where's your navy coat?" Mrs. Hamilcar asked him harshly.

"I didn't wear any coat tonight. Or did I?" he asked, immediately made unsure of himself under Mrs. Hamilcar's penetrating stare.

"You wore your new navy gabardine."

"What did it look like?"

"It had sleeves, and buttons down the front."

A light of revelation spread over William's face.

"Was that my coat? Everybody kept insisting it was mine and trying to put it on me but I assured them that I had never seen it before in my life."

He got it back and wore it to a party. This time, at least, he was alert enough to come home with a coat, a tan gabardine coat that looked like one he used to own. It was dirty and torn, but at least it had the virtue of familiarity, which might induce him to cling to it perhaps through the brisker part of early spring weather. Some time later, at a camp reunion, a subconscious memory of his navy coat must have emerged without warning, for he came home with a very creditable navy coat and hung it up without comment, quite as if he had started the evening with it. It was a little long, but in good condition. The memory of the tan gabardine seemed to have vanished for good, along with the wallet that had been in it.

This indiscriminate picking up and putting down of topcoats, as well as of raincoats and other apparel, occasionally confused him by presenting him with a strange new identity. He would dip his hand into his jacket pocket and pull out a small memo book belonging to Roger Cunningham. Most people would make the obvious deduction that the wrong jacket had somehow settled upon the right person. But William, who was quite unaware of having ever taken off his jacket in the public library, could only assume that the jacket was the right jacket but that the wrong fellow, in this case Roger Cunningham, had somehow held temporary residence in it. Mrs. Hamilcar often came upon him staring in baffled dismay at just such a strange name written into his rubbers or labeled on his gloves. Or he would squint unhappily at a small date book.

"Do I date with girls yet?" he would ask Mrs. Hamilcar.

Mrs. Hamilcar didn't know and went to ask Mr. Hamilcar, but Mr. Hamilcar just gave her a withering glance and stalked out of the house.

The next night William was pondering the date book again with a worried frown.

"Who is Minnie?" he asked Mrs. Hamilcar.

"I don't know," said Mrs. Hamilcar sharply, because he was always asking her who everybody was and she was pretty tired of it. "A mouse, I guess. Why?"

"I have a date with her tonight and I just can't seem to remember who she is and where I met her."

When this kind of thing happened, Mrs. Hamilcar would usually just let him sweat it out, in the vain hope that it would make him more careful next time.

Even when the jacket was indubitably his own, with his own name tape inside its neck, there were odd objects to be found in his pockets, deposited from time to time by some supernatural agency. His astonished hand would come up with a variety of gifts and prizes such as gold key-holders, tissue-wrapped wallets, and pearl-handled jackknives.

"Look at that!" Mrs. Hamilcar would say furiously to her husband, displaying a gold medal inscribed with the year and William's name. "He doesn't know what it's for or how he got it."

"You spoil him," said Mr. Hamilcar, who was extraordinarily efficient both in his office and in his home, and always disposed of problems the moment they arose.

Once William came home from camp with a trunkful of the wrong clothing. For years thereafter the Hamilcars' weekly laundry sorting was haunted by a strange ghostly presence who was never visible, but whose shorts, handkerchiefs and pajamas had clearly been worn and tossed into one of the hampers. William said he hadn't the faintest idea who Clifford Teil was. Secretly he wondered if his mother, who was inclined to eccentricity and a poor memory (she could never keep in her head the formula for the relationship of mass to energy), had not ordered the wrong name tapes by mistake one day and was now too ashamed to admit it.

Years later, in adult life, William was at a cocktail party and was introduced to a Clifford Teil, a short, frightened man with stiffly brushed hair and a moist face. William, who knew nobody else of the many people presented to him (he had not really been invited but had discovered the invitation in the inside pocket of a raincoat he found himself wearing and assumed was his), grasped Teil's hand effusively.

"Oh, how great to find you here," he shouted enthusiastically.

Mr. Teil stared at him terrified and spilled half of a martini that he had been holding.

Confident that any friend of his with whose name he seemed so comfortably familiar must surely be a mathematician, William plunged into a cheerful explanation of the azimuth of a celestial body, a calculation which he himself found very amusing. Mr. Teil, who was a florist, found himself growing faint at the end of ten minutes. But quite suddenly William, who had come to the party without a topcoat, murmured thoughtfully, "Guess I'd better pick up my topcoat before the mob gets at the coatrack. See you," and left.

Unfathomable, too, was the disposition of time to take devious twists the instant the back of his consciousness was turned. There was the uneasy moment, fraught with ambiguity and wrong choices, in which he would find himself with his trousers on the lower half of his body and his pajama tops on the upper. Swimming up toward such a paradox after half an hour of fruitful reverie during which he found how he would trisect the line using the compass without the ruler (he later discovered that Napoleon had done it), he faced the perplexing problem of whether he was dressing or undressing, and failing to notice in his shade-darkened room such unmistakable signs of morning as the bustling trucks, the thump of the newspaper on the apartment door, and the smell of coffee, he promptly removed his trousers, put on the other half of his pajamas, opened the window, set his alarm for seven the next morning, and went to sleep, just as Mrs. Hamilcar came to call him for breakfast.

And as for the disposition of the world to rearrange itself under his nose into a disordered pattern, like a jigsaw puzzle that has been suddenly jostled, there was the frightening incident that had occurred one summer at camp. It was almost noon. He had come back from swimming, had dressed, and was lying on his bed thinking up several ways other than the usual of determining a right-angled triangle given the radii of the inscribed and circumscribed circles, when gradually his senses stirred with a vague alarm. It took some time for the unease to cut across the humming cords of his thought, but one thread after another was torn until his musings fell in shreds and he jerked upright, profoundly oppressed. At first, as the familiar scene took shape before his eyes—the five beds, the scattered towels, his tennis racket hanging on its nail—he failed to realize what was wrong. Then quite suddenly he knew. There was a great terrible silence as if the world had stopped.

His own bunk was empty, but the boys may have gone to play ping-pong before the noon meal. Oddly, the path outside his bunk was deserted too. He began to wonder if the dinner siren had sounded after all. His counselor would be angry. His small tan face puckered with worry as he started running up the hill toward the great open square which held the mess hall. It was frightening to be in the wrong place at the wrong time and his heart beat hard as he leaped up the porch steps and threw open the screen door of the dining room.

The huge empty hall, the bare tables, the silent chairs leaped at him as from an ambush. He fell back against the wall and leaned there panting for a while. No sound came from the kitchen. His memory, demoralized, raced backward, touching at each prominent activity as at a talisman. He remembered breakfast. He recalled clean-up. They had surely played baseball. He had caught a foul fly. Swimming. Then blur. Had he left them all at the lake?

He started running again, past the empty ping-pong tables, the deserted baseketball court, the tennis courts, white-lined and waiting, and did not need to reach the water's edge to know that the lake was as hushed as though it still awaited discovery by the white man.

A rehearsal. Or an assembly! Of course. That would explain the quiet. It must have been announced when he had not been listening. They would all be there. The mirage cooled his forehead, slowed his hammering pulse as he ran more slowly through the trees and over the rock toward the recreation hall. It was quiet here, the trees dripping with dark. He could expect silence from the disciplines of the rigidly controlled camp assemblies, but as he entered he recognized the stillness in which the heart hears itself when it is alone. The small stage creaked with the tread of ghosts and the piano bared its white teeth in a lonely yawn.

He was not young enough to cry nor old enough to faint. He did not fear being alone or the wary shadows of the trees. Like the lame boy of Hamelin he was frightened only by the dreadful notoriety of being the only survivor of an uncanny disaster that had spirited away within a few minutes of a sunny morning an entire camp of one hundred and eighty-five boys, thirty counselors and numerous kitchen and maintenance personnel. His mother had been annoyed enough when he had lagged behind during her last visit and missed flag-raising. What would she think now that he had failed to participate in the enigmatic obliteration which had attacked the entire lively population of his summer quarters? Filled with guilt and remorse he sat down in one of the empty seats that faced the deserted stage and began to search for rational solutions to his riddle.

He considered whether they might have gone away on a cookout or an overnight hike, but on reflection he realized that only a limited group at a time would embark on such an outing, not possibly the whole camp. He dealt next with the possibility that it was September and that they had all gone home to the city. With this in mind he returned to his bunk, but the piles of shorts and shirts in the cupboards, the well-made beds, and the towels on the floor quickly demolished this hypothesis.

Perhaps there was a war on. They had been suddenly alerted and had taken shelter at some prearranged place, with no time to make sure he was with them. He scanned the sky for planes, but nothing more lethal than a bird swooped confidently through the glowing blue circle. Still it was a possibility. He went into the office, a forbidden place, now treacherously empty, and dialed operator. The sound of life, however cold and impersonal, was wonderfully reassuring.

"Is there a war on?" he quavered in a cracking treble.

"What number did you want, please?" asked life.

Since he did not know and was always rather baffled by the telephone, he hung up.

Somehow he would have to acquaint the authorities with the unnatural event which had islanded him. He could write to his mother, the chief of all authorities, but he realized with a surge of pride at his own hard-headed pragmatism, that there was nobody here to take the letter to town. Besides he couldn't think only of himself. The whole world would be wondering what had happened to so many people. He must go to Pittsfield, the nearest large city, and tell everything he knew. He pictured the citizens crowding about him, besieging him with questions, as in a Greek tragedy.

At last, bursting with responsibility, he started off on the only road away from camp, searching the ground and trees for clues with unpracticed eyes that saw nothing. He had walked for perhaps an hour when suddenly he heard a boy's matter-of-fact voice quite close to him and turned to round a large bush. There they all were, reincarnated at last, as mysteriously and suddenly as they had vanished in the first place, their familiar faces, which he had never expected to see again, unbelievably insensible of any crisis. They had eaten and were resting, silence being imposed as usual by the counselors.

When Mrs. Hamilcar had read William's next letter, she took it at once to Mr. Hamilcar.

"William's camp disappeared," she said gloomily. "First his socks, then his blankets, and now the whole camp."

"Spoiled. Spoiled," muttered Mr. Hamilcar, quite as if William had been given so many camps to play with that it was only out of carelessness fostered by overindulgence that he had misplaced one.

A second letter came from the camp director. Some time during each summer all the boys were separated into two teams for the customary color war. At this particular camp the color war began traditionally with a dramatic, unannounced, opening ceremony that burst each year with greater éclat. This year, as the boys after swimming had been idling in their bunks or on the open stretches awaiting the lunch siren, quite suddenly a great noise arose from the surrounding trees and from every side the camp was invaded by counselors dressed in fanciful costumes and rousing every sleeping insect for miles around with the extraordinary clamor of their brass band. There were bagpipes, trumpets, big horns and enormous drums. At the very first blast of this unparalleled cacophony, the boys streaked from cabins to add their excited shrieks of excitement and partisanship to the color war parade. Soon every single inhabitant in the camp, including the baby of the director's wife and the small dog belonging to the cook, were in the screaming, singing, booming, blaring line which crawled all about the flag field, snaked around every cabin, danced and crashed across the baseball field and finally dragged its entire clangorous length in among the frightened trees on the path to the prepared cookout—that is, every single inhabitant but William.

This explanation from the camp director was not one to reassure Mrs. Hamilcar. The memory of the incident, long after it had happened, lay always close at hand and seemed to bear an ominous pertinence to many unrelated matters.

For example, Mr. Hamilcar liked his son to be well groomed, and indeed when finally turned out for an occasion William managed to look quite attractive, particularly if the last topcoat he had picked up was not too short in the sleeves. An unfortunate habit of stuffing one trouser leg inside his sock, or even the occasional absence of a belt in his trousers was, after all, a remediable flaw. What really caught the attention was a sartorial error, tiny enough but persistent, which finally took its place as one more of the unfathomable features of William's life.

There had been a period when Mrs. Hamilcar thought William would never master the intricacies of tie-making. For a while it was hit and miss, and William at eight and nine years old might show up at school with the tie hanging from the back of his neck, or with the two lengths so uneven that one end dangled about his knees. But the day did come when the problem appealed to him as one that he truly wished to solve. He asked his father how to make a Windsor knot and leveled his entire attention on Mr. Hamilcar's demonstration. Mr. Hamilcar was brisk, authoritative and severe. He was always accusing Mrs. Hamilcar of being too soft with William and was pleased to have this opportunity to display his own manner of conducting a father-son interview with an effective didactic approach. He and William walked around and around each other, passing lengths of tie about each other's necks. At one point they both might have strangled if Mrs. Hamilcar had not cut the tie in two.

The very next morning William tried it out himself with unexpected dexterity and produced a very neat knot with well-approximated lengths. Mrs. Hamilcar was lost in admiration. William, after all, was a boy like any other boy. Perhaps some day he would even come home with the same topcoat in which he had ventured forth.

But alas, William's Windsor knots were cursed with a fatal delayed twist, not immediately apparent to the naked eye. It took about an hour for the perversity to emerge. If you tried, and Mrs. Hamilcar often did, to watch for the transformation to happen under your eyes, you were never able to catch it, but suddenly there it would be. Somehow or other the narrow underneath length of this exemplarily made tie worked itself around to come out on top of the wider portion which should have been topside.

Mrs. Hamilcar thought at first that it was an accident and couldn't possibly happen again. She watched William make his tie without saying anything about her fears, for he himself had not noticed the ultimate eccentric disposition of his handiwork.

"If there's one thing you'll have to admit I do very well, it's making a Windsor tie," he said when his eyes met hers in the mirror. She nodded bravely and he did not notice how pale she was.

When he had finished, she looked closely at the finished product. It was perfect. The knot was straight, no twists in it to uncurl into disarray later. The top length lay neatly, apparently contentedly, over the lower length. William went jauntily to breakfast. An hour later the bottom part was on top, jumping about aggressively like an inferior junior partner.

Mrs. Hamilcar appealed at last to Mr. Hamilcar.

"You'll have to do something about William's ties," she said. "The bottom comes out on the top."

"You let him have his own way too much," said Mr. Hamilcar. Together they thought of their dissatisfaction in William.

The next few mornings William was a little surprised to find his mother and father standing by in what appeared to him to be affectionate admiration while he made his Windsor tie in the mirror.

"Perfect," said Mr. Hamilcar with a vindictive glance in Mrs. Hamilcar's direction.

An hour later, while they all dawdled at the table over the Sunday papers, Mrs. Hamilcar nudged her husband and pointed to William's tie. The bottom was on top. The very sight of it made Mr. Hamilcar furious.

"Why don't we ever have anything but French toast for Sunday breakfast!" he shouted, thumping the table.

He spent the rest of the day knotting ties around the four posts of the bed. He tied every conceivable type of knot, made his passes in every conceivable order, tied knots as wearer and knots as beholder and knots as a mirror image of himself. But all the ties which started life with the top part uppermost, still maintained this dull juxtaposition after an hour. Mr. Hamilcar ended with frustration and a slight feeling of envy.

"You've got to hand it to the kid," he said at last to Mrs. Hamilcar. "It's something he puts into it that does the trick." Then, loath to give up, he tried two or three more knots, giving his fingers a clever little flick and twist at the end, somewhat like the curious twist a baseball pitcher gives to a ball that will swing perversely away from the batter precisely at the end of its flight. Unsuccessful in this too, Mr. Hamilcar dolefully untied all his ties from the bedposts and gave them to Mrs. Hamilcar to have them pressed, since their appearance had not been improved by the experiments to which they had been subjected.

Mrs. Hamilcar could not find in herself any real esteem for William's new accomplishment. She asked many of her friends about it. One suggested bow ties and another told her William might try starting with his tie bottom side up. William scorned bow ties as being much too primitive for somebody who could make a Windsor knot, and the second suggestion seemed derisive. William, since he never glanced at himself in a mirror after the morning exercises, continued to have no idea of the odd turn his ties were taking.

Occasionally Mrs. Hamilcar would pick up one of the many science fiction stories that littered William's room. In these stories people were always cracking out somehow into the fourth dimension and then barging back at thoroughly inconvenient times, as in the middle of a formal dinner when everybody had given them up for dead and the supply of broiled chickens was already inadequate, or to find themselves five hundred years younger, or with their skins inside out, or with everything in their old room reversed somehow. If Mrs. Hamilcar could have induced herself to think in such extravagant terms, she might have believed that here was a possible explanation for William's tie. It was enough to know that sometime during the process of twist and knot and final pat of tie-making there came a deep and dreadful pause during which William, if not in a fourth dimension, was as surely in a spot beyond space, where time stood still and only number was true. So automatic was his tie-making that it was hard to catch the moment of his departure, but depart he did, and it was during his absence, she was sure, that the fateful detour was imparted to his cravat.

The caprices of his ties and the picaresque adventures of his coats filled Mrs. Hamilcar with angry impatience, and as the day approached when William was to leave for prep school she was conscious of a growing despair. The mountainous details of living still seemed to escape her son. The thought of turning him loose without some last attempt to anchor his attention in reality seemed almost irresponsible on the part of a mother who thought of herself as provident. She therefore determined to drive into his consciousness an awareness of every article that he would take with him. Nothing would go with him to prep school that he did not think of taking himself.

With this plan in mind Mrs. Hamilcar watched William closely to see if he would come himself to entertain preparations for the approaching departure. But apparently he expected that by some miracle he and his room, intact with all his effects of dress, study and toilet, would be transferred to his new abode without his lifting a finger or even bothering to say a magic word. Finally she had the trunk brought up and left conspicuously open in the middle of his room.

"Oh, yes," he said pleasantly, "I guess I have to take some things."

"Yes," she said, closing her eyes tragically.

"Let's see now." He looked vaguely around the room and his eyes lit on his bookcase.

"Oh, no," said Mrs. Hamilcar. "Books are the last."

"What do I start with then?"

"I'm not going to tell you," said Mrs. Hamilcar, folding her arms grimly. "If you don't remember, you won't have it. Just picture yourself getting up in the morning and go through a day and think of what you'll use."

"Well," he said, blithely telescoping some of the most significant moments of the day, "I get up in the morning and go to school."

He went to the desk looking quite smugly satisfied with himself and took out five pencils, a compass, a slide rule and two ballpoint pens. He put them in the trunk and then fell into a deep reverie during which he worked on a proof that equations of the fifth degree could not be solved. Mrs. Hamilcar decided to start embroidering the tablecloth that had been in her linen closet since she had married. It was going to be a long siege watching William pack. By nightfall he had put in a few rather obvious articles of his clothing.

"Just picture it," said Mrs. Hamilcar, egging him on. "You come into a bare room. Nothing in it but a bed, a desk, a bookcase and a chair."

"I'll need ink," said William.

"Ink. Very good, but not really basic. There's a complete basic category that you haven't even started."

"Desk lamp!"

"Also fairly good. Get a grocer's box and put it in, but that's not it. I wish you'd get away from the desk and move around the room a little."

"Window shades!"

"No!"

"I'm away from the desk. I look out the window. I move around further. I come to the bed."

"Yes?"

"I sit down on it and look around the room," he said, sitting on his own bed and looking around.

"Fine, fine."

"I lie down a while to help me think better," he said, stretching out

"Oh God."

At two in the morning he knocked at her bedroom door.

"What is it?" she called out, while Mr. Hamilcar, who had just gotten to bed and didn't sleep too well, grumbled angrily.

"Sheets!" called William. "Sheets and blankets!"

"Excellent," groaned Mrs. Hamilcar.

"What's the matter with him?" asked Mr. Hamilcar irritably.

"He thought of sheets and blankets."

"So did I," he snarled, "but a lot of good it does me."

It took William ten days to pack his trunk. Every once in a while he would look at Mrs. Hamilcar and say, "Well, I guess that's everything, isn't it?"

Mrs. Hamilcar would swing her foot and say bitterly, "If you think so."

"I've left something out."

"Perhaps."

"Something basic?"

"Moderately."

"Useful during the day?"

"Many people think so."

"To wear?"

"If it's your whim."

"Do I have it on now?"

"As luck would have it."

He checked over his clothes, beginning from the inside and working out. Suddenly he clamped a hand to his brow.

"Socks! Of course. Socks!"

He got them out of the drawer. They were new colored Argyles which Mrs. Hamilcar had bought for him.

"Please look at them very carefully," she said. "The last socks you had were black, red and gray. These are black, green and gray. Stare at them for a while and say, 'These are *my* socks. These are *my* socks.' I don't want you to write to me that you discovered some strange socks in the drawer which you handed over to the lost and found and where on earth are your socks."

William could not deny that there was a strong possibility that he would do exactly that. He therefore willingly stood in front of the collection of socks, staring fixedly at them and repeating over and over again, "These are *my* socks. These are *my* socks."

Just then Mr. Hamilcar, who had found himself that morning a little short of socks, appeared at the door and looked enviously at the great array.

"These are *my* socks. These are *my* socks," said William.

"He's a selfish pig," shouted Mr. Hamilcar furiously, and slammed shut the door.

Sometimes Mr. Hamilcar, who rarely knew what they were talking about, happened to hear them in the midst of their guessing game.

"I'm thinking of something that is used under certain meteorological conditions," said Mrs. Hamilcar.

"Do I wear it or look at it on a wall?" asked William.

It was at this point that Mr. Hamilcar began to listen.

"You wear it," said Mrs. Hamilcar between cracked swollen lips.

William looked deeply puzzled.

"I packed my raincoat," he said.

"Rubbers!" shouted Mr. Hamilcar, leaping from his seat like an eager student with the right answer.

Mrs. Hamilcar stuck her embroidery needle into the arm of her chair and stamped her foot with a feeling akin to that which Rumpelstiltskin must have suffered.

"You told him! You told him!"

Once she was called to the phone at her hairdresser's. She went to it with several pounds of fixtures on her head.

"Hello?" she said.

"Shirts," said a voice and hung up.

When the trunk was finally locked and sent off, Mrs. Hamilcar could picture William going through his school days and nights in relative comfort. If he found himself inconvenienced by having no pillowcases, having to use Kleenex in place of the towels he had forgotten and to tiptoe around the gymnasium in his socks instead of in sneakers, he could write and ask for the missing articles. She would be glad to send them, content that the lesson had been learned.

At last the day of departure arrived. As they waited for the train to pull out, Mrs. Hamilcar looked closely at the other boys, presumably going to the same school. They looked resolute, competent and contained. Behind their farewell expressions lay careful inventories of the contents of their trunks. They patted their upper left breastpockets where they knew their railroad tickets lay. They would know when the train left and would not be surprised when it arrived at its destination. They would count off wittingly as they picked up overnight bags, tennis rackets, coats, magazines and books. Intact, their attention dealt with the moment before them. Conscious, *integri vitae*, what a contrast they made to William with his inverted tie.

They would check in at the right desk at school, pocket their doorkeys carefully and find the right rooms immediately. They would unpack, putting all the things in the right places. They would not put pajamas in the desk drawers. They would put two sheets on the bed before they put a blanket on top. They would wear thin short-sleeved shirts until the weather turned cold and then unerringly pick out the long-sleeved shirts for the rest of the winter. They would read the notices on the bulletin boards and would not turn up for the English midterm when it was over. They knew what sweaters were for, could replace broken shoelaces, and understood laundry.

You would have thought Mr. Hamilcar was going to school. Patiently, his face bewildered, his lips dry with nervousness, he asked Mrs. Hamilcar all the necessary questions.

"What about dinner?" he asked hoarsely.

"The dining room will be open at six. They have to ask for their food card from the house governor and then line up in the basement for their table assignments."

He was carrying all William's necessary papers.

"I don't see the vaccination certificate." His hands trembled as he fumbled with the papers.

"I clipped it to the room reservation receipt and his baggage receipt. There. See it?"

"And when is registration?"

"Tomorrow at nine in room 307. Then there's an assembly." Mrs. Hamilcar spoke slowly and clearly. She and Mr. Hamilcar now knew all the arrangements. William had a faint smile on his face as he walked ahead of them, quite oblivious of the things Mr. Hamilcar carried and the things Mrs. Hamilcar knew.

"William," said Mrs. Hamilcar, "you must make friends on

the train. Pick out someone likely and ask him his name."

"I will," said William cheerfully.

"And when you're in school, try not to think, dear. You'll be all right if you don't think."

"All right."

"Watch for your trunk. If it doesn't arrive in your room, you must make inquiries, you must . . ." Her voice failed as she realized that he would surely never notice either the nonarrival or the arrival of his trunk.

Besides he was already gone, lost to her. His eyes were lackluster. ". . . But suppose I choose a negative square for the constant simply because it will turn out later to be more convenient that way. I'll know nothing about the actual value of $-k_1^2$ until I try to meet the boundary conditions. So now my equation is . . ."

Mrs. Hamilcar touched the bottom of her discontent, and gave him up, as it were, forever. He would never, never be correctly wired to the common posts of ordered human life. Oh, he was hopeless, hopeless.

Yet almost at the same instant that she reached this nadir of defeat, seeing him as she had so often seen him, estranged from the urgent moment, impassive to the insecurities of travel and matriculation, with the familiar half-smile betraying his secret preoccupation, it occurred to her quite unexpectedly that it was not he who was unmoored but all the rest. For their connections were to people and things which now would be left behind, while William, who had always seemed to her so deplorably broken off, now alone appeared related to permanence as he stood quiet against the jostling crowd, in ecstatic contemplation, not of a railroad station that in a moment would be swept away, but of a portion of universal everlasting truth.

Whether this new view of her son was revelation or rationalization under the strain of farewell she could not tell, but her unhappy rejection of him, sometimes bitter and sometimes amused, which she had harbored for at least ten of his thirteen years, suddenly dissolved.

Turning to Mr. Hamilcar she raised her voice above the noise of departure to say, "William has great connections but they are not the usual ones."

And while Mr. and Mrs. Hamilcar often misunderstood

each other in small matters and would answer irrelevantly to unambiguous remarks, in matters of survival their language took a mutually comprehensible form; Mr. Hamilcar did not find a vulgar connotation in this statement, but understood exactly what his wife meant, and like her, took heart.

Suddenly to their horror there was a loud cry of "All aboard." Mr. Hamilcar jumped on the train, then jumped off and pushed William on.

"Give him his things," shrieked Mrs. Hamilcar, and feverishly they plied him with his various accessories of journey.

"Good-bye."

"Good-bye."

Mrs. Hamilcar clutched him briefly and he kissed her on the cheek. Mr. Hamilcar clapped him on the shoulder, then clapped him on the shoulder again. As he walked into the car and looked about for a seat, he could see them following him along the platform, watching him anxiously. Poor things. How distraught they looked. And everything was so simple. He wasn't quite clear what one did about food there, but he'd run into a drugstore for a sandwich. As for his railroad ticket which didn't seem to be in the side pocket where he was sure he had put it, he was quite certain it would turn up somewhere. He sat down, his valise, coat, papers, and books on his lap while he turned to smile at them out the window.

His mother was signaling to him, making the letters of the alphabet with her fingers. She had taught it to him a long time ago as something that might some day prove useful if he were trapped in a mine or kidnapped by spies. Now she spelled out to him, "Write." He nodded and smiled. "Make friends," she signaled. He nodded and smiled again. Then she was gone, racing toward the front of the car and peering at each face along the way. No doubt she was searching for some old lady to befriend him and see that he took his valise with him. He certainly wasn't going to leave his valise behind. After all, it had all his clothes for the next six months. His father gazed at him steadfastly as if he were trying to memorize something. Then the train gave a lurch and started very slowly, just as Mrs. Hamilcar reappeared at his window and tapped sharply. He looked at her expectantly. She ran alongside the train, spelling out with her fingers, "Sit next to boy in front. A friend."

He smiled and nodded to make her very happy and immediately got up and changed his place. She seemed reassured and stopped running and in a moment was gone with the station and Mr. Hamilcar, who seemed to have finished memorizing at last and was trudging away, his head quite low on his chest.

The boy in front, next to whom he now took his seat, seemed quite unaware as he put his valise up, hung his coat, and sat down beside him. He couldn't imagine what his mother could have meant by saying he was a friend. He was sure he had never seen him before and there wasn't anything remarkably promising about his fat pink cheeks and unintelligent-looking curly hair. The boy fumbled in his briefcase and pulled out, not the expected water pistol, but a book. It was *Elementary Subfinite Groups*. Pleased, William looked hard at the fellow to see if he was going to mind his reading over his shoulder. The fellow looked up briefly, smiled easily, and returned to his book. William sighed with pleasure. The fellow seemed friendly enough. He began to read over his shoulder, noting only with half an eye that the narrow underside of his host's tie was fluttering on top of the wider end.

13

The Father-Thing

PHILIP K. DICK

There is a charming story told of King Frederick William I of Prussia (1713–1740), a gross, boorish, penny-pinching individual who felt himself to be the father of his people and expected to be regarded as such. He had the habit of walking the streets of Berlin with a stout cudgel, and using said cudgel as an instrument of correction if he saw anything of which he disapproved. Naturally the citizenry sought business elsewhere when they spied his stout figure on the horizon.

Frederick William, annoyed at the growing emptiness of the streets, snatched at a wizened individual one day, as he was about to worm his way down an alley. "Why are you hastening away?" demanded Frederick William.

"Please, sire," said the trembling man. "I fear you."

"Fear me!" cried the outraged monarch. "You're suppose to love me." And lifting his cudgel high, he chased the unfortunate down the street, laying on vigorously and yelling, "Love me, scum, love me!"

And how many ordinary fathers do the same? How many of them are wound-up springs of vengeance and punishment who, after unwinding, having expended their aggressions on a person forbidden to strike back or even to defend himself, sit back and expect love?

If it weren't that children could look forward to having children of their own some day, there might be more parricides.

It is the glory of science fiction that even the oldest of emotions, such as the imperfectly repressed feelings of aggression a child feels against the all-powerful father, can be given a fresh and sometimes frightful cast.

Let Philip Dick bring you the description of a child in mortal and horrifying combat with (after a fashion) his father.

"Dinner's ready," commanded Mrs. Walton. "Go get your father and tell him to wash his hands. The same applies to you, young man." She carried a steaming casserole to the neatly set table. "You'll find him out in the garage."

Charles hesitated. He was only eight years old, and the problem bothering him would have confounded Hillel. "I . . ." he began uncertainly.

"What's wrong?" June Walton caught the uneasy tone in her son's voice and her matronly bosom fluttered with sudden alarm. "Isn't Ted out in the garage? For heaven's sake, he was sharpening the hedge shears a minute ago. He didn't go over to the Andersons', did he? I told him dinner was practically on the table."

"He's in the garage," Charles said. "But he's . . . talking to himself."

"Talking to himself!" Mrs. Walton removed her bright plastic apron and hung it over the doorknob. "Ted? Why, he never talks to himself. Go tell him to come in here." She poured boiling black coffee in the little blue-and-white china cups and began ladling out creamed corn. "What's wrong with you? Go tell him!"

"I don't know which of them to tell," Charles blurted out desperately. "They both look alike."

June Walton's fingers lost their hold on the aluminum pan; for a moment the creamed corn slushed dangerously. "Young man—" she began angrily, but at that moment Ted Walton came striding into the kitchen, inhaling and sniffing and rubbing his hands together.

"Ah," he cried happily. "Lamb stew."

"Beef stew," June murmured. "Ted, what were you doing out there?"

Ted threw himself down at his place and unfolded his napkin. "I got the shears sharpened like a razor. Oiled and sharpened. Better not touch them—they'll cut your hand off." He was a good-looking man in his early thirties; thick blond hair, strong arms, competent hands, square face, and flashing brown eyes. "Man, this stew looks good. Hard day at the office—Friday, you know. Stuff piles up and we have to get all the accounts out by five. Al McKinley claims the department could handle twenty percent more stuff if we organized our lunch hours; staggered them so somebody was there all the time." He beckoned Charles over. "Sit down and let's go."

Mrs. Walton served the frozen peas. "Ted," she said, as she slowly took her seat, "is there anything on your mind?"

"On my mind?" He blinked. "No, nothing unusual. Just the regular stuff. Why?"

Uneasily June Walton glanced over at her son. Charles was sitting bolt-upright at his place, face expressionless, white as chalk. He hadn't moved, hadn't unfolded his napkin or even touched his milk. A tension was in the air; she could feel it. Charles had pulled his chair away from his father's; he was huddled in a tense little bundle as far from his father as possible. His lips were moving, but she couldn't catch what he was saying.

"What is it?" she demanded, leaning toward him.

"The other one," Charles was muttering under his breath. "The other one came in."

"What do you mean, dear?" June Walton asked out loud. "What other one?"

Ted jerked. A strange expression flitted across his face. It vanished at once; but in the brief instant Ted Walton's face lost all familiarity. Something alien and cold gleamed out, a twisting, wriggling mass. The eyes blurred and receded, as an archaic sheen filmed over them. The ordinary look of a tired, middle-aged husband was gone.

And then it was back—or nearly back. Ted grinned and began to wolf down his stew and frozen peas and creamed corn. He laughed, stirred his coffee, kidded, and ate. But something terrible was wrong.

"The other one," Charles muttered, face white, hands beginning to tremble. Suddenly he leaped up and backed away from the table. "Get away!" he shouted. "Get out of here!"

"Hey," Ted rumbled ominously. "What's got into you?" He pointed sternly at the boy's chair. "You sit down there and eat your dinner, young man. Your mother didn't fix it for nothing."

Charles turned and ran out of the kitchen, upstairs to his room. June Walton gasped and fluttered in dismay. "What in the world—"

Ted went on eating. His face was grim; his eyes were hard and dark. "That kid," he grated, "is going to have to learn a few things. Maybe he and I need to have a little private conference together."

Charles crouched and listened.

The father-thing was coming up the stairs, nearer and nearer. "Charles!" it shouted angrily. "Are you up there?"

He didn't answer. Soundlessly he moved back into his room and pulled the door shut. His heart was pounding heavily. The father-thing had reached the landing; in a moment it would come in his room.

He hurried to the window. He was terrified; it was already fumbling in the dark hall for the knob. He lifted the window and climbed out on the roof. With a grunt he dropped into the flower garden that ran by the front door, staggered and gasped, then leaped to his feet and ran from the light that streamed out the window, a patch of yellow in the evening darkness.

He found the garage; it loomed up ahead, a black square against the skyline. Breathing quickly, he fumbled in his pocket for his flashlight, then cautiously slid the door up and entered.

The garage was empty. The car was parked out front. To the left was his father's workbench. Hammers and saws on the wooden walls. In the back were the lawnmower, rake, shovel, hoe. A drum of kerosene. License plates nailed up everywhere. Floor was concrete and dirt; a great oil slick stained the center, tufts of weeds greasy and black in the flickering beam of the flashlight.

Just inside the door was a big trash barrel. On top of the barrel were stacks of soggy newspapers and magazines, moldy and damp. A thick stench of decay issued from them as Charles began to move them around. Spiders dropped to the cement and scampered off; he crushed them with his foot and went on looking.

The sight made him shriek. He dropped the flashlight and leaped wildly back. The garage was plunged into instant gloom. He forced himself to kneel down, and for an ageless moment, he groped in the darkness for the light, among the spiders and greasy weeds. Finally he had it again. He managed to turn the beam down into the barrel, down the well he had made by pushing back the piles of magazines.

The father-thing had stuffed it down in the very bottom of the barrel. Among the old leaves and torn-up cardboard, the rotting remains of magazines and curtains, rubbish from the attic his mother had lugged down here with the idea of burning someday. It still looked a little like his father enough for him to recognize. He had found it—and the sight made him sick at his stomach. He hung onto the barrel and shut his eyes until finally he was able to look again. In the barrel were the remains of his father, his real father. Bits the father-thing had no use for. Bits it had discarded.

He got the rake and pushed it down to stir the remains. They were dry. They cracked and broke at the touch of the rake. They were like a discarded snake skin, flaky and crumbling, rustling at the touch. *An empty skin.* The insides were gone. The important part. This was all that remained, just the brittle, cracking skin, wadded down at the bottom of the trash barrel in a little heap. This was all the father-thing had left; it had eaten the rest. Taken the insides—and his father's place.

A sound.

He dropped the rake and hurried to the door. The father-thing was coming down the path, toward the garage. Its shoes crushed the gravel; it felt its way along uncertainly. "Charles!" it called angrily. "Are you in there? Wait'll I get my hands on you, young man!"

His mother's ample, nervous shape was outlined in the bright doorway of the house. "Ted, please don't hurt him. He's all upset about something."

"I'm not going to hurt him," the father-thing rasped; it halted to strike a match. "I'm just going to have a little talk with him. He needs to learn better manners. Leaving the table like that and running out at night, climbing down the roof—"

Charles slipped from the garage; the glare of the match caught his moving shape, and with a bellow the father-thing lunged forward.

"Come here!"

Charles ran. He knew the ground better than the father-thing; it knew a lot, had taken a lot when it got his father's insides, but nobody knew the way like *he* did. He reached the fence, climbed it, leaped into the Andersons' yard, raced past their clothesline, down the path around the side of their house, and out on Maple Street.

He listened, crouched down and not breathing. The father-thing hadn't come after him. It had gone back. Or it was coming around the sidewalk.

He took a deep, shuddering breath. He had to keep moving. Sooner or later it would find him. He glanced right and left, made sure it wasn't watching, and then started off at a rapid dog-trot.

"What do you want?" Tony Peretti demanded belligerently. Tony was fourteen. He was sitting at the table in the oak-paneled Peretti dining room, books and pencils scattered around him, half a ham-and-peanut-butter sandwich and a coke beside him. "You're Walton, aren't you?"

Tony Peretti had a job uncrating stoves and refrigerators after school at Johnson's Appliance Shop, downtown. He was big and blunt-faced. Black hair, olive skin, white teeth. A couple of times he had beaten up Charles; he had beaten up every kid in the neighborhood.

Charles twisted. "Say, Peretti. Do me a favor?"

"What do you want?" Peretti was annoyed. "You looking for a bruise?"

Gazing unhappily down, his fists clenched, Charles explained what had happened in short, mumbled words.

When he had finished, Peretti let out a low whistle. "No kidding."

"It's true." He nodded quickly. "I'll show you. Come on and I'll show you."

Peretti got slowly to his feet. "Yeah, show me. I want to see."

He got his b.b. gun from his room, and the two of them walked silently up the dark street, toward Charles's house. Neither of them said much. Peretti was deep in thought, serious and solemn-faced. Charles was still dazed; his mind was completely blank.

They turned down the Anderson driveway, cut through the backyard, climbed the fence, and lowered themselves cautiously into Charles's backyard. There was no movement. The yard was silent. The front door of the house was closed.

They peered through the living room window. The shades were down, but a narrow crack of yellow streamed out. Sitting on the couch was Mrs. Walton, sewing a cotton T-shirt. There was a sad, troubled look on her large face. She worked listlessly, without interest. Opposite her was the father-thing. Leaning back in his father's easy chair, its shoes off, reading the evening newspaper. The TV was on, playing to itself in the corner. A can of beer rested on the arm of the easy chair. The father-thing sat exactly as his own father had sat; it had learned a lot.

"Looks just like him," Peretti whispered suspiciously. "You sure you're not bulling me?"

Charles led him to the garage and showed him the trash barrel. Peretti reached his long tanned arms down and carefully pulled up the dry, flaking remains. They spread out, unfolded, until the whole figure of his father was outlined. Peretti laid the remains on the floor and pieced broken parts back into place.

The remains were colorless. Almost transparent. An amber yellow, thin as paper. Dry and utterly lifeless.

"That's all," Charles said. Tears welled up in his eyes. "That's all that's left of him. The thing has the insides."

Peretti had turned pale. Shakily he crammed the remains back in the trash barrel. "This is really something," he muttered. "You say you saw the two of them together?"

"Talking. They looked exactly alike. I ran inside." Charles wiped the tears away and sniveled; he couldn't hold it back any longer. "It ate him while I was inside. Then it came in the house. It pretended it was him. But it isn't. It killed him and ate his insides."

For a moment Peretti was silent. "I'll tell you something," he said suddenly. "I've heard about this sort of thing. It's a bad business. You have to use your head and not get scared. You're not scared, are you?"

"No," Charles managed to mutter.

"The first thing we have to do is figure out how to kill it." He rattled his b.b. gun. "I don't know if this'll work. It must be plenty tough to get hold of your father. He was a big man." Peretti considered. "Let's get out of here. It might come back. They say that's what a murderer does."

They left the garage. Peretti crouched down and peeked through the window again. Mrs. Walton had got to her feet. She was talking anxiously. Vague sounds filtered out. The father-thing threw down its newspaper. They were arguing.

"For God's sake!" the father-thing shouted. "Don't do anything stupid like that."

"Something's wrong," Mrs. Walton moaned. "Something terrible. Just let me call the hospital and see."

"Don't call anybody. He's all right. Probably up the street playing."

"He's never out this late. He never disobeys. He was terribly upset—afraid of you! I don't blame him." Her voice broke with misery. "What's wrong with you? You're so strange." She moved out of the room, into the hall. "I'm going to call some of the neighbors."

The father-thing glared after her until she had disappeared. Then a terrifying thing happened. Charles gasped; even Peretti grunted under his breath.

"Look," Charles muttered. "What—"

"Golly," Peretti said, black eyes wide.

As soon as Mrs. Walton was gone from the room, the father-thing sagged in its chair. It became limp. Its mouth fell open. Its eyes peered vacantly. Its head fell forward, like a discarded rag doll.

Peretti moved away from the window. "That's it," he whispered. "That's the whole thing."

"What is it?" Charles demanded. He was shocked and bewildered. "It looked like somebody turned off its power."

"Exactly." Peretti nodded slowly, grim and shaken. "It's controlled from outside."

Horror settled over Charles. "You mean, something outside our world?"

Peretti shook his head with disgust. "Outside the house! In the yard. You know how to find?"

"Not very well." Charles pulled his mind together. "But I know somebody who's good at finding." He forced his mind to summon the name. "Bobby Daniels."

"That little colored kid? Is he good at finding?"

"The best."

"All right," Peretti said. "Let's go get him. We have to find the thing that's outside. That made *it* in there, and keeps it going . . ."

"It's near the garage," Peretti said to the small, thin-faced Negro boy who crouched beside them in the darkness. "When it got him, he was in the garage. So look there."

"In the garage?" Daniels asked.

"*Around* the garage. Walton's already gone over the garage, inside. Look around outside. Nearby."

There was a small bed of flowers growing by the garage, and a great tangle of bamboo and discarded debris between the garage and the back of the house. The moon had come out; a cold, misty light filtered down over everything. "If we don't find it pretty soon," Daniels said, "I got to go back home. I can't stay up much later." He wasn't any older than Charles. Perhaps nine.

"All right," Peretti agreed. "Then get looking."

The three of them spread out and began to go over the ground with care. Daniels worked with incredible speed; his thin little body moved in a blur of motion as he crawled among the flowers, turned over rocks, peered under the house, separated stalks of plants, ran his expert hands over leaves and stems, in tangles of compost and weeds. No inch was missed.

Peretti halted after a short time. "I'll guard. It might be dangerous. The father-thing might come and try to stop us." He posted himself on the back step with his b.b. gun while Charles and Bobby Daniels searched. Charles worked slowly. He was tired, and his body was cold and numb. It seemed impossible, the father-thing and what had happened to his own father, his real father. But terror spurred him on; what if it happened to his mother, or to him? Or to everyone? Maybe the whole world.

"I found it!" Daniels called in a thin, high voice. "You all come around here quick!"

Peretti raised his gun and got up cautiously. Charles hurried over; he turned the flickering yellow beam of his flashlight where Daniels stood.

The Negro boy had raised a concrete stone. In the moist, rotting soil the light gleamed on a metallic body. A thin, jointed thing with endless crooked legs was digging frantically. Plated, like an ant; a red-brown bug that rapidly disappeared before their eyes. Its rows of legs scabbled and clutched. The ground gave rapidly under it. Its wicked-looking tail twisted furiously as it struggled down the tunnel it had made.

Peretti ran into the garage and grabbed up the rake. He pinned down the tail of the bug with it. "Quick! Shoot it with the b.b. gun!"

Daniels snatched the gun and took aim. The first shot tore the tail of the bug loose. It writhed and twisted frantically; its tail dragged uselessly and some of its legs broke off. It was a foot long, like a great millipede. It struggled desperately to escape down its hole.

"Shoot again," Peretti ordered.

Daniels fumbled with the gun. The bug slithered and hissed. Its head jerked back and forth; it twisted and bit at the rake holding it down. Its wicked specks of eyes gleamed with hatred. For a moment it struck futilely at the rake; then abruptly, without warning, it thrashed in a frantic convulsion that made them all draw away in fear.

Something buzzed through Charles's brain. A loud humming, metallic and harsh, a billion metal wires dancing and vibrating at once. He was tossed about violently by the force; the banging crash of metal made him deaf and confused. He stumbled to his feet and backed off; the others were doing the same, white-faced and shaken.

"If we can't kill it with the gun," Peretti gasped, "we can drown it. Or burn it. Or stick a pin through its brain." He fought to hold onto the rake, to keep the bug pinned down.

"I have a jar of formaldehyde," Daniels muttered. His fingers fumbled nervously with the b.b. gun. "How do this thing work? I can't seem to—"

Charles grabbed the gun from him. "I'll kill it." He squatted down, one eye to the sight, and gripped the trigger. The bug lashed and struggled. Its force-field hammered in his ears, but he hung onto the gun. His finger tightened . . .

"All right, Charles," the father-thing said. Powerful fingers gripped him, a paralyzing pressure around his wrists. The gun fell to the ground as he struggled futilely. The father-thing shoved against Peretti. The boy leaped away and the bug, free of the rake, slithered triumphantly down its tunnel.

"You have a spanking coming, Charles," the father-thing droned on. "What got into you? Your poor mother's out of her mind with worry."

It had been there, hiding in the shadows. Crouched in the darkness watching them. Its calm, emotionless voice, a dreadful parody of his father's, rumbled close to his ear as it pulled him relentlessly toward the garage. Its cold breath blew in his face, an icy-sweet odor, like decaying soil. Its strength was immense; there was nothing he could do.

"Don't fight me," it said calmly. "Come along, into the garage. This is for your own good. I know best, Charles."

"Did you find him?" his mother called anxiously, opening the back door.

"Yes, I found him."

"What are you going to do?"

"A little spanking." The father-thing pushed up the garage door. "In the garage." In the half-light a faint smile, humorless and utterly without emotion, touched its lips. "You go back in the living room, June. I'll take care of this. It's more in my line. You never did like punishing him."

The back door reluctantly closed. As the light cut off, Peretti bent down and groped for the b.b. gun. The father-thing instantly froze.

"Go on home, boys," it rasped.

Peretti stood undecided, gripping the b.b. gun.

"Get going," the father-thing repeated. "Put down that toy and get out of here." It moved slowly toward Peretti, gripping Charles with one hand, reaching toward Peretti with the other. "No b.b. guns allowed in town, sonny. Your father know you have that? There's a city ordinance. I think you better give me that before—"

Peretti shot it in the eye.

The father-thing grunted and pawed at its ruined eye. Abruptly it slashed out at Peretti. Peretti moved down the driveway, trying to cock the gun. The father-thing lunged. Its powerful fingers snatched the gun from Peretti's hands. Silently the father-thing mashed the gun against the wall of the house.

Charles broke away and ran numbly off. Where could he hide? It was between him and the house. Already, it was coming back toward him, a black shape creeping carefully, peering into the darkness, trying to make him out. Charles retreated. If there were only some place he could hide . . .

The bamboo.

He crept quickly into the bamboo. The stalks were huge and old. They closed after him with a faint rustle. The father-thing was fumbling in its pocket; it lit a match, then the whole pack flared up. "Charles," it said, "I know you're here, someplace. There's no use hiding. You're only making it more difficult."

His heart hammering, Charles crouched among the bamboo. Here, debris and filth rotted. Weeds, garbage, papers, boxes, old clothing, boards, tin cans, bottles. Spiders and salamanders squirmed around him. The bamboo swayed with the night wind. Insects and filth.

And something else.

A shape, a silent, unmoving shape that grew up from the mound of filth like some nocturnal mushroom. A white column, a pulpy mass that glistened moistly in the moonlight. Webs covered it, a moldy cocoon. It had vague arms and legs. An indistinct half-shaped head. As yet, the features hadn't formed. But he could tell what it was.

A mother-thing. Growing here in the filth and dampness, between the garage and the house. Behind the towering bamboo.

It was almost ready. Another few days and it would reach maturity. It was still a larva, white and soft and pulpy. But the sun would dry and warm it. Harden its shell. Turn it dark and strong. It would emerge from its cocoon, and one day when his mother came by the garage . . .

Behind the mother-thing were other pulpy white larvae, recently laid by the bug. Small. Just coming into existence. He could see where the father-thing had broken off; the place where it had grown. It had matured here. And in the garage, his father had met it.

Charles began to move numbly away, past the rotting boards, the filth and debris, the pulpy mushroom larvae. Weakly he reached out to take hold of the fence—and scrambled back.

Another one. Another larva. He hadn't seen this one, at first. It wasn't white. It had already turned dark. The web, the pulpy softness, the moistness, were gone. It was ready. It stirred a little, moved its arm feebly.

The Charles-thing.

The bamboo separated, and the father-thing's hand clamped firmly around the boy's wrist. "You stay right here," it said. "This is exactly the place for you. Don't move." With its other hand it tore at the remains of the cocoon binding the Charles-thing. "I'll help it out—it's still a little weak."

The last shred of moist gray was stripped back, and the Charles-thing tottered out. It floundered uncertainly, as the father-thing cleared a path for it toward Charles.

"This way," the father-thing grunted. "I'll hold him for you. When you're fed you'll be stronger."

The Charles-thing's mouth opened and closed. It reached greedily toward Charles. The boy struggled wildly, but the father-thing's immense hand held him down.

"Stop that, young man," the father-thing commanded. "It'll be a lot easier for you if you—"

It screamed and convulsed. It let go of Charles and staggered back. Its body twitched violently. It crashed against the garage, limbs jerking. For a time it rolled and flopped in a dance of agony. It whimpered, moaned, tried to crawl away. Gradually it became quiet. The Charles-thing settled down in a silent heap. It lay stupidly among the bamboo and rotting debris, body slack, face empty and blank.

At last the father-thing ceased to stir. There was only the faint rustle of the bamboo in the night wind.

Charles got up awkwardly. He stepped down onto the cement driveway. Peretti and Daniels approached, wide-eyed and cautious. "Don't go near it," Daniels ordered sharply. "It ain't dead yet. Takes a little while."

"What did you do?" Charles muttered.

Daniels set down the drum of kerosene with a gasp of relief. "Found this in the garage. We Daniels always used kerosene on our mosquitoes, back in Virginia."

"Daniels poured kerosene down the bug's tunnel," Peretti explained, still awed. "It was his idea."

Daniels kicked cautiously at the contorted body of the father-thing. "It's dead, now. Died as soon as the bug died."

"I guess the others'll die too," Peretti said. He pushed aside the bamboo to examine the larvae growing here and there among the debris. The Charles-thing didn't move at all, as Peretti jabbed the end of a stick into its chest. "This one's dead."

"We better make sure," Daniels said grimly. He picked up the heavy drum of kerosene and lugged it to the edge of the bamboo. "It dropped some matches in the driveway. You get them, Peretti."

They looked at each other.

"Sure," Peretti said softly.

"We better turn on the hose," Charles said. "To make sure it doesn't spread."

"Let's get going," Peretti said impatiently. He was already moving off. Charles quickly followed him and they began searching for the matches, in the moonlit darkness.

14

Star Bright

MARK CLIFTON

As we all know—or think we know—child prodigies have a hard time of it. The theory goes that they find themselves in the company of dull children whom they consider infinitely boring and by whom they are hated. What's more, they are misunderstood and persecuted by adults.

Reverse the situation and look at it from the youngster's point of view. He is hated by other children and persecuted by adults: Does it not automatically follow that he must consider himself better *than the others?*

Has there ever been a reasonably bright child who has not, at least once in a while, harbored the thought that he was an ugly duckling who was going to burgeon into a swan and show them all, darn them?

I have eagerly searched my own childhood to find traces of just such a romance in it. Surely I was very bright (wasn't I?) and surely I was hated and persecuted (wasn't I?) and surely I showed them all, darn them (didn't I?).

Actually, though, I must either abandon honesty or deny romance. I was *bright, but I realized it, my parents realized it, and my teachers realized it. Nobody persecuted me. If the other kids sometimes disliked me it was only because I was sometimes unlikable. Nor did I ever* show *anybody, darn them, because everyone (including myself) was sure I would all along, so that I didn't have the indescribable pleasure of surprising anyone.*

Adieu, romance.

But it's all a matter of degree. Asimov-smart is, after all, just a-little-bit-smart. What about a kid who was really *smart?*

Let Mark Clifton introduce you to one of those. (I assure you it's no pleasant thing for me to read the story and realize I'm only a Tween at best.)

Friday, June 11

At three years of age, a little girl shouldn't have enough functioning intelligence to cut out and paste together a Moebius Strip.

Or, if she did it by accident, she surely shouldn't have enough reasoning ability to pick up one of her crayons and carefully trace the continuous line to prove it has only one surface.

And if by some strange coincidence she did, and it was still just an accident, how can I account for this generally active daughter of mine—and I do mean *active*—sitting for a solid half hour with her chin cupped in her hand, staring off into space, thinking with such concentration that it was almost painful to watch?

I was in my reading chair, going over some work. Star was sitting on the floor, in the circle of my light, with her blunt-nosed scissors and her scraps of paper.

Her long silence made me glance down at her as she was taping the two ends of the paper together. At that point I thought it was an accident that she had given a half twist to the paper strip before joining the circle. I smiled to myself as she picked it up in her chubby fingers.

"A little child forms the enigma of the ages," I mused.

But instead of throwing the strip aside, or tearing it apart as any other child would do, she carefully turned it over and around—studying it from all sides.

Then she picked up one of her crayons and began tracing the line. She did it as though she were substantiating a conclusion already reached!

It was a bitter confirmation for me. I had been refusing to face it for a long time, but I could ignore it no longer.

Star was a High I.Q.

For half an hour I watched her while she sat on the floor, one knee bent under her, her chin in her hand, unmoving. Her eyes were wide with wonderment, looking into the potentialities of the phenomenon she had found.

It had been a tough struggle, taking care of her since my wife's death. Now this added problem. If only she could have been normally dull, like other children!

I made up my mind while I watched her. If a child is afflicted, then let's face it, she's afflicted. A parent must teach her to compensate. At least she could be prepared for the bitterness I'd known. She could learn early to take it in stride.

I could use the measurements available, get the degree of intelligence, and in that way grasp the extent of my problem. A twenty-point jump in I.Q. creates an entirely different set of problems. The 140 child lives in a world nothing at all like that of the 100 child, and a world which the 120 child can but vaguely sense. The problems which vex and challenge the 160 pass over the 140 as a bird flies over a field mouse. I must not make the mistake of posing the problems of one if she is the other. I must know. In the meantime, I must treat it casually.

"That's called the Moebius Strip, Star," I interrupted her thoughts.

She came out of her reveries with a start. I didn't like the quick way her eyes sought mine—almost furtively, as though she had been caught doing something bad.

"Somebody already make it?" she disappointedly asked.

She knew what she had discovered! Something inside me spilled over with grief, and something else caught at me with dread.

I kept my voice casual. "A man by the name of Moebius. A long time ago. I'll tell you about him sometime when you're older."

"Now. While I'm little," she commanded, with a frown. "And don't tell. Read me."

What did she mean by that? Oh, she must be simply paraphrasing me at those times in the past when I've wanted the facts and not garbled generalizations. It could only be that!

"Okay, young lady." I lifted an eyebrow and glared at her in mock ferociousness, which usually sent her into gales of laughter. "I'll slow you down!"

She remained completely sober.

I turned to the subject in a physics book. It's not in simple language, by any means, and I read it as rapidly as I could speak. My thought was to make her admit she didn't understand it, so I could translate it into basic language.

Her reaction?

"You read too slow, Daddy," she complained. She was childishly irritable about it. "You say a word. Then I think a long time. Then you say another word."

I knew what she meant. I remember, when I was a child, my thoughts used to dart in and out among the slowly droning words of any adult. Whole patterns of universes would appear and disappear in those brief moments.

"So?" I asked.

"So," she mocked me impishly. "You teach me to read. Then I can think quick as I want."

"Quickly," I corrected in a weak voice. "The word is 'quickly,' an adverb."

She looked at me impatiently, as if she saw through this allegedly adult device to show up a youngster's ignorance. I felt like the dope!

September 1

A great deal has happened the past few months. I have tried a number of times to bring the conversation around to discuss Star's affliction with her. But she is amazingly adroit at heading me off, as though she already knows what I am trying to say and isn't concerned. Perhaps, in spite of her brilliance, she's too young to realize the hostility of the world toward intelligence.

Some of the visiting neighbors have been amused to see her sit on the floor with an encyclopedia as big as she is, rapidly turning the pages. Only Star and I know she is reading the pages as rapidly as she can turn them. I've brushed away the neighbors' comments with: "She likes to look at the pictures."

They talk to her in baby talk—and she answers in baby talk! How does she know enough to do that?

I have spent the months making an exhaustive record of her I.Q. measurements, aptitude speeds, reaction, tables, all the recommended paraphernalia for measuring something we know nothing about.

The tables are screwy, or Star is beyond all measurement.

All right, Pete Holmes, how are you going to pose those problems and combat them for her, when you have no conception of what they might be? But I must have a conception. I've got to be able to comprehend at least a little of what she may face. I simply couldn't stand by and do nothing.

Easy, though. Nobody knows better than you the futility of trying to compete out of your class. How many students, workers, and employers have tried to compete with you? You've watched them and pitied them, comparing them to a donkey trying to run the Kentucky Derby.

How does it feel to be in the place of the donkey, for a change? You've always blamed them for not realizing they shouldn't try to compete.

But this is my own daughter! I *must* understand.

October 1

Star is now four years old, and according to State Law her mind has now developed enough so that she may attend nursery school. Again I tried to prepare her for what she might face. She listened through about two sentences and changed the subject. I can't tell about Star. Does she already know the answers? Or does she not even realize there is a problem?

I was in a sweat of worry when I took her to her first day at school yesterday morning. Last night I was sitting in my chair, reading. After she had put her dolls away, she went to the bookshelves and brought down a book of fairy tales.

That is another peculiarity of hers. She has an unmeasurably quick perception, yet she has all the normal reactions of a little girl. She likes her dolls, fairy stories, playing grownup. No, she's not a monster.

She brought the book of fairy tales over to me.

"Daddy, read me a story," she asked quite seriously.

I looked at her in amazement. "Since when? Go read your own story."

She lifted an eyebrow in imitation of my own characteristic gesture.

"Children of my age do not read," she instructed pedantically. "I can't learn to read until I am in the first grade. It is very hard to do and I am much too little."

She had found the answer to her affliction—conformity! She had already learned to conceal her intelligence. So many of us break our hearts before we learn that.

But you don't have to conceal it from me, Star! Not from me!

Oh, well, I could go along with the gag, if that was what she wanted.

"Did you like nursery school?" I asked the standard question.

"Oh, yes," she exclaimed enthusiastically. "It was fun."

"And what did you learn today, little girl?"

She played it straight back to me. "Not much. I tried to cut out paper dolls, but the scissors kept slipping." Was there an elfin deviltry back of her sober expression?

"Now, look," I cautioned, "don't overdo it. That's as bad as being too quick. The idea is that everybody has to be just about standard average. That's the only thing we will tolerate.

It is expected that a little girl of four should know how to cut out paper dolls properly."

"Oh?" she questioned, and looked thoughtful. "I guess that's the hard part, isn't it, Daddy—to know how much you ought to know?"

"Yes, that's the hard part," I agreed fervently.

"But it's all right," she reassured me. "One of the Stupids showed me how to cut them out, so now that little girl likes me. She just took charge of me then and told the other kids they should like me too. So of course they did because she's leader. I think I did right, after all."

"Oh, no!" I breathed to myself. She knew how to manipulate other people already. Then my thought whirled around another concept. It was the first time she had verbally classified normal people as "Stupids," but it had slipped out so easily that I knew she'd been thinking to herself for a long time. Then my whirling thoughts hit a third implication.

"Yes, maybe it was the right thing," I conceded. "Where the little girl was concerned, that is. But don't forget you were being observed by a grownup teacher in the room. And she's smarter."

"You mean she's older, Daddy," Star corrected me.

"Smarter, too, maybe. You can't tell."

"I can," she sighed. "She's just older."

I think it was growing fear which made me defensive. "That's good," I said emphatically. "That's very good. You can learn a lot from her then. It takes an awful lot of study to learn how to be stupid."

My own troublesome business life came to mind and I thought to myself, "I sometimes think I'll never learn it."

I swear I didn't say it aloud. But Star patted me consolingly and answered as though I'd spoken.

"That's because you're only fairly bright, Daddy. You're a Tween, and that's harder than being really bright."

"A Tween? What's a Tween?" I was bumbling to hide my confusion.

"That's what I mean, Daddy," she answered in exasperation. "You don't grasp quickly. An In Between, of course. The other people are Stupids, I'm a Bright, and you're a Tween. I made those names up when I was little."

Good God! Besides being unmeasurably bright, she's a telepath!

All right, Pete, there you are. On reasoning processes you might stand a chance—but not telepathy!

"Star," I said on impulse, "can you read people's minds?"

"Of course, Daddy," she answered, as if I'd asked a foolishly obvious question.

"Can you teach me?"

She looked at me impishly. "You're already learning it a little. But you're so slow! You see, you didn't even know you were learning."

Her voice took on a wistful note, a tone of loneliness. "I wish—" she said, and paused.

"What do you wish?"

"You see what I mean, Daddy? You try, but you're slow."

All the same, I knew. I knew she was already longing for a companion whose mind could match her own.

A father is prepared to lose his daughter eventually, Star, but not so soon.

Not so soon . . .

June again

Some new people have moved in next door. Star says their name is Howell. Bill and Ruth Howell. They have a son, Robert, who looks maybe a year older than Star, who will soon be five.

Star seems to have taken up with Robert right away. He is a well-mannered boy and good company for Star.

I'm worried, though. Star had something to do with their moving in next door. I'm convinced of that. I'm also convinced, even from the little I've seen of him, that Robert is a Bright and a telepath.

Could it be that, failing to find quick accord with my mind, Star has reached out and out until she made contact with a telepath companion?

No, that's too fantastic. Even if it were so, how could she shape circumstances so she could bring Robert to live next door to her? The Howells came from another city. It just happened that the people who lived next door moved out and the house was put up for sale.

Just happened? How frequently do we find such abnormal Brights? What are the chances of one *just happening* to move in next door to another?

I know he is a telepath because, as I write this, I sense him reading it.

I even catch his thought: "Oh, pardon me, Mr. Holmes. I didn't intend to peek. Really I didn't."

Did I imagine that? Or is Star building a skill in my mind?

"It isn't nice to look into another person's mind unless you're asked, Robert," I thought back, rather severely. It was purely an experiment.

"I know it, Mr. Holmes. I apologize." He is in his bed in his house, across the driveway.

"No, Daddy, he really didn't mean to." And Star is in her bed in this house.

It is impossible to write how I feel. There comes a time when words are empty husks. But mixed with my expectant dread is a threat of gratitude for having been taught to be even stumblingly telepathic.

Saturday, August 11

I've thought of a gag. I haven't seen Jim Pietre in a month of Sundays, not since he was awarded that research fellowship with the museum. It will be good to pull him out of his hole, and this little piece of advertising junk Star dropped should be just the thing.

Strange about the gadget. The Awful Secret Talisman of the Mystic Junior G-Men, no doubt. Still, it doesn't have anything about crackles and pops printed on it. Merely an odd-looking coin, not even true round, bronze by the look of it. Crude. They must stamp them out by the million without ever changing a die.

But it is just the thing to send to Jim to get a rise out of him. He could always appreciate a good practical joke. Wonder how he'd feel to know he was only a Tween.

Monday, August 13

Sitting here at my study desk, I've been staring into space for an hour. I don't know what to think.

It was about noon today when Jim Pietre called the office on the phone.

"Now, look, Pete," he started out, "what kind of gag are you pulling?"

I chortled to myself and pulled the dead pan on him. "What do you mean, boy?" I asked back into the phone. "Gag? What kind of gag? What are you talking about?"

"A coin. A coin." He was impatient. "You remember you sent me a coin in the mail?"

"Oh, yeah, that." I pretended to remember. "Look, you're an important research analyst on metals—too damned important to keep in touch with your old friends—so I thought I'd make a bid for your attention thataway."

"All right, give," he said in a low voice. "Where did you get it?" He was serious.

"Come off it, Jim. Are you practicing to be a stuffed shirt? I admit it's a rib. Something Star dropped the other day. A manufacturer's idea of kid advertising, no doubt."

"I'm in dead earnest, Peter," he answered. "It's no advertising gadget."

"It means something?"

In college Jim could take a practical joke and make six out of it.

"I don't know what it means. Where did Star get it?" He was being pretty crisp about it.

"Oh, I don't know," I said. I was getting a little fed up; the joke wasn't going according to plan. "Never asked her. You know how kids clutter up the place with their things. No father even tries to keep track of all the junk that can be bought with three boxtops and a dime."

"This was not bought with three boxtops and a dime," he spaced his words evenly. "This was not bought anywhere, for any price. In fact, if you want to be logical about it, this coin doesn't exist at all."

I laughed out loud. This was more like the old Jim.

"Okay, so you've turned the gag back on me. Let's call it quits. How about coming over to supper some night soon?"

"I'm coming over, my friend." He remained grim as he said it. "And I'm coming over tonight. As soon as you will be home. It's no gag I'm pulling. Can you get that through your stubborn head? You say you got it from Star, and of course I believe you. But it's no toy. It's the real thing." Then, as if in profound puzzlement, "Only it isn't."

A feeling of dread was settling upon me. Once you cried "Uncle" to Jim, he always let up.

"Suppose you tell me what you mean," I answered soberly.

"That's more like it, Pete. Here's what we know about the coin so far. It is apparently pre-Egyptian. It's hand-cast. It's made out of one of the lost bronzes. We fix it at around four thousand years old."

"That ought to be easy to solve," I argued. "Probably some coin collector is screaming all over the place for it. No doubt lost it and Star found it. Must be lots of old coins like that in museums and in private collections."

I was rationalizing more for my own benefit than for Jim. He would know all those things without my mentioning them. He waited until I had finished.

"Step two," he went on. "We've got one of the top coin men in the world here at the museum. As soon as I saw what the metal was, I took it to him. Now hold onto your chair, Pete. He says there is no coin like it in the world, either museum or private collection."

"You museum boys get beside yourselves at times. Come down to earth. Sometime, somewhere, some collector picked it up in some exotic place and kept it quiet. I don't have to tell you how some collectors are—sitting in a dark room, gloating over some worthless bauble, not telling a soul about it—"

"All right, wise guy," he interrupted. "Step three. That coin is at least four thousand years old *and it's also brand-new!* Let's hear you explain that away."

"New?" I asked weakly. "I don't get it."

"Old coins show wear. The edges get rounded with handling. The surface oxidizes. The molecular structure changes, crystalizes. This coin shows no wear, no oxidation, no molecular change. This coin might have been struck yesterday. *Where did Star get it?*"

"Hold it a minute," I pleaded.

I began to think back. Saturday morning. Star and Robert had been playing a game. Come to think of it, that was a peculiar game. Mighty peculiar.

Star would run into the house and stand in front of the encyclopedia shelf. I could hear Robert counting loudly at the base tree outside in the backyard. She would stare at the encyclopedia for a moment.

Once I heard her mumble: "That's a good place."

Or maybe she merely thought it and I caught the thought. I'm doing that quite a bit of late.

Then she would run outside again. A moment later, Robert would run in and stand in front of the same shelf. Then he also would run outside again. There would bc silence for several minutes. The silence would rupture with a burst of laughing and shouting. Soon, Star would come in again.

"How does he find me?" I heard her think once. "I can't reason it, and I can't ESP it out of him."

It was during one of their silences when Ruth called over to me.

"Hey, Pete! Do you know where the kids are? Time for their milk and cookies."

The Howells are awfully good to Star, bless 'em. I got up and went over to the window.

"I don't know, Ruth," I called back. "They were in and out only a few minutes ago."

"Well, I'm not worried," she said. She came through the kitchen door and stood on the back steps. "They know better than to cross the street by themselves. They're too little for that. So I guess they're over at Marily's. When they come back, tell 'em to come and get it."

"Okay, Ruth," I answered.

She opened the screen door again and went back into her kitchen. I left the window and returned to my work.

A little later, both the kids came running into the house. I managed to capture them long enough to tell them about the cookies and milk.

"Beat you there!" Robert shouted to Star.

There was a scuffle and they ran out the front door. I noticed then that Star had dropped the coin and I picked it up and sent it to Jim Pietre.

"Hello, Jim," I said into the phone. "Are you still there?"

"Yep, still waiting for an answer," he said.

"Jim, I think you'd better come over to the house right away. I'll leave my office now and meet you there. Can you get away?"

"Can I get away?" he exclaimed. "Boss says to trace this coin down and do nothing else. See you in fifteen minutes."

He hung up. Thoughtfully I replaced the receiver and went out to my car. I was pulling into my block from one arterial when I saw Jim's car pulling in from a block away. I stopped at the curb and waited for him. I didn't see the kids anywhere out front.

Jim climbed out of his car, and I never saw such an eager look of anticipation on a man's face before. I didn't realize I was showing my dread, but when he saw my face, he became serious.

"What is it, Pete? What on Earth is it?" he almost whispered.

"I don't know. At least I'm not sure. Come on inside the house."

We let ourselves in the front, and I took Jim into the study. It has a large window opening on the back garden, and the scene was very clear.

At first it was an innocent scene—so innocent and peaceful. Just three little children in the backyard playing hide and seek. Marily, a neighbor's child, was stepping up to the base tree.

"Now look, you kids," she was saying. "You hide where I can find you or I won't play."

"But where can we go, Marily?" Robert was arguing loudly. Like all little boys, he seems to carry on his conversations at the top of his lungs. "There's the garage, and there's those trees and bushes. You have to look everywhere, Marily."

"And there's going to be other buildings and trees and bushes there afterward," Star called out with glee. "You gotta look behind them too."

"Yeah!" Robert took up the teasing refrain. "And there's been lots and lots of buildings and trees there before—especially trees. You gotta look behind them too."

Marily tossed her head petulantly. "I don't know what you're talking about, and I don't care. Just hide where I can find you, that's all."

She hid her face at the tree and started counting. If I had been alone, I would have been sure my eyesight had failed me, or that I was the victim of hallucinations. But Jim was standing there and saw it too.

Marily started counting, yet the other two didn't run away. Star reached out and took Robert's hand and they merely stood there. For an instant they seemed to shimmer and—*they disappeared without moving a step!*

Marily finished her counting and ran around to the few possible hiding places in the yard. When she couldn't find them, she started to blubber and pushed through the hedge to Ruth's back door.

"They runned away from me again," she whined through the screen at Ruth.

Jim and I stood staring out the window. I glanced at him. His face was set and pale, but probably no worse than my own.

We saw the instant shimmer again. Star, and then immediately Robert, materialized from the air and ran up to the tree, shouting, "Safe! Safe!"

Marily let out a bawl and ran home to her mother.

I called Star and Robert into the house. They came, still holding hands, a little shamefaced, a little defiant.

How to begin? What in hell could I say?

"It's not exactly fair," I told them. "Marily can't follow you there." I was shooting in the dark, but I had at least a glimmering to go by.

Star turned pale enough for the freckles on her little nose to stand out under her tan. Robert blushed and turned to her fiercely.

"I told you so, Star. I *told* you so! I said it wasn't sporting," he accused. He turned to me. "Marily can't play good hide-and-seek anyway. She's only a Stupid."

"Let's forget that for a minute, Robert." I turned to her. "Star, just where did you go?"

"Oh, it's nothing, Daddy." She spoke defensively, belittling the whole thing. "We just go a little ways when we play with her. She ought to be able to find us a little ways."

"That's evading the issue. *Where* do you go—and *how* do you go?"

Jim stepped forward and showed her the bronze coin I'd sent him.

"You see, Star," he said quietly, "we've found this."

"I shouldn't have to tell you my game." She was almost in tears. "You're both just Tweens. You couldn't understand." Then, struck with contrition, she turned to me. "Daddy, I've tried and tried to ESP. you. Truly I did. But you don't ESP worth anything." She slipped her hand through Robert's arm. "Robert does it very nicely," she said primly, as though she were complimenting him on using his fork the right way. "He must be better than I am, because I don't know how he finds me."

"I'll tell you how I do it, Star," Robert exclaimed eagerly. It was as if he were trying to make amends now that grownups had caught on. "You don't use any imagination. I never saw anybody with so little imagination!"

"I do too have imagination," she countered loudly. "I thought up the game, didn't I? I told you how to do it, didn't I?"

"Yeah, yeah!" he shouted back. "But you always have to look at a book to ESP what's in it, so you leave an ESP smudge. I just go to the encyclopedia and ESP where you did—and I go to that place—and there you are. It's simple."

Star's mouth dropped open in consternation.

"I never thought of that," she said.

Jim and I stood there, letting the meaning of what they were saying penetrate slowly into our incredulous minds.

"Anyway," Robert was saying, "you haven't any imagination." He sank down cross-legged on the floor. "You can't teleport yourself to any place that's never been."

She went over to squat down beside him. "I can too! What about the Moon People? They haven't been yet."

He looked at her with childish disgust.

"Oh, Star, they have so been. You know that." He spread his hands out as though he were a baseball referee. "That time hasn't been yet for your daddy here, for instance, but it's already been for somebody like—well, say, like those things from Arcturus."

"Well, neither have you teleported yourself to some place that never was," Star was arguing back. "So there."

Waving Jim to one chair, I sank down into another. At least the arms of the chair felt solid beneath my hands.

"Now look, kids," I interrupted their evasive tactics, "let's start at the beginning. I gather you've figured a way to travel to places in the past or future."

"Well, of course, Daddy." Star shrugged the statement aside nonchalantly. "We just TP ourselves by ESP anywhere we want to go. It doesn't do any harm."

And these were the children who were too little to cross the street!

I have been through times of shock before. This was the same—somehow, the mind becomes too stunned to react beyond a point. One simply plows through the rest, the best he can, almost normally.

"Okay, okay," I said, and was surprised to hear the same tone I would have used over an argument about the biggest piece of cake. "I don't know whether it's harmful or not. I'll have to think it over. Right now, just tell me how you do it."

"It would be so much easier if I could ESP it to you," Star said doubtfully.

"Well, pretend I'm a Stupid and tell me in words."

"You remember the Moebius Strip?" she asked very slowly and carefully, starting with the first and most basic point in almost the way one explains to an ordinary child.

Yes, I remembered it. And I remembered how long ago it was that she had discovered it. Over a year, and her busy, brilliant mind had been exploring its possibilities ever since. And I thought she had forgotten it!

"That's where you join the ends of a strip of paper together with a half twist to make one surface," she went on, as though jogging my undependable, slow memory.

"Yes," I answered. "We all know the Moebius Strip."

Jim looked startled. I had never told him about the incident.

"Next you take a sheet and you give it a half twist and join the edge to itself all over to make a funny kind of holder."

"Klein's Bottle," Jim supplied.

She looked at him in relief.

"Oh, you know about that," she said. "That makes it easier. Well, then, the next step. You take a cube—" Her face clouded with doubt again, and she explained, "You can't do this with your hands. You've gotta ESP it done, because it's an imaginary cube anyway."

She looked at us questioningly. I nodded for her to continue.

"And you ESP the twisted cube all together the same way you did Klein's Bottle. Now if you do that big enough, all around you, so you're sort of half twisted in the middle, then you can TP yourself anywhere you want to go. And that's all there is to it," she finished hurriedly.

"Where have you gone?" I asked her quietly.

The technique of doing it would take some thinking. I knew enough physics to know that was the way the dimensions were built up. The line, the plane, the cube—Euclidian physics. The Moebius Strip, the Klein Bottle, the unnamed twisted cube—Einsteinian physics. Yes, it was possible.

"Oh, we've gone all over," Star answered vaguely. "The Romans and the Egyptians—places like that."

"You picked up a coin in one of those places?" Jim asked. He was doing a good job of keeping his voice casual. I knew the excitement he must be feeling, the vision of the wealth of knowledge which must be opening before his eyes.

"I found it, Daddy," Star answered Jim's question. She was about to cry. "I found it in the dirt, and Robert was about to catch me. I forgot I had it when I went away from there so fast." She looked at me pleadingly. "I didn't mean to steal it, Daddy. I never stole anything, anywhere. And I was going to take it back and put it right where I found it. Truly I was. But I dropped it again, and then I ESP'd that you had it. I guess I was awful naughty."

I brushed my hand across my forehead.

"Let's skip the question of good and bad for a minute," I said, my head throbbing. "What about this business of going into the future?"

Robert spoke up, his eyes shining. "There isn't any future, Mr. Holmes. That's what I keep telling Star, but she can't reason—she's just a girl. It'll all pass. Everything is always past."

Jim stared at him, as though thunderstruck, and opened his mouth to protest. I shook my head warningly.

"Suppose you tell me about that, Robert," I said.

"Well," he began on a rising note, frowning, "it's kinda hard to explain at that. Star's a Bright and even she doesn't understand it exactly. But, you see, I'm older." He looked at her with superiority. Then, with a change of mood, he defended her. "But when she gets as old as I am, she'll understand it okay."

He patted her shoulder consolingly. He was all of six years old.

"You go back into the past. Back past Egypt and Atlantis. That's recent," he said with scorn. "And on back, and on back, and all of a sudden it's future."

"That isn't the way *I* did it." Star tossed her head contrarily. "I *reasoned* the future. I reasoned what would come next, and I went there, and then I reasoned again. And on and on. I can too reason."

"It's the same future," Robert told us dogmatically. "It has to be, because that's all that ever happened." He turned to Star. "The reason you never could find any Garden of Eden is because there wasn't any Adam and Eve." Then to me, "And man didn't come from the apes, either. Man started himself."

Jim almost strangled as he leaned forward, his face red and his eyes bulging.

"How?" he choked out.

Robert sent his gaze into the far distance.

"Well," he said, "a long time from now—you know what I mean, as a Stupid would think of Time-From-Now—men got into a mess. Quite a mess—

"There were some people in that time who figured out the same kind of traveling Star and I do. So when the world was about to blow up and form a new star, a lot of them teleported themselves back to when the Earth was young, and they started over again."

Jim just stared at Robert, unable to speak.

"I don't get it," I said.

"Not everybody could do it," Robert explained patiently. "Just a few Brights. But they enclosed a lot of other people and took them along." He became a little vague at this point. "I guess later on the Brights lost interest in the Stupids or something. Anyway, the Stupids sank down lower and lower and became like animals." He held his nose briefly. "They smelled worse. They worshiped the Brights as gods."

Robert looked at me and shrugged.

"I don't know all that happened. I've only been there a few times. It's not very interesting. Anyway," he finished, "the Brights finally disappeared."

"I'd sure like to know where they went." Star sighed. It was a lonely sigh. I helplessly took her hand and gave my attention back to Robert.

"I still don't quite understand," I said.

He grabbed up some scissors, a piece of cellophane tape, a sheet of paper. Quickly he cut a strip, gave it a half twist, and taped it together. Then rapidly, on the Moebius Strip, he wrote: "Cave men, This men, That men, Mu Men, Atlantis Men, Egyptians, History Men, Us Now Men, Atom Men, Moon Men, Planet Men, Star Men–"

"There," he said. "That's all the room there is on the strip. I've written clear around it. Right after Star Men comes Cave Men. It's all one thing, joined together. It isn't future, and it isn't past, either. It just plain *is*. Don't you see?"

"I'd sure like to know how the Brights got off the strip," Star said wistfully.

I had all I could take.

"Look, kids," I pleaded, "I don't know whether this game's dangerous or not. Maybe you'll wind up in a lion's mouth, or something."

"Oh, no, Daddy!" Star shrilled in glee. "We'd just TP ourselves right out of there."

"But fast," Robert chortled in agreement.

"Anyway, I've got to think it over," I said stubbornly. "I'm only a Tween, but, Star, I'm your daddy and you're just a little girl, so you have to mind me."

"I always mind you," she said virtuously.

"You do, eh?" I asked. "What about going off the block? Visiting the Greeks and Star Men isn't my idea of staying on the block."

"But you didn't say that, Daddy. You said not to cross the street. And I never did cross the street. Did we, Robert? Did we?"

"We didn't cross a single street, Mr. Holmes," he insisted.

"My God!" said Jim, and he went on trying to light a cigarette.

"All right, all *right!* No more leaving this time, then," I warned.

"Wait!" It was a cry of anguish from Jim. He broke the cigarette in sudden frustration and threw it in an ashtray. "The museum, Pete," he pleaded. "Think what it would mean. Pictures, specimens, voice recordings. And not only from historical places, but Star men, Pete. *Star men!* Wouldn't it be all right for them to go places they know are safe? I wouldn't ask them to take risks, but—"

"No, Jim," I said regretfully. "It's your museum, but this is my daughter."

"Sure," he breathed. "I guess I'd feel the same way."

I turned back to the youngsters.

"Star, Robert," I said to them both, "I want your promise that you will not leave this time, until I let you. Now I couldn't punish you if you broke your promise, because I couldn't follow you. But I want your promise on your word of honor you won't leave this time."

"We promise." They each held up a hand, as if swearing in court. "No more leaving this time."

I let the kids go back outside into the yard. Jim and I looked at one another for a long while, breathing hard enough to have been running.

"I'm sorry," I said at last.

"I know," he answered. "So am I. But I don't blame you. I simply forgot, for a moment, how much a daughter could mean to a man." He was silent, and then added, with the humorous quirk back at the corner of his lips, "I can just see myself reporting this interview to the museum."

"You don't intend to, do you?" I asked, alarmed.

"And get myself canned or laughed at? I'm not that stupid."

September 10

Am I actually getting it? I had a flash for an instant. I was concentrating on Caesar's triumphant march into Rome. For the briefest of instants, *there it was!* I was standing on the roadway, watching. But, most peculiar, it was still a picture; I was the only thing moving. And then, just as abruptly, I lost it.

Was it only a hallucination? Something brought about by intense concentration and wishful thinking?

Now let's see. You visualize a cube. Then you ESP it a half twist and seal the edges together– No, when it has the half twist there's only one surface. You seal that surface all around you . . .

Sometimes I think I have it. Sometimes I despair. If only I were a Bright instead of a Tween!

October 23

I don't see how I managed to make so much work of teleporting myself. It's the simplest thing in the world, no effort at all. Why, a child could do it! That sounds like a gag, considering that it was two children who showed me how, but I mean the whole thing is easy enough for even almost any kid to learn. The problem is understanding the steps . . . no, not understanding, because I can't say I do, but working out the steps in the process.

There's no danger, either. No wonder it felt like a still picture at first, for the speeding up is incredible. That bullet I got in the way of, for instance–I was able to go and meet it and walk along beside it while it traveled through the air. To the men who were dueling, I must have been no more than an instantaneous streak of movement.

That's why the youngsters laughed at the suggestion of danger. Even if they materialized right in the middle of an atomic blast, it is so slow by comparison that they could TP right out again before they got hurt. The blast can't travel any faster than the speed of light, you see, while there is no limit to the speed of thought.

But I still haven't given them permission to teleport themselves out of this time yet. I want to go over the ages pretty carefully before I do; I'm not taking any chances, even though I don't see how they could wind up in any trouble. Still, Robert claimed the Brights went from the future back into the beginning, which means they could be going through time and overtake any of the three of us, and one of them might be hostile . . .

I feel like a louse, not taking Jim's cameras, specimen boxes, and recorders along. But there's time for that. Plenty of time, once I get the feel of history without being encumbered by all that stuff to carry.

Speaking of time and history—what a rotten job historians have done! For instance:

George III of England was neither crazy nor a moron. He wasn't a particularly nice guy, I'll admit—I don't see how anybody could be with the amount of flattery I saw—but he was the victim of empire expansion and the ferment of the Industrial Revolution. So were all the other European rulers at the time, though. He certainly did better than Louis of France. At least George kept his job and his head.

On the other hand, John Wilkes Booth was definitely psychotic. He could have been cured if they'd had our methods of psychotherapy then, and Lincoln, of course, wouldn't have been assassinated. It was almost a compulsion to prevent the killing, but I didn't dare . . . God knows what effect it would have had on history. Strange thing, Lincoln looked less surprised than anybody else when he was shot, sad, yes, and hurt emotionally at least as much as physically, yet you'd swear he was expecting it.

Cheops was *plenty* worried about the number of slaves who died while the pyramid was being built. They weren't easy to replace. He gave them four hours off in the hottest part of the day, and I don't think any slaves in the country were fed or housed better.

I never found any signs of Atlantis or Lemuria, just tales of lands far off—a few hundred miles was a big distance then, remember—that had sunk beneath the sea. With the Ancients' exaggerated notion of geography, a big island was the same as a continent. Some islands did disappear, naturally, drowning a few thousand villagers and herdsmen. That must have been the source of the legends.

Columbus was a stubborn cuss. He was thinking of turning back when the sailors mutinied, which made him obstinate. I still can't see what was eating Genghis Khan and Alexander the Great—it would have been a big help to know the languages, because their big campaigns started off more like vacation or exploration trips. Helen of Troy was attractive enough, considering, but she was just an excuse to fight.

There were several attempts to federate the Indian tribes before the white man and the Five Nations, but going after wives and slaves ruined the movement every time. I think they could have kept America if they had been united and, it goes without saying, knew the deal they were going to get. At any rate, they might have traded for weapons and tools and industrialized the country somewhat in the way the Japanese did. I admit that's only speculation, but this would certainly have been a different world if they'd succeeded!

One day I'll put it all in a comprehensive and *corrected* history of mankind, *complete with photographs*, and then let the "experts" argue themselves into nervous breakdowns over it.

I didn't get very far into the future. Nowhere near the Star Men, or, for that matter, back to the beginning that Robert told us about. It's a matter of reasoning out the path and I'm not a Bright. I'll take Robert and Star along as guides, when and if.

What I did see of the future wasn't so good, but it wasn't so bad, either. The real mess obviously doesn't happen until the Star Men show up very far ahead in history, if Robert is right, and I think he is. I can't guess what the trouble will be, but it must be something ghastly if they won't be able to get out of it even with the enormously advanced technology they'll have. Or maybe that's the answer. It's almost true of us now.

November, Friday 14

The Howells have gone for a weekend trip and left Robert in my care. He's a good kid and no trouble. He and Star have kept their promise, but they're up to something else. I can sense it and that feeling of expectant dread is back with me.

They've been secretive of late. I catch them concentrating intensely, sighing with vexation, and then breaking out into unexplained giggles.

"Remember your promise," I warned Star while Robert was in the room.

"We're not going to break it, Daddy," she answered seriously.

They both chorused, "No more leaving this time."

But they both broke into giggles!

I'll have to watch them. What good it would do, I don't

know. They're up to something, yet how can I stop them? Shut them in their rooms? Tan their hides?

I wonder what someone else would recommend.

The kids are gone!

I've been waiting an hour for them. I know they wouldn't stay away so long if they could get back. There must be something they've run into. Bright as they are, they're still only children.

I have some clues. They promised me they wouldn't go out of this present time. With all her mischievousness, Star has never broken a promise to me—as her typically feminine mind interprets it, that is. So I know they are in our own time. On several occasions Star has brought it up, wondering where the Old Ones, the Bright Ones, have gone—how they got off the Moebius Strip.

That's the clue. How can I get off the Moebius Strip and remain in the present?

A cube won't do it. There we have a mere journey along the single surface. We have a line, we have a plane, we have a cube. And then we have a supercube—a tesseract. That is the logical progression of mathematics. The Bright Ones must have pursued that line of reasoning.

Now I've got to do the same, but without the advantage of being a Bright. Still, it's not the same as expecting a normally intelligent person to produce a work of genius. (Genius by our standards, of course, which I suppose Robert and Star would classify as Tween.) Anyone with a pretty fair I.Q. and proper education and training can follow a genius' logic, provided the steps are there and especially if it has a practical application. What he can't do is initiate and complete that structure of logic. I don't have to, either—that was done for me by a pair of Brights and I "simply" have to apply their findings.

Now let's see if I can.

By reducing the present-past-future of man to a Moebius Strip, we have sheared away a dimension. It is a two-dimensional strip, because it has no depth. (Naturally it would be impossible for a Moebius Strip to have depth; it has only one surface.)

Reducing it to two dimensions makes it possible to travel anywhere you want to go on it via the third dimension. And you're in the third dimension when you enfold yourself in the twisted cube.

Let's go a step higher, into one more dimension. In short, the tesseract. To get the equivalent of a Moebius Strip with depth, you have to go into the fourth dimension, which, it seems to me, is the only way the Bright Ones could get off this closed cycle of past-present-future-past. They must have reasoned that one more notch up the dimensions was all they needed. It is equally obvious that Star and Robert have followed the same line of reasoning; they wouldn't break their promise not to leave the present—and getting off the Moebius Strip into *another* present would, in a sort of devious way, be keeping that promise.

I'm putting all this speculation down for you, Jim Pietre, knowing first that you're a Tween like myself, and second that you're sure to have been doing a lot of thinking about what happened after I sent you the coin Star dropped. I'm hoping you can explain all this to Bill and Ruth Howell—or enough, in any case, to let them understand the truth about their son Robert and my daughter Star, and where the children may have gone.

I'm leaving these notes where you will find them, when you and Bill and Ruth search the house and grounds for us. If you read this, it will be because I have failed in my search for the youngsters. There is also the possibility that I'll find them and that we won't be able to get back onto this Moebius Strip. Perhaps time has a different value there, or doesn't exist at all. What it's like off the Strip is anybody's guess.

Bill and Ruth: I wish I might give you hope that I will bring Robert back to you. But all I can do is wish. It may be no more than wishing upon a star—my Star.

I'm trying now to take six cubes and fold them in on one another so that every angle is a right angle.

It's not easy, but I can do it, using every bit of concentration I've learned from the kids. All right, I have the six cubes and I have every angle a right angle.

Now if, in the folding, I ESP the tesseract a half twist around myself and—

15

All Summer in a Day

RAY BRADBURY

What can one say about Ray Bradbury. He is entirely in a class by himself. So entirely, that even I myself must reluctantly admit it.

Ray and I were both on an "Open End" program—a television talk program, in case you've forgotten—when the subject under discussion was "Life on Other Worlds."

Twice in the course of the show, the moderator introduced Ray as "the dean of science fiction." Now he was not referring to age, of course, since Ray is some six weeks younger than I am and there are a great many science fiction writers (well, a few, anyway) who are years and years and years older than either of us.

He could only be referring to Ray as the best science fiction writer and, of course, it is always difficult for me to sit still and hear someone else being referred to in such a fashion in my very own presence. It rouses the monster in me. But if it must happen, let it happen in connection with Ray.

On the outside, Ray looks sweet and gentle and pleasantly ordinary. Inside, however, there is something oddly trenchant and unusual about him. He just doesn't think like anyone else. At least, his stories always bear the highly individual Bradbury stamp and it always seems to me that no one else but he could possibly have written them.

The occasion of the TV show was the first time I had met Ray since the first World Science Fiction Convention in 1939, when he had not yet published a single story and when, he told me, he looked up at me in awe because I had published three. I hope we don't have to wait so long for the next meeting.

And while we wait, let Ray Bradbury introduce you to some children on Venus, and to the unspeakable tragedy that befell one of them.

"Ready?"

"Ready."

"Now?"

"Soon."

"Do the scientists really know? Will it happen today, will it?"

"Look, look; see for yourself!"

The children pressed to each other like so many roses, so many weeds, intermixed, peering out for a look at the hidden sun.

It rained.

It had been raining for seven years; thousands upon thousands of days compounded and filled from one end to the other with rain, with the drum and gush of water, with the sweet crystal fall of showers and the concussion of storms so heavy they were tidal waves come over the islands. A thousand forests had been crushed under the rain and grown up a thousand times to be crushed again. And this was the way life was forever on the planet Venus, and this was the schoolroom of the children of the rocket men and women who had come to a raining world to set up civilization and live out their lives.

"It's stopping, it's stopping!"

"Yes, yes!"

Margot stood apart from them, from these children who could never remember a time when there wasn't rain and rain and rain. They were all nine years old, and if there had been a day, seven years ago, when the sun came out for an hour and showed its face to the stunned world, they could not recall. Sometimes, at night, she head them stir, in remembrance, and she knew they were dreaming and remembering gold or a yellow crayon or a coin large enough to buy the world with. She knew that they thought they remembered a warmness, like a blushing in the face, in the body, in the arms and legs and trembling hands. But then they always awoke to the tatting drum, the endless shaking down of clear bead necklaces upon the roof, the walk, the gardens, the forest, and their dreams were gone.

All day yesterday they had read in class, about the sun. About how like a lemon it was, and how hot. And they had written small stories or essays or poems about it:

I think the sun is a flower,
That blooms for just one hour.

That was Margot's poem, read in a quiet voice in the still classroom while the rain was falling outside.

"Aw, you didn't write that!" protested one of the boys.

"I did," said Margot. "I *did*."

"William!" said the teacher.

But that was yesterday. Now, the rain was slackening, and the children were crushed to the great thick windows.

"Where's teacher?"

"She'll be back."

"She'd better hurry, we'll miss it!"

They turned on themselves, like a feverish wheel, all tumbling spokes.

Margot stood alone. She was a very frail girl who looked as if she had been lost in the rain for years and the rain had washed out the blue from her eyes and the red from her mouth and the yellow from her hair. She was an old photograph dusted from an album, whitened away, and if she spoke at all her voice would be a ghost. Now she stood, separate, staring at the rain and the loud wet world beyond the huge glass.

"What're *you* looking at?" said William.

Margot said nothing.

"Speak when you're spoken to." He gave her a shove. But she did not move; rather, she let herself be moved only by him and nothing else.

They edged away from her, they would not look at her. She felt them go away. And this was because she would play no games with them in the echoing tunnels of the underground city. If they tagged her and ran, she stood blinking after them and did not follow. When the class sang songs about happiness and life and games, her lips barely moved. Only when they sang about the sun and the summer did her lips move, as she watched the drenched windows.

And then, of course, the biggest crime of all was that she had come here only five years ago from Earth, and she remembered the sun and the way the sun was and the sky was, when she was four, in Ohio. And they, they had been on Venus all their lives, and they had been only two years old when last the sun came out, and had long since forgotten the color and heat of it and the way that it really was. But Margot remembered.

"It's like a penny," she said, once, eyes closed.

"No, it's not!" the children cried.

"It's like a fire," she said, "in the stove."

"You're lying, you don't remember!" cried the children.

But she remembered and stood quietly apart from all of them, and watched the patterning windows. And once, a month ago, she had refused to shower in the school shower rooms, had clutched her hands to her ears and over her head, screaming the water mustn't touch her head. So after that, dimly, dimly, she sensed it, she was different and they knew her difference and kept away.

There was talk that her father and mother were taking her back to Earth next year; it seemed vital to her that they do so, though it would mean the loss of thousands of dollars to her family. And so the children hated her for all these reasons, of big and little consequence. They hated her pale snow face, her waiting silence, her thinness and her possible future.

"Get away!" The boy gave her another push. "What're you waiting for?"

Then, for the first time, she turned and looked at him. And what she was waiting for was in her eyes.

"Well, don't wait around here!" cried the boy, savagely. "You won't see nothing!"

Her lips moved.

"Nothing!" he cried. "It was all a joke, wasn't it?" He turned to the other children. "Nothing's happening today. *Is* it?"

They all blinked at him and then, understanding, laughed and shook their heads. "Nothing, nothing!"

"Oh, but," Margot whispered, her eyes helpless. "But, this is the day, the scientists predict, they say, they *know*, the sun . . ."

"All a joke!" said the boy, and seized her roughly. "Hey, everyone, let's put her in a closet before teacher comes!"

"No," said Margot, falling back.

They surged about her, caught her up and bore her, protesting, and then pleading, and then crying, back into a tunnel, a room, a closet, where they slammed and locked the door. They stood looking at the door and saw it tremble from her beating and throwing herself against it. They heard her muffled cries. Then, smiling, they turned and went out and back down the tunnel, just as the teacher arrived.

"Ready, children?" She glanced at her watch.

"Yes!" said everyone.

"Are we all here?"

"Yes!"

The rain slackened still more.

They crowded to the huge door.

The rain stopped.

It was as if, in the midst of a film concerning an avalanche, a tornado, a hurricane, a volcanic eruption, something had, first, gone wrong with the sound apparatus, thus muffling and finally cutting off all noise, all of the blasts and repercussions and thunders, and then secondly, ripped the film from the projector and inserted in its place a peaceful tropical slide which did not move or tremor. The world ground to a standstill. The silence was so immense and unbelievable that you felt that your ears had been stuffed or you had lost your hearing altogether. The children put their hands to their ears. They stood apart. The door slid back and the smell of the silent, waiting world came in to them.

The sun came out.

It was the color of flaming bronze and it was very large. And the sky around it was a blazing blue tile color. And the jungle burned with sunlight as the children, released from their spell, rushed out, yelling, into the summertime.

"Now, don't go too far," called the teacher after them. "You've only one hour, you know. You wouldn't want to get caught out!"

But they were running and turning their faces up to the sky and feeling the sun on their cheeks like a warm iron; they were taking off their jackets and letting the sun burn their arms.

"Oh, it's better than the sun lamps, isn't it?"

"Much, much better!"

They stopped running and stood in the great jungle that covered Venus, that grew and never stopped growing, tumultuously, even as you watched it. It was a nest of octopuses, clustering up great arms of fleshlike weed, wavering, flowering in this brief spring. It was the color of rubber and ash, this jungle, from the many years without sun. It was the color of stones and white cheeses and ink.

The children lay out, laughing, on the jungle mattress, and heard it sigh and squeak under them, resilient and alive. They ran among the trees, they slipped and fell, they pushed each other, they played hide-and-seek and tag, but most of all they squinted at the sun until tears ran down their faces, they put their hands up at that yellowness and that amazing blueness and they breathed of the fresh fresh air and listened and listened to the silence which suspended them in a blessed sea of no sound and no motion. They looked at everything and savored everything. Then, wildly, like animals escaped from their caves, they ran and ran in shouting circles. They ran for an hour and did not stop running.

And then—

In the midst of their running, one of the girls wailed.

Everyone stopped.

The girl, standing in the open, held out her hand.

"Oh, look, look," she said, trembling.

They came slowly to look at her opened palm.

In the center of it, cupped and huge, was a single raindrop.

She began to cry, looking at it.

They glanced quickly at the sky.

"Oh. Oh."

A few cold drops fell on their noses and their cheeks and their mouths. The sun faded behind a stir of mist. A wind blew cool around them. They turned and started to walk back toward the underground house, their hands at their sides, their smiles vanishing away.

A boom of thunder startled them and like leaves before a new hurricane, they tumbled upon each other and ran. Lightning struck ten miles away, five miles away, a mile, a half mile. The sky darkened into midnight in a flash.

They stood in the doorway of the undergound for a moment until it was raining hard. Then they closed the door and heard the gigantic sound of the rain falling in tons and avalanches everywhere and forever.

"Will it be seven more years?"

"Yes. Seven."

Then one of them gave a little cry.

"Margot!"

"What?"

"She's still in the closet where we locked her."

"Margot."

They stood as if someone had driven them, like so many stakes, into the floor. They looked at each other and then looked away. They glanced out at the world that was raining now and raining and raining steadily. They could not meet each other's glances. Their faces were solemn and pale. They looked at their hands and feet, their faces down.

"Margot."

One of the girls said, "Well . . . ?"

No one moved.

"Go on," whispered the girl.

They walked slowly down the hall in the sound of cold rain. They turned through the doorway to the room, in the sound of the storm and thunder, lightning on their faces, blue and terrible. They walked over to the closet door slowly and stood by it.

Behind the closet door was only silence.

They unlocked the door, even more slowly, and let Margot out.

16

It's a *Good* Life

JEROME BIXBY

My sharpest memory of Jerome Bixby dates back some sixteen years when both of us lived in New York and were members of the "Hydra Club" (surely the most delightful association of science fiction personalities ever crammed into a single room). While conversation ran deep and high, Jerry played the piano to himself as he often did. He played very well.

He was playing "Greensleeves," at the sound of which I invariably melt into a sense of romantic tragedy. Since I sing in an indifferent fashion, I found myself singing sadly and soulfully in time to his music.

A dreadful silence fell upon the room suddenly, and Jerry muted the piano, so that, with my eyes flashing in terror this way and that, I found myself engaged in what seemed virtually an operatic solo; and, moreover, one I felt compelled to finish. I have never quite recovered and now I lock the bathroom door whenever I sing in the shower.

A second connection is both more recent and more distant. The great science fiction movie called The Fantastic Voyage *(dealing with a miniaturized germ-sized submarine with a surgical crew aboard which is injected into a patient's blood stream to perform a delicate operation from within) involves both of us. Jerry, in California, helped write the screenplay and when that was quite done, I, in Massachusetts, wrote a novelization of the movie treatment.*

In many ways it's been a good life for both of us but not in the sense intended by the title of the truly grisly tale you are about to read. There are hells far beyond the purely physical torture-chambers imagined by Dante, so let Jerome Bixby introduce you to one in which a young child is cast in the role of Satan.

Aunt Amy was out on the front porch, rocking back and forth in the high-backed chair and fanning herself, when Bill Soames rode his bicycle up the road and stopped in front of the house.

Perspiring under the afternoon "sun," Bill lifted the box of groceries out of the big basket over the front wheel of the bike, and came up the front walk.

Little Anthony was sitting on the lawn, playing with a rat. He had caught the rat down in the basement—he had made it think that it smelled cheese, the most rich-smelling and crumbly delicious cheese a rat had ever thought it smelled, and it had come out of its hole, and now Anthony had hold of it with his mind and was making it do tricks.

When the rat saw Bill Soames coming, it tried to run, but

Anthony thought at it, and it turned a flip-flop on the grass and lay trembling, its eyes gleaming in small black terror.

Bill Soames hurried past Anthony and reached the front steps, mumbling. He always mumbled when he came to the Fremont house, or passed it by, or even thought of it. Everybody did. They thought about silly things, things that didn't mean very much, like two-and-two-is-four-and-twice-is-eight and so on; they tried to jumble up their thoughts and keep them skipping back and forth, so Anthony couldn't read their minds. The mumbling helped. Because if Anthony got anything strong out of your thought, he might take a notion to do something about it—like curing your wife's sick headaches or your kid's mumps, or getting your old milk cow back on schedule, or fixing the privy. And while Anthony mightn't actually mean any harm, he couldn't be expected to have much notion of what was the right thing to do in such cases.

That was if he liked you. He might try to help you, in his way. And that could be pretty horrible.

If he didn't like you . . . well, that could be worse.

Bill Soames set the box of groceries on the porch railing, and stopped his mumbling long enough to say, "Everythin' you wanted, Miss Amy."

"Oh, fine, William," Amy Fremont said lightly. "My, ain't it terrible hot today?"

Bill Soames almost cringed. His eyes pleaded with her. He shook his head violently *no*, and then interrupted his mumbling again, though obviously he didn't want to: "Oh, don't say that, Miss Amy . . . it's fine, just fine. A real *good* day!"

Amy Fremont got up from the rocking chair, and came across the porch. She was a tall woman, thin, a smiling vacancy in her eyes. About a year ago Anthony had gotten mad at her because she'd told him he shouldn't have turned the cat into a cat-rug, and although he had always obeyed her more than anyone else, which was hardly at all, this time he'd snapped at her. With his mind. And that had been the end of Amy Fremont's bright eyes, and the end of Amy Fremont as everyone had known her. And that was when word got around in Peaksville (population: 46) that even the members of Anthony's own family weren't safe. After that, everyone was twice as careful.

Someday Anthony might undo what he'd done to Aunt Amy. Anthony's Mom and Pop hoped he would. When he was older, and maybe sorry. If it was possible, that is. Because Aunt Amy had changed a lot, and besides, now Anthony wouldn't obey anyone.

"Land alive, William," Aunt Amy said, "you don't have to mumble like that. Anthony wouldn't hurt you. My goodness, Anthony likes you!" She raised her voice and called to Anthony, who had tired of the rat and was making it eat itself. "Don't you, dear? Don't you like Mr. Soames?"

Anthony looked across the lawn at the grocery man—a bright, wet, purple gaze. He didn't say anything. Bill Soames tried to smile at him. After a second Anthony returned his attention to the rat. It had already devoured its tail, or at least chewed it off—for Anthony had made it bite faster than it could swallow, and little pink and red furry pieces lay around it on the green grass. Now the rat was having trouble reaching its hindquarters.

Mumbling silently, thinking of nothing in particular as hard as he could, Bill Soames went stiff-legged down the walk, mounted his bicycle and pedaled off.

"We'll see you tonight, William," Aunt Amy called after him.

As Bill Soames pumped the pedals, he was wishing deep down that he could pump twice as fast, to get away from Anthony all the faster, and away from Aunt Amy, who sometimes just forgot how *careful* you had to be. And he shouldn't have thought that. Because Anthony caught it. He caught the desire to get away from the Fremont house as if it was something *bad,* and his purple gaze blinked, and he snapped a small, sulky thought after Bill Soames—just a small one, because he was in a good mood today, and besides, he liked Bill Soames, or at least didn't dislike him, at least today. Bill Soames wanted to go away—so, petulantly, Anthony helped him.

Pedaling with superhuman speed—or rather, appearing to, because in reality the bicycle was pedaling *him*—Bill Soames vanished down the road in a cloud of dust, his thin, terrified wail drifting back across the summerlike heat.

Anthony looked at the rat. It had devoured half its belly,

and had died from pain. He thought it into a grave out deep in the cornfield—his father had once said, smiling, that he might as well do that with the things he killed—and went around the house, casting his odd shadow in the hot, brassy light from above.

In the kitchen Aunt Amy was unpacking the groceries. She put the Mason-jarred goods on the shelves, and the meat and milk in the icebox, and the beet sugar and coarse flour in big cans under the sink. She put the cardboard box in the corner, by the door, for Mr. Soames to pick up next time he came. It was stained and battered and torn and worn fuzzy, but it was one of the few left in Peaksville. In faded red letters it said *Campbell's Soup*. The last cans of soup, or of anything else, had been eaten long ago, except for a small communal hoard which the villagers dipped into for special occasions—but the box lingered on, like a coffin, and when it and the other boxes were gone, the men would have to make some out of wood.

Aunt Amy went out in back, where Anthony's Mom—Aunt Amy's sister—sat in the shade of the house, shelling peas. The peas, every time Mom ran a finger along a pod, went *lollop-lollop-lollop* into the pan on her lap.

"William brought the groceries," Aunt Amy said. She sat down wearily in the straight-backed chair beside Mom, and began fanning herself again. She wasn't really old; but ever since Anthony had snapped at her with his mind, something had seemed to be wrong with her body as well as her mind, and she was tired all the time.

"Oh, good," said Mom. *Lollop* went the fat peas into the pan.

Everyone in Peaksville always said, "Oh fine," or "Good," or "Say, that's swell!" when almost anything happened or was mentioned, even unhappy things like accidents or even deaths. They'd always say, "Good," because if they didn't try to cover up how they really felt, Anthony might overhear with his mind and then nobody knew what might happen. Like the time Mrs. Kent's husband, Sam, had come walking back from the graveyard, because Anthony liked Mrs. Kent and had heard her mourning.

Lollop.

"Tonight's television night," said Aunt Amy. "I'm glad. I look forward to it so much every week. I wonder what we'll see tonight?"

"Did Bill bring the meat?" asked Mom.

"Yes." Aunt Amy fanned herself, looking up at the featureless brassy glare of the sky. "Goodness, it's so hot! I wish Anthony would make it just a little cooler—"

"Amy!"

"Oh!" Mom's sharp tone had penetrated, where Bill Soames's agonized expression had failed. Aunt Amy put one thin hand to her mouth in exaggerated alarm. "Oh . . . I'm sorry, dear." Her pale blue eyes shuttled around, right and left, to see if Anthony was in sight. Not that it would make any difference if he was or wasn't—he didn't have to be near you to know what you were thinking. Usually, though, unless he had his attention on somebody, he would be occupied with thoughts of his own.

But some things attracted his attention—you could never be sure just what.

"This weather's just *fine,*" Mom said.

Lollop.

"Oh, yes," Aunt Amy said. "It's a wonderful day. I wouldn't want it changed for the world!"

Lollop.

Lollop.

"What time is it?" Mom said.

Aunt Amy was sitting where she could see through the kitchen window to the alarm clock on the shelf above the stove. "Four-thirty," she said.

Lollop.

"I want tonight to be something special," Mom said. "Did Bill bring a good lean roast?"

"Good and lean, dear. They butchered just today, you know, and sent us over the best piece."

"Dan Hollis will be *so* surprised when he finds out that tonight's television party is a birthday party for him too!"

"Oh *I* think he will! Are you sure nobody's told him?"

"Everybody swore they wouldn't."

"That'll be real nice," Aunt Amy nodded, looking off across the cornfield. "A birthday party."

"Well . . ." Mom put the pan of peas down beside her, stood up and brushed her apron. "I'd better get the roast on. Then we can set the table." She picked up the peas.

Anthony came around the corner of the house. He didn't look at them, but continued on down through the carefully kept garden—*all* the gardens in Peaksville were carefully kept, very carefully kept—and went past the rusting, useless hulk that had been the Fremont family car, and went smoothly over the fence and out into the cornfield.

"Isn't this a lovely day!" said Mom, a little loudly, as they went toward the back door.

Aunt Amy fanned herself. "A beautiful day, dear. Just *fine!*"

Out in the cornfield, Anthony walked between the tall, rustling rows of green stalks. He liked to smell the corn. The alive corn overhead, and the old dead corn underfoot. Rich Ohio earth, thick with weeds and brown, dry-rotting ears of corn, pressed between his bare toes with every step—he had made it rain last night so everything would smell and feel nice today.

He walked clear to the edge of the cornfield, and over to where a grove of shadowy green trees covered cool, moist, dark ground and lots of leafy undergrowth and jumbled moss-covered rocks and a small spring that made a clear, clean pool. Here Anthony liked to rest and watch the birds and insects and small animals that rustled and scampered and chirped about. He liked to lie on the cool ground and look up through the moving greenness overhead, and watch the insects flit in the hazy soft sunbeams that stood like slanting, glowing bars between ground and treetops. Somehow, he liked the thoughts of the little creatures in this place better than the thoughts outside; and while the thoughts he picked up here weren't very strong or very clear, he could get enough out of them to know what the little creatures liked and wanted, and he spent a lot of time making the grove more like what they wanted it to be. The spring hadn't always been here; but one time he had found thirst in one small furry mind, and had brought subterranean water to the surface in a clear cold flow, and had watched blinking as the creature drank, feeling its pleasure. Later he had made the pool, when he found a small urge to swim.

He had made rocks and trees and bushes and caves, and sunlight here and shadows there, because he had felt in all the tiny minds around him the desire—or the instinctive want—for this kind of resting place, and that kind of mating place, and this kind of place to play, and that kind of home.

And somehow the creatures from all the fields and pastures around the grove had seemed to know that this was a good place, for there were always more of them coming in—every time Anthony came out here there were more creatures than the last time, and more desires and needs to be tended to. Every time there would be some kind of creature he had never seen before, and he would find its mind, and see what it wanted, and then give it to it.

He liked to help them. He liked to feel their simple gratification.

Today, he rested beneath a thick elm, and lifted his purple gaze to a red and black bird that had just come to the grove. It twittered on a branch over his head, and hopped back and forth, and thought its tiny thoughts, and Anthony made a big, soft nest for it, and pretty soon it hopped in.

A long, brown, sleek-furred animal was drinking at the pool. Anthony found its mind next. The animal was thinking about a smaller creature that was scurrying along the ground on the other side of the pool, grubbing for insects. The little creature didn't know that it was in danger. The long, brown animal finished drinking and tensed its legs to leap, and Anthony thought it into a grave in the cornfield.

He didn't like those kinds of thoughts. They reminded him of the thoughts outside the grove. A long time ago some of the people outside had thought that way about *him*, and one night they'd hidden and waited for him to come back from the grove—and he'd just thought them all into the cornfield. Since then, the rest of the people hadn't thought that way—at least, very clearly. Now their thoughts were all mixed up and confusing whenever they thought about him or near him, so he didn't pay much attention.

He liked to help them, too, sometimes—but it wasn't simple, or very gratifying either. They never thought happy thoughts when he did—just the jumble. So he spent more time out here.

He watched all the birds and insects and furry creatures for a while, and played with a bird, making it soar and dip and streak madly around tree trunks until, accidentally, when another bird caught his attention for a moment, he ran it into a rock. Petulantly he thought the rock into a grave in the cornfield, but he couldn't do anything more with the bird. Not because it was dead, though it was, but because it had a broken wing. So he went back to the house. He didn't feel like walking back through the cornfield, so he just *went* to the house, right down into the basement.

It was nice down here. Nice and dark and damp and sort of fragrant, because once Mom had been making preserves in a rack along the far wall and then she'd stopped coming down ever since Anthony had started spending time here, and the preserves had spoiled and leaked down and spread over the dirt floor, and Anthony liked the smell.

He caught another rat, making it smell cheese, and after he played with it, he thought it into a grave right beside the long animal he'd killed in the grove. Aunt Amy hated rats, and so he killed a lot of them, because he liked Aunt Amy most of all and sometimes did things that Aunt Amy wanted. Her mind was more like the little furry minds out in the grove. She hadn't thought anything bad at all about him for a long time.

After the rat, he played with a big black spider in the corner under the stairs, making it run back and forth until its web shook and shimmered in the light from the cellar window like a reflection in silvery water. Then he drove fruit flies into the web until the spider was frantic trying to wind them all up. The spider liked flies, and its thoughts were stronger than theirs, so he did it. There were something bad in the way it liked flies, but it wasn't clear—and besides, Aunt Amy hated flies too.

He heard footsteps overhead—Mom moving around in the kitchen. He blinked his purple gaze, and almost decided to make her hold still—but instead he went up to the attic, and, after looking out the circular window for a while at the front lawn and the dusty road and Henderson's tip-waving wheatfield beyond, he curled into an unlikely shape and went partly to sleep.

Soon people would be coming for television, he heard Mom think.

He went more to sleep. He liked television night. Aunt Amy had always liked television a lot, so one time he had thought some for her, and a few other people had been there at the time, and Aunt Amy had felt disappointed when they wanted to leave. He'd done something to them for that—and now everybody came to television.

He liked all the attention he got when they did.

Anthony's father came home around six-thirty, looking tired and dirty and bloody. He'd been over in Dunn's pasture with the other men, helping pick out the cow to be slaughtered this month and doing the job, and then butchering the meat and salting it away in Soames's icehouse. Not a job he cared for, but every man had his turn. Yesterday he had helped scythe down old McIntyre's wheat. Tomorrow they would start threshing. By hand. Everything in Peaksville had to be done by hand.

He kissed his wife on the cheek and sat down at the kitchen table. He smiled and said, "Where's Anthony?"

"Around someplacc," Mom said.

Aunt Amy was over at the wood-burning stove, stirring the big pot of peas. Mom went back to the oven and opened it and basted the roast.

"Well, it's been a *good* day," Dad said. By rote. Then he looked at the mixing bowl and breadboard on the table. He sniffed at the dough. "M'm," he said. "I could eat a loaf all by myself, I'm so hungry."

"No one told Dan Hollis about its being a birthday party, did they?" his wife asked.

"Nope. We kept as quiet as mummies."

"We've fixed up such a lovely surprise!"

"Um? What?"

"Well . . . you know how much Dan likes music. Well, last week Thelma Dunn found a *record* in her attic!"

"No!"

"Yes! And we had Ethel sort of ask—you know, without really *asking*—if he had that one. And he said no. Isn't that a wonderful surprise?"

"Well, now, it sure is. A record, imagine! That's a real nice thing to find! What record is it?"

"Perry Como, singing *You Are My Sunshine*."

"Well, I'll be darned. I always liked that tune." Some raw carrots were lying on the table. Dad picked up a small one, scrubbed it on his chest, and took a bite. "How did Thelma happen to find it?"

"Oh, you know . . . just looking around for new things."

"M'm." Dad chewed the carrot. "Say, who has that picture we found a while back? I kind of liked it—that old clipper sailing along—"

"The Smiths. Next week the Sipichs get it and they give the Smiths old McIntyre's music box, and we give the Sipichs—" And she went down the tentative order of things that would exchange hands among the women at church this Sunday.

He nodded. "Looks like we can't have the picture for a while, I guess. Look, honey, you might try to get that detective book back from the Reillys. I was so busy the week we had it, I never got to finish all the stories."

"I'll try," his wife said doubtfully. "But I hear the van Husens have a stereoscope they found in the cellar." Her voice was just a little accusing. "They had it two whole months before they told anybody about it . . ."

"Say," Dad said, looking interested. "That'd be nice, too. Lots of pictures?"

"I suppose so. I'll see on Sunday. I'd like to have it—but we still owe the van Husens for their canary. I don't know why that bird had to pick *our* house to die . . . it must have been sick when we got it. Now there's just no satisfying Betty van Husen—she even hinted she'd like our *piano* for a while!"

"Well, honey, you try for the stereoscope—or just anything you think we'll like." At last he swallowed the carrot. It had been a little young and tough. Anthony's whims about the weather made it so that people never knew what crops would come up, or what shape they'd be in if they did. All they could do was plant a lot; and always enough of something came up any one season to live on. Just once there had been a grain surplus; tons of it had been hauled to the edge of Peaksville and dumped off into the nothingness. Otherwise, nobody could have breathed when it started to spoil.

"You know," Dad went on. "It's nice to have the new things around. "It's nice to think that there's probably still a lot of stuff nobody's found yet, in cellars and attics and barns and down behind things. They help, somehow. As much as anything can help—"

"Sh-h!" Mom glanced nervously around.

"Oh," Dad said, smiling hastily. "It's all right! The new things are *good!* It's *nice* to be able to have something around you've never seen before, and know that something you've given somebody else is making them happy . . . that's a real *good* thing."

"A good thing," his wife echoed.

"Pretty soon," Aunt Amy said, from the stove, "there won't be any more new things. We'll have found everything there is to find. Goodness, that'll be too bad—"

"Amy!"

"Well . . ." Her pale eyes were shallow and fixed, a sign of her recurrent vagueness. "It will be kind of a shame . . . no new things . . ."

"Don't *talk* like that," Mom said, trembling. "Amy, be *quiet!"*

"It's *good,"* said Dad, in the loud, familiar, wanting-to-be-overheard tone of voice. "Such talk is *good.* It's okay, honey—don't you see? It's good for Amy to talk any way she wants. It's good for her to feel bad. Everything's good. Everything *has* to be good."

Anthony's mother was pale. And so was Aunt Amy—the peril of the moment had suddenly penetrated the clouds surrounding her mind. Sometimes it was difficult to handle words so that they might not prove disastrous. You just never *knew.* There were so many things it was wise not to say, or even think—but remonstration for saying or thinking them might be just as bad, if Anthony heard and decided to do anything about it. You could just never tell what Anthony was liable to do.

Everything had to be good. Had to be fine just as it was, even if it wasn't. Always. Because any change might be worse. So terribly much worse.

"Oh, my goodness, yes, of course it's good," Mom said. "You talk any way you want to, Amy, and it's just fine. Of course, you want to remember that some ways are *better* than others . . ."

Aunt Amy stirred the peas, fright in her pale eyes.

"Oh, yes," she said. "But I don't feel like talking right now. It . . . it's *good* that I don't feel like talking."

Dad said tiredly, smiling, "I'm going out and wash up."

They started arriving around eight o'clock. By that time Mom and Aunt Amy had the big table in the dining room set, and two more tables off to the side. The candles were burning, and the chairs situated, and Dad had a big fire going in the fireplace.

The first to arrive were the Sipichs, John and Mary. John wore his best suit, and was well scrubbed and pink-faced after his day in McIntyre's pasture. The suit was neatly pressed, but getting threadbare at elbows and cuffs. Old McIntyre was working on a loom, designing it out of schoolbooks, but so far it was slow going. McIntyre was a capable man with wood and tools, but a loom was a big order when you couldn't get metal parts. McIntyre had been one of the ones who, at first, had wanted to try to get Anthony to make things the villagers needed, like clothes and canned goods and medical supplies and gasoline. Since then, he felt that what had happened to the whole Terrance family and Joe Kinney was his fault, and he worked hard trying to make it up to the rest of them. And since then, no one had tried to get Anthony to do anything.

Mary Sipich was a small, cheerful woman in a simple dress. She immediately set about helping Mom and Aunt Amy put the finishing touches on the dinner.

The next arrivals were the Smiths and Dunns, who lived right next to each other down the road, only a few yards from the nothingness. They drove up in the Smiths' wagon, drawn by their old horse.

Then the Reillys showed up, from across the darkened wheat-field, and the evening really began. Pat Reilly sat down at the big upright in the front room, and began to play from the popular sheet music on the rack. He played softly, as expressively as he could—and nobody sang. Anthony liked piano playing a whole lot, but not singing; often he would come up from the basement, or down from the attic, or just *come*, and sit on top of the piano, nodding his head as Pat played *Lover* or *Boulevard of Broken Dreams* or *Night and Day*. He seemed to prefer ballads, sweet-sounding songs—but the one time somebody had started to sing, Anthony had looked over from the top of the piano and done something that made everybody afraid of singing from then on. Later they'd decided that the piano was what Anthony had heard first, before anybody had ever tried to sing, and now anything else added to it didn't sound right and distracted him from his pleasure.

So, every television night, Pat would play the piano, and that was the beginning of the evening. Wherever Anthony was, the music would make him happy, and put him in a good mood, and he would know that they were gathering for television and waiting for him.

By eight-thirty everybody had shown up, except for the seventeen children and Mrs. Soames who was off watching them in the schoolhouse at the far end of town. The children of Peaksville were never, never allowed near the Fremont house—not since little Fred Smith had tried to play with Anthony on a dare. The younger children weren't even told about Anthony. The others had mostly forgotten about him, or were told that he was a nice, nice goblin but they must never go near him.

Dan and Ethel Hollis came late, and Dan walked in not suspecting a thing. Pat Reilly had played the piano until his hands ached—he'd worked pretty hard with them today—and now he got up, and everybody gathered around to wish Dan Hollis a happy birthday.

"Well, I'll be darned." Dan grinned. "This is swell, I wasn't expecting this at all . . . gosh, this is *swell!*"

They gave him his presents—mostly things they had made by hand, though some were things that people had possessed as their own and now gave him as his. John Sipich gave him a watch charm, hand-carved out of a piece of hickory wood. Dan's watch had broken down a year or so ago, and there was nobody in the village who knew how to fix it, but he still carried it around because it had been his grandfather's and was a fine old heavy thing of gold and silver. He attached the charm to the chain, while everybody laughed and said John had done a nice job of carving. Then Mary Sipich gave him a knitted necktie, which he put on, removing the one he'd worn.

The Reillys gave him a little box they had made, to keep

things in. They didn't say what things, but Dan said he'd keep his personal jewelry in it. The Reillys had made it out of a cigar box, carefully peeled of its paper and lined on the inside with velvet. The outside had been polished, and carefully if not expertly carved by Pat—but his carving got complimented too. Dan Hollis received many other gifts—a pipe, a pair of shoelaces, a tie pin, a knit pair of socks, some fudge, a pair of garters made from old suspenders.

He unwrapped each gift with vast pleasure, and wore as many of them as he could right there, even the garters. He lit up the pipe, and said he'd never had a better smoke, which wasn't quite true, because the pipe wasn't broken in yet. Pete Manners had had it lying around ever since he'd received it as a gift four years ago from an out-of-town relative who hadn't known he'd stopped smoking.

Dan put the tobacco into the bowl very carefully. Tobacco was precious. It was only pure luck that Pat Reilly had decided to try to grow some in his backyard just before what had happened to Peaksville had happened. It didn't grow very well, and then they had to cure it and shred it and all, and it was just precious stuff. Everybody in town used wooden holders old McIntyre had made, to save on butts.

Last of all, Thelma Dunn gave Dan Hollis the record she had found.

Dan's eyes misted even before he opened the package. He knew it was a record.

"Gosh," he said softly. "What one is it? I'm almost afraid to look . . ."

"You haven't got it, darling," Ethel Hollis smiled. "Don't you remember, I asked about *You Are My Sunshine?*"

"Oh, gosh," Dan said again. Carefully he removed the wrapping and stood there fondling the record, running his big hands over the worn grooves with their tiny, dulling crosswise scratches. He looked around the room, eyes shining, and they all smiled back, knowing how delighted he was.

"Happy birthday, darling!" Ethel said, throwing her arms around him and kissing him.

He clutched the record in both hands, holding it off to one side as she pressed against him. "Hey," he laughed, pulling back his head. "Be careful . . . I'm holding a priceless object!" He looked around again, over his wife's arms, which were still around his neck. His eyes were hungry. "Look . . . do you think we could play it? Lord, what I'd give to hear some new music . . . just the first part, the orchestra part, before Como sings?"

Faces sobered. After a minute, John Sipich said, "I don't think we'd better, Dan. After all, we don't know just where the singer comes in—it'd be taking too much of a chance. Better wait till you get home."

Dan Hollis reluctantly put the record on the buffet with all his other presents. "It's *good*," he said automatically, but disappointedly, "that I can't play it here."

"Oh, yes," said Sipich. "It's good." To compensate for Dan's disappointed tone, he repeated, "It's *good*."

They ate dinner, the candles lighting their smiling faces, and ate it all right down to the last delicious drop of gravy. They complimented Mom and Aunt Amy on the roast beef, and the peas and carrots, and the tender corn on the cob. The corn hadn't come from the Fremont's cornfield, naturally—everybody knew what was out there, and the field was going to weeds.

Then they polished off the dessert—homemade ice cream and cookies. And then they sat back, in the flickering light of the candles, and chatted waiting for television.

There never was a lot of mumbling on television night—everybody came and had a good dinner at the Fremonts', and that was nice, and afterwards there was television, and nobody really thought much about that—it just had to be put up with. So it was a pleasant enough get-together, aside from your having to watch what you said just as carefully as you always did everyplace. If a dangerous thought came into your mind, you just started mumbling, even right in the middle of a sentence. When you did that, the others just ignored you until you felt happier again and stopped.

Anthony liked television night. He had done only two or three awful things on television night in the whole past year.

Mom had put a bottle of brandy on the table, and they each had a tiny glass of it. Liquor was even more precious than tobacco. The villagers could make wine, but the grapes weren't right, and certainly the techniques weren't, and it wasn't very good wine. There were only a few bottles of real liquor left in the village—four rye, three Scotch, three brandy, nine real wine, and half a bottle of Drambuie belonging to old McIntyre (only for marriages)—and when those were gone, that was it.

Afterward, everybody wished that the brandy hadn't been brought out. Because Dan Hollis drank more of it than he should have, and mixed it with a lot of the homemade wine. Nobody thought anything about it at first, because he didn't show it much outside, and it was his birthday party and a happy party, and Anthony liked these get-togethers and shouldn't see any reason to do anything even if he was listening.

But Dan Hollis got high, and did a fool thing. If they'd seen it coming, they'd have taken him outside and walked him around.

The first thing they knew, Dan stopped laughing right in the middle of the story about how Thelma Dunn had found the Perry Como record and dropped it and it hadn't broken because she'd moved faster than she ever had before in her life and caught it. He was fondling the record again, and looking longingly at the Fremonts' gramophone over in the corner, and suddenly he stopped laughing and his face got slack, and then it got ugly, and he said, "Oh, *damn!*"

Immediately the room was still. So still they could hear the whirring movement of the grandfather's clock out in the hall. Pat Reilly had been playing the piano, softly. He stopped, his hands poised over the yellowed keys.

The candles on the dining room table flickered in a cool breeze that blew through the lace curtains over the bay window.

"Keep playing, Pat," Anthony's father said softly.

Pat started again. He played *Night and Day*, but his eyes were sidewise on Dan Hollis, and he missed notes.

Dan stood in the middle of the room, holding the record. In his other hand he held a glass of brandy so hard his hand shook.

They were all looking at him.

"*Damn*," he said again, and he made it sound like a dirty word.

Reverend Younger, who had been talking with Mom and

Aunt Amy by the dining room door began to pray. His hands were clasped, and his eyes were closed.

John Sipich moved forward. "Now, Dan . . . it's *good* for you to talk that way. But you don't want to talk too much, you know."

Dan shook off the hand Sipich put on his arm.

"Can't even play my record," he said loudly. He looked down at the record, and then around at their faces. "Oh, *damn* it . . ."

He threw the glassful of brandy against the wall. It splattered and ran down the wallpaper in streaks.

Some of the women gasped.

"Dan," Sipich said in a whisper. "Dan, cut it out—"

Pat Reilly was playing *Night and Day* louder, to cover up the sounds of the talk. It wouldn't do any good, though, if Anthony was listening.

Dan Hollis went over to the piano and stood by Pat's shoulder, swaying a little.

"Pat," he said. "Don't play *that*. Play *this*." And he began to sing. Softly, hoarsely, miserably: "Happy birthday to me . . . Happy birthday to me . . ."

"Dan!" Ethel Hollis screamed. She tried to run across the room to him. Mary Sipich grabbed her arm and held her back. "Dan," Ethel screamed again. "Stop—"

"Be quiet!" hissed Mary Sipich, and pushed her toward one of the men, who put his hand over her mouth and held her still.

"—Happy Birthday, dear Danny," Dan sang. "Happy birthday to me!" He stopped and looked down at Pat Reilly. "Play it, Pat. Play it, so I can sing right . . . you know I can't carry a tune unless somebody plays it!"

Pat Reilly put his hands on the keys and began *Lover*—in a low waltz tempo, the way Anthony liked it. Pat's face was white. His hands fumbled.

Dan Hollis stared over at the dining room door. At Anthony's mother, and at Anthony's father who had gone to join her.

"You had him," he said. Tears gleamed on his cheeks as the candlelight caught them. "*You* had to go and *have* him . . ."

He closed his eyes, and the tears squeezed out. He sang loudly, "You are my sunshine . . . my only sunshine . . . you make me happy . . . when I am blue . . ."

Anthony came into the room.

Pat stopped playing. He froze. Everybody froze. The breeze rippled the curtains. Ethel Hollis couldn't even try to scream —she had fainted.

"Please don't take my sunshine . . . away . . ." Dan's voice faltered into silence. His eyes widened. He put both hands out in front of him, the empty glass in one, the record in the other. He hiccupped, and said, "*No*—"

"Bad man," Anthony said, and thought Dan Hollis into something like nothing anyone would have believed possible, and then he thought the thing into a grave deep, deep in the cornfield.

The glass and record thumped on the rug. Neither broke.

Anthony's purple gaze went around the room.

Some of the people began mumbling. They all tried to smile. The sound of mumbling filled the room like a far-off approval. Out of the murmuring came one or two clear voices:

"Oh, it's a very *good* thing," said John Sipich.

"A good thing," said Anthony's father, smiling. He'd had more practice in smiling than most of them. "A wonderful thing."

"It's swell . . . just swell," said Pat Reilly, tears leaking from eyes and nose, and he began to play the piano again, softly, his trembling hands feeling for *Night and Day*.

Anthony climbed up on top of the piano, and Pat played for two hours.

Afterward, they watched television. They all went into the front room, and lit just a few candles, and pulled up chairs around the set. It was a small-screen set, and they couldn't all sit close enough to it to see, but that didn't matter. They didn't even turn the set on. It wouldn't have worked anyway, there being no electricity in Peaksville.

They just sat silently, and watched the twisting, writhing shapes on the screen, and listened to the sounds that came out of the speaker, and none of them had any idea of what it was all about. They never did. It was always the same.

"It's real nice," Aunt Amy said once, her pale eyes on the meaningless flickers and shadows. "But I like it a little better when there were cities outside and we could get real—"

"Why, Amy!" said Mom. "It's good for you to say such a thing. Very good. But how can you mean it? Why, this television is *much* better than anything we ever used to get!"

"Yes," chimed in John Sipich. "It's fine. It's the best show we've ever seen!"

He sat on the couch, with two other men, holding Ethel Hollis flat against the cushions, holding her arms and legs and putting their hands over her mouth, so she couldn't start screaming again.

"It's really *good!*" he said again.

Mom looked out of the front window, across the darkened road, across Henderson's darkened wheatfield to the vast, endless, gray nothingness in which the little village of Peaksville floated like a soul—the huge nothingness that was most evident at night, when Anthony's brassy day had gone.

It did no good to wonder where they were . . . no good at all. Peaksville was just someplace. Someplace away from the world. It was wherever it had been since that day three years ago when Anthony had crept from her womb and old Doc Bates—God rest him—had screamed and dropped him and tried to kill him, and Anthony had whined and done the thing. Had taken the village someplace. Or had destroyed the world and left only the village, nobody knew which.

It did no good to wonder about it. Nothing at all did any good—except to live as they must live. Must always, always live, if Anthony would let them.

These thoughts were dangerous, she thought.

She began to mumble. The others started mumbling too. They had all been thinking, evidently.

The men on the couch whispered and whispered to Ethel Hollis and when they took their hands away, she mumbled too.

While Anthony sat on top of the set and made television, they sat around and mumbled and watched the meaningless, flickering shapes far into the night.

Next day it snowed, and killed off half the crops—but it was a *good* day.

17

The Place of the Gods

STEPHEN VINCENT BENÉT

I hate to make damaging admissions where people can hear me, but the truth is that I am hopelessly square in my appreciation of poetry. My taste seems to have stopped short in nineteenth-century romanticism and I can read and reread with finger-licking pleasure such mawkish items as Noyes' "The Barrel-Organ" and Tennyson's "Ballad of the Revenge" and weep over them, too. This goes along with my liking for the minor mode in music and for strokes of tragic irony in drama.

There's something ineffably romantic, in short, in having one's emotions wrung; or, at least, I find it so. And what can be more wringing than the death, not only of an individual, but of a whole civilization? A verse that always, without fail, sends chills up and down my vertebrae is from Kipling's "Recessional":

Far-called, our navies melt away—
On dune and headland sinks the fire—
Lo, all our pomp of yesterday
Is one with Nineveh and Tyre!

Two hundred years after the fall and utter destruction of Nineveh, a passing Greek army had to ask what the mound of ruins was, so thoroughly had the city been forgotten.

Surely that couldn't happen today to us. Our libraries, our archives, our records, our endless spate of words cannot disappear.

But then our destructive ability has risen to match our passion for record-making. It is no longer chemical fire and flashing sword we need fear, but nuclear fire and flashing artillery.

Let Stephen Vincent Benét, then, introduce you to a time after the Bombs have fallen, and to adventure with a young man who has old, old discoveries to make.

The north and the west and the south are good hunting ground, but it is forbidden to go east. It is forbidden to go to any of the Dead Places except to search for metal, and then he who touches the metal must be a priest or the son of a priest. Afterward, both the man and the metal must be purified. These are the rules and the laws; they are well made. It is forbidden to cross the great river and look upon the place that was the Place of the Gods; this is most strictly forbidden. We do not even say its name, though we know its name. It is there that spirits live, and demons; it is there that there are the ashes of the Great Burning. These things are forbidden; they have been forbidden since the beginning of time.

My father is a priest; I am the son of a priest. I have been in the Dead Places near us with my father. At first I was afraid. When my father went into the house to search for the metal, I stood by the door, and my heart felt small and weak. It was a dead man's house, a spirit house. It did not have the smell of man, though there were old bones in a corner. But it is not fitting that a priest's son should show fear. I looked at the bones in the shadow and kept my voice still.

Then my father came out with the metal—a good, strong piece. He looked at me with both eyes, but I had not run away. He gave me the metal to hold. I took it and did not die. So he knew that I was truly his son and would be a priest in my time. That was when I was very young. Nevertheless, my brothers would not have done it, though they are good hunters. After that, they gave me the good piece of meat and the warm corner by the fire. My father watched over me; he was glad that I should be a priest. But when I boasted or wept without reason, he punished me more strictly than my brothers. That was right.

After a time, I myself was allowed to go into the dead houses and search for metal. So I learned the ways of those houses, and if I saw bones, I was no longer afraid. The bones are light and old; sometimes they will fall into dust if you touch them. But that is a great sin.

I was taught the chants and the spells. I was taught how to stop the running of blood from a wound, and many secrets. A priest must know many secrets—that was what my father said. If the hunters think we know all things by chants and spells, they may believe so; it does not hurt them. I was taught how to read in the old books and how to make the old writings; that was hard and took a long time. My knowledge made me happy; it was like a fire in my heart. Most of all, I liked to hear of the Old Days and the stories of the gods. I asked myself many questions that I could not answer, but it was good to ask them. At night, I would lie awake and listen to the wind; it seemed to me that it was the voice of the gods as they flew through the air.

We are not ignorant like the Forest People; our women spin wool on the wheel, our priests wear a white robe. We do not eat grubs from the tree, we have not forgotten the old writings, although they are hard to understand. Nevertheless, my knowledge and my lack of knowledge burned in me; I wished to know more. When I was a man at last, I came to my father and said, "It is time for me to go on my journey. Give me leave."

He looked at me for a long time, stroking his beard, then he said at last, "Yes. It is time."

That night, in the house of priesthood, I asked for and received purification. My body hurt, but my spirit was a cool stone. It was my father himself who questioned me about my dreams.

He bade me look into the smoke of the fire and see. I saw and told what I saw. It was what I have always seen—a river and, beyond it, a great Dead Place, and in it the gods walking. I have always thought about that. His eyes were stern when I told him; he was no longer my father but a priest. He said, "This is a strong dream."

"It is mine," I said, while the smoke waved and my head felt light. They were singing the Star song in the outer chamber, and it was like the buzzing of bees in my head.

He asked me how the gods were dressed, and I told him how they were dressed. We know how they were dressed from the book, but I saw them as if they were before me. When I had finished, he threw the sticks three times and studied them as they fell.

"This is a very strong dream," he said. "It may eat you up."

"I am not afraid," I said, and looked at him with both eyes. My voice sounded thin in my ears, but that was because of the smoke.

He touched me on the breast and the forehead. He gave me the bow and the three arrows.

"Take them," he said. "It is forbidden to travel east. It is forbidden to cross the great river. It is forbidden to go to the Place of the Gods. All these things are forbidden."

"All these things are forbidden," I said, but it was my voice that spoke, and not my spirit. He looked at me again.

"My son," he said, "once I had young dreams. If your dream does not eat you up, you may be a great priest. If it eats you, you are still my son. Now go on your journey."

I went fasting, as is the law. My body hurt, but not my

heart. When the dawn came, I was out of sight of the village. I prayed and purified myself, waiting for a sign. The sign was an eagle. It flew east.

Sometimes signs are sent by bad spirits. I waited again on the flat rock, fasting, taking no food. I was very still; I could feel the sky above me and the earth beneath. I waited till the sun was beginning to sink. Then three deer passed in the valley, going east; they did not wind me or see me. There was a white fawn with them—a very great sign.

I followed them at a distance, waiting for what would happen. My heart was troubled about going east, yet I knew that I must go. My head hummed with my fasting; I did not even see the panther spring upon the white fawn. But before I knew it, the bow was in my hand. I shouted and the panther lifted his head from the fawn. It is not easy to kill a panther with one arrow, but the arrow went through his eye and into his brain. He died as he tried to spring; he rolled over, tearing at the ground. Then I knew I was meant to go east; I knew that was my journey. When the night came, I made my fire and roasted meat.

It is eight suns' journey to the east and a man passes by many Dead Places. The Forest People are afraid of them, but I am not. Once I made my fire on the edge of a Dead Place at night and, next morning, in the dead house, I found a good knife, little rusted. That was small to what came afterward, but it made my heart feel big. Always when I looked for game, it was in front of my arrow, and twice I passed hunting parties of the Forest People without their knowing. So I knew my magic was strong and my journey clean, in spite of the law.

Toward the setting of the eighth sun, I came to the banks of the great river. It was half a day's journey after I had left the god road; we do not use the god roads now, for they are falling apart into great blocks of stone, and the forest is safer going. A long way off, I had seen the water through trees, but the trees were thick. At last I came out upon an open place at the top of a cliff. There was the great river below, like a giant in the sun. It is very long, very wide. It could eat all the streams we know and still be thirsty. Its name is Ou-dis-sun, the Sacred, the Long. No man of my tribe has seen it; not even my father, the priest. It was magic and I prayed.

Then I raised my eyes and looked south. It was there—the Place of the Gods.

How can I tell what it was like? You do not know. It was there, in the red light, and they were too big to be houses. It was there, with the red light upon it, mighty and ruined. I knew that in another moment the gods would see me. I covered my eyes with my hands and crept back into the forest.

Surely, that was enough to do, and live. Surely, it was enough to spend the night upon the cliff. The Forest People themselves do not come near. Yet, all through the night, I knew that I should have to cross the river and walk in the Place of the Gods, although the gods ate me up. My magic did not help me at all, and yet there was a fire in my bowels, a fire in my mind. When the sun rose, I thought, "My journey has been clean. Now I will go home from my journey." But even as I thought so, I knew I could not. If I went to the Place of the Gods, I would surely die, but if I did not go, I could never be at peace with my spirit again. It is better to lose one's life than one's spirit, if one is a priest and the son of a priest.

Nevertheless, as I made the raft, the tears ran out of my eyes. The Forest People could have killed me without fight, if they had come upon me then, but they did not come. When the raft was made, I said the sayings for the dead and painted myself for death. My heart was cold as a frog and my knees like water, but the burning in my mind would not let me have peace. As I pushed the raft from the shore, I began my death song; I had the right. It was a fine song. I sang:

"I am John, son of John. My people are the Hill People. They are the men.
I go into the Dead Places, but I am not slain.
I take the metal from the Dead Places, but I am not blasted.
I travel upon the god roads and am not afraid. E-yah! I have killed the panther, I have killed the fawn!
E-yah! I have come to the great river. No man has come there before.
It is forbidden to go east, but I have gone; forbidden to go on the great river, but I am there.
Open your hearts you spirits, and hear my song.

Now I go to the Place of the Gods; I shall not return.
My body is painted for death and my limbs weak, but my
heart is big as I go to the Place of the Gods!"

All the same, when I came to the Place of the Gods, I was afraid, afraid. The current of the great river is very strong; it gripped my raft with its hands. That was magic, for the river itself is wide and calm. I could feel evil spirits about me in the bright morning; I could feel their breath on my neck as I was swept down the stream. Never have I been so much alone. I tried to think of my knowledge, but it was a squirrel's heap of winter nuts. There was no strength in my knowledge any more and I felt small and naked as a new-hatched bird—alone upon the great river, the servant of the gods.

Yet, after a while, my eyes were opened and I saw. I saw both banks of the river; I saw that once there had been god roads across it, though now they were broken and fallen like broken vines. Very great they were, and wonderful and broken—broken in the time of the Great Burning, when the fire fell out of the sky. And always the current took me nearer to the Place of the Gods, and the huge ruins rose higher before my eyes.

I do not know the customs of rivers; we are the People of the Hills. I tried to guide my raft with the pole, but it spun about. I thought the river meant to take me past the Place of the Gods and out into the Bitter Water of the legends.

I grew angry then; my heart felt strong. I said aloud, "I am a priest and the son of a priest!" The gods heard me; they showed me how to paddle with the pole on one side of the raft. The current changed itself; I drew near to the Place of the Gods.

When I was very near, my raft struck and turned over. I can swim in our lakes; I swam to the shore. There was a great spike of rusted metal sticking out into the river; I hauled myself up upon it and sat there, panting. I had saved my bow and two arrows and the knife I found in the Dead Place, but that was all. My raft went whirling downstream toward the Bitter Water. I looked after it, and thought if it had trod me under, at least I would be safely dead. Nevertheless, when I had dried my bow-string and restrung it, I walked forward to the Place of the Gods.

It felt like ground underfoot; it did not burn me. It is not true—what some of the tales say—that the ground there burns forever, for I have been there. Here and there were the marks and stains of the Great Burning on the ruins, that is true. But they were old marks and old stains. It is not true, either—what some of our priests say—that it is an island covered with fogs and enchantments. It is not. It is a great Dead Place—greater than any Dead Place we know. Everywhere in it there are god roads; though most are cracked and broken. Everywhere there are the ruins of the high towers of the gods.

How shall I tell what I saw? I went carefully, my strung bow in my hand, my skin ready for danger. There should have been the wailings of spirits and the shrieks of demons, but there were not. It was very silent and sunny where I had landed; the wind and the rain and the birds that drop seeds had done their work; the grass grew in the cracks of the broken stone. It is a fair island; no wonder the gods built there. If I had come there a god, I also would have built.

How shall I tell what I saw? The towers are not all broken; here and there one still stands, like a great tree in a forest, and the birds nest high. But the towers themselves look blind, for the gods are gone. I saw a fish hawk, catching fish in the river. I saw a little dance of white butterflies over a great heap of broken stones and columns. I went there and looked about me; there was a carved stone with cut letters, broken in half. I can read letters, but I could not understand these. They said UBTREAS. There was also the shattered image of a man or a god. It had been made of white stone and he wore his hair tied back like a woman's. His name was ASHING, as I read on the cracked half of a stone. I thought it wise to pray to ASHING, though I do not know that god.

How shall I tell what I saw? There was no smell of man left on stone or metal. Nor were there many trees in that wilderness of stone. There are many pigeons, nesting and dropping in the towers; the gods must have loved them, or, perhaps, they used them for sacrifice. There are wild cats that roam the god roads, green-eyed, unfraid of man. At night they wail like demons, but they are not demons. The wild dogs are more dangerous, for they hunt in a pack, but them I did not meet till later. Everywhere there are the carved stones, carved with magical numbers and words.

I went north; I did not try to hide myself. When a god or a demon saw me, then I would die, but meanwhile I was no longer afraid. My hunger for knowledge burned in me; there was so much that I could not understand. After a while, I knew that my belly was hungry. I could have hunted for my meat, but I did not hunt. It is known that the gods did not hunt as we do; they got their food from enchanted boxes and jars. Sometimes these are still found in the Dead Places. Once, when I was a child and foolish, I opened such a jar and tasted it and found the food sweet. But my father found out and punished me for it strictly; for, often, that food is death. Now, though, I had long gone past what was forbidden, and I entered the likeliest towers, looking for the food of the gods.

I found it at last in the ruins of a great temple in the midcity. A mighty temple it must have been, for the roof was painted like the sky at night with its stars—that much I could see, though the colors were faint and dim. It went down into great caves and tunnels—perhaps they kept their slaves there. But when I started to climb down, I heard the squeaking of rats, so I did not go. Rats are unclean, and there must have been many tribes of them, from the squeaking. But near there I found food, in the heart of a ruin, behind a door that still opened. I ate only the fruits from the jars; they had a very sweet taste. There was drink, too, in bottles of glass; the drink of the gods is strong and made my head swim. After I had eaten and drunk, I slept on the top of a stone, my bow at my side.

When I woke, the sun was low. Looking down from where I lay, I saw a dog sitting on his haunches. His tongue hung out of his mouth; he looked as if he were laughing. He was a big dog with a gray-brown coat, as big as a wolf. I sprang up and shouted at him, but he did not move; he just sat there as if he were laughing. I did not like that. When I reached for a stone to throw, he moved swiftly out of the way of the stone. He was not afraid of me; he looked at me as if I were meat. No doubt I could have killed him with an arrow, but I did not know if there were others. Moreover, night was falling.

I looked about me. Not far away there was a great, broken

god road, leading north. The towers were high enough, but not so high, and while many of the dead houses were wrecked, there were some that stood. I went toward this god road, keeping to the heights of the ruins, while the dog followed. When I had reached the god road, I saw that there were others behind him. If I had slept later, they would have come upon me asleep and torn out my throat. As it was, they were sure enough of me; they did not hurry. When I went into the dead house, they kept watch at the entrance; doubtless they thought they would have a fine hunt. But a dog cannot open a door, and I knew, from the books, that the gods did not like to live on the ground but on high.

I had just found a door I could open when the dogs decided to rush. Ha! They were surprised when I shut the door in their faces; it was a good door, of strong metal. I could hear their foolish baying beyond it, but I did not stop to answer them. I was in darkness; I found stairs and climbed. There were many stairs, turning around till my head was dizzy. At the top was another door; I found the knob and opened it. I was in a long small chamber. On one side of it was a bronze door that could not be opened, for it had no handle. Perhaps there was a magic word to open it, but I did not have the word. I turned to the door in the opposite side of the wall. The lock of it was broken and I opened it and went in.

Within, there was a place of great riches. The god who lived there must have been a powerful god. The first room was a small anteroom. I waited there for some time, telling the spirits of the place that I came in peace and not as a robber. When it seemed to me that they had had time to hear me, I went on. Ah, what riches! Few, even, of the windows had been broken; it was all as it had been. The great windows that looked over the city had not been broken at all, though they were dusty and streaked with many years. There were coverings on the floors, the colors not greatly faded, and the chairs were soft and deep. There were pictures upon the walls, very strange, very wonderful. I remember one of a bunch of flowers in a jar; if you came close to it, you could see nothing but bits of color, but if you stood away from it, the flowers might have been picked yesterday. It made my heart feel strange to look at this picture, and to look at the figure of a bird, in some hard clay, on a table and see it so like our birds. Everywhere there were books and writings, many in tongues that I could not read. The god who lived there must have been a wise god, and full of knowledge. I felt I had a right there, as I sought knowledge also.

Nevertheless, it was strange. There was a washing place, but no water; perhaps the gods washed in air. There was a cooking place, but no wood, and though there was a machine to cook food, there was no place to put fire in it. Nor were there candles or lamps. There were things that looked like lamps, but they had neither oil nor wick. All these things were magic, but I touched them and lived; the magic had gone out of them. Let me tell one thing to show. In the washing place, a thing said "Hot," but it was not hot to the touch; another thing said "Cold," but it was not cold. This must have been a strong magic, but the magic was gone. I do not understand—they had ways—I wish that I knew.

It was close and dry and dusty in the house of the god. I have said the magic was gone, but that is not true; it had gone from the magic things, but it had not gone from the place. I felt the spirits about me, weighing upon me. Nor had I ever slept in a Dead Place before, and yet, tonight, I must sleep there. When I thought of it, my tongue felt dry in my throat, in spite of my wish for knowledge. Almost I would have gone down again and faced the dogs, but I did not.

I had not gone through all the rooms when the darkness fell. When it fell, I went back to the big room looking over the city and made fire. There was a place to make fire and a box with wood in it, though I do not think they cooked there. I wrapped myself in a floor covering and slept in front of the fire.

Now I tell what is very strong magic. I woke in the midst of the night. When I woke, the fire had gone out and I was cold. It seemed to me that all around me there were whisperings and voices. I closed my eyes to shut them out. Some will say that I slept again, but I do not think that I slept. I could feel the spirits drawing my spirit out of my body as a fish is drawn on a line.

Why should I lie about it? I am a priest and the son of a priest. If there are spirits, as they say, in the small Dead Places near us, what spirits must there not be in that great Place of the Gods? And would not they wish to speak after such long years? I know that I felt myself drawn as a fish is drawn on a line. I had stepped out of my body; I could see my body asleep in front of the cold fire, but it was not I. I was drawn to look out upon the city of the gods.

It should have been dark, for it was night, but it was not dark. Everywhere there were lights—lines of light, circles and blurs of light—ten thousand torches would not have been the same. The sky itself was alight; you could barely see the stars for the glow in the sky. I thought to myself, "This is strong magic," and trembled. There was a roaring in my ears like the rushing of rivers. Then my eyes grew used to the light and my ears to the sound. I knew that I was seeing the city as it had been when the gods were alive.

That was a sight indeed! Yes, that was a sight! I could not have seen it in the body—my body would have died. Everywhere went the gods, on foot and in chariots; there were gods beyond number and counting, and their chariots blocked the streets. They had turned night to day for their pleasure; they did not sleep with the sun. The noise of their coming and going was the noise of many waters. It was magic what they could do; it was magic what they did.

I looked out of another window; the great vines of their bridges were mended and the god roads went east and west. Restless, restless were the gods, and always in motion! They burrowed tunnels under rivers; they flew in the air. With unbelievable tools they did giant works; no part of the earth was safe from them, for, if they wished for a thing, they summoned it from the other side of the world. And always, as they labored and rested, as they feasted and made love, there was a drum in their ears—the pulse of the giant city, beating and beating like a man's heart.

Were they happy? What is happiness to the gods? They were great, they were mighty, they were wonderful and terrible. As I looked upon them and their magic, I felt like a child; but a little more, it seemed to me, and they would lay their hands upon the stars. I saw them with wisdom beyond wisdom and knowledge beyond knowledge. And yet not all they did was well done, and yet their wisdom could not but grow until all was peace.

Then I saw their fate come upon them, and that was terrible past speech. It came upon them as they walked the streets of their city. I have been in the fights with the Forest People; I have seen men die. But this was not like that. When gods war with gods, they use weapons we do not know. It was fire falling out of the sky and a mist that poisoned. It was the time of the Great Burning and the Destruction. They ran about like ants in the streets—poor gods, poor gods! Then the towers began to fall. A few escaped—yes, a few. The legends tell it. But even after the city had become a Dead Place, for many years the poison was still in the ground. I saw it happen; I saw the last of them die. It was darkness over the broken city and I wept.

All this, I saw. I saw it as I have told it; though not in the body. When I woke in the morning, I was hungry, but I did not think first of my hunger, for my heart was perplexed and confused. I knew the reason for the Dead Places, but I did not see why it had happened. It seemed to me it should not have happened, with all the magic they had. I went through the house looking for an answer. There was so much in the house I could not understand, and yet I am a priest and the son of a priest. It was like being on the side of the great river at night, with no light to show the way.

Then I saw the dead god. He was sitting in his chair by the window, in a room I had not entered before, and, for the first moment, I thought that he was alive. Then I saw the skin on the back of his hand—it was like dry leather. The room was shut, hot and dry; no doubt that had kept him as he was. At first I was afraid to approach him; then the fear left me. He was sitting, looking out over his city; he was dressed in the clothes of the gods. His age was neither young nor old; I could not tell his age. But there was wisdom in his face, and great sadness. You could see that he would not run away. He had sat at his window, watching his city die; then he himself had died. But it is better to lose one's life than one's spirit; and you could see from the face that his spirit had not been lost. I knew that, if I touched him, he would fall into dust; and yet, there was something unconquered in the face.

That is all of my story, for then I knew he was a man. I knew then that they had been men, neither gods nor demons. It is a great knowledge, hard to tell and believe. They were men; they went a dark road, but they were men. I had no fear after that. I had no fear going home, though twice I fought off the dogs and once I was hunted for two days by the Forest People. When I saw my father again, I prayed and was purified.

He touched my lips and my breast; he said, "You went away a boy. You come back a man and a priest."

I said, "Father, they were men! I have been in the Place of the Gods and seen it! Now slay me if it is the law, but still I know they were men."

He looked at me out of both eyes. He said, "The law is not always the same shape. You have done what you have done. I could not have done it in my time, but you come after me. Tell!"

I told and he listened. After that, I wished to tell all the people, but he showed me otherwise. He said, "Truth is a hard deer to hunt. If you eat too much truth at once, you may die of the truth. It was not idly that our fathers forbade the Dead Places." He was right; it is better the truth should come little by little. I have learned that, being a priest. Perhaps, in the old days they ate knowledge too fast.

Nevertheless, we make a beginning. It is not for the metal alone we go to the Dead Places now; there are the books and the writings. They are hard to learn. And the magic tools are broken, but we can look at them and wonder. At least, we make a beginning. And, when I am chief priest we shall go beyond the great river. We shall go to the Place of the Gods—the place Newyork—not one man but a company. We shall walk in the broken streets and say its name aloud, without fear. We shall look for the images of gods and find the god ASHING and the others—the gods LINCOLN and BILTMORE and MOSES. But they were men who built the city; they were not gods or demons. They were men. I remember the dead man's face. They were men who were here before us. We must build again.

18

The Ugly Little Boy

ISAAC ASIMOV

Sometimes, when I am feeling a little uncertain, I wonder if it isn't immodest for an editor of an anthology to include one of his own stories—and it is, it is!

But I guess I had better adjust myself to my own immodesty, for I am not only including this story, but I am saying right now that I like it better than any other story in the collection.

After all, isn't it more important for me to be honest than modest?

As a matter of fact, a writer is necessarily immodest or he couldn't possibly be a writer. What on earth can convince a person that anyone would not only be willing to read the words he has committed to paper, but would actually pay money for the privilege? Only an enormous, an overwhelming immodesty.

I had spent half a dozen years of youth writing, without ever daring to let anyone see the product of my Muse but myself. There's modesty for you; it leads to nothing.

Then at eighteen, something snapped within me and immodesty burgeoned into immediate full bloom. I gathered together the story I had just written and brought it to an editor, expecting—well, not really expecting but hoping—that he would pay me a bright, shiny, copper penny for every single glorious word I had written, even including little ones like "the" and "of" and "a."

He didn't. He sent the story back to me the very next day, but with such a kind letter that I was thereafter permanently frozen into immodesty. From the day of that rejection forward, I have made a career of offering to sell my words—only it's been a long time since I charge a mere penny for one of them.

Anyway, let me introduce you to an ugly little boy . . .

Edith Fellowes smoothed her working smock as she always did before opening the elaborately locked door and stepping across the invisible dividing line between the *is* and the *is not*. She carried her notebook and her pen although she no longer took notes except when she felt the absolute need for some report.

This time she also carried a suitcase. ("Games for the boy," she had said, smiling, to the guard—who had long since stopped even thinking of questioning her and who waved her on.)

And, as always, the ugly little boy knew that she had entered and came running to her, crying, "Miss Fellowes—Miss Fellowes—" in his soft, slurring way.

"Timmie," she said, and passed her hand over the shaggy, brown hair on his misshapen little head. "What's wrong?"

He said, "Will Jerry be back to play again? I'm sorry about what happened."

"Never mind that now, Timmie. Is that why you've been crying?"

He looked away. "Not just about that, Miss Fellowes. I dreamed again."

"The same dream?" Miss Fellowes' lips set. Of course, the Jerry affair would bring back the dream.

He nodded. His too large teeth showed as he tried to smile and the lips of his forward-thrusting mouth stretched wide. "When will I be big enough to go out there, Miss Fellowes?"

"Soon," she said softly, feeling her heart break. "Soon."

Miss Fellowes let him take her hand and enjoyed the warm touch of the thick dry skin of his palm. He led her through the three rooms that made up the whole of Stasis Section One—comfortable enough, yes, but an eternal prison for the ugly little boy all the seven (was it seven?) years of his life.

He led her to the one window, looking out onto a scrubby woodland section of the world of *is* (now hidden by night), where a fence and painted instructions allowed no men to wander without permission.

He pressed his nose against the window. "Out there, Miss Fellowes?"

"Better places. Nicer places," she said sadly as she looked at his poor little imprisoned face outlined in profile against the window. The forehead retreated flatly and his hair lay down in tufts upon it. The back of his skull bulged and seemed to make the head overheavy so that it sagged and bent forward, forcing the whole body into a stoop. Already, bony ridges were beginning to bulge the skin above his eyes. His wide mouth thrust forward more prominently than did his wide and flattened nose and he had no chin to speak of, only a jawbone that curved smoothly down and back. He was small for his years and his stumpy legs were bowed.

He was a very ugly little boy and Edith Fellowes loved him dearly.

Her own face was behind his line of vision, so she allowed her lips the luxury of a tremor.

They would *not* kill him. She would do anything to prevent

it. Anything. She opened the suitcase and began taking out the clothes it contained.

Edith Fellowes had crossed the threshold of Stasis, Inc., for the first time just a little over three years before. She hadn't, at that time, the slightest idea as to what Stasis meant or what the place did. No one did then, except those who worked there. In fact, it was only the day after she arrived that the news broke upon the world.

At the time, it was just that they had advertised for a woman with knowledge of physiology, experience with clinical chemistry, and a love for children. Edith Fellowes had been a nurse in a maternity ward and believed she fulfilled those qualifications.

Gerald Hoskins, whose name plate on the desk included a Ph.D. after the name, scratched his cheek with his thumb and looked at her steadily.

Miss Fellowes automatically stiffened and felt her face (with its slightly asymmetric nose and its a-trifle-too-heavy eyebrows) twitch.

He's no dreamboat himself, she thought resentfully. He's getting fat and bald and he's got a sullen mouth. –But the salary mentioned had been considerably higher than she expected, so she waited.

Hoskins said, "Now do you really love children?"

"I wouldn't say I did if I didn't."

"Or do you just love pretty children? Nice chubby children with cute little button-noses and gurgly ways?"

Miss Fellowes said, "Children are children, Dr. Hoskins, and the ones that aren't pretty are just the ones who may happen to need help most."

"Then suppose we take you on–"

"You mean you're offering me the job now?"

He smiled briefly, and for a moment, his broad face had an absentminded charm about it. He said, "I make quick decisions. So far the offer is tentative, however. I may make as quick a decision to let you go. Are you ready to take the chance?"

Miss Fellowes clutched at her purse and calculated just as swiftly as she could, then ignored calculations and followed impulse. "All right."

"Fine. We're going to form the Stasis tonight and I think you had better be there to take over at once. That will be at eight p.m. and I'd appreciate it if you could be here at seven-thirty."

"But what—"

"Fine. Fine. That will be all now." On signal, a smiling secretary came in to usher her out.

Miss Fellowes stared back at Dr. Hoskins' closed door for a moment. What was Stasis? What had this large barn of a building—with its badged employees, its makeshift corridors, and its unmistakable air of engineering—to do with children?

She wondered if she should go back that evening or stay away and teach that arrogant man a lesson. But she knew she would be back if only out of sheer frustration. She would have to find out about the children.

She came back at seven-thirty and did not have to announce herself. One after another, men and women seemed to know her and to know her function. She found herself all but placed on skids as she was moved inward.

Dr. Hoskins was there, but he only looked at her distantly and murmured, "Miss Fellowes."

He did not even suggest that she take a seat, but she drew one calmly up to the railing and sat down.

They were on a balcony, looking down into a large pit, filled with instruments that looked like a cross between the control panel of a spaceship and the working face of a computer. On one side were partitions that seemed to make up an unceilinged apartment, a giant dollhouse into the rooms of which she could look from above.

She could see an electronic cooker and a freeze-space unit in one room and a washroom arrangement off another. And surely the object she made out in another room could only be part of a bed, a small bed.

Hoskins was speaking to another man and, with Miss Fellowes, they made up the total occupancy of the balcony. Hoskins did not offer to introduce the other man, and Miss Fellowes eyed him surreptitiously. He was thin and quite fine-looking in a middle-aged way. He had a small mustache and keen eyes that seemed to busy themselves with everything.

He was saying, "I won't pretend for one moment that I understand all this, Dr. Hoskins; I mean, except as a layman, a reasonably intelligent layman, may be expected to understand it. Still, if there's one part I understand less than another, it's this matter of selectivity. You can only reach out so far; that seems sensible; things get dimmer the further you go; it takes more energy. —But then, you can only reach out so near. That's the puzzling part."

"I can make it seem less paradoxical, Deveney, if you will allow me to use an analogy."

(Miss Fellowes placed the new man the moment she heard his name, and despite herself was impressed. This was obviously Candide Deveney, the science writer of the Telenews, who was notoriously at the scene of every major scientific break-through. She even recognized his face as one she saw on the news-plate when the landing on Mars had been announced. —So Dr. Hoskins must have something important here.)

"By all means use an analogy," said Deveney ruefully, "if you think it will help."

"Well, then, you can't read a book with ordinary-sized print if it is held six feet from your eyes, but you can read it if you hold it one foot from your eyes. So far, the closer the better. If you bring the book to within one inch of your eyes, however, you've lost it again. There is such a thing as being too close, you see."

"Hmm," said Deveney.

"Or take another example. Your right shoulder is about thirty inches from the tip of your right forefinger and you can place your right forefinger on your right shoulder. Your right elbow is only half the distance from the tip of your right forefinger; it should by all ordinary logic be easier to reach, and yet you cannot place your right finger on your right elbow. Again, there is such a thing as being too close."

Deveney said, "May I use these analogies in my story?"

"Well, of course. Only too glad. I've been waiting long enough for someone like you to have a story. I'll give you anything else you want. It is time, finally, that we want the world looking over our shoulder. They'll see something."

(Miss Fellowes found herself admiring his calm certainty despite herself. There was strength there.)

Deveney said, "How far out will you reach?"

"Forty thousand years."

Miss Fellowes drew in her breath sharply.

Years?

There was tension in the air. The men at the controls scarcely moved. One man at a microphone spoke into it in a soft monotone, in short phrases that made no sense to Miss Fellowes.

Deveney, leaning over the balcony railing with an intent stare, said, "Will we see anything, Dr. Hoskins?"

"What? No. Nothing till the job is done. We detect indirectly, something on the principle of radar, except that we use mesons rather than radiation. Mesons reach backward under the proper conditions. Some are reflected and we must analyze the reflections."

"That sounds difficult."

Hoskins smiled again, briefly as always. "It is the end product of fifty years of research; forty years of it before I entered the field. —Yes, it's difficult."

The man at the microphone raised one hand.

Hoskins said, "We've had the fix on one particular moment in time for weeks; breaking it, remaking it after calculating our own movements in time; making certain that we could handle time-flow with sufficient precision. This must work now."

But his forehead glistened.

Edith Fellowes found herself out of her seat and at the balcony railing, but there was nothing to see.

The man at the microphone said quietly, "Now."

There was a space of silence sufficient for one breath and then the sound of a terrified little boy's scream from the dollhouse rooms. Terror! Piercing terror!

Miss Fellowes' head twisted in the direction of the cry. A child was involved. She had forgotten.

And Hoskins' fist pounded on the railing and he said in a tight voice, trembling with triumph, "*Did* it."

Miss Fellowes was urged down the short, spiral flight of steps by the hard press of Hoskins' palm between her shoulder blades. He did not speak to her.

The men who had been at the controls were standing about now, smiling, smoking, watching the three as they entered on the main floor. A very soft buzz sounded from the direction of the dollhouse.

Hoskins said to Deveney, "It's perfectly safe to enter Stasis. I've done it a thousand times. There's a queer sensation which is momentary and means nothing."

He stepped through an open door in mute demonstration, and Deveney, smiling stiffly and drawing an obviously deep breath, followed him.

Hoskins said, "Miss Fellowes! Please!" He crooked his forefinger impatiently.

Miss Fellowes nodded and stepped stiffly through. It was as though a ripple went through her, an internal tickle.

But once inside all seemed normal. There was the smell of the fresh wood of the dollhouse and—of—of soil somehow.

There was silence now, no voice at least, but there was the dry shuffling of feet, a scrabbling as of a hand over wood—then a low moan.

"Where is it?" asked Miss Fellowes in distress. Didn't these fool men *care?*

The boy was in the bedroom; at least the room with the bed in it.

It was standing naked, with its small, dirt-smeared chest heaving raggedly. A bushel of dirt and coarse grass spread over the floor at his bare brown feet. The smell of soil came from it and a touch of something fetid.

Hoskins followed her horrified glance and said with annoyance, "You can't pluck a boy cleanly out of time, Miss Fellowes. We had to take some of the surroundings with it for safety. Or would you have preferred to have it arrive here minus a leg or with only half a head?"

"*Please!*" said Miss Fellowes, in an agony of revulsion. "Are we just to stand here? The poor child is frightened. And it's *filthy.*"

She was quite correct. It was smeared with encrusted dirt and grease and had a scratch on its thigh that looked red and sore.

As Hoskins approached him, the boy, who seemed to be something over three years in age, hunched low and backed away rapidly. He lifted his upper lip and snarled in a hissing fashion like a cat. With a rapid gesture, Hoskins seized both the child's arms and lifted him, writhing and screaming, from the floor.

Miss Fellowes said, "Hold him, now. He needs a warm bath first. He needs to be cleaned. Have you the equipment? If so, have it brought here, and I'll need to have help in handling him just at first. Then, too, for heaven's sake, have all this trash and filth removed."

She was giving the orders now and she felt perfectly good about that. And because now she was an efficient nurse, rather than a confused spectator, she looked at the child with a clinical eye—and hesitated for one shocked moment. She saw past the dirt and shrieking, past the thrashing of limbs and useless twisting. She saw the boy himself.

It was the ugliest little boy she had ever seen. It was horribly ugly from misshapen head to bandy legs.

She got the boy cleaned with three men helping her and with others milling about in their efforts to clean the room. She worked in silence and with a sense of outrage, annoyed by the continued strugglings and outcries of the boy and by the undignified drenchings of soapy water to which she was subjected.

Dr. Hoskins had hinted that the child would not be pretty, but that was far from stating that it would be repulsively deformed. And there was a stench about the boy that soap and water was only alleviating little by little.

She had the strong desire to thrust the boy, soaped as he was, into Hoskins' arms and walk out; but there was the pride of profession. She had accepted an assignment after all. —And there would be the look in his eyes. A cold look that would read: Only pretty children, Miss Fellowes?

He was standing apart from them, watching coolly from a distance with a half-smile on his face when he caught her eyes, as though amused at her outrage.

She decided she would wait a while before quitting. To do so now would only demean her.

Then, when the boy was a bearable pink and smelled of scented soap, she felt better anyway. His cries changed to whimpers of exhaustion as he watched carefully, eyes moving in quick frightened suspicion from one to another of those in the room. His cleanness accentuated his thin nakedness as he shivered with cold after the bath.

Miss Fellowes said sharply, "Bring me a nightgown for the child!"

A nightgown appeared at once. It was as though everything were ready and yet nothing were ready unless she gave orders; as though they were deliberately leaving this in her charge without help, to test her.

The newsman, Deveney, approached and said, "I'll hold him, Miss. You won't get it on yourself."

"Thank you," said Miss Fellowes. And it was a battle indeed, but the nightgown went on, and when the boy made as though to rip it off, she slapped his hand sharply.

The boy reddened, but did not cry. He stared at her and the splayed fingers of one hand moved slowly across the flannel of the nightgown, feeling the strangeness of it.

Miss Fellowes thought desperately: Well, what next?

Everyone seemed in suspended animation, waiting for her—even the ugly little boy.

Miss Fellowes said sharply, "Have you provided food? Milk?"

They had. A mobile unit was wheeled in, with its refrigeration compartment containing three quarts of milk, with a warming unit and a supply of fortifications in the form of vitamin drops, copper-cobalt-iron syrup and others she had no time to be concerned with. There was a variety of canned self-warming junior foods.

She used milk, simply milk, to begin with. The radar unit heated the milk to a set temperature in a matter of ten seconds and clicked off, and she put some in a saucer. She had a certainty about the boy's savagery. He wouldn't know how to handle a cup.

Miss Fellowes nodded and said to the boy, "Drink. Drink." She made a gesture as though to raise the milk to her mouth. The boy's eyes followed but he made no move.

Suddenly, the nurse resorted to direct measures. She seized the boy's upper arm in one hand and dipped the other in the milk. She dashed the milk across his lips, so that it dripped down cheeks and receding chin.

For a moment, the child uttered a high-pitched cry, then his tongue moved over his wetted lips. Miss Fellowes stepped back.

The boy approached the saucer, bent toward it, then looked up and behind sharply as though expecting a crouching enemy;

bent again and licked at the milk eagerly, like a cat. He made a slurping noise. He did not use his hands to lift the saucer.

Miss Fellowes allowed a bit of the revulsion she felt show on her face. She couldn't help it.

Deveney caught that, perhaps. He said, "Does the nurse know, Dr. Hoskins?"

"Know what?" demanded Miss Fellowes.

Deveney hesitated, but Hoskins (again that look of detached amusement on his face) said, "Well, tell her."

Deveney addressed Miss Fellowes. "You may not suspect it, Miss, but you happen to be the first civilized woman in history ever to be taking care of a Neanderthal youngster."

She turned on Hoskins with a kind of controlled ferocity. "You might have told me, Doctor."

"Why? What difference does it make?"

"You said a child."

"Isn't that a child? Have you ever had a puppy or a kitten, Miss Fellowes? Are those closer to the human? If that were a baby chimpanzee, would you be repelled? You're a nurse, Miss Fellowes. Your record places you in a maternity ward for three years. Have you ever refused to take care of a deformed infant?"

Miss Fellowes felt her case slipping away. She said, with much less decision, "You might have told me."

"And you would have refused the position? Well, do you refuse it now?" He gazed at her coolly, while Deveney watched from the other side of the room, and the Neanderthal child, having finished the milk and licked the plate, looked up at her with a wet face and wide, longing eyes.

The boy pointed to the milk and suddenly burst out in a short series of sounds repeated over and over; sounds made up of gutturals and elaborate tongue-clickings.

Miss Fellowes said, in surprise, "Why, he talks."

"Of course," said Hoskins. "Homo neanderthalensis is not a truly separate species, but rather a subspecies of Homo sapiens. Why shouldn't he talk? He's probably asking for more milk."

Automatically, Miss Fellowes reached for the bottle of milk, but Hoskins seized her wrist. "Now, Miss Fellowes, before we go any further, are you staying on the job?"

Miss Fellowes shook free in annoyance, "Won't you feed him if I don't? I'll stay with him—for a while."

She poured the milk.

Hoskins said, "We are going to leave you with the boy, Miss Fellowes. This is the only door to Stasis Number One and it is elaborately locked and guarded. I'll want you to learn the details of the lock which will, of course, be keyed to your fingerprints as they are already keyed to mine. The spaces overhead"—he looked upward to the open ceilings of the dollhouse—"are also guarded and we will be warned if anything untoward takes place in here."

Miss Fellowes said indignantly, "You mean I'll be under view." She thought suddenly of her own survey of the room interiors from the balcony.

"No, no," said Hoskins seriously, "your privacy will be respected completely. The view will consist of electronic symbolism only, which only a computer will deal with. Now you will stay with him tonight, Miss Fellowes, and every night until further notice. You will be relieved during the day according to some schedule you will find convenient. We will allow you to arrange that."

Miss Fellowes looked about the dollhouse with a puzzled expression. "But why all this, Dr. Hoskins? Is the boy dangerous?"

"It's a matter of energy, Miss Fellowes. He must never be allowed to leave these rooms. Never. Not for an instant. Not for any reason. Not to save his life. Not even to save *your* life, Miss Fellowes. Is that clear?"

Miss Fellowes raised her chin. "I understand the orders, Dr. Hoskins, and the nursing profession is accustomed to placing its duties ahead of self-preservation."

"Good. You can alway signal if you need anyone." And the two men left.

Miss Fellowes turned to the boy. He was watching her and there was still milk in the saucer. Laboriously she tried to show him how to lift the saucer and place it to his lips. He resisted, but let her touch him without crying out.

Always, his frightened eyes were on her, watching, watching for the one false move. She found herself soothing him, trying to move her hand very slowly toward his hair, letting him see it every inch of the way, see there was no harm in it.

And she succeeded in stroking his hair for an instant.

She said, "I'm going to have to show you how to use the bathroom. Do you think you can learn?"

She spoke quietly, kindly, knowing he would not understand the words but hoping he would respond to the calmness of the tone.

The boy launched into a clicking phrase again.

She said, "May I take your hand?"

She held out hers and the boy looked at it. She left it outstretched and waited. The boy's own hand crept forward toward hers.

"That's right," she said.

It approached within an inch of hers and then the boy's courage failed him. He snatched it back.

"Well," said Miss Fellowes calmly, "we'll try again later. Would you like to sit down here?" She patted the mattress of the bed.

The hours passed slowly and progress was minute. She did not succeed either with bathroom or with the bed. In fact, after the child had given unmistakable signs of sleepiness he lay down on the bare ground and then, with a quick movement, rolled beneath the bed.

She bent to look at him and his eyes gleamed out at her as he tongue-clicked at her.

"All right," she said, "if you feel safer there, you sleep there."

She closed the door to the bedroom and retired to the cot that had been placed for her use in the largest room. At her insistence, a makeshift canopy had been stretched over it. She thought: Those stupid men will have to place a mirror in this room and a larger chest of drawers and a separate washroom if they expect me to spend nights here.

It was difficult to sleep. She found herself straining to hear possible sounds in the next room. He couldn't get out, could he? The walls were sheer and impossibly high but suppose the child could climb like a monkey? Well, Hoskins said there were observational devices watching through the ceiling.

Suddenly she thought: Can he be dangerous? Physically dangerous?

Surely Hoskins couldn't have meant that. Surely he would not have left her here alone, if—

She tried to laugh at herself. He was only a three- or four-year-old child. Still, she had not succeeded in cutting his nails. If he should attack her with nails and teeth while she slept—

Her breath came quickly. Oh, ridiculous, and yet—

She listened with painful attentiveness, and this time she heard the sound.

The boy was crying.

Not shrieking in fear or anger; not yelling or screaming. It was crying softly, and the cry was the heartbroken sobbing of a lonely, lonely child.

For the first time, Miss Fellowes thought with a pang: Poor thing!

Of course, it was a child; what did the shape of its head matter? It was a child that had been orphaned as no child had ever been orphaned before. Not only its mother and father were gone, but all its species. Snatched callously out of time, it was now the only creature of its kind in the world. The last. The only.

She felt pity for it strengthen, and with it shame at her own callousness. Tucking her own nightgown carefully about her calves (incongruously, she thought: Tomorrow I'll have to bring in a bathrobe) she got out of bed and went into the boy's room.

"Little boy," she called in a whisper. "Little boy."

She was about to reach under the bed, but she thought of a possible bite and did not. Instead, she turned on the night light and moved the bed.

The poor thing was huddled in the corner, knees up against his chin, looking up at her with blurred and apprehensive eyes.

In the dim light, she was not aware of his repulsiveness.

"Poor boy," she said, "poor boy." She felt him stiffen as she stroked his hair, then relax. "Poor boy. May I hold you?"

She sat down on the floor next to him and slowly and rhythmically stroked his hair, his cheek, his arm. Softly she began to sing a slow and gentle song.

He lifted his head at that, staring at her mouth in the dimness, as though wondering at the sound.

She maneuvered him closer while he listened to her. Slowly, she pressed gently against the side of his head, until it rested on her shoulder. She put her arm under his thighs and with a smooth and unhurried motion lifted him into her lap.

She continued singing, the same simple verse over and over, while she rocked back and forth, back and forth.

He stopped crying, and after a while the smooth burr of his breathing showed he was asleep.

With infinite care, she pushed his bed back against the wall and laid him down. She covered him and stared down. His face looked so peaceful and little-boy as he slept. It didn't matter so much that it was so ugly. Really.

She began to tiptoe out, then thought: If he wakes up?

She came back, battled irresolutely with herself, then sighed and slowly got into bed with the child.

It was too small for her. She was cramped and uneasy at the lack of canopy, but the child's hand crept into hers and, somehow, she fell asleep in that position.

She awoke with a start and a wild impulse to scream. The latter she just managed to suppress into a gurgle. The boy was looking at her, wide-eyed. It took her a long moment to remember getting into bed with him, and now, slowly, without unfixing her eyes from his, she stretched one leg carefully and let it touch the floor, then the other one.

She cast a quick and apprehensive glance toward the open ceiling, then tensed her muscles for quick disengagement.

But at that moment, the boy's stubby fingers reached out and touched her lips. He said something.

She shrank at the touch. He was terribly ugly in the light of day.

The boy spoke again. He opened his own mouth and gestured with his hands as though something were coming out.

Miss Fellows guessed at the meaning and said tremulously, "Do you want me to sing?"

The boy said nothing but stared at her mouth.

In a voice slightly off key with tension, Miss Fellowes began the little song she had sung the night before and the ugly little boy smiled. He swayed clumsily in rough time to the music and made a little gurgly sound that might have been the beginnings of a laugh.

Miss Fellowes sighed inwardly. Music hath charms to soothe the savage breast. It might help . . .

She said, "You wait. Let me get myself fixed up. It will just take a minute. Then I'll make breakfast for you."

She worked rapidly, conscious of the lack of ceiling at all times. The boy remained in bed, watching her when she was in view. She smiled at him at those times and waved. At the end, he waved back, and she found herself being charmed by that.

Finally she said, "Would you like oatmeal with milk?" It took a moment to prepare, and then she beckoned to him.

Whether he understood the gesture or followed the aroma, Miss Fellowes did not know, but he got out of bed.

She tried to show him how to use a spoon but he shrank away from it in fright. (Time enough, she thought.) She compromised on insisting that he lift the bowl in his hands. He did it clumsily enough and it was incredibly messy but most of it did get into him.

She tried the drinking milk in a glass this time, and the little boy whined when he found the opening too small for him to get his face into conveniently. She held his hand, forcing it around the glass, making him tip it, forcing his mouth to the rim.

Again a mess but again most went into him, and she was used to messes.

The washroom, to her surprise and relief, was a less frustrating matter. He understood what it was she expected him to do.

She found herself patting his head, saying, "Good boy. Smart boy."

And to Miss Fellowes' exceeding pleasure, the boy smiled at that.

She thought: When he smiles, he's quite bearable. Really.

Later in the day, the gentlemen of the press arrived.

She held the boy in her arms and he clung to her wildly while across the open door they set cameras to work. The commotion frightened the boy and he began to cry, but it was ten minutes before Miss Fellowes was allowed to retreat and put the boy in the next room.

She emerged again, flushed with indignation, walked out of the apartment (for the first time in eighteen hours) and closed the door behind her. "I think you've had enough. It will take me a while to quiet him. Go away."

"Sure, sure," said the gentleman from the *Times-Herald*. "But is that really a Neanderthal or is this some kind of gag?"

"I assure you," said Hoskins' voice, suddenly, from the background, "that this is no gag. The child is authentic Homo neanderthalensis."

"Is it a boy or a girl?"

"Boy," said Miss Fellowes briefly.

"Ape-boy," said the gentleman from the *News*. "That's what we've got here. Ape-boy. How does he act, Nurse?"

"He acts exactly like a little boy," snapped Miss Fellowes, annoyed into the defensive, "and he is not an ape-boy. His name is—is Timothy, Timmie—and he is perfectly normal in his behavior."

She had chosen the name Timothy at a venture. It was the first that had occurred to her.

"Timmie the Ape-boy," said the gentleman from the *News* and, as it turned out, Timmie the Ape-boy was the name under which the child became known to the world.

The gentleman from the *Globe* turned to Hoskins and said, "Doc, what do you expect to do with the ape-boy?"

Hoskins shrugged. "My original plan was completed when I proved it possible to bring him here. However, the anthropologists will be very interested, I imagine, and the physiologists. We have here, after all, a creature which is at the edge of being human. We should learn a great deal about ourselves and our ancestry from him."

"How long will you keep him?"

"Until such a time as we need the space more than we need him. Quite a while, perhaps."

The gentleman from the *News* said, "Can you bring it out into the open so we can set up sub-etheric equipment and put on a real show?"

"I'm sorry, but the child cannot be removed from Stasis."

"Exactly what is Stasis?"

"Ah." Hoskins permitted himself one of his short smiles. "That would take a great deal of explanation, gentlemen. In Stasis, time as we know it doesn't exist. Those rooms are inside an invisible bubble that is not exactly part of our Universe. That is why the child could be plucked out of time as it was."

"Well, wait now," said the gentleman from the *News* discontentedly, "what are you giving us? The nurse goes into the room and out of it."

"And so can any of you," said Hoskins matter-of-factly. "You would be moving parallel to the lines of temporal force and no great energy gain or loss would be involved. The child, however, was taken from the far past. It moved across the lines and gained temporal potential. To move it into the Universe and into our own time would absorb enough energy to burn out every line in the place and probably blank out all power in the city of Washington. We had to store trash brought with him on the premises and will have to remove it little by little."

The newsmen were writing down sentences busily as Hoskins spoke to them. They did not understand and they were sure their readers would not, but it sounded scientific and that was what counted.

The gentleman from the *Times-Herald* said, "Would you be available for an all-circuit interview tonight?"

"I think so," said Hoskins at once, and they all moved off.

Miss Fellowes looked after them. She understood all this about Stasis and temporal force as little as the newsmen but she managed to get this much. Timmie's imprisonment (she found herself suddenly thinking of the little boy as Timmie) was a real one and not one imposed by the arbitrary fiat of Hoskins. Apparently it was impossible to let him out of Stasis at all, ever.

Poor child. Poor child.

She was suddenly aware of his crying and she hastened in to console him.

Miss Fellowes did not have a chance to see Hoskins on the all-circuit hookup, and though his interview was beamed to every part of the world and even to the outpost on the Moon, it did not penetrate the apartment in which Miss Fellowes and the ugly little boy lived.

But he was down the next morning, radiant and joyful.

Miss Fellowes said, "Did the interview go well?"

"Extremely. And how is—Timmie?"

Miss Fellowes found herself pleased at the use of the name. "Doing quite well. Now come out here, Timmie, the nice gentleman will not hurt you."

But Timmie stayed in the other room, with a lock of his matted hair showing behind the barrier of the door and, occasionally, the corner of an eye.

"Actually," said Miss Fellowes, "he is settling down amazingly. He is quite intelligent."

"Are you surprised?"

She hesitated just a moment, then said, "Yes, I am. I suppose I thought he was an ape-boy."

"Well, ape-boy or not, he's done a great deal for us. He's put Stasis, Inc., on the map. We're in, Miss Fellowes, we're in." It was as though he had to express his triumph to someone, even if only to Miss Fellowes.

"Oh?" She let him talk.

He put his hands in his pockets and said, "We've been working on a shoestring for ten years, scrounging funds a penny at a time wherever we could. We had to shoot the works on one big show. It was everything, or nothing. And when I say the works, I mean it. This attempt to bring in a Neanderthal took every cent we could borrow or steal, and some of it *was* stolen—funds for other projects, used for this one without permission. If that experiment hadn't succeeded, I'd have been through."

Miss Fellowes said abruptly, "Is that why there are no ceilings?"

"Eh?" Hoskins looked up.

"Was there no money for ceilings?"

"Oh. Well, that wasn't the only reason. We didn't really know in advance how old the Neanderthal might be exactly. We can detect only dimly in time, and he might have been large and savage. It was possible we might have had to deal with him from a distance, like a caged animal."

"But since that hasn't turned out to be so, I suppose you can build a ceiling now."

"Now, yes. We have plenty of money, now. Funds have been promised from every source. This is all wonderful, Miss Fellowes." His broad face gleamed with a smile that lasted and when he left, even his back seemed to be smiling.

Miss Fellowes thought: He's quite a nice man when he's off guard and forgets about being scientific.

She wondered for an idle moment if he were married, then dismissed the thought in self-embarrassment.

"Timmie," she called. "Come here, Timmie."

In the months that passed, Miss Fellowes felt herself grow to be an integral part of Stasis, Inc. She was given a small office of her own with her name on the door, an office quite close to the dollhouse—as she never stopped calling Timmie's Stasis bubble. She was given a substantial raise. The dollhouse was covered by a ceiling; its furnishings were elaborated and improved; a second washroom was added—and even so, she gained an apartment of her own on the institute grounds and, on occasion, did not stay with Timmie during the night. An intercom was set up between the dollhouse and her apartment and Timmie learned how to use it.

Miss Fellowes got used to Timmie. She even grew less conscious of his ugliness. One day she found herself staring at an ordinary boy in the street and finding something bulgy and unattractive in his high domed forehead and jutting chin. She had to shake herself to break the spell.

It was more pleasant to grow used to Hoskins' occasional visits. It was obvious he welcomed escape from his increasingly harried role as head of Stasis, Inc., and that he took a sentimental interest in the child who had started it all, but it seemed to Miss Fellowes that he also enjoyed talking to her.

(She had learned some facts about Hoskins, too. He had invented the method of analyzing the reflection of the past-penetrating mesonic beam; he had invented the method of establishing Stasis; his coldness was only an effort to hide a kindly nature; and, oh yes, he *was* married.)

What Miss Fellowes could *not* get used to was the fact that she was engaged in a scientific experiment. Despite all she could do, she found herself getting personally involved to the point of quarreling with the physiologists.

On one occasion Hoskins came down and found her in the midst of a hot urge to kill. They had no right; they had no *right*– Even if he *was* a Neanderthal, he still wasn't an animal.

She was staring after them in a blind fury; staring out the open door and listening to Timmie's sobbing, when she noticed Hoskins standing before her. He might have been there for minutes.

He said, "May I come in?"

She nodded curtly, then hurried to Timmie, who clung to her, curling his little bandy legs–still thin, so thin–about her.

Hoskins watched, then said gravely, "He seems quite unhappy."

Miss Fellowes said, "I don't blame him. They're at him every day now with their blood samples and their probings. They keep him on synthetic diets that I wouldn't feed a pig."

"It's the sort of thing they can't try on a human, you know."

"And they can't try it on Timmie, either. Dr. Hoskins, I insist. You told me it was Timmie's coming that put Stasis, Inc., on the map. If you have any gratitude for that at all, you've *got* to keep them away from the poor thing at least until he's old enough to understand a little more. After he's had a bad session with them, he has nightmares, he can't sleep. Now I warn you"–she reached a sudden peak of fury–"I'm not letting them in here anymore."

(She realized that she had screamed that, but she couldn't help it.)

She said more quietly, "I know he's Neanderthal, but there's a great deal we don't appreciate about Neanderthals. I've read up on them. They had a culture of their own. Some of the greatest human inventions arose in Neanderthal times. The domestication of animals, for instance; the wheel; various techniques in grinding stone. They even had spiritual yearnings. They buried their dead and buried possessions with the body, showing they believed in a life after death. It amounts to the fact that they invented religion. Doesn't that mean Timmie has a right to human treatment?"

She patted the little boy gently on his buttocks and sent him off into his playroom. As the door was opened, Hoskins smiled briefly at the display of toys that could be seen.

Miss Fellowes said defensively, "The poor child deserves his toys. It's all he has and he earns them with what he goes through."

"No, no. No objections, I assure you. I was just thinking how you've changed since the first day, when you were quite angry I had foisted a Neanderthal on you."

Miss Fellowes said in a low voice, "I suppose I didn't . . ." and faded off.

Hoskins changed the subject, "How old would you say he is, Miss Fellowes?"

She said, "I can't say, since we don't know how Neanderthals develop. In size he'd only be three but Neanderthals are smaller generally and with all the tampering they do with him, he probably isn't growing. The way he's learning English, though, I'd say he was well over four."

"Really? I haven't noticed anything about learning English in the reports."

"He won't speak to anyone but me. For now, anyway. He's terribly afraid of others, and no wonder. But he can ask for an article of food; he can indicate any need practically; and he understands almost anything I say. Of course"—she watched him shrewdly, trying to estimate if this was the time—"his development may not continue."

"Why not?"

"Any child needs stimulation and this one lives a life of solitary confinement. I do what I can, but I'm not with him all the time and I'm not all he needs. What I mean, Dr. Hoskins, is that he needs another boy to play with."

Hoskins nodded slowly. "Unfortunately, there's only one of him, isn't there? Poor child."

Miss Fellowes warmed to him at once. She said, "You do like Timmie, don't you?" It was so nice to have someone else feel like that.

"Oh, yes," said Hoskins, and with his guard down, she could see the weariness in his eyes.

Miss Fellowes dropped her plans to push the matter at once. She said, with real concern, "You look worn out, Dr. Hoskins."

"Do I, Miss Fellowes? I'll have to practice looking more life-like then."

"I suppose Stasis, Inc., is very busy and that that keeps you very busy."

Hoskins shrugged. "You suppose right. It's a matter of animal, vegetable, and mineral in equal parts, Miss Fellowes. But then, I suppose you haven't ever seen our displays."

"Actually, I haven't. But it's not because I'm not interested. It's just that I've been so busy."

"Well, you're not all that busy right now," he said with impulsive decision. "I'll call for you tomorrow at eleven and give you a personal tour. How's that?"

She smiled happily. "I'd love it."

He nodded and smiled in his turn and left.

Miss Fellowes hummed at intervals for the rest of the day. Really—to think so was ridiculous, of course—but really, it was almost like—like making a date.

He was quite on time the next day, smiling and pleasant. She had replaced her nurse's uniform with a dress. One of conservative cut, to be sure, but she hadn't felt so feminine in years.

He complimented her on her appearance with staid formality and she accepted with equally formal grace. It was really a perfect prelude, she thought. And then the additional thought came, prelude to what?

She shut that off by hastening to say good-bye to Timmie and to assure him she would be back soon. She made sure he knew all about what and where lunch was.

Hoskins took her into the new wing, into which she had never yet gone. It still had the odor of newness about it and the sound of construction, softly heard, was indication enough that it was still being extended.

"Animal, vegetable, and mineral," said Hoskins, as he had the day before. "Animal right there; our most spectacular exhibits."

The space was divided into many rooms, each a separate Stasis bubble. Hoskins brought her to the view-glass of one and she looked in. What she saw impressed her first as a scaled, tailed chicken. Skittering on two thin legs it ran from wall to wall with its delicate birdlike head, surmounted by a bony keel like the comb of a rooster, looking this way and that. The paws on its small forelimbs clenched and unclenched constantly.

Hoskins said, "It's our dinosaur. We've had it for months. I don't know when we'll be able to let go of it."

"Dinosaur?"

"Did you expect a giant?"

She dimpled. "One does, I suppose. I know some of them are small."

"A small one is all we aimed for, believe me. Generally, it's under investigation, but this seems to be an open hour. Some interesting things have been discovered. For instance, it is not entirely cold-blooded. It has an imperfect method of maintaining internal temperatures higher than that of its environment. Unfortunately it's a male. Ever since we brought it in we've been trying to get a fix on another that may be female, but we've had no luck yet."

"Why female?"

He looked at her quizzically. "So that we might have a fighting chance to obtain fertile eggs, and baby dinosaurs."

"Of course."

He led her to the trilobite section. "That's Professor Dwayne of Washington University," he said. "He's a nuclear chemist. If I recall correctly, he's taking an isotope ratio on the oxygen of the water."

"Why?"

"It's primeval water; at least half a billion years old. The isotope ratio gives the temperature of the ocean at that time. He himself happens to ignore the trilobites, but others are chiefly concerned in dissecting them. They're the lucky ones because all they need are scalpels and microscopes. Dwayne has to set up a mass spectrograph each time he conducts an experiment."

"Why's that? Can't he—"

"No, he can't. He can't take anything out of the room as far as can be helped."

There were samples of primordial plant life too and chunks of rock formations. Those were the vegetable and mineral. And every specimen had its investigator. It was like a museum, a museum brought to life and serving as a superactive center of research.

"And you have to supervise all of this, Dr. Hoskins?"

"Only indirectly, Miss Fellowes. I have subordinates, thank heaven. My own interest is entirely in the theoretical aspects of the matter: the nature of Time, the technique of mesonic intertemporal detection and so on. I would exchange all this for a method of detecting objects closer in Time than ten thousand years ago. If we could get into historical times—"

He was interrupted by a commotion at one of the distant booths, a thin voice raised querulously. He frowned, muttered hastily, "Excuse me," and hastened off.

Miss Fellowes followed as best she could without actually running.

An elderly man, thinly bearded and red-faced, was saying, "I had vital aspects of my investigations to complete. Don't you understand that?"

A uniformed technician with the interwoven SI monogram—for Stasis, Inc.—on his lab coat, said, "Dr. Hoskins, it was arranged with Professor Ademewski at the beginning that the specimen could only remain here two weeks."

"I did not know then how long my investigations would take. I'm not a prophet," said Ademewski heatedly.

Dr. Hoskins said, "You understand, Professor, we have limited space; we must keep specimens rotating. That piece of chalcopyrite must go back; there are men waiting for the next specimen."

"Why can't I have it for myself, then? Let me take it out of there."

"You know you can't have it."

"A piece of chalcopyrite, a miserable five-kilogram piece? Why not?"

"We can't afford the energy expense!" said Hoskins brusquely. "You know that."

The technician interrupted. "The point is, Dr. Hoskins, that he tried to remove the rock against the rules and I almost punctured Stasis while he was in there, not knowing he was in there."

There was a short silence and Dr. Hoskins turned on the investigator with a cold formality. "Is that so, Professor?"

Professor Ademewski coughed. "I saw no harm . . ."

Hoskins reached up to a hand-pull dangling just within reach, outside the specimen room in question. He pulled it.

Miss Fellowes, who had been peering in, looking at the totally undistinguished sample of rock that occasioned the dispute, drew in her breath sharply as its existence flickered out. The room was empty.

Hoskins said, "Professor, your permit to investigate matters in Stasis will be permanently voided. I am sorry."

"But wait—"

"I am sorry. You have violated one of the stringent rules."

"I will appeal to the International Association . . ."

"Appeal away. In a case like this, you will find I can't be overruled."

He turned away deliberately, leaving the professor still protesting, and said to Miss Fellowes, his face still white with anger, "Would you care to have lunch with me, Miss Fellowes?"

He took her into the small administration alcove of the cafeteria. He greeted others and introduced Miss Fellowes with complete ease, although she herself felt painfully self-conscious.

What must they think, she thought, and tried desperately to appear businesslike.

She said, "Do you have that kind of trouble often, Dr. Hoskins? I mean like that you just had with the professor?" She took her fork in hand and began eating.

"No," said Hoskins forcefully. "That was the first time. Of course I'm always having to argue men out of removing specimens but this is the first time one actually tried to *do* it."

"I remember you once talked about the energy it would consume."

"That's right. Of course, we've tried to take it into account. Accidents will happen and so we've got special power sources designed to stand the drain of accidental removal from Stasis, but that doesn't mean we want to see a year's supply of energy gone in half a second, or can afford to without having our plans of expansion delayed for years. Besides, imagine the professor's being in the room while Stasis was about to be punctured."

"What would have happened to him if it had been?"

"Well, we've experimented with inanimate objects and with mice and they've disappeared. Presumably they've traveled back in Time; carried along, so to speak, by the pull of the object simultaneously snapping back into its natural time. For that reason, we have to anchor objects within Stasis that we don't want to move and that's a complicated procedure. The professor would not have been anchored and he would have gone back to the Pliocene at the moment when we abstracted the rock—plus, of course, the two weeks it had remained here in the present."

"How dreadful it would have been."

"Not on account of the professor, I assure you. If he were fool enough to do what he did, it would serve him right. But imagine the effect it would have on the public if the fact came out. All people would need is to become aware of the dangers involved and funds could be choked off like that." He snapped his fingers and played moodily with his food.

Miss Fellowes said, "Couldn't you get him back? The way you got the rock in the first place?"

"No, because once an object is returned, the original fix is lost unless we deliberately plan to retain it and there was no reason to do that in this case. There never is. Finding the professor again would mean relocating a specific fix and that would be like dropping a line into the oceanic abyss for the purpose of dredging up a particular fish. My God, when I think of the precautions we take to prevent accidents, it makes me mad. We have every individual Stasis unit set up with its own puncturing device. We have to, since each unit has its separate fix and must be collapsible independently. The point is, though, none of the puncturing devices is ever activated until the last minute. And then we deliberately make activation impossible except by the pull of a rope carefully led outside the Stasis. The pull is a gross mechanical motion that requires a strong effort, not something that is likely to be done accidentally."

Miss Fellowes said, "But doesn't it—change history to move something in and out of Time?"

Hoskins shrugged. "Theoretically, yes; actually, except in unusual cases, no. We move objects out of Stasis all the time. Air molecules. Bacteria. Dust. About ten percent of our energy consumption goes to make up micro-losses of that nature. But moving even large objects in Time sets up changes that damp out. Take that chalcopyrite from the Pliocene. Because of its absence for two weeks some insect didn't find the shelter it might have found and is killed. That could initiate a whole series of changes, but the mathematics of Stasis indicates that this is a converging series. The amount of change diminishes with time and then things are as before."

"You mean, reality heals itself?"

"In a manner of speaking. Abstract a human from Time or send one back, and you make a larger wound. If the individual is an ordinary one, that wound still heals itself. Of course, there are a great many people who write to us each day and want us to bring Abraham Lincoln into the present, or Mohammed, or Lenin. *That* can't be done, of course. Even if we could find them, the change in reality in moving one of the history molders would be too great to be healed. There are ways of calculating when a change is likely to be too great and we avoid even approaching that limit."

Miss Fellowes said, "Then, Timmie—"

"No, he presents no problem in that direction. Reality is safe. But"—he gave her a quick, sharp glance, then went on—"But never mind. Yesterday you said Timmie needed companionship."

"Yes," Miss Fellowes smiled her delight. "I didn't think you paid that any attention."

"Of course I did. I'm fond of the child. I appreciate your feelings for him and I was concerned enough to want to explain to you. Now I have; you've seen what we do; you've gotten some insight into the difficulties involved; so you know why, with the best will in the world, we can't supply companionship for Timmie."

"You can't?" said Miss Fellowes, with sudden dismay.

"But I've just explained. We couldn't possibly expect to find another Neanderthal his age without incredible luck, and if we could, it wouldn't be fair to multiply risks by having another human being in Stasis."

Miss Fellowes put down her spoon and said energetically, "But, Dr. Hoskins, that is not at all what I meant. I don't want you to bring another Neanderthal into the present. I know that's impossible. But it isn't impossible to bring another child to play with Timmie."

Hoskins stared at her in concern. "A *human* child?"

"*Another* child," said Miss Fellowes, completely hostile now. "Timmie is human."

"I couldn't dream of such a thing."

"Why not? Why couldn't you? What is wrong with the notion? You pulled that child out of Time and made him an eternal prisoner. Don't you owe him something? Dr. Hoskins, if there is any man who, in this world, is that child's father in every sense but the biological, it is you. Why can't you do this little thing for him?"

Hoskins said, "His *father?*" He rose, somewhat unsteadily, to his feet. "Miss Fellowes, I think I'll take you back now, if you don't mind."

They returned to the dollhouse in a complete silence that neither broke.

It was a long time after that before she saw Hoskins again, except for an occasional glimpse in passing. She was sorry about that at times; then, at other times, when Timmie was more than usually woebegone or when he spent silent hours at the window with its prospect of little more than nothing, she thought, fiercely: Stupid man.

Timmie's speech grew better and more precise each day. It never entirely lost a certain soft, slurriness that Miss Fellowes found rather endearing. In times of excitement, he fell back into tongue-clicking but those times were becoming fewer. He must be forgetting the days before he came into the present, except for dreams.

As he grew older, the physiologists grew less interested and the psychologists more so. Miss Fellowes was not sure that she did not like the new group even less than the first. The needles were gone; the injections and withdrawals of fluid; the special diets. But now Timmie was made to overcome barriers to reach food and water. He had to lift panels, move bars, reach for cords. And the mild electric shocks made him cry and drove Miss Fellowes to distraction.

She did not wish to appeal to Hoskins; she did not wish to have to go to him; for each time she thought of him, she thought of his face over the luncheon table that last time. Her eyes moistened and she thought: Stupid, *stupid* man.

And then one day Hoskins' voice sounded unexpectedly, calling into the dollhouse, "Miss Fellowes."

She came out coldly, smoothing her nurse's uniform, then stopped in confusion at finding herself in the presence of a pale woman, slender and of middle height. The woman's fair hair and complexion gave her an appearance of fragility. Standing behind her and clutching at her skirt was a round-faced, large-eyed child of four.

Hoskins said, "Dear, this is Miss Fellowes, the nurse in charge of the boy. Miss Fellowes, this is my wife."

(Was this his wife? She was not as Miss Fellowes had imagined her to be. But then, why not? A man like Hoskins would choose a weak thing to be his foil. If that was what he wanted . . .)

She forced a matter-of-fact greeting. "Good afternoon, Mrs. Hoskins. Is this your—your little boy?"

(*That* was a surprise. She had thought of Hoskins as a husband, but not as a father, except, of course . . . She suddenly caught Hoskins' grave eyes and flushed.)

Hoskins said, "Yes, this is my boy, Jerry. Say hello to Miss Fellowes, Jerry."

(Had he stressed the word "this" just a bit? Was he saying *this* was his son and not—)

Jerry receded a bit further into the folds of the maternal skirt and muttered his hello. Mrs. Hoskins' eyes were searching over Miss Fellowes' shoulders, peering into the room, looking for something.

Hoskins said, "Well, let's go in. Come, dear. There's a trifling discomfort at the threshold, but it passes."

Miss Fellowes said, "Do you want Jerry to come in too?"

"Of course. He is to be Timmie's playmate. You said that Timmie needed a playmate. Or have you forgotten?"

"But—" She looked at him with a colossal, surprised wonder. "*Your* boy?"

He said peevishly, "Well, who's boy, then? Isn't this what you want? Come on in, dear. Come on in."

Mrs. Hoskins lifted Jerry into her arms with a distinct effort and, hesitantly, stepped over the threshold. Jerry squirmed as she did so, disliking the sensation.

Mrs. Hoskins said in a thin voice, "Is the creature here? I don't see him."

Miss Fellowes called, "Timmie. Come out."

Timmie peered around the edge of the door, staring up at the little boy who was visiting him. The muscles in Mrs. Hoskins' arms tensed visibly.

She said to her husband, "Gerald, are you sure it's safe?"

Miss Fellowes said at once, "If you mean is Timmie safe, why, of course he is. He's a gentle little boy."

"But he's a sa—savage."

(The ape-boy stories in the newspapers!) Miss Fellowes said emphatically, "He is not a savage. He is just as quiet and reasonable as you can possibly expect a five-and-a-half-year-old to be. It is very generous of you, Mrs. Hoskins, to agree to allow your boy to play with Timmie but please have no fears about it."

Mrs. Hoskins said with mild heat, "I'm not sure that I agree."

"We've had it out, dear," said Hoskins. "Let's not bring up the matter for new argument. Put Jerry down."

Mrs. Hoskins did so and the boy backed against her, staring at the pair of eyes which were staring back at him from the next room.

"Come here, Timmie," said Miss Fellowes. "Don't be afraid."

Slowly, Timmie stepped into the room. Hoskins bent to disengage Jerry's fingers from his mother's skirt. "Step back, dear. Give the children a chance."

The youngsters faced one another. Although the younger, Jerry was nevertheless an inch taller, and in the presence of his straightness and his high-held, well-proportioned head, Timmie's grotesqueries were suddenly almost as pronounced as they had been in the first days.

Miss Fellowes' lips quivered.

It was the little Neanderthal who spoke first, in childish treble. "What's your name?" And Timmie thrust his face suddenly forward as though to inspect the other's features more closely.

Startled, Jerry responded with a vigorous shove that sent Timmie tumbling. Both began crying loudly and Mrs. Hoskins snatched up her child, while Miss Fellowes, flushed with repressed anger, lifted Timmie and comforted him.

Mrs. Hoskins said, "They just instinctively don't like one another."

"No more instinctively," said her husband wearily, "than any two children dislike each other. Now put Jerry down and let him get used to the situation. In fact, we had better leave. Miss Fellowes can bring Jerry to my office after a while and I'll have him taken home."

The two children spent the next hour very aware of each other. Jerry cried for his mother, struck out at Miss Fellowes and, finally, allowed himself to be comforted with a lollipop. Timmie sucked at another, and at the end of an hour, Miss Fellowes had them playing with the same set of blocks, though at opposite ends of the room.

She found herself almost maudlinly grateful to Hoskins when she brought Jerry to him.

She searched for ways to thank him but his very formality was a rebuff. Perhaps he could not forgive her for making him feel like a cruel father. Perhaps the bringing of his own child was an attempt, after all, to prove himself both a kind father to Timmie and, also, not his father at all. Both at the same time!

So all she could say was, "Thank you. Thank you very much."

And all he could say was, "It's all right. Don't mention it."

It became a settled routine. Twice a week, Jerry was brought in for an hour's play, later extended to two hours' play. The children learned each other's names and ways and played together.

And yet, after the first rush of gratitude, Miss Fellowes found herself disliking Jerry. He was larger and heavier and in all things dominant, forcing Timmie into a completely secondary role. All that reconciled her to the situation was the fact that, despite difficulties, Timmie looked forward with more and more delight to the periodic appearances of his playfellow.

It was all he had, she mourned to herself.

And once, as she watched them, she thought: Hoskins' two children, one by his wife and one by Stasis.

While she herself . . .

Heavens, she thought, putting her fists to her temples and feeling ashamed: I'm jealous!

"Miss Fellowes," said Timmie (carefully—she had never allowed him to call her anything else), "when will I go to school?"

She looked down at those eager brown eyes turned up to hers and passed her hand softly through his thick, curly hair. It was the most disheveled portion of his appearance, for she cut his hair herself while he sat restlessly under the scissors. She did not ask for professional help, for the very clumsiness of the cut served to mask the retreating fore part of the skull and the bulging hinder part.

She said, "Where did you hear about school?"

"Jerry goes to school. Kin-der-gar-ten." He said it carefully. "There are lots of places he goes. Outside. When can I go outside, Miss Fellowes?"

A small pain centered in Miss Fellowes' heart. Of course, she saw, there would be no way of avoiding the inevitability of Timmie's hearing more and more of the outer world he could never enter.

She said, with an attempt at gaiety, "Why, whatever would you do in kindergarten, Timmie?"

"Jerry says they play games, they have picture tapes. He says there are lots of children. He says—he says—" A thought, then a triumphant upholding of both small hands with the fingers splayed apart. "He says this many."

Miss Fellowes said, "Would you like picture tapes? I can get you picture tapes. Very nice ones. And music tapes, too." So that Timmie was temporarily comforted.

He pored over the picture tapes in Jerry's absence and Miss Fellowes read to him out of ordinary books by the hours.

There was so much to explain in even the simplest story, so much that was outside the perspective of his three rooms. Timmie took to having his dreams more often now that the outside was being introduced to him.

They were always the same, about the outside. He tried haltingly to describe them to Miss Fellowes. In his dreams, he was outside, an empty outside, but very large, with children and queer indescribable objects half-digested in his thought out of bookish descriptions half-understood, or out of distant Neanderthal memories half-recalled.

But the children and objects ignored him and though he was in the world, he was never part of it, but was as alone as though he were in his own room—and would wake up crying.

Miss Fellowes tried to laugh at the dreams, but there were nights in her own apartment when she cried, too.

One day, as Miss Fellowes read, Timmie put his hand under her chin and lifted it gently so that her eyes left the book and met his.

He said, "How do you know what to say, Miss Fellowes?"

She said, "You see these marks? They tell me what to say. These marks make words."

He stared at them long and curiously, taking the book out of her hands. "Some of these marks are the same."

She laughed with pleasure at this sign of his shrewdness and said, "So they are. Would you like to have me show you how to make the marks?"

"All right. That would be a nice game."

It did not occur to her that he could learn to read. Up to the very moment that he read a book to her, it did not occur to her that he could learn to read.

Then, weeks later, the enormity of what had been done struck her. Timmie sat in her lap, following word by word the printing in a child's book, reading to her. He was reading to her!

She struggled to her feet in amazement and said, "Now Timmie, I'll be back later. I want to see Dr. Hoskins."

Excited nearly to frenzy, it seemed to her she might have an answer to Timmie's unhappiness. If Timmie could not leave to enter the world, the world must be brought into those three rooms to Timmie—the whole world in books and film and sound. He must be educated to his full capacity. So much the world owed him.

She found Hoskins in a mood that was oddly analogous to her own; a kind of triumph and glory. His offices were unusually busy, and for a moment, she thought she would not get to see him, as she stood abashed in the anteroom.

But he saw her, and a smile spread over his broad face. "Miss Fellowes, come here."

He spoke rapidly into the intercom, then shut it off. "Have you heard? No, of course, you couldn't have. We've done it. We've actually done it. We have intertemporal detection at close range."

"You mean," she tried to detach her thought from her own good news for a moment, "that you can get a person from historical times into the present?"

"That's just what I mean. We have a fix on a fourteenth-century individual right now. Imagine. *Imagine!* If you could only know how glad I'll be to shift from the eternal concentration on the Mesozoic, replace the paleontologists with the historians— But there's something you wish to say to me, eh? Well, go ahead; go ahead. You find me in a good mood. Anything you want you can have."

Miss Fellowes smiled. "I'm glad. Because I wonder if we might not establish a system of instruction for Timmie?"

"Instruction? In what?"

"Well, in everything. A school. So that he might learn."

"But *can* he learn?"

"Certainly, he *is* learning. He can read. I've taught him so much myself."

Hoskins sat there, seeming suddenly depressed. "I don't know, Miss Fellowes."

She said, "You just said that anything I wanted—"

"I know and I should not have. You see, Miss Fellowes, I'm sure you must realize that we cannot maintain the Timmie experiment forever."

She stared at him with sudden horror, not really understanding what he had said. How did he mean "cannot maintain"? With an agonizing flash of recollection, she recalled Professor Ademewski and his mineral specimen that was taken away after two weeks. She said, "But you're talking about a boy. Not about a rock . . ."

Dr. Hoskins said uneasily, "Even a boy can't be given undue importance, Miss Fellowes. Now that we expect individuals out of historical time, we will need Stasis space, all we can get."

She didn't grasp it. "But you can't. Timmie—Timmie—"

"Now, Miss Fellowes, please don't upset yourself. Timmie won't go right away; perhaps not for months. Meanwhile we'll do what we can."

She was still staring at him.

"Let me get you something, Miss Fellowes."

"No," she whispered. "I don't need anything." She arose in a kind of nightmare and left.

Timmie, she thought, you will *not* die. You will *not* die.

It was all very well to hold tensely to the thought that Timmie must not die, but how was that to be arranged? In the first weeks Miss Fellowes clung only to the hope that the attempt to bring forward a man from the fourteenth century would fail completely. Hoskins' theories might be wrong or his practice defective. Then things could go on as before.

Certainly that was not the hope of the rest of the world and, irrationally, Miss Fellowes hated the world for it. "Project Middle Ages" reached a climax of white-hot publicity. The press and the public had hungered for something like this. Stasis, Inc., had lacked the necessary sensation for a long time now. A new rock or another ancient fish failed to stir them. But *this* was *it*.

A historical human; an adult speaking a known language; someone who could open a new page of history to the scholar.

Zero-time was coming and this time it was not a question of three onlookers from a balcony. This time there would be a world-wide audience. This time the technicians of Stasis, Inc., would play their role before nearly all of mankind.

Miss Fellowes was herself all but savage with waiting. When young Jerry Hoskins showed up for his scheduled playtime with Timmie, she scarcely recognized him. He was not the one she was waiting for.

(The secretary who brought him left hurriedly after the barest nod for Miss Fellowes. She was rushing for a good place from which to watch the climax of Project Middle Ages. And so ought Miss Fellowes with far better reason, she thought bitterly, if only that stupid girl would arrive.)

Jerry Hoskins sidled toward her, embarrassed. "Miss Fellowes?" He took the reproduction of a news-strip out of his pocket.

"Yes? What is it, Jerry?"

"Is this a picture of Timmie?"

Miss Fellowes stared at him, then snatched the strip from Jerry's hand. The excitement of Project Middle Ages had brought about a pale revival of interest in Timmie on the part of the press.

Jerry watched her narrowly, then said, "It says Timmie is an ape-boy. What does that mean?"

Miss Fellowes caught the youngster's wrist and repressed the impulse to shake him. "Never say that, Jerry. Never, do you understand? It is a nasty word and you mustn't use it."

Jerry struggled out of her grip, frightened.

Miss Fellowes tore up the news-strip with a vicious twist of the wrist. "Now go inside and play with Timmie. He's got a new book to show you."

And then, finally, the girl appeared. Miss Fellowes did not know her. None of the usual stand-ins she had used when business took her elsewhere was available now, not with Project Middle Ages at climax, but Hoskins' secretary had promised to find *someone* and this must be the girl.

Miss Fellowes tried to keep querulousness out of her voice. "Are you the girl assigned to Stasis Section One?"

"Yes, I'm Mandy Terris. You're Miss Fellowes, aren't you?"

"That's right."

"I'm sorry I'm late. There's just so much excitement."

"I know. Now I want you—"

Mandy said, "You'll be watching, I suppose." Her thin, vacuously pretty face filled with envy.

"Never mind that. Now I want you to come inside and meet Timmie and Jerry. They will be playing for the next two hours so they'll be giving you no trouble. They've got milk handy and plenty of toys. In fact, it will be better if you leave them alone as much as possible. Now I'll show you where everything is located and—"

"Is it Timmie that's the ape-b—"

"Timmie is the Stasis subject," said Miss Fellowes firmly.

"I mean, he's the one who's not supposed to get out, is that right?"

"Yes. Now, come in. There isn't much time."

And when she finally left, Mandy Terris called after her

shrilly, "I hope you get a good seat and, golly, I sure hope it works."

Miss Fellowes did not trust herself to make a reasonable response. She hurried on without looking back.

But the delay meant she did *not* get a good seat. She got no nearer than the wall-viewing-plate in the assembly hall. Bitterly she regretted that. If she could have been on the spot; if she could somehow have reached out for some sensitive portion of the instrumentations; if she were in some way able to wreck the experiment—

She found the strength to beat down her madness. Simple destruction would have done no good. They would have rebuilt and reconstructed and made the effort again. And she would never be allowed to return to Timmie.

Nothing would help. Nothing but that the experiment itself fail; that it break down irretrievably.

So she waited through the countdown, watching every move on the giant screen, scanning the faces of the technicians as the focus shifted from one to the other, watching for the look of worry and uncertainty that would mark something going unexpectedly wrong; watching, watching—

There was no such look. The count reached zero, and very quietly, very unassumingly, the experiment succeeded!

In the new Stasis that had been established there stood a bearded, stoop-shouldered peasant of indeterminate age, in ragged dirty clothing and wooden shoes, staring in dull horror at the sudden mad change that had flung itself over him.

And while the world went mad with jubilation, Miss Fellowes stood frozen in sorrow, jostled and pushed, all but trampled; surrounded by triumph while bowed down with defeat.

And when the loudspeaker called her name with strident force, it sounded it three times before she responded.

"Miss Fellowes. Miss Fellowes. You are wanted in Stasis Section One immediately. Miss Fellowes. Miss Fell—"

"Let me through!" she cried breathlessly, while the loudspeaker continued its repetitions without pause. She forced her way through the crowds with wild energy, beating at it, striking out with closed fists, flailing, moving toward the door in a nightmare slowness.

Mandy Terris was in tears. "I don't know how it happened. I just went down to the edge of the corridor to watch a pocket-viewing-plate they had put up. Just for a minute. And then before I could move or do anything—" She cried out in sudden accusation, "You said they would make no trouble; you *said* to leave them alone—"

Miss Fellowes, disheveled and trembling uncontrollably, glared at her. "Where's Timmie?"

A nurse was swabbing the arm of a wailing Jerry with disinfectant and another was preparing an antitetanus shot. There was blood on Jerry's clothes.

"He bit me, Miss Fellowes," Jerry cried in rage. "He *bit* me."

But Miss Fellowes didn't even see him.

"What did you do with Timmie?" she cried out.

"I locked him in the bathroom," said Mandy. "I just threw the little monster in there and locked him in."

Miss Fellowes ran into the dollhouse. She fumbled at the bathroom door. It took an eternity to get it open and to find the ugly little boy cowering in the corner.

"Don't whip me, Miss Fellowes," he whispered. His eyes were red. His lips were quivering. "I didn't mean to do it."

"Oh, Timmie, who told you about whips?" She caught him to her, hugging him wildly.

He said tremulously, "She said, with a long rope. She said you would hit me and hit me."

"You won't be. She was wicked to say so. But what happened? What happened?"

"He called me an ape-boy. He said I wasn't a real boy. He said I was an animal." Timmie dissolved in a flood of tears. "He said he wasn't going to play with a monkey anymore. I said I wasn't a monkey; I *wasn't* a monkey. He said I was all funny-looking. He said I was horrible ugly. He kept saying and saying and I bit him."

They were both crying now. Miss Fellowes sobbed, "But it isn't true. You know that, Timmie. You're a real boy. You're a dear real boy and the best boy in the world. And no one, *no* one will ever take you away from me."

It was easy to make up her mind, now; easy to know what to do. Only it had to be done quickly. Hoskins wouldn't wait much longer, with his own son mangled—

No, it would have to be done this night, *this* night; with the place four-fifths asleep and the remaining fifth intellectually drunk over Project Middle Ages.

It would be an unusual time for her to return but not an unheard of one. The guard knew her well and would not dream of questioning her. He would think nothing of her carrying a suitcase. She rehearsed the noncommittal phrase, "Games for the boy," and the calm smile.

Why shouldn't he believe that?

He did. When she entered the dollhouse again, Timmie was still awake, and she maintained a desperate normality to avoid frightening him. She talked about his dreams with him and listened to him ask wistfully after Jerry.

There would be few to see her afterward, none to question the bundle she would be carrying. Timmie would be very quiet and then it would be a *fait accompli*. It would be done and what would be the use of trying to undo it. They would leave her be. They would leave them both be.

She opened the suitcase, took out the overcoat, the woolen cap with the ear-flaps and the rest.

Timmie said, with the beginning of alarm, "Why are you putting all these clothes on me, Miss Fellowes?"

She said, "I am going to take you outside, Timmie. To where your dreams are."

"My dreams?" His face twisted in sudden yearning, yet fear was there, too.

"You won't be afraid. You'll be with me. You won't be afraid if you're with me, will you, Timmie?"

"No, Miss Fellowes." He buried his little misshapen head against her side, and under her enclosing arm she could feel his small heart thud.

It was midnight and she lifted him into her arms. She disconnected the alarm and opened the door softly.

And she screamed, for facing her across the open door was Hoskins!

There were two men with him and he stared at her, as astonished as she.

Miss Fellowes recovered first by a second and made a quick attempt to push past him; but even with the second's delay he had time. He caught her roughly and hurled her back against a chest of drawers. He waved the men in and confronted her, blocking the door.

"I didn't expect this. Are you completely insane?"

She had managed to interpose her shoulder so that it, rather than Timmie, had struck the chest. She said pleadingly, "What harm can it do if I take him, Dr. Hoskins? You can't put energy loss ahead of a human life?"

Firmly, Hoskins took Timmie out of her arms. "An energy loss this size would mean millions of dollars lost out of the pockets of investors. It would mean a terrible setback for Stasis, Inc. It would mean eventual publicity about a sentimental nurse destroying all that for the sake of an ape-boy."

"*Ape-boy!*" said Miss Fellowes in helpless fury.

"That's what the reporters would call him," said Hoskins.

One of the men emerged now, looping a nylon rope through eyelets along the upper portion of the wall.

Miss Fellowes remembered the rope that Hoskins had pulled outside the room containing Professor Ademewski's rock specimen so long ago.

She cried out, "No!"

But Hoskins put Timmie down and gently removed the overcoat he was wearing. "You stay here, Timmie. Nothing will happen to you. We're just going outside for a moment. All right?"

Timmie, white and wordless, managed to nod.

Hoskins steered Miss Fellowes out of the dollhouse ahead of himself. For the moment Miss Fellowes was beyond resistance. Dully she noticed the hand-pull being adjusted outside the dollhouse.

"I'm sorry, Miss Fellowes," said Hoskins. "I would have spared you this. I planned it for the night so that you would know only when it was over."

She said in a weary whisper, "Because your son was hurt. Because he tormented this child into striking out at him."

"No. Believe me. I understand about the incident today and I know it was Jerry's fault. But the story has leaked out. It would have to with the press surrounding us on this day of all days. I can't risk having a distorted story about negligence and savage Neanderthalers, so-called, distract from the success of

Project Middle Ages. Timmie has to go soon anyway; he might as well go now and give the sensationalists as small a peg as possible on which to hang their trash."

"It's not like sending a rock back. You'll be killing a human being."

"Not killing. There'll be no sensation. He'll simply be a Neanderthal boy in a Neanderthal world. He will no longer be a prisoner and alien. He will have a chance at a free life."

"What chance? He's only seven years old, used to being taken care of, fed, clothed, sheltered. He will be alone. His tribe may not be at the point where he left them now that four years have passed. And if they were, they would not recognize him. He will have to take care of himself. How will he know how?"

Hoskins shook his head in hopeless negative. "Lord, Miss Fellowes, do you think we haven't thought of that? Do you think we would have brought in a child if it weren't that it was the first successful fix of a human or near-human we made and that we did not dare to take the chance of unfixing him and finding another fix as good? Why do you suppose we kept Timmie as long as we did, if it were not for our reluctance to send a child back into the past. It's just"—his voice took on a desperate urgency—"that we can wait no longer. Timmie stands in the way of expansion! Timmie is a source of possible bad publicity; we are on the threshold of great things, and I'm sorry, Miss Fellowes, but we can't let Timmie block us. We cannot. We cannot. I'm sorry, Miss Fellowes."

"Well, then," said Miss Fellowes sadly. "Let me say good-bye. Give me five minutes to say good-bye. Spare me that much."

Hoskins hesitated. "Go ahead."

Timmie ran to her. For the last time he ran to her and for the last time Miss Fellowes clasped him in her arms.

For a moment she hugged him blindly. She caught at a chair with the toe of one foot, moved it against the wall, sat down.

"Don't be afraid, Timmie."

"I'm not afraid if you're here, Miss Fellowes. Is that man mad at me, the man out there?"

"No, he isn't. He just doesn't understand about us. Timmie, do you know what a mother is?"

"Like Jerry's mother?"

"Did he tell you about his mother?"

"Sometimes. I think maybe a mother is a lady who takes care of you and who's very nice to you and who does good things."

"That's right. Have you ever wanted a mother, Timmie?"

Timmie pulled his head away from her so that he could look into her face. Slowly, he put his hand to her cheek and hair and stroked her, as long, long ago she had stroked him. He said, "Aren't you my mother?"

"Oh, Timmie."

"Are you angry because I asked?"

"No. Of course not."

"Because I know your name is Miss Fellowes, but—but sometimes, I call you 'Mother' inside. Is that all right?"

"Yes. Yes. It's all right. And I won't leave you anymore and nothing will hurt you. I'll be with you to care for you always. Call me Mother, so I can hear you."

"Mother," said Timmie contentedly, leaning his cheek against hers.

She rose, and, still holding him, stepped up on the chair. The sudden beginning of a shout from outside went unheard and, with her free hand, she yanked with all her weight at the cord where it hung suspended between two eyelets.

And Stasis was punctured and the room was empty.

ABOUT THE EDITOR AND ARTIST

Widely known for both his science fiction and his serious scientific essays, Isaac Asimov has written over seventy books on subjects ranging from physics to mythology, from mathematics to the Bible. Born in Russia in 1920, Dr. Asimov came to Brooklyn with his family at the age of three, received his Ph.D. from Columbia University in 1948, and the following year joined the faculty of Boston University School of Medicine, where he is now associate professor of biochemistry.

Emanuel Schongut received his B.F.A. and M.F.A. degrees from the Pratt Institute (where he now teaches) and later studied at the Art Students League and the Pratt Graphic Art Center. He has designed and illustrated a number of book jackets, and his illustrations have appeared in *Harper's* and *Ingenue* magazines.